Legends of Orkney
Series

The RED SUN

Published by SparkPress, a BookSparks imprint,
A division of SparkPoint Studio, LLC
Tempe, Arizona, USA, 85281
www.gosparkpress.com

Published 2015
Printed in the United States of America
ISBN: 978-1-940716-26-8

Library of Congress Control Number: 2015938507

Cover design © Tabitha Lahr
Cover Illustration by Jonathan Stroh
Interior design by Tabitha Lahr

Legends of Orkney

THE RED SUN

ALANE ADAMS

spark press

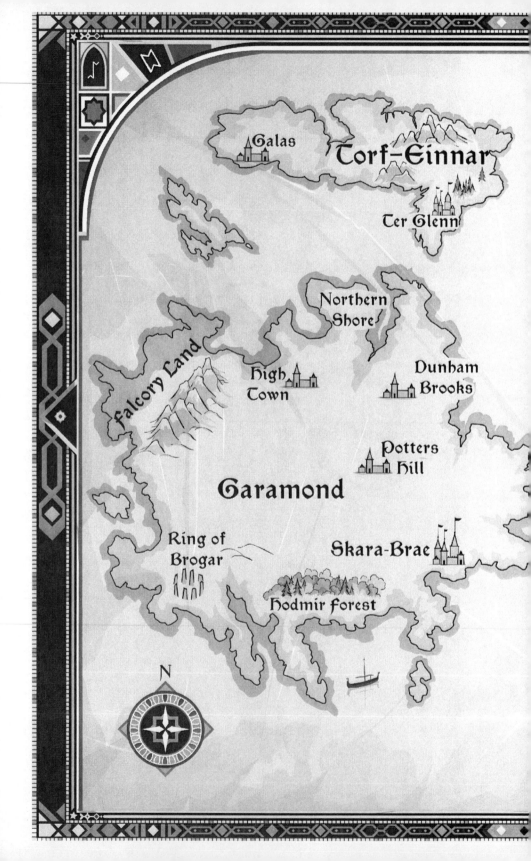

Asgard

Pantros

Tarkana Fortress

Balfour Island

Orkney

For Alex

Prologue

The setting sun cast a farewell glow across the green and fertile countryside. Basking in the radiance, Robert Barconian watched the day's end from a window in his new farmhouse on the outskirts of Skara Brae. At thirty-two, Robert had seen his fair share of sunsets, but they never grew old for him.

By Odin's blood, Orkney is glorious this time of year, Robert thought.

After a difficult winter, spring was finally in the air. The days were longer now. Soon, crops would need planting and tending. The fence would need repairs to keep animals from feasting on early buds. Robert envisioned his life as a farmer with a smile. It would be a new adventure. An adventure, unlike many in his past, he could safely share with his wife and child.

"Is he asleep?" Robert whispered to Abigail, who gently rocked their seven-day-old son, Samuel, in her arms while she walked circles around the hand-carved bassinet.

"Yes," she replied, "but I don't want to put him down just yet."

And to think some doubted Abby would make a great mother, Robert recalled. He took no small pride in knowing those naysayers were all wrong.

Robert returned his gaze to the fertile acreage outside the window. That dirt was now his family's future. The soil was rocky in spots, but with this much afternoon sun there was no reason they could not claim a bumper crop come harvest time. "I'm thinking black cabbage and squashmor," Robert whispered to Abigail, as she passed by him on another lap around the baby's bed. "Maybe even some jookberries for the—"

Outside, a flock of crows broke Robert's reverie. Flapping and cawing and scattering, spooked from a gnarled tree at the farm's fenced border. Robert thought he caught a glimpse of a figure, indistinct, before it disappeared into the tree's twisted shadows.

"No," Abigail teased, bringing his attention back, "you are not corrupting our son with your jookberry addiction." She finally stopped circling. "Now, if you had said gally melons, *that* I could support."

Robert shook his head, amused, as she laid the infant down in the bassinet. The truth was that neither parent could wait to share their favorite foods with young Samuel, not to mention cherished places and childhood stories. Robert kissed his index finger and touched it to his son's forehead. "Grow up fast, my boy," he said half-seriously. "There's much to see and much to do."

After Abigail carefully tucked Samuel beneath a blanket bearing the Orkadian crest, a white heron clasping an olive branch, she floated a question.

"I know you have your heart set on homesteading, but do you really think the High Council will let you trade your sword for a . . . well, for a hoe?"

Robert bristled. "The Council does not control me." His voice raised with his ire. "I'll do what's best for my family, politics be damned."

"Shh," Abigail chided with a smile as she waited at the doorway for her husband. "With any luck, our son will have more common sense than his parents."

"I told you, Abby," Robert reminded her on their way to the kitchen, "you have to forget what they're saying. Every word, erase it from your mind. If we can't trust our hearts, what can we trust?" He sealed the question with a kiss. "Call when dinner is ready."

Robert left through the front door, soaking up the last rays of sun as he strode across his untilled land to the border fence where he had seen the mysterious figure beneath the old tree. There were footprints. Narrow and heeled. Clearly made by a woman.

Glancing back at his farmhouse, now cloaked in twilight, Robert noticed something amiss. A window was open—Samuel's bedroom window.

That was closed before, he recalled. *How could . . . ?*

Before he could finish his thought, a wailing cry came from inside the baby's room.

Robert ran across the dirt field, feet barely touching the ground.

Never had he heard his son cry like this. The sound distressed every fiber of his being, made worse by a dread revelation. *I never thought it would happen this soon.*

He burst in through the front door and sprinted to Samuel's room, where he found Abigail cradling the bawling baby tightly in her arms.

"Is he all right?" Robert barked breathlessly.

"A Deathstalker. In his bed! Kill it!"

Robert moved quickly to the bassinet. He peered in, only to rear back in alarm. There was a violet-colored scorpion with black pincers and a stinger-tipped tail skittering across the blanket.

"Be careful, Robert!"

Without hesitation, Robert reached in and gathered up the blanket to capture the creature inside; then he flung the cloth to the floor and stomped with both feet until a sickly crunch announced an end to the threat.

He took a moment to regain his breath. "Thank Odin it didn't sting him."

Abigail had begun to quiet Samuel, now sobbing only fitfully.

"It did sting him." Abigail lifted Samuel's tiny foot to reveal a swollen red mark on the boy's heel.

"I don't understand. Deathstalkers are always fatal."

Abigail covered the baby back up as she moved to the open window. She paused there, looking as if the world were caving in on her. Then she closed the window firmly and turned to Robert.

"We have to leave. Tonight."

"Leave? But those cursed witches will find us wherever we go."

"That is why we have to leave the Ninth Realm, Robert."

Confused, he searched her eyes. "What are you not telling me?"

"To survive that creature. . . . Our son has more power than you can imagine. We're all in danger now."

With a heavy sigh, Robert nodded in resignation. As Abigail pulled together an overnight bag, he glanced out the window one last time at his would-be farm, now shrouded in darkness. Their future as homesteaders would have to wait.

"I know who can take us," Robert said, following his wife from the room. "An old sailor."

"Can he be trusted?" she asked, hurrying down the hallway.

"Without a doubt." Robert joined Abigail in the master bedroom. "But we'll take no chances," he added, removing his broad, sheathed sword from the closet.

While Abigail stuffed a change of clothes for both of them into the overnight bag, Robert pulled on his High Council coat and gear. His mind raced ahead. He had never been to Midgard—the Earth realm. He was nervous but determined.

Wherever we settle, he silently vowed, *I will be the best father a boy can have.*

Chapter One

The day started out like every other day in the life of Sam Baron, which is to say it was as boring and predictable as the sun rising over the Blue Mountains. Sam rolled up to school five minutes past the bell and parked his bike. The brick buildings of Pilot Rock Junior High glistened from the heavy Oregon rain that had fallen during the night. In the distance, the giant boulder the town was named for loomed like a swollen tick.

Sam splashed through puddles and entered the building. The hallways were deserted, but he wasn't worried. Good old Mr. Platz didn't mind if Sam was a little late, as long as he brought his English teacher some of his old *Gamer* magazines.

He strolled into class and was surprised to see kids sitting on desks, throwing wads of paper, and chattering like hyenas. There was no sign of Platz. A crowd of boys had formed a dogpile by the window. Sam dropped his backpack on his seat in front of Keely Hatch. A quiet girl who kept to herself, Keely had her nose buried in a book.

"Where's Howie?" Sam asked.

Keely went on reading and pointed to the back.

Sam gritted his teeth. Howie got picked on. A lot. He was skinny, and his pants were usually an inch or three too short. Top that off with oversized glasses and a mop of curly hair, and he might as well have spray-painted a bull's-eye on his chest.

"Be careful," Keely cautioned as Sam brushed past. "Ronnie's in a mood."

A pair of familiar red tennis shoes stuck out from the bottom of the dogpile. Sam waded in, yanking aside the first two boys. Howie lay on his back. The class bully, Ronnie Polk, was on top of him, squashing a grape jelly sandwich all over Howie's face.

Sam yanked Ronnie off and spun him around. The startled look on Ronnie's face was priceless, as if he was about to wet his pants when he saw who it was. Kids started chanting, "*Fight, fight!*"

A twinge of guilt made Sam loosen his hold. He had already flattened Ronnie's nose once a few months back. Another incident, and his mom was going to pack him off to military school. But Ronnie had other ideas. He twisted free and punched Sam hard in the stomach. The air went out of Sam with an *oof*. Blood zinged between his ears. Grabbing Ronnie by the shirt, Sam cocked his fist back to reflatten Ronnie's nose, when the door opened with a bang.

A woman walked in on spindly high heels, dressed in a black suit cinched tight around the waist. Her ebony-colored hair was tied back in a sleek bun. Dropping a leather satchel on the desk, she turned to face the class, folding her arms primly. She arched one eyebrow at Sam, and he realized he was still holding Ronnie by his collar. Sam dropped the boy, sure he was about to be suspended.

"Sit down."

She rapped out the command with quiet authority. Kids scattered to their seats. Sam helped Howie to his feet. Chunks of grape jelly dripped from his friend's face. Sam handed Howie his glasses, and they slunk to their desks.

"My name is Ms. Endera," she announced to the silent room. "I will be taking over for Mr. Platz."

"What happened to Mr. Platz?" a girl up front asked.

Ms. Endera looked down her thin nose and said, "Why don't I show you? Raise your hand if you would like to see a magic trick."

Hands shot up. This was a lot more fun than grammar lessons. Ms. Endera rummaged in her black satchel and pulled out a silk handkerchief. "Observe." She put the scrap of fabric over her left hand and waved her other hand in a circle. "*Fein kinter, reptilia,*" she whispered.

Ms. Endera whipped the handkerchief away, and on her palm sat a fat green lizard. Its pink tongue slithered out of its mouth. The class oohed and clapped as she raised the reptile up high. "Here is your Mr. Platz. As you can see, someone has turned him into a lizard."

The class burst into laughter, but Sam half rose out of his chair. The lizard's eyes looked so forlorn, he almost believed it was their missing teacher.

Howie grabbed Sam and yanked him back down. "Dude, how'd she do that?" he whispered.

Sam had no idea, but it was kinda strange.

"When's he coming back?" Keely asked.

The room quieted, and Ms. Endera's eyes narrowed as she put the lizard away in her bag. "I don't believe poor Mr. Platz is going to be able to return. Let's play a little game, shall we?" She clapped her hands. "Everyone stand up. Come, come, out of your chairs." The students slouched to their feet, standing awkwardly next to their desks.

"Now, if you are a girl, you may sit down."

The girls grabbed their seats and giggled as if they had just won a prize.

Ms. Endera held up a finger. "If your father has blond hair, take a seat."

Seven of the boys sat down.

Sam shuffled from foot to foot. It was like an awful game of musical chairs. Only five boys remained.

She resumed her pacing. "If your father was at back-to-school night, please sit down." Three more were excused, leaving only Sam and Ronnie Polk. The bully shot Sam a nasty look, like it was Sam's fault Ronnie was left standing with him.

"You." She pointed at Ronnie. "Where was your father?"

Ronnie scowled. "At home, watching the play-offs. He says back-to-school night is lame."

She waved him into his chair. "And you?" She scrutinized Sam closely. "The boy with the temper. What is your name?"

"Sam. Sam Baron." A bead of sweat rose up on his brow. This was embarrassing.

"Mr. Baron, where was your father?"

"Working on a fishing boat in Alaska," he lied. She didn't need to know his dad had walked out two years ago without so much as a note.

Ronnie snorted loudly. "His dad took off 'cause Sam's so ugly."

Sam would gladly have punched Ronnie right then and there, but Ms. Endera came to his rescue. She stalked over on those spindly heels of hers and leaned over Ronnie's desk.

"Then your father must be a mountain troll—or has your nose always been that crooked?"

Ronnie turned red and sank down in his seat as titters of laughter spread across the class. Sam relaxed, taking the opportunity to take his seat. Maybe this Ms. Endera wasn't so bad.

They spent the rest of the period writing an essay about the kind of work their dads did. Sam filled a couple of pages on how to bait a hook, before the bell rang. As he gathered his stuff, Ms. Endera tapped him on the shoulder.

"I'd like a word after class."

The room emptied, leaving just the two of them. She sat on the edge of her desk, a tentative smile on her face. "I hope I didn't make you uncomfortable. I find it breaks the ice to play a little game."

Sam didn't want to tell her it had been a pretty lame game, not when she had come to his rescue. So he just said it was cool.

Ms. Endera crooked her finger, inviting him closer. "I have a secret," she said softly. "I'm looking for someone. A boy. About your age."

"Who?"

"Perhaps you," she said, searching his eyes intently.

Sam took a step back. His "crazy" sensors were sending off loud warnings. "I gotta go," he said, grabbing his backpack. He turned to make a break for it, but she was fast. In a blink, she was between Sam and the door.

She poked her finger into his chest. At her touch, a jolt of pain shot through Sam. "Are you a Son of Odin, Mr. Baron?"

"What? No," Sam gritted out. "I don't know what you're talking about."

She pressed harder. Iron bands wrapped around his torso until he felt like he couldn't breathe.

"I saw how you wanted to tear that boy apart," she crooned in a low voice. "Are you the one I'm looking for?"

Sam tried to shout for help, but his tongue felt nailed to the roof of his mouth.

Thankfully, the door burst open as the next class crowded in, filling the room with noise. Ms. Endera vanished, appearing on the other side of the classroom. Sam didn't stop to wonder how she had done that. He fled as fast as his feet could carry him.

Safely outside, he leaned against the wall, trying to slow his racing heart.

"Teacher's pet," Howie said, punching him on the arm.

"Shut up, Howie."

"You shut up, Mr. Baron, or I'll turn you into a lizard." Howie pitched his voice higher, mimicking Ms. Endera and waving his arms around. *"Finker pinker, reptile stinker."*

Sam couldn't help it; he smiled, feeling the haze of fear lift. "You okay?" he asked.

Howie shrugged, his skinny shoulders jutting sharply under

his tee. "Never better. Grape jelly facials are all the rage. Hey, check out the new kid."

Sam looked up. A boy stood uncertainly in the hall, clutching his schedule. His long black hair was tied neatly in a ponytail. He wore a flannel shirt over faded jeans. With his almond skin, he was obviously Umatilla. Strange. The Native American kids usually stuck to the reservation school.

Their eyes met. The other boy's nostrils flared, as if he recognized Sam, but Sam could swear he had never seen the kid before. One thing was certain: the day was turning out to be anything but boring.

Chapter Two

S am spent the day puzzling over his strange encounter with Ms. Endera. It was like she had turned him into a brain-dead zombie with that fingernail trick. He had been paralyzed, unable even to breathe. And how had she moved like a phantom from one side of the room to the other? As the last bell of the day rang, Sam found himself moving though the packed hallway in a daze. He was so busy thinking about Ms. Endera's eerie green eyes that he didn't see Ronnie Polk and his little gang of thugs lurking.

Next thing he knew, Ronnie slammed him up against a locker.

"Hey, Baron, seen your dad lately?" Ronnie laughed in Sam's face, spraying him with spittle. Half his lunch was stuck in his braces.

Two of Ronnie's pals pinned Sam's arms back.

"Back off, Ronnie," Sam said, trying to keep calm.

But Ronnie just sneered. "I'm gonna flatten *your* nose this time. See how you like it."

Ronnie pulled his fist back. Sam flinched, waiting for the punch, but a slender hand caught Ronnie's in a tight grip.

"Leave him alone." Keely stood there, her hazel eyes fierce as she stared Ronnie down.

The bully looked surprised; then his lip curled into a snarl. "Buzz off," he said, jerking free and knocking the books out of Keely's other hand, "before I rearrange your face."

A flush of anger rose up in Sam, making his cheeks sting. Picking on him was one thing, but picking on a girl? A burning sensation spread through his body, making every inch of his skin tingle. Strange words lit up in his brain, echoing in an incessant chant. With a sudden surge of rage, Sam tore his arms loose and grabbed Ronnie, pushing him backward so hard the boy hit the far wall with a thump. Like exploding firecrackers, the lockers around them blew open with loud cracks.

"I will finish you," Sam breathed, his fingers wrapped tightly around Ronnie's collar, "if you ever threaten her again."

Ronnie paled, shrinking two sizes. And just like that, Sam's anger faded. The flush in his face returned to normal, and the tingling subsided. He released Ronnie, suddenly ashamed over his outburst, and stepped back. The bully looked green, but he and his crew knocked over a trash can, shouting at the other kids in the hall as they made their escape.

Keely gaped at the open lockers as Sam bent down to pick up her books.

"How did you do that?" she asked.

Sam struggled to return his heart rate to normal. It had happened again, that unexpected flash of anger that took over his brain. He must have slammed Ronnie hard enough to make the lockers fly open. "I didn't need your help," he responded, handing the books to her. "I had it under control."

Keely shook her head, tossing her blond hair over one shoulder. "Really? Because it looked like Ronnie was about to give you a black eye." She hesitated, then blurted out, "I'm going to the library later, if you want to, you know, study or something. We have that geometry test Friday, and . . ."

"Yeah, I suck at math," Sam finished for her, smiling so she could see that his dazzling lack of math skills didn't bother him. "Thanks. But I have to warn you, I don't know a trapezoid from a tarantula."

Keely rolled her eyes but gave him a smile as she backed away, clutching her books. "Six o'clock, Baron. Don't be late."

Sam grinned, watching her go. Keely had kept to herself since she had moved to Pilot Rock the year before, but today she had shown real spunk. And Sam really needed the help with math.

The sound of distant thunder got him going. He hurried outside to his bike, eyeing the dark clouds overhead, then let out a groan. His back tire was flat—make that shredded. A chunk of rubber was missing, as if something had taken a bite out of it. He put his hand on the tire and came away with a wad of sticky fluid. He tried to shake it off, but it was as thick as gorilla snot.

Did Ronnie sabotage my bike? Sam thought, staring at the damage. A shadow fell over him. He looked up to see the new Umatilla kid hovering.

"What happened?" the kid asked. His dark eyes darted from Sam to the bike.

Sam scratched his head. "You got me. Something took a bite out of my tire."

The other boy knelt down, running his hand over the rim. He rubbed his fingers in the gorilla snot, bringing it to his nose to sniff it. "This is bad," he said, standing. He wiped his hand on his jeans. "You're being hunted."

"Hunted?" Sam's voice rose an octave. "By who?"

"Don't worry. It's my honor to protect you."

He looked so serious, Sam did not have the heart to laugh, but the kid was clearly out of his mind.

"I'm Leo," the boy said, and stuck out his hand.

Sam hesitated and then offered his own hand. "Sam."

As they shook, Leo's sleeve pulled away, revealing a long scar on the inside of his forearm. It looked like his arm had been torn up pretty badly. Leo caught Sam's glance and pulled his sleeve down.

Sam tried to be polite. "No offense, Leo, but I think I'll be fine. The most dangerous things around here are the rats in the cafeteria."

Leo looked like he wanted to argue, but Sam gave him a wave and started to push his wobbly bike down the street. He half expected the kid to follow him, but when he looked over his shoulder, Leo was gone.

Sam shook his head, perplexed. Some slobbery dog had probably mistaken his tire for a chew toy. Heavy drops began to fall, rolling down his neck and under his jacket. He lowered his head as the wind picked up and blew rain into his eyes.

By the time Sam made it to his driveway, his clothes were plastered to his skin and his fingers felt like skinny Popsicles. He fumbled with the key to open the side door to the garage and trundled the bike inside.

That's when his day got even weirder. By a factor of ten.

A bearded dwarf dressed in burlap stood where his mom's car usually parked, pointing a large sword at Sam. Thick reddish whiskers bristled around his nose. His sharp blue eyes seemed to miss nothing as he looked Sam up and down.

Sam raised his hands, hoping the dwarf wouldn't see how scared he was. "I-I don't have any money," he stuttered.

"What's your name, boy?"

Sam backed away. "Sam. Sam Baron."

The dwarf came closer, pressing the tip of the blade to Sam's stomach. "You're supposed to be dead."

"Well, sorry to disappoint," Sam joked, hoping the dwarf wasn't about to run him through.

The dwarf continued to glare at him. Then he sheathed his sword and shook his head. "So the rumors were true. This changes everything. Name's Rego." He bowed slightly. "I served under your father."

In a single heartbeat, Sam went from scared out of his wits to indignant. "My dad doesn't live here anymore, so you can go serve him somewhere else. Feel free to show yourself out." Dropping his hands, Sam nodded at the sword. "Unless you're planning to use that on me, I have a tire to fix."

Without waiting for an answer, Sam turned his back on the strange dwarf. His heart was pounding, but he was determined to act normal. He picked up his bike and flipped it over on the bench, kneading the rubber off the rim. Definite teeth marks had scored the aluminum. What kind of crazy animal attacked bicycle tires?

"We don't have much time, so it's vital that you listen to me," Rego said gravely. "Your life is in danger, Samuel. Something treacherous stalks you in Pilot Rock"—he stopped, squinting at the scratches on Sam's rim—"and from the look of things, it's already got your scent."

That Leo kid had said the same thing. Frowning, Sam opened a cupboard to get a new tire, when a giant bird burst out, knocking him over. It flew into Sam's face like it was trying to claw out his eyes.

Sam threw his arms up. "Get it away!" he yelled, batting at it, but Rego just let out a hearty laugh.

"That's where you've been hiding, Lagos." Rego gave a low whistle. The winged thing immediately withdrew and glided over to the dwarf's shoulder, where it perched daintily.

Sam risked a proper look at it. The bird was twice as big as a hawk, with cinnamon-orange feathers on its wings and a snow-white chest. Its beak looked sharp enough to rip his face off.

"What is that thing?" Sam asked, slowly picking himself up off the ground.

"She's a *iolar*." It rolled off Rego's tongue like *yo-lar*. "Noblest creature in the Ninth Realm." He ran his hand along her wing, smoothing her plumes with his fingers and crooning softly to her in a singsong language. "Go on, make friends with her."

Sam extended his hand tentatively and stroked the front of

Lagos's chest with his knuckles. Her heartbeat was steady and strong. He pulled his hand back. "So . . . who are you, again?"

Before Rego could answer, Lagos cocked her head toward the window and let out an alarming squawk. Rego's whole demeanor changed instantly. He unsheathed his sword, and his voice lowered to a growl.

"Let's just say I'm a friend of the family." Rego began slowly backing away toward the door. "I swore an oath to your father to protect you, and I never take an oath unless I'm willing to stake my life on it. But you must be careful, Samuel. The stones don't lie. You are in great danger." Then he tossed something into the air.

Sam caught it easily. It was a smooth rock, like the kind found in a riverbed. On its face was the scratched symbol of a jagged $\int$ shape. When Sam looked up, the dwarf was gone.

Chapter Three

Sam paced from one end of the house to the other, trying to understand both how a dwarf had ended up in his garage and why an Umatilla boy had warned him that he was being hunted. Not to mention his substitute English teacher was, well, strange, to say the least. Sam stared at the phone, tempted to call his mom, but she would just worry. His math book sat on the table. Sam made a decision. He would go see Keely at the library and then come straight home.

The rain had stopped, leaving scattered puddles that reflected the light from the streetlamps. Ordinarily, Sam wasn't afraid of riding in the dark. Pilot Rock was about the most boring town in the world. But tonight, his nerves were on edge as he pedaled down the darkened streets, imagining that he saw something lurking in the shadows of every tree he passed.

He was three blocks from the library when a strange howl split the silence of the night. The sound made the hair on the back of his neck stand up. Sam skidded his bike to a stop across from the dumpy town park. He could make out the swing set outlined against the white sand of the playground.

There. In the bushes fronting the park. Was that a rustle?

"Hello?" Sam couldn't see anything through the dense brush. His blood chilled. Was it the same animal that had tried to eat his tire? The animal that Leo and Rego said was hunting him?

Sam hesitated, biting down on his lip. It might be foolish, but he had to know. He couldn't run away like a scared kitten. Leaving his bike, he crossed the street and then jumped back as Leo himself stepped out of a bush. The boy held a long wooden lance in his hands. The grip was wrapped in leather, like deerskin. Its sharp metal tip glinted in the streetlight.

"Leo?" Sam let out the breath he had been holding, relieved and irritated he had been frightened by nothing. "Jeez, what's the deal? Are you following me?"

But Leo's eyes were trained on a spot just over Sam's shoulder. "Run," he said, shoving Sam behind him.

Sam turned in time to see a king-size wolf step out of the bushes and onto the sidewalk. Soot black, it had enormous paws the size of Sam's baseball mitt. A long snout jutted from a head that was squared and capped by tall, pointed ears. Fangs glistened in the weak light of the streetlamp as it snarled at the boys. And those eyes: feral, wild, and hungry.

Nimbly twirling the lance, Leo snapped it to a stop and held it in front of him as he crouched low. "Don't worry, Sam. My father has entrusted me with your protection. I won't let you down."

He jabbed at the fierce creature with his weapon, but it snapped its jaws, breaking the lance in half like a toothpick. Then the wolf coiled itself and sprang over Leo, straight at Sam. Terror froze Sam to the spot. All he could see was a set of glowing green eyes bearing down, claws outstretched, when a large figure knocked him to the ground. Sam scuffed his face on the pavement as the beast sailed past, skidding to a landing on the other side.

"Stay down," the man said, before jumping to his feet. He was another Umatilla, older, but with the same long black hair and caramel skin as Leo. Three more Umatilla appeared out of the bushes. They surrounded Sam, holding sturdier lances than the one Leo had brandished.

"Dad! What are you doing here?" Leo asked, grabbing his broken lance and holding it in front of him.

"You should have told me a Shun Kara had returned," his father rebuked.

The men shouted and jabbed at the beast, driving it back. The wolf kept circling, trying to move in. Finally, with a howl that hurt Sam's ears, it loped off into the dark, fading into the shadows.

Leo stuck out his hand to help Sam up. "I'm sorry, Sam. This was my fault."

"What was that thing?" Sam said, feeling the sting where his cheek had scraped the ground.

Leo's father cut in. "That was a Shun Kara. The black wolf. If my son had warned me, you would have been properly protected. I'm Chief Pate-wa. You have my word: it won't happen again. From now on, my people will be standing by to keep you safe."

The other Umatilla men stood in a circle, staring silently at Sam. Leo's head hung low. Sam knew he should thank them, but he backed away, feeling spooked by the chief's words.

"I can take care of myself. Just leave me alone."

"Wait, Sam!" Leo shouted after him, but Sam ran to his bike and shoved off. He pedaled furiously, imagining the clicking sounds of nails loping along the pavement, gaining on him with every step.

The bright lights of the library were the most welcome sight Sam had ever seen. Locking his bike to the rail, he barreled up the steps, not breathing until he was safe inside the building. He found Keely on the third floor, bent over a math book. Her hair had fallen over her face like a blond curtain.

She looked up with a smile, then frowned when she saw the scrape on Sam's face. "Don't tell me you ran into Ronnie Polk."

"No. Just something . . . stupid. Forget it." Sam didn't want to think about that wolf or Leo's strange need to protect him. It had to be some kind of Umatilla tribal thing.

"What is it with you and Ronnie, anyway?" she asked, laying her pencil down.

Sam flushed. "We got into it last summer. At my twelfth birthday party." He grew silent as he dredged up the memory of that day. One minute, he had been enjoying his slice of cake; the next, he'd had Ronnie down on the ground, pounding his face into the dirt like a tent stake.

"What did he do?"

"It's not what he did. It's what he said." Sam stared at his hands as he recalled the words. "He was mouthing off, saying my dad left town to be with his real family."

"Ouch."

"Yeah. I might have overreacted. Howie said I turned bright red." All Sam remembered was that the sun had felt too hot, like he was burning up inside. The cake had slipped out of his fingers, and a roar in his ears had sent him into a boiling rage. He had never felt so much anger at one time.

Sam looked at Keely. "To be honest, I don't even remember hitting him; it just happened so fast." Sam left out the part where Ronnie had called him a freak as the boy's mother rushed him away, glaring at Sam as if he were some kind of monster.

"So, what's the story with your dad?" she asked softly.

Thinking of his dad was like stepping on a thumbtack. "He took off. Two years ago. No note, no warning—just left town."

Keely said nothing at first; then she covered his hand with hers. "I'm sorry. I know how that must feel."

Sam seriously doubted that. Hoping to change the subject, he took the odd stone the dwarf had given him from his pocket and tossed it on the table. "I found this today. You ever see anything like it?"

"This looks like a rune stone," Keely said, picking it up and studying it. "Runes are part of Norse mythology. I did a project on them in sixth grade."

She set the stone down and disappeared into the racks, eventually returning with a heavy, leather-bound book. She laid it out on the table, flipping through its pages. Sam scooted his chair closer to look over her shoulder. She smelled of cherry Chap-Stick. It was nice. The sheets were filled with drawings of fierce-looking men and strange, mythical animals.

"Here it is," she said, turning to a page with a list of symbols. She pointed at the image of a sharply pointed S, just like the one scratched on the rock.

"What does it say?"

She studied the text. "This one stands for *Sigel*. It says, 'The holder of this stone is the source of energy for the sun.'"

"What does that mean?"

Keely shrugged. "The runes aren't literal. You interpret them according to the person and the wisdom being sought." She flipped through more pages.

"Who's that?" Sam pointed at a picture of an old man with a long beard and muscled arms, dangling from the branch of a large tree.

"That's Odin. He was the most powerful god in Norse culture."

Sam's heart skipped a beat at the mention of Odin. What had Ms. Endera said? She was looking for a Son of Odin? "This Odin, did he have sons?"

"Sure, Odin had lots of sons and daughters. Haven't you ever heard of Thor?"

Sam couldn't stop a chuckle. "If Ms. Endera's after a movie star, then she's got the wrong guy."

"Thor is based on a Norse myth," Keely persisted. "Odin was his father."

"Fine. Are any of these sons still alive?"

"Technically, the Norse gods are all dead. They walked the earth until an ultimate battle called Ragnarok, but some people believe they still exist in one of the other realms."

"What other realms?"

She leaned in intently, folding her hands. "Odin created these nine realms, like worlds within worlds, each one separate from the other. The underworld was part of the lower realms. Our world, the world of mankind, was somewhere in the middle, and Asgard, the home of the gods, was at the top." Her eyes shone with excitement as she told the tale.

"Do you believe that?"

Keely hesitated, and the light dimmed in her eyes. She shut the book with a snap. "Doesn't matter what I believe. This isn't going to help you pass your math test." She held out the rune stone, but Sam shook his head.

"You keep it." He didn't want any reminders of his strange day.

She looked pleased, tucking it away in her bag before babbling on about angles and polygons.

Sam hardly heard a word she said. Overnight, Pilot Rock had gone from a boring little town to the epicenter of strangeness. And he had a feeling this was only the beginning.

Chapter Four

That night, Sam dreamed that his substitute English teacher was chasing him down the hallway at school. As Ms. Endera got closer, she changed into a black wolf with glittering green eyes, reaching for him with sharpened nails. He awoke with a start, tangled in the sheets.

Lying back on his pillow, Sam stared up at the ceiling, thinking about good old Mr. Platz. Why would a teacher pack up and leave in the middle of a semester without saying goodbye? Maybe if Sam figured that out, he could shake the nagging feeling that Ms. Endera had actually turned Mr. Platz into a lizard.

Because that was crazy.

Unable to go back to sleep, Sam threw off the sheets and got dressed. He crept down the hall past his mom's bedroom. He could see her asleep, still dressed, on top of the covers. His mom worked the night shift at the local mill and came home long after he had gone to bed. Sam hesitated, then went in and pulled a blanket over her.

The sun was just rising when he set out for Platz's house on his bike. He had been there once before with Howie to drop off a late assignment, and they had ended up playing a round of Zombie Wars with his teacher. The guy had crazy gaming skills and had shown them some secret back doors to upping levels. Sam figured he had just enough time to knock on Platz's door, beg his teacher to come back, and make it to school before the bell rang.

Relieved to see his teacher's aging Camaro in the driveway, Sam left his bike and crept across the lawn, leaving footprints in the crisp layer of frost. He peeked in the front window. A sofa lay tipped on its side. Papers were strewn all over the floor. It looked like the place had been ransacked.

He tried the door. Locked. He was about to go around back, when the garage rumbled open. Diving into the bushes, he peered over the top and saw Ms. Endera come out and walk to Platz's car.

What was Ms. Endera doing at Platz's house?

She carried a small wire cage holding the lizard she had shown them in class. Sam stared at the creature and felt a connection as the lizard's eyes locked with his. A jolt of sadness and fear shot through him, as if the lizard were trying to communicate with him. Ms. Endera stopped, her head turning toward the lawn. Sam ducked down lower.

"Is someone there?" she called.

Sam froze, his heart jerking like a yo-yo. Ms. Endera studied the lawn. He had stupidly left footprints, he realized with a silent groan. But just as he was about to jump out and offer some lame explanation, Ms. Endera tossed the cage on the seat and started the car, throwing the Camaro in reverse, and backed right over Sam's bike. Sam watched helplessly as the tires squashed his rim and the Camaro roared off down the street.

He waited a moment to be sure that she was gone, then retrieved his mangled bike. Far from feeling better, Sam was now dead certain that this Ms. Endera was somehow behind Mr. Platz's disappearance. Stashing the bike in Platz's side yard, Sam began hoofing it to school. He could think of a million things he would rather do, but he had to get some answers. And this lady teacher seemed to be at the center of the recent strange events.

He slipped in the side door just in time for the first bell.

Kids milled about, talking aimlessly, like it was just another normal day at school. Sam wanted to shout out the truth, that their substitute teacher was some kind of enchantress, but instead, he headed for his locker and angrily spun the combination and opened the door.

A fanged creature with black wings and razor-sharp talons launched itself at him, ensnaring the front of Sam's shirt. Its wings flapped in his face as it tried to sink its teeth into Sam's neck. A thin stream of slime dripped from its fangs. Sam caught a glimpse of red eyes as he screamed, putting his hands around it and wrestling it away from his neck. Then, as suddenly as it had appeared, it flew up into the heating vent and vanished, leaving Sam fighting with nothing but air.

Traffic in the hallway ground to a halt as every kid stared at Sam as if he had the plague. Howie came up and put his hand on Sam's shoulder. "Dude, what's with all the screaming?"

"Didn't you see it?" Sam gasped. "That thing attacked me."

Howie raised an eyebrow. "What thing?" He looked inside Sam's locker. "You losing your marbles?"

Sam gingerly fingered the tiny tears in his shirt. No way had he imagined that.

The warning bell rang, and students darted in every direction.

"Get it together, my man. You don't want to be late to English, or Ms. Endera might turn you into a lizard," Howie razzed.

Sam grabbed Howie by the arm. "There's something going on with her. I went to Platz's house this morning, and she was there. We need to find out what she's up to."

But Howie backed away from him, his cheeks reddening. "Is there a problem, Mr. Baron?" Ms. Endera's voice sounded in Sam's ear.

She had snuck up on him like a dark shadow. Sam turned and met the glittering look in her eyes. His courage wavered.

"There's no problem, Ms. Endera."

"Good. Come along, boys. You don't want to miss today's lesson. It's going to be very enlightening."

Sam watched her go, her heels clicking and clacking down the hall.

"Thanks a lot," Howie muttered, slinking along behind her.

But Sam didn't follow, his feet rooted in place. He had such a feeling of dread, such an aversion to going to class, that he literally couldn't move. The second bell rang, and the halls emptied. He started to walk then, feeling like a prisoner going to the gallows. He stopped outside the door of the classroom. He could see Ms. Endera inside, stalking back and forth in front of the chalkboard. A cold sweat broke out on his forehead. He wanted to puke right there, wishing himself a deadly disease that would get him out of class.

As he reached for the handle, the fire alarm on the wall gave him an idea. Before he could change his mind, Sam lifted the lever and took a step back, slightly panicked, as the alarm started to sound shrilly.

Doors flung open in the hallway. Sam nearly wept with relief as students poured out, jostling him as they hurried for the exit. Ms. Endera's eyes met his over the crowd of students leaving her class, and he couldn't help grinning. But his smile faded as she glared at him like she wanted to eat his liver. Sam backed away, but not before he saw her pointing at him and tilting her head back to laugh.

———(◈◈◈)———

At lunchtime, Sam waited in line at the cafeteria, trying not to think about lizards or wolves or substitute teachers. He was surprised to see Keely sitting at a table with Leo and Howie, laughing at everything they said. Sam stuck his plate out, not caring what the lunch lady put on it, watching Keely's hands flutter in the air as she told some story.

She waved him over to her table, and Sam took a seat. Howie was spooning up chocolate pudding. Howie liked to eat dessert first.

"That looks delicious," Leo said politely, nodding at Sam's plate.

Sam looked down. He had a big slop of spaghetti and meatballs. Great—he was probably going to get sauce all over his face. He stabbed at a meatball as they resumed talking. Everyone seemed to like the new guy, Leo. Even Howie asked nonstop questions about the reservation.

Sam fumed in silence, wishing someone would ask him if he was okay, if he had been attacked by any strange creatures that flew out of his locker, and whether their missing teacher was really a lizard. He grew more and more angry as he tried to stab the meatball that kept sliding around on his plate.

Something was off. The noodles seemed to be moving. He would stab at the meatball, and it would slide away. Sam held his fork up and watched as the noodles inched along like worms, slithering around and around. He looked to see if anyone else had noticed, but the cafeteria had gone quiet, even though kids were still talking and laughing and eating their lunches. It was as if Sam was locked in his own world. He looked back at his plate and watched the noodles spin and dance, forming a tunnel in the center like a vortex. The meatballs swirled around the bottom. Sam stared, fascinated by what was happening, and then it suddenly blew up into his face, spattering him with noodles and red sauce. One meatball landed on his head.

The roar of laughter penetrated his haze. Sam wiped the sauce away from his eyes with one hand. Leo stared, and Keely's mouth hung open. And then she started laughing and Howie joined in. Leo continued to stare, a frown marring his features.

"Sam, what the heck?" Keely said, giggling at him.

A wave of rage washed over him, blanking out Sam's thoughts

and leaving behind feelings so primal he wanted to howl. He started to rise out of his seat, when he saw Ms. Endera leaning against a wall in the corner of the cafeteria, her eyes on him like burning emeralds.

She had done this to him. She had made him look a fool. He was certain.

Ms. Endera moved away, but not before he caught a glimpse of the satchel she carried over her shoulder. A scaly lizard's head poked out, desperately trying to escape. She roughly shoved the reptile back down and departed.

After lunch, Sam spent the day like a shadow, bouncing from class to class and staying as far away from Ms. Endera as he could.

When the final bell rang, he hurried to leave the building and ran straight into Keely.

"What's the matter with you?" Keely blocked the door, looking impatient. "You act like you've seen a ghost."

"I'm fine. I just need to go. Howie's waiting for me," Sam lied, listening for the clicking of Ms. Endera's heels.

"He's going to be a while. Ms. Endera asked him to help her with something."

Fear spiked through him. Sam gripped her arm. "Where were they going?"

"Lay off! It's like you're about to explode."

She was right. Sam did feel like he was about to blow his lid, because nothing was making any sense. He relaxed his grip. "I'm sorry. It's just . . . you wouldn't understand."

"Try me."

Sam studied her face. "Okay, what would you say if I told you that I think Ms. Endera really did turn Mr. Platz into a lizard?" There. He had said it out loud.

Predictably, Keely rolled her eyes. "Sam, if this is some kind of a joke—"

"It's not a joke. She's after me for some reason, and I think she's using Howie as bait."

Keely took a deep breath. "You know how crazy that sounds, right?"

"Look, I don't expect you to believe me—I wouldn't believe me, either. Just tell me where Howie is."

"She told him to meet her in the gym."

Without another word, Sam rushed off in that direction.

"Sam, wait!" Keely caught up to him and yanked him to a halt. "I want to help."

"Then come on," he said, grabbing her hand and running. "We have to stop her."

Outside the gymnasium, they peered in through the glass door panels. The place was dark. It looked deserted.

"They're not in there," Keely said.

Sam ignored her and pushed open the door. The gym smelled of sweat and old leather. Voices sounded from the other side of the room. Sam dragged Keely out of sight under the bleachers. They crept forward to peer through one of the rows.

The lights snapped on. Howie walked alongside Ms. Endera across the basketball court, carrying a ladder. He seemed to be chattering away, like nothing was amiss.

"He's fine," Keely whispered.

"Wait," Sam whispered back. "Let's just make sure."

Howie put the ladder under the backboard and climbed up. He stood on the top, teetering slightly, then reached and lifted something off the back of the rim.

Sam leaned forward for a better look. It was Ms. Endera's lizard, clinging to the metal basketball rim.

Sam was so surprised, he raised up, bumping his head against the bench above him.

"You can come out, Mr. Baron," Ms. Endera called. "Your friend, too."

Reluctantly, Keely and Sam crawled out from under the bleachers and stood next to a rack of balls. Howie climbed down with the lizard, looking at Sam as if he were from another planet.

"Isn't this convenient," Ms. Endera said to Sam. "Now I don't have to come looking for you."

The lizard jumped out of Howie's hands onto the floor, scampering for the exit door. Ms. Endera waggled her fingers and zapped it with a crackling green light that leaped from her fingertips. The lizard began to grow, its legs extending and its snout enlarging. As its torso thickened and stretched, its head grew larger and a row of ugly teeth sprouted. Thick scales covered its body. It rose up on muscular hind legs, towering six feet tall as it pawed the air with its front claws.

"Sam, what is that?" Keely said, clutching his arm so tightly that her nails dug into his skin.

"I don't know."

The lizard turned toward Howie. "Run, Howie!" Sam shouted, but Howie didn't move. His hands hung at his sides; his jaw hung open in utter shock.

Sam tackled his friend as the giant lizard tried to bite Howie's head off with its razor-sharp teeth. Then Keely screamed. The lizard had dropped to all fours and was waddling at high speed toward her.

Sam pulled Howie to his feet, and they rushed to Keely's side. The reptile reared up on its hind legs and let out a snarling roar, beating its chest with its clawed hands. It snapped its jaws at them as it prowled forward, backing them up against the bleachers.

"Take Keely and make a run for it!" Sam shouted at Howie.

"No way! I'm not leaving you!" Howie hollered back.

Just then, a voice shouted from the other side of the gym. Leo stood in the open doorway of the boys' locker room.

"This way, Sam!"

Chapter Five

Sam grabbed the rack of basketballs and knocked it over, tripping the giant lizard with the jumble of rolling balls. Running hard, they burst through the double doors into the locker room.

"Follow me," Leo said.

Metal overhead lights dimly lit the sprawling space. They raced down the center aisle past rows of lockers. Ducking down a row at random, Keely and Howie crouched behind one bay while Sam and Leo pressed up against the next. The lizard entered the room, its claws clicking on the cement floor.

"Come out, come out; I just want to talk!" Ms. Endera called. "There's nothing to be afraid of!"

Keely and Howie looked at Sam hopefully, but he shook his head. Ms. Endera was lying through her teeth.

The lizard jumped on top of the lockers with a thump that shook the rafters. Sam's friends looked terrified, huddling down as if they could make themselves disappear. The monster was jumping from bay to bay, searching for them. It was only a matter of time before it discovered their hiding spot.

Sam could hear the lizard lumbering down their row. Sweat rolled down his temples. If he just sat there, they were going to be an all-you-can-eat lizard buffet. He had no choice. Before Leo could guess his intentions, Sam jumped out into the aisle and waved his arms.

"Here I am, lizard-man—try to catch me." Sam jumped onto the bench and then levered himself up to the top of the lockers as the lizard snapped at him, narrowly missing him. He ran down the bay, then took a running leap at the next set of lockers. Sam laughed as his feet hit the metal with a thump. The lizard jumped after him but fell short, slamming into the ground. The exit door was in sight. Sam picked up the pace as he raced along the locker tops, and then he nearly choked, flinging his arms back to stop himself from falling as Endera appeared in front of him in a puff of green smoke.

"Hello, Sam."

"Leave me alone," he said, backing away. But behind him, the Platz-lizard thing was making its way toward him.

"Oh, but I've come all this way just to see you." She reached out a hand and grabbed him by his shirt. "And I can't bear to leave without you."

Whatever she was going to do next was lost in a sudden cacophony of noise as Sam's three crazed friends ran toward them, bearing metal trash cans and beating them, hollering at the top of their lungs. Endera turned her head sharply toward the noise. Her hand came up, and a blast of green fire shot out of her palm, straight at Sam's friends. Leo had the sense to raise the lid of his trash can like a shield. The blast of fire ricocheted off and shot up into the rafters. It must have hit one of the fire sprinklers, because before Sam could catch his breath, water poured down on them and the fire bells began to clang.

Sam was about to give Endera a taste of his knuckles, when she vanished in a puff of smoke, taking her ugly lizard with her. He spun around, searching, but Ms. Endera was nowhere to be seen. "She's gone!" he shouted.

Leo helped Keely up, while Howie clambered to his feet. Sam

jumped down to join them. Water from the sprinklers poured down, soaking them to the skin. They stared at each other in disbelief.

Leo spoke first. "We should go before someone comes."

They headed for a side door that opened onto the practice field and ran all the way to the bleachers.

"You guys okay?" Sam asked, shaking the water out of his hair.

Howie gave him a weak thumbs-up, but Keely started shouting.

"Are you crazy? A giant lizard just attacked us. I'm the opposite of okay. What was that thing?"

Sam shrugged. "I told you, I think Ms. Endera turned Platz into a lizard."

She looked at Howie, who just shrugged, then back at Sam. "How? And how did she make it grow like that?"

"I don't know," Sam said.

"Sam, you need to be more careful," Leo cautioned. "Endera is not who she pretends to be."

Sam laughed. "Yeah, I kinda figured that out when she zapped that lizard into a monster."

Leo flushed. "I'm sorry," he began, but Howie slapped him on the back.

"Thanks for saving our bacon, bro."

Keely paced along the fence. "We have to tell someone what happened."

"Tell them what, Keely?" Sam argued. "Our new English teacher turned our old one into a lizard, and it tried to eat us? Who's going to believe that?"

Keely stopped pacing and glared at him. "Well, we have to do something!"

Leo stepped forward. "My father will know what to do. My people know this Ms. Endera. She has been hunting Sam."

"Hunting him? Why?" Keely asked.

Leo looked embarrassed. "I don't know. My father hasn't trusted me with the whole story."

They were all silent for a moment, until Howie chimed in: "So . . . anyone up for a Chuggies run?"

Chuggies was Pilot Rock's local hamburger joint. Howie's uncle owned it and gave them free fries.

"You want to eat a burger after nearly being eaten alive?" Keely asked in disbelief. "What's wrong with you?"

Howie looked to Sam for support. "I don't know. I guess life-and-death situations make me hungry."

The high-pitched sound of a bird trilling had Leo looking over his shoulder. "My father is close by. I have to find him and tell him what happened. But I should stay with Sam—"

"Don't worry about me, Leo. I'll be fine."

Leo hesitated. Then the trilling sounded again, and he backed away. "Stick with the others, Sam. I'll see you later." Then he ran off.

Keely tightened up her backpack. "I have to get dinner ready for my dad, so I'm out."

"Can't your mom do it?" Sam asked. "You heard Leo: we should stick together until we figure this out."

Keely's face tightened, and something flickered in her eyes. "No. My mom can't do it. She's not here. I mean . . . she's dead."

Sam flushed. *Insert foot in mouth and swallow*, he thought.

"Sorry," he said awkwardly, but she was already walking away. Howie smacked him in the back of the head and hurried to catch up to her.

Howie lived two blocks from school. When they got to his street, he stopped to salute them. "Keep away from man-eating lizards," he cracked.

"Lock your door," Sam warned.

Howie laughed, backing away. "Dude, I live with ten people. Have you seen my brothers? They'd eat that lizard for breakfast."

Sam waited until Howie was safely inside, then hurried after Keely. "Sorry about your mom," he started, as he fell in step beside her.

"Forget it. It's not your fault."

For once, Sam wished he had the right words, but nothing came to mind. They walked in silence for a while. She stopped in front of a red brick house.

"This is me," she said.

"Okay, well, double-bolt the door, all right? I don't want a lizard to eat you."

She didn't smile, just headed up the cement path, her head down, like she was someplace else.

———————⟨⟩———————

Sam entered through the front door and caught the familiar smell of a burnt casserole.

"Mom, I'm home!"

"In the kitchen," she called out.

Sam dropped his bag by the door. His mom was just pulling dinner out of the oven. She looked flustered. Her T-shirt was spattered with tomato sauce, and her long black hair was tied back in a ponytail, but most of it had come loose.

"Here, let me get it." Sam grabbed an oven mitt and lifted the heavy dish onto the counter. The macaroni casserole had its usual blackened crust over the top.

"I burned it again," she lamented. "I'll never understand that oven. How was your day?" she asked, turning to smile at him.

"It was school." He gave her a quick hug. "Long, boring, and teachers breathing down my neck."

She held him at arm's length. "Why are there holes in your shirt?" She frowned, poking at the small tears. "Have you been fighting again?"

Sam hated that look in her eyes, like he had disappointed her. He stepped back. "No. It's a long story. Let's eat. I'm starved."

"Don't change the subject. I'm off tonight, so I've got plenty of time to listen."

Sam raised his eyebrows. "You got a night off?"

"Yup." She slid two plates out of the cupboard. "I had this feeling you missed me, so I asked for a break."

"Great!" he said, and meant it. He wished she had a better life. His mom worked long nights at the lumber mill, dispatching trucks. She was stuck working there because his dad had left them with nothing. Her eyes held a sadness that never went away. It had been there ever since the day two years ago when his father hadn't come home.

They sat down at the table and began to eat.

"So, if you weren't fighting, what happened to your shirt?" she asked over a forkful of casserole.

Sam opted for the truth. "A giant bat attacked me," he said, looking her in the eye. "And then it disappeared like that—poof!"

She grew completely still; then, as he had hoped, she laughed. "Ha, ha, very funny," she said. "Fine, none of my business. How are things at school?"

"I've got a new English teacher. And this girl, Keely, is helping me with math."

"Is she cute? The girl, not the teacher."

Sam rolled his eyes. No way was he talking to his mom about girls.

The doorbell rang as they cleared the dishes.

"I'll get it," he offered.

Sam opened the door. It was Rego, the dwarf from the garage.

"I need to speak with your mother," he said.

"She's not home." Sam tried to shut the door, but Rego stuck his boot in the way, wedging it open. Before Sam could wrestle it closed, his mom came up behind him.

"Rego, what's happened? Why are you here?"

And that's how Sam found out that his mom knew much more about the incredible events of Sam's day than he ever could have imagined.

Chapter Six

Inside the red brick house, Keely checked her watch for the tenth time. Her dad should have been home by now. She sat at the dining room table, set for two. The candle she had lit sputtered fitfully. She had not eaten, hoping he would show up. It was his favorite. Roast beef and steamed spinach. The meal was cold now.

Her hands shook as she made a mental list of reasons today's events in the gym could be explained. One, she had been exposed to some kind of tainted food at lunch and was hallucinating. Two, she had contracted a foreign virus and was currently in a feverish coma, having a vivid dream. Three, Sam was right, and Ms. Endera had turned their old teacher into a lizard. None of her choices was comforting in the least. She leaned forward and blew out the candle.

The thought of eating alone curled her stomach. She had tried to fill the gap left by her mom, but it was hard. Even harder for her dad, she remembered, awash with guilt. Her eyes flicked to the picture of the three of them that sat on the hutch. Happier times. Before the tumor. Before the crushing sadness.

Sighing, she picked up the plates and took them to the kitchen, dumping them in the sink. It was tough enough losing one parent, but she felt alone in the world. Her hair needed trimming. She had outgrown most of her clothes. But she was too embarrassed to say anything to her dad. Not when she was to blame. If only she had seen how much pain her mom was in, maybe she could have done something. That's what Keely kept telling herself.

The doorbell rang, interrupting her guilty thoughts. Her dad must be home at last, she thought, skipping to the door and opening it.

Ms. Endera stood on the porch, a malicious grin on her face.

"Hello, Keely. How would you like to take a trip?" Ms. Endera opened her hand and blew some black powder into Keely's face. Keely sneezed, and then all feeling left her body.

⚬⚬⚬

Howie's homecoming was unspectacular. The household was in its usual state of chaos. When you were number eight of ten siblings, you tended to get overlooked. Howie's parents had named their brood alphabetically, in order to better remember their names: Andrew, Brianna, Cody, Daniel, Ellen, the twins—Frankie and Gemma—then Howie, Isabella, and Jessie. The older ones hogged the TV, the bathroom, and the attention of their parents; the youngest two hogged whatever was left, leaving Howie with zippo.

"Hi, Mom," he said, trying unsuccessfully to give her a hug as she moved away to prevent one of the twins from grabbing the dish in her hands.

"Howie, be a dear and get the table set."

Four of his siblings were sprawled on the couch, watching TV. Howie sighed and opened the silverware drawer. "A giant lizard attacked me today," he said loudly as he set the table. "I think it was my old English teacher."

"That's nice, Howie," his mom said absently.

"Yeah, I thought so, too," he said softly, carefully placing the silverware in its proper place.

Everyone in Howie's family ignored his tall tales. They knew he made up stories because nothing exciting ever happened to him. He simply couldn't compete with his siblings. They all had some kind of special talent. Andrew and Cody were football stars. Brianna and Ellen ruled the soccer field. Daniel and the twins were gifted pianists and flute players. Even Izzie and Jessie were excelling at ballet lessons. Howie had nothing—not a single trophy, award, or prize to show for his childhood, besides a meager collection of participation ribbons.

His mom put her fingers to her mouth and let out a loud whistle, signaling that dinner was ready. There was a stampede to the table. Howie sank into a seat at the end, waiting for the food to be passed. By the time the platter of roast beef reached him, there was only one gristly piece left. He went to stab it with his fork, but his brother Cody grabbed it with two hands, winking at him as he bit into it.

"Sorry, bro; every man for himself."

Before Howie could complain, Jessie started crying because Izzie had taken her biscuit. The house erupted in yelling, shouting, and screaming. Giving up, Howie slunk away from the table, hoping to find something in the fridge to take to his room. As he studied the containers of leftovers, a scratching noise came at the back door, then the sound of rattling, as if someone were trying to open it.

Half hoping it was the Platz-lizard thing so he could show everyone that his story was true, Howie went to the door and pulled the curtain aside. The porch was empty. Probably the neighbor's cat digging in the trash again. *Great*, he thought. *I'll be the one who has to clean it up.* But when Howie opened the door to shoo it away, he came face-to-face with Ms. Endera.

"Hello, Howie." She opened her hand. She had a handful of dirt, or at least that was the last thing Howie remembered. She blew it in his face, and the lights went out in his brain.

While Sam's mom, Abigail, made a pot of coffee, Sam stared across the table at Rego, who, in turn, watched his *iolar*, Lagos. The bird was perched on top of the refrigerator, gazing vigilantly out the window. The wheezing hum of the central heating system echoed the tension in the room.

Abigail joined them, gripping her cup like it was a lifeline to sanity.

"What's the news, Rego?"

"News? Abigail, surely you know the news is sitting right here." He jabbed a finger at Sam. "The boy's alive. You led us to believe he was dead."

She flushed. "It was safer that way. You know why."

"I'll have to take him back with me."

She shook her head firmly. "He's not going back."

Sam looked between them, completely confused by the conversation and by the fact that his mom seemed to be on a first-name basis with this dwarf. "Does anybody want to explain where 'back' is?"

Rego ignored him. "Abigail, milady, the High Council will want to know he lives."

She jumped up and started pacing. "If I send him back, the witches will find a way to get to him. I'll take him away from here, somewhere safe."

"The witches have already found him," Rego thundered. "Endera Tarkana is here. And she's brought her black wolves with her to hunt the boy."

"How?" She looked at Sam.

He shrugged. "I told you. I have a new English teacher."

"And?" Her face was white as she waited for him to go on.

Sam flushed, mumbling the rest. "And I think she turned Mr. Platz into a lizard. It sort of tried to eat me today."

"Sam, you should have told me. And you"—she whirled on Rego—"you left him out there with those black monsters. He could have been killed!"

Rego's shoulders stiffened. "I was guarding the stonefire, milady, so no more of those infernal spellcasters could cross over. Chief Pate-wa and his tribe were watching over Sam. I made sure of it."

"I've heard enough. I'm taking Sam away. Tonight." She grabbed her purse, fumbling for the keys.

"The red sun is back."

At the dwarf's quiet words, Abigail turned even whiter, as if all the blood had left her body. "No. No, it's not possible."

"Tell that to the farmers who have lost their crops this year because of its poisonous rays. The boy must come back. Surely you can see that."

Sam couldn't take it any longer. "Stop!" he shouted. "No one's taking me anywhere." He looked from his mom to the dwarf. "Not until somebody tells me what's going on here. I mean, witches and wolves? Man-eating lizards? Tell me this is some kind of bad dream, and that I'm going to wake up soon. Please."

"Sam." His mom sat down and took his hand. "I don't know where to begin—"

"Boy, your mother and father are from another realm called Orkney," Rego cut in. "Your father's a descendant of Odin, and your mother—"

"Rego, don't!" Abigail interrupted.

"He needs to know," Rego insisted, his eyes fixed on Sam. "Your mother is a witch. Your parents crossed through the stonefire when you were a tiny thing to protect you from the rest of them witches, like Endera Tarkana. The witches killed your father, and now they're after you. Oops"—he looked at Abigail's stricken face—"I've said too much."

"Robert's dead?" she whispered.

Sam barely took in the part where Rego had said his mother was a witch. All he heard was the part about his father being dead. His heart turned into a chunk of ice. He had always imagined his dad living it up somewhere, playing the slots in Vegas or fly-fishing on the California coast. Dead was something different altogether.

Chapter Seven

"Rego! Answers. Now," Abigail demanded.

The dwarf licked his lips before answering. "Two years ago, when Lord Barconian returned to help lead the battle against the witches, it did not go as planned."

Sam's mind reeled. "Lord Barconian? Was that his real name?" He looked from Rego to his mom.

Abigail nodded, her hands twisting in her lap. "All this time . . . when he didn't come back, I hoped he was still alive, still fighting. What happened?"

"The witches tricked him into going to the Ring of Brogar," Rego said grimly.

Sam gripped the table, feeling dizzy. "What's the Ring of Brogar?"

"It's an ancient circle of giant stones. Centuries ago, six of the most powerful witches were trapped inside them as punishment for their crimes. Endera lured your father there with the promise of peace, a way to end the war between us and the witches. The Council warned him not to trust her, but your father was a stubborn man. Once he entered the ring, the witches sprang their trap. Lord Barconian's troops were being slaughtered. He surrendered himself in exchange for the lives of his men." Rego took a deep breath. "The witches must have incinerated him with their damnable magic."

"And his men? Did they escape alive?" Abigail's voice was tinged with faint hope.

"No, milady, the witches laid waste to them without a shred of mercy." The dwarf gritted his teeth at the bitter memory. "By the time we arrived with reinforcements, there were just the remains. We were burying them when we heard a voice. It was my brother, Amicus, trapped under the bodies of five men. He lost an arm, but he survived to tell us what happened."

Abigail sagged with despair. "Endera always swore she'd have her revenge. She tried to take Robert from me when we were engaged; then, when he wouldn't accept her advances, she promised to take my son, driving us from our home to this place. It seems she got her revenge after all."

"We found this . . ." Rego pulled out a worn leather pouch and untied the string, tipping the contents onto the table. A rock the size of a quail's egg rolled out. It looked like ordinary granite with rough, uneven edges.

Sam picked up the stone with trembling hands and studied its golden flecks. He remembered it well. His father had worn the pouch around his neck every day. He said Sam's grandfather had given it to him. Sam let the rock drop on the table.

"Is all this true?" Sam whispered, lifting his eyes to look at his mother.

"Honey . . ." She laid her hand on his arm, but Sam recoiled in disgust, jumping to his feet.

"You're a witch, like Ms. Endera?"

"Sam, let me explain."

"No." He backed away. "You knew. You knew all along why Dad left. And you never said anything. I thought he abandoned us, and you just let me hate him. How could you do that?"

Abigail looked stricken. "I don't know, Sam. How could I explain I was a witch and we were from another realm?"

"Well, you should have said something!" Sam yelled. "Anything would have been better than letting me believe he didn't care about us."

He couldn't stay in the same room as his mother. Sam ran out of the kitchen and flung open the front door, ready to run as far away as possible, but a flood of black-winged creatures flew in, knocking him backward.

His scream echoed through the house. They clawed at Sam's face, trying to scratch out his eyes. He covered his head with his arms. The same kind of creature had attacked him at his locker.

Rego burst in, sword drawn, and started flailing at them. "Shreeks," he muttered. "Filthy witches' spawn. Endera's had them tracking your every move."

Sam's mom crowded in behind Rego as a new swarm of shreeks erupted out of the chimney. They flew like a black ribbon across the room, heading straight for Sam.

"Rego!" he yelped. "Do something."

The dwarf slashed at them, sending them squealing and spinning away, but more poured in through the front door. Lagos swooped in and sniped at them, tearing them to pieces with her claws, but there were too many. Sam grabbed a lamp by the neck and swung it at a cloud of shreeks. He missed and nearly hit Rego on the head.

"Get him out of here," Abigail said to Rego. "I can handle them."

Rego put his hand on Sam's back and shoved him toward the kitchen.

Sam reached for her. "No, Mom, we can't leave you."

But Abigail seemed to be in a trance. Her head was cocked to the side, and she held her hands out, murmuring words that tugged at Sam like a faint memory. A strange blue glow emanated from her palms and then shot out in a streak of light. As the shreeks hit the light, they evaporated into a puff of white smoke.

Sam watched in awe as his mother doubled over, breathless, as though she had just been punched in the stomach.

"Come on, lad," said Rego. "Out you go."

They spilled onto the porch as a dusty brown pickup careened across the grass and screeched to a halt, gouging rivets in the lawn. Leo and three Umatilla men jumped out of the back. They grabbed Sam's arms and lifted him into the truck bed. As Rego levered himself in, the vehicle took off.

A cloud of shreeks swirled above the house, pouring down the chimney like ebony rain. Sam lunged for the side, determined to jump, but the men held him back.

"We can't just leave her there!" Sam cried in a panic.

Rego rested against the wall of the truck bed, cleaning shreek skin from his nails with the tip of his knife. "Your mother can take care of herself, boy."

Sam struggled to pull free, but the Umatilla just stared at him silently, their faces unyielding. He appealed to Leo. "Help me. I need to go home."

Leo nodded. "Yes. It's time, Sam. My father is preparing the way."

Sam's hands trembled when he realized Leo wasn't talking about Sam's little house in Pilot Rock. He was talking about this other realm, this place called Orkney. "You swear on your life she'll be okay?" he said to Rego. "Swear it."

Rego drew his fingers in an X across his leather vest. "By Odin's blood, I swear it."

Sam relaxed a little, then tried to orient himself to the blur of scenery passing by outside. "Where are we going?"

Leo explained proudly. "On the top of Pilot Rock is a sacred stone that can open the doorway between this world and Orkney. My father is a guardian. He will light the stonefire and help you cross over safely."

"Stonefire? What is that?"

"An ancient method of travel between the realms. Don't worry, Sam. It's going to be all right." Leo put a sympathetic hand on Sam's shoulder.

Sam didn't know what to say. He sat staring at the horizon as the truck bounced down the highway toward the reservation. Tears blurred his eyes. His father was dead. And his mother was most definitely a witch. She had used magic to wipe out those shreeks. Some crazy things had happened in the past few days, but that was the craziest.

They left the main road and entered a dirt lane, heading deep into the Umatilla wastelands. The familiar boulder loomed ahead as twilight settled over them, cooling the air. A glow came from atop Pilot Rock. A large blaze burned, lighting up the night sky.

Leo's father was up there, preparing an ancient portal so that Sam could go "home" to a place he had never heard of. When the truck finally pulled to a stop, Sam jumped down onto wobbly legs. Leo looped a polished wooden bow and a quiver full of arrows over his shoulder. He handed Sam a serrated knife in a leather case.

"Take this. The Shun Kara may be here."

Sam held it, trying to understand. "Why are you helping me? Have we met before?"

A muscle twitched in Leo's jaw. "One day, you will understand. My people are connected to your world. We still believe in the ancient gods. When they need our help, we are their allies."

Rego yelled at them to get moving. The other men would stay behind to guard the trail. The way was narrow and rocky. One false step, and he would plunge off the side into an abyss. Halfway up, Sam stumbled over something in his path.

A red tennis shoe.

"Wait," he said, kneeling down to pick it up. Recognition hit him like a punch in the gut. "This is Howie's." He looked from Leo to Rego. "What's Howie's shoe doing here?"

Rego's face tightened. "There's sure to be trouble ahead, lads; stay on your toes."

They continued on, hurrying now with renewed urgency. As they neared the top, shouts rang out. There was a loud pop and an explosion. Rocks tumbled down around Sam, knocking him off the edge of the trail. He grabbed a branch as he went over the side, kicking furiously to find his footing. Then Leo was there, pulling him back onto solid ground.

"Hurry, Sam—the portal has been opened."

The smell of smoke reached them as they crested the boulder. The top was smooth and flat, barren of trees and shrubs. In the center, leaping flames burned a phosphorescent orange around a stone the size of a refrigerator. The stone glowed with a silvery light that shimmered and flickered, as if the rock were transparent. This must be the stonefire.

The doorway to another world.

Two days ago, Sam would never have believed it. Now, he barely glanced at it. He was more concerned with finding Howie and dealing with the three enormous black wolves that stood in front of the stone, defying them to pass.

The Shun Kara paced back and forth in the dancing firelight, fangs bared, growling deep in their chests. Leo's father faced off against the beasts, a sturdy lance his only weapon. A bloody gash ran down his leg.

"Dad, are you okay?" Leo ran to join his father, and the first Shun Kara attacked, loping straight for Leo. Before it could crouch and leap, Chief Pate-wa impaled the beast in the shoulder, taking it down in a lifeless lump. Leo reached his father, putting his shoulder under the chief's arm.

"Get Sam out of here!" the chief shouted. "It's not safe for him."

Sam understood when Ms. Endera stepped out of the shadows, holding Howie and Keely by the scruffs of their necks.

Keely screamed Sam's name when she saw him.

Ms. Endera sent him a triumphant glare before letting out an evil peal of laughter.

Sam started to run forward, but Rego tripped him and knocked him to the ground. He looked up to see Endera step into the flames, dragging his friends with her through the shimmering stone.

"Keely!" he shouted, stretching his hand out, but she was gone, along with Howie. Furious, he rolled onto his back. "Why'd you do that?" he shouted at Rego.

Rego hauled him to his feet. "Don't be a fool, lad. She's using your friends to get you to follow her. She's got a trap waiting on the other side."

"Listen to him, Samuel," the chief shouted, leaning on Leo for support. "The witches don't want your friends; they want you."

Another Shun Kara broke from the pair and ran straight for Sam. He fumbled for the knife at his side, but Leo already had an arrow notched. He let it loose, and the arrow embedded in the beast's shoulder. It rolled to a stop at Sam's feet.

Sam looked at Leo. His new friend nodded, offering silent support. Sam gathered his courage. Nothing was going to stop him from going after Howie and Keely. He took a step forward, then stopped as Endera's giant lizard came from behind the stone. It roared, standing like an alligator on two legs, beating its chest with its clawed front feet. Lizard-Platz was blocking the entrance to the stonefire. The lone Shun Kara prowled between them.

"Step aside, Sam. We have to kill that thing," Rego said, holding his sword.

"No way!" Sam yelled. "That's Mr. Platz. You can't harm him."

"Sorry, lad. He's not your Mr. Platz anymore."

The lizard beat its chest again. And then its roar choked off into a squeak. Suddenly, it began to change; its talons retracted, and its snout shrank down. Hair began to sprout on its head, and then, a moment later, Mr. Platz stood there, looking dazed and confused.

"Sam?" He staggered a bit as he peered across the plateau at his student. "Where am I?"

Sam was as surprised to see Platz as his old teacher was to see him. Endera's exit must have broken the spell keeping Platz in his lizard form. But the English teacher was still in grave danger.

"Watch out, Mr. Platz!"

The Shun Kara had turned and started loping toward the disoriented teacher. Sam didn't stop to think. He ran, tackling the wolf as it leaped at his teacher, and tumbled into the stonefire with it. Sam fell into heat and flames, ready to be scorched, but there was only coldness and pain as the beast's claws scraped his belly. He took Leo's knife and plunged it into the mat of black fur. Then the world went dark.

Chapter Eight

ndera Tarkana let out a shriek of elation as she emerged from the stonefire. Dropping the two squealing children, she filled her lungs with air after their suffocating journey. She watched with amusement as Howie frantically patted out the flames on his raggedy clothes. The girl was more demure, or maybe she was in shock. She got to her feet, looking around her silently. Only the clenched fists at her sides revealed that she was seething inwardly. Good. Keely would need strength to withstand what was coming. Endera let out a low whistle. From the shadows of the trees surrounding the stone portal, a bevy of witches appeared.

"Where is the Barconian boy?" The commanding voice came from Hestera. As the eldest member of their coven, Hestera fancied herself in charge. She hobbled toward them, bent over a knobby cane topped by a magnificent emerald-colored stone. "Does he live or not?"

Endera sauntered forward to greet her. "Hestera, dear sister, were you not even a little worried about me?" She pouted playfully.

The old witch bared her teeth. "Your survival was never in doubt, Endera. You always find a way. This cannot be the boy." She sniffed Howie up and down. "He smells weak."

"Back off, you bag of bones." Howie put on a brave face, but Endera could see his fear. His bottom lip quivered, and his pupils were dilated. He had just made a fatal mistake, however. Before she could intercede, Hestera struck like a snake.

"You dare speak to me like that?" Hestera's bony hand shot out to wrap around Howie's throat as she dragged him closer. The boy's face turned purple as her grip tightened.

"Leave him alone!" Keely kicked at Hestera until a pair of witches grabbed her by the arms and held her back. "Make her stop," she yelled at Endera. "Why did you bring us here if you're just going to kill us?"

The girl had a point. Endera clapped loudly. "Hestera, enough."

The old witch whirled on Endera. "You waste our time. This child is not a Son of Odin." She continued to squeeze the boy's throat. He began to go limp.

Endera stepped forward, laying her hand on Hestera's arm. "Patience, Hestera. These children are the bait in our trap. The boy we seek will be coming through that portal any moment." She pointed back at the stone. "You will see. You will all see."

"Then we wait here and kill him!" Hestera cried, releasing Howie. He dropped to his knees, his hands on the grass as he sucked in huge gulps of air. The other witches murmured in agreement.

"The Son of Odin is under my protection," Endera commanded. "If he dies, we can't achieve our goals."

"You and your plans," Hestera mocked. "That boy is a threat. We cannot afford to let him live."

"He has no idea of his potential. Take these brats back to the dungeons. Leave me with some of my sisters, and I will have the boy eating out of our hands. If my plan succeeds, we will gain unfathomable power. If I fail, you can kill him personally and feed his corpse to the Shun Kara."

Hestera hesitated, and then finally relented.

Behind Endera, the stone began to glow and crackle with electricity.

Endera shooed the others toward the trees. "Quickly, before we are seen."

In a puff of green smoke, the witches vanished, taking the captives with them. Endera and the small remaining band faded into the woods, disappearing from sight as the stone began to open.

From the shadows, Endera paused to be sure the Barconian boy made it safely through. She watched as Sam tumbled into sight with a Shun Kara wolf on top of him. Her stomach clenched. It would do her no good if one of her pets harmed the boy, but the beast lay still and unmoving, a knife sticking out of its ribs. With another thump, the nosy dwarf tumbled through, landing next to the boy and jumping to his feet. He checked Sam and then took a seat on a stump. Satisfied, Endera hurried after her sister witches. Her plan to bring the boy to Orkney had succeeded. The next step was to help him discover who he really was.

A foul animal stench filled Sam's nostrils, rousing him from his stupor. He felt as if a load of bricks had landed on his chest. Gasping for air, he opened his eyes and saw the gaping mouth of a Shun Kara. Yelling loudly, he pushed off the brute and then scrambled away on all fours. The animal rolled over onto the grass as limp as a dishrag, the hilt of Sam's knife buried in its rib cage. Its sticky blood covered his hands and arms. Sam wiped his hands on the grass, trying to get his heart rate back to normal.

Across from him, Rego sat on a tree stump, whittling. In the tree behind him, Lagos ruffled her singed feathers.

"You could have gotten it off me," Sam said, feeling wobbly. He put his head between his knees and took several deep breaths.

"Aye, I could have," Rego agreed, continuing to whittle. "But I didn't want to disturb your beauty sleep," he quipped, his whiskers twitching.

"This isn't funny," Sam said, raising his head. "That witch has my friends. Howie and Keely could be dead already." He staggered to his feet, fighting dizziness. "We have to go after them." Bright spots danced in front of his eyes. Traveling through the stonefire had left him light-headed.

"They're long gone. Smell that sulfur? They spirited themselves away. And your friends aren't dead, lad. Not yet. The witch didn't bring them all this way just to kill them—though it probably would have been better for them if she had," he added.

"What's that supposed to mean?"

"It means nothing good ever comes from a witch."

Sam took a proper look around. So this was Orkney. Place didn't seem half bad. The day was warm. He filled his lungs with air from this new world. It was kind of crazy, but he was excited. The air had a faint pungent odor like the burnt sage from his mom's cooking. A large stone stood nearby, charred and cracked from their passage. Sam couldn't remember much of the journey; he had been too busy trying not to get eaten by the Shun Kara. He did remember a sense of falling and a lack of oxygen.

By the looks of it, they were on top of a large boulder like the one back in Pilot Rock. In fact, the closer Sam looked, the more he realized it *was* the same boulder. Only now, the big rock wasn't perched on the edge of the barren Umatilla wasteland. Below them, rolling green hills spread out like a lush carpet. Sheep grazed peacefully among the rocky cairns that lined the landscape. In the distance, white-capped waves crashed against the coastline under an azure sky. Sam could only shake his head in amazement. It defied explanation, but after he had seen Mr. Platz change back from being a lizard, anything seemed possible.

Sam squinted up at the sky, and that's when his excitement turned to dust. Blood-red veins ran across the face of the sun, splitting off into thinner capillaries. He frowned, trying to make sense of it. His head felt like someone had dropped a sledgehammer on it. A wave of nausea came over him so strongly that he thought he would faint.

He tried to drag his eyes away, but he was transfixed as waves of envy, rage, and a sense of pleasure flooded him at the same time. As he stared at the sun, another plump vein sprouted, sending a fresh trail spiking across its yellow face.

Without warning, Sam's legs were swept out from under him, and he landed on his back with a loud *woomph*. He looked up at Rego and shouted, "What's your problem?"

"Don't be daft, boy. You can't stare at the sun and not get poisoned by it."

Not wanting to alienate the only person he knew in this place, Sam did his best to tamp down his temper. He picked himself up, brushing off the dirt. "What happened to it?"

"Witches," Rego said, as if that explained it. "Here, this belongs to you now." He tossed Sam the leather pouch Sam's father had worn. It had a drawstring knotted in a long loop. Sam hefted it, feeling the weight of the rock inside.

"What's so special about it?" He hesitated. Part of him wanted to throw it back at Rego, but another part craved a little piece of his dad. Finally, he slipped the pouch around his neck. The weight felt reassuring and heavy.

"It's what remains of Odin's Stone. A powerful talisman of the gods. The witches ground it into dust years ago to destroy its power. This remnant survived. It's small, but it still contains Odin's breath. Your father would have wanted you to have it."

Lifting Lagos onto his arm, Rego stroked her feathers, then launched her into the air. "You're my eyes now, Lagos." She sprang off his wrist and took to the sky, circling once above them before heading away. He shouldered his pack. "We should be moving. There's still a long journey ahead." Without waiting for Sam's answer, the dwarf began trudging down a narrow trail.

"Wait up." Sam took a step and looked down at his feet.

Sooty toes stuck out through burned holes in his socks. "Snap, where are my shoes?"

"Didn't make it through the fire," Rego said over his shoulder.

Sam's clothes were singed black around the edges. The only thing to survive intact was Leo's knife. It stuck out of the side of the beast. Reluctant to touch it, but even more reluctant to leave it behind, Sam put his foot on the wolf's shoulder and pulled with both hands. The knife slipped out with a repulsive sucking noise. He wiped the blade on the ground several times to remove the blood, then stuffed it in the sheath at his waist.

Rego was a distant blur on the trail. Sam picked his way over sharp stones, wincing with every step until he caught up with the dwarf.

"Where are we?" he asked.

"Where do you think? Orkney." Rego said it like that should mean something to Sam, then kept on trudging down the trail. Annoyed, Sam grabbed Rego by the shoulder and spun him around.

"I know that, but where is it? How did we get here? Why are the witches after me? How can witches even exist?"

Rego was silent as Sam finished his string of questions, staring at Sam with something close to pity in his eyes.

"Please. I just want to understand," Sam added quietly, dropping his hand.

The dwarf sighed and took a seat on a rock. Sam sat down across from him on the ground.

"To understand the present, you have to start in the past when the world was young and gods like Odin walked freely on the earth." Rego took an apple out of his satchel and began peeling the green skin.

"So the gods are real?" Sam leaned forward, feeling his breath catch in his chest.

Rego laughed. "Of course they're real. The world didn't make itself. Odin is the father of creation. Keeper of mankind."

Sam remembered the book Keely had shown him in the library. "Is it true he divided the world into nine realms?"

"Yup, each one separated from the other by a thin veil. In the center is your world, the realm Odin called Midgard. Home of men, but also in those early days, home to all kinds of magic folk, including the witches. Odin watched over them like they were his children." Rego carved a slice of apple and handed it to Sam.

He chewed it, savoring the familiar, if somewhat tarter, taste. "What changed?"

"A powerful he-witch named Rubicus is what changed. Rubicus wanted to control the nine realms for himself."

"Sounds like he wanted to be a god," Sam joked. "Bet Odin didn't like that."

Rego glared at him. "No. Odin didn't like it one stinking bit. But Rubicus had big plans. He thought if he poisoned the sun, Odin would surrender to him."

Sam swallowed the mouthful of apple. "What happened?"

"Rubicus found a source of dark magic powerful enough to curse the sun. As the veins spread, the sun began poisoning everything in the land. War broke out between the witches and the gods. The spell got beyond Rubicus's control. It was terrible. No one could stop it, not even Odin. All of Midgard was in danger of extinction."

Sam was speechless. "So what did Odin do?"

Rego snorted loudly. "He cut off Rubicus's head and mounted it on a stake outside the witches' fortress."

"Ouch!" Sam's eyes flickered to the poisoned sun. "So what made it come back?"

Rego tossed away the apple core. "Odin never found the source of the dark magic. A few months ago, the first red vein appeared on the sun. The High Council thinks the witches found the source and used it to finish what Rubicus started." Rego hesitated. Sam thought he was going to say something else important, but the dwarf scowled. "We're wasting time yapping." He reshouldered his pack and began tromping down the trail.

Sam hurried after him, slowed by his bare feet. The poisoned sun beat down, drilling into his head like he was at the dentist getting a cavity filled. The trail seemed endless, winding between large boulders. His feet were cut and raw by the time he caught up with the dwarf.

"At the house, you said the witches were after me," he called out to the back of Rego's head. "Why am I so important to them?"

Rego stopped in his tracks. Sam thought he was going to answer his question, but the dwarf was focused on the clearing ahead. A horse whinnied close by. They weren't alone. A group of men clustered around a small encampment in a clump of trees across the open space. Red banners were planted in the ground. A shout went out when they caught sight of the pair. Best of all, Sam could smell a whiff of something delicious cooking.

Rego started to stride toward them, but Sam grabbed his arm. "Come on, Rego. What's so special about me?"

The dwarf jerked his arm free, blue eyes fierce as he spat out the words. "After Odin cut off Rubicus's head, he swore vengeance on the witches. He cursed them to never again bear a male child."

It took a moment for the words to sink in, and then Sam's eyes lit up. "So my mom can't be a witch, right?"

Rego just grunted. "She's a witch all right, a descendant of Rubicus, himself. Your father descended from Odin. Somehow, they overcame his curse. Some say it was the strength of their bloodlines, others the power of their 'love.'" He said the last part with a touch of disgust. "I say it makes no matter how it happened. You, Samuel Baron, are the first son born to a witch in a very long time. And now the witches want to know whose side you're on."

"Whose side I'm on? Well, not theirs; that's for sure," Sam said hotly.

Rego looked at him a long time before answering. "We can only hope. But in the meantime, I suggest you keep your piehole shut about all this. Not everyone is going to be happy you're still alive."

A dwarf strode out to greet them, his lone arm extended. Rego clasped him heartily, pounded him on the back, and then turned to Sam. "Samuel, this here's my brother, Amicus."

Amicus raised one bushy eyebrow. "So the rumors were true." Amicus extended his hand, and Sam shook it. The dwarf's grip nearly crushed Sam's fingers.

A soldier came forward. He was twenty or so and blond, dressed in a white shirt of fine linen and simple leggings tucked into tall, black leather boots. He wore a vest of loose metal mesh that bore the symbol of a white heron on the chest.

"Milord." He bowed low in front of Sam. "Our hope has been restored to us. It is good to have you back on Orkadian soil."

"Thanks. I'm Sam." He stuck out his hand.

The soldier looked surprised. "Yes, Sam, I know who you are. I am Teren, Captain of the Orkadian Guard." He grabbed Sam's hand with both of his and shook it vigorously. He turned to the other men. "Samuel Elias Barconian, Lord of the Ninth Realm, Son of Odin, has returned to us."

The men, about a dozen of them, let out a resounding cheer and raised their swords high. The horses neighed noisily, and one of them reared up.

Now, this was a homecoming. Lord of the Ninth Realm? Rego must have left out that part of his story.

Chapter Nine

Captain Teren ushered Sam into a silken tent and left him to wash up in a large bowl of steaming water. It was a relief to get out of that cursed sun. He stripped off his charred pants and then soaked his feet, washing away the grime and dried wolf's blood. A set of clothes had been laid out for him: black breeches like Teren's, a white shirt, and a pair of boots that were a size too big but better than going barefoot. Sam looked down at his new outfit and thought he must look like quite the swashbuckling musketeer. He pretended to slash the air with a sword and heard a giggle.

"Who's there?" he called, feeling foolish.

The giggle repeated, and Sam waded deeper into the tent. There were piles of animal skins, saddles stacked up, and tubs of cookware. The room was bigger than he had thought and partitioned by a silk screen. He pulled it aside.

A girl, no more than eight or so, crouched behind the screen. She held her hand over her mouth as she tried to stifle her laughter.

"Are you spying on me?" Sam asked, irritated and a little embarrassed.

"No, this is my tent," she said, standing up. She had bare feet. Her dress was clean but worn.

"Your tent? It looks like a storage tent."

"I'm Mavery." She stuck out her hand. Her hair was black and uneven, as if she had cut it herself. She had shiny black eyes like those of a crow.

"I'm Sam." He reached for her hand, only to find that he was holding a trout and Mavery had disappeared.

"What the—"

The giggle came from behind him. Sam whipped around. "How did you do that?" The fish wriggled and slipped out of his hand onto the ground.

Captain Teren entered at that moment. "*Feregen*, Mavery. You know better than to use your witchery around camp. Get out before I tan that backside of yours."

The girl scampered to the door, sticking her tongue out at Teren behind his back before slipping away.

Sam had to smile. She was an imp, but he liked her already.

"Milord, are you feeling ready to begin our journey?" Teren asked.

"Sure, but call me Sam. Where are we going?"

"To Skara Brae, milord. The capital city. The High Council is most anxious to meet with you." Teren held open the door of the tent and waited for Sam to exit.

Sam stepped out to find that the camp had literally dropped to the ground while he was changing. Behind him, he heard the slithering of ropes being released as the tent he had just bathed in came down.

He spied Rego sitting on a horse, talking to his brother, Amicus. Sam walked over to Rego's mount. The pony was smaller than the others, a ruddy red color with short, thick legs and long, pointy ears. It reminded Sam of a cross between a mule and a Shetland pony. Amicus rode a similar mount.

"There's a little problem," Sam said uneasily.

"What now, boy?" Rego asked.

"I don't know how to, you know . . ." He jerked his head at the horses.

"Don't know how to what?"

"The horses. I don't know how to ride them," he confessed.

Rego let out a laugh. "And here I thought you were Lord of the Ninth Realm." He kicked his pony in the side and moved off. "You'll figure it out soon enough," he called over his shoulder.

Sam glared at his back. That dwarf really got on his nerves.

Amicus was no help. He gave Sam a wink and kicked his pony to catch up to Rego.

One of Teren's men led over a stallion, tall and majestic, black as night. It reared up, pawing at the air with its hooves as it pulled against the lead.

I'm going to die, Sam thought.

"Oh no, not that one," he said, shaking his head. "I need an old one, a slow one, preferably one that doesn't buck."

The man just shrugged and led the horse away. A boy in dungarees and a cap, not much older than Sam, appeared with a sturdy brown mare.

"Here you go, milord," he said. "Seamus was just being a daft jerk. This beauty will be steady and easy on your bum."

"Thank you." Sam felt eternally grateful. "What's your name?"

"I'm Davis, sir. Here, let me help you up." He grasped Sam's foot and helped hoist him into the saddle, adjusting the stirrups before handing him the reins. "Now, point them where you want to go, and she'll follow. Pull back when you want to stop."

Sam tested the reins. "Seems easy enough."

Davis tugged on his cap and slapped the mare on the flank. She jolted forward and joined the line of horses heading down the trail. A whistle came from the tree next to Sam. In its lowest branch, Mavery squatted on a limb. She pursed her lips together and began to blow, and a golden-brown globe floated toward him. He watched as it got closer, fascinated by the shimmering colors, until it popped in his face, spraying him with a sticky liquid. He dabbed his finger on his face and licked it.

Maple syrup.

He rode off to the sound of her giggle.

———— (O⧓O) ————

The trail converged with a river that twisted its way through the forest. The rushing water sent up a spray as it tumbled over boulders, showering the air with a mist that made Sam's clothes cling to his skin. The thicket of trees kept out much of the sunlight; the trunks were painted green with moss. He began to shiver. Something stung his neck. He slapped it, looking down at his hand. Great—even Orkney had mosquitoes.

Captain Teren rode up next to him.

"Well, Samuel, what do you think of your homeland?"

"It's a lot like the Blue Mountains near Pilot Rock, where I grew up," Sam said, grateful for the company. "I used to go camping there with my dad."

"What did your parents tell you about this place—the Ninth Realm?"

Sam shrugged. "Not much. Actually, nothing. I guess they thought I wouldn't believe them."

Teren smiled, flashing white teeth. "Then allow me to give you a history lesson. Did Rego tell you about Rubicus?"

"Yeah. He's the guy who started that." Sam pointed at the freaky red-streaked sun.

Teren nodded grimly. "Rubicus had a daughter named Catriona. She was determined to finish what Rubicus had started. She went to war with mankind, and she would have won if not for Hermodan."

Sam looked over at the soldier. "Hermodan? Who was he?"

"Hermodan was the King of Orkney. Not this Orkney. The Orkney of your world. Back then, it was a small chain of islands near a place you call Scotland. But Hermodan was no ordinary mortal. He was a direct descendant of Odin."

"A Son of Odin," Sam whispered. His horse let out a whinny, as if it understood the name.

"Aye. Like you and your father. His birthright made him capable of crossing to Asgard to ask Odin for his help. Hermodan returned with Odin's Stone, a talisman powerful enough to fight the witches."

Sam's fingers crept up to the pouch around his neck. No wonder his dad had kept it close. The tiny chunk of granite used to hold great power.

Teren continued. "Hermodan used the magic in Odin's Stone to trap Catriona and five of her most powerful witch-sisters inside the stones that make up the Ring of Brogar."

Fresh grief shot through Sam. "That's where my dad was killed. But how does that explain this place?"

"Odin feared magic would be the undoing of mankind. He wanted to destroy it forever. It was Hermodan who pleaded for mercy for the magic folk who had fought on the side of good. He offered part of his kingdom as sanctuary, a handful of islands that could be lifted from your world and cast, here, into the Ninth Realm of Odin. Every magical thing, creature, stick, and stone would go with it, thus protecting mankind. And still preserving magic."

Sam couldn't speak. The idea was fantastic. Take islands from his world and just remove them? *No wonder Rubicus wanted to be a god*, Sam thought. "But why did Odin bring the witches here, too? Why not just get rid of them if they were such a problem?"

Teren sighed. "Hermodan believed there was some good to be found in them. The elven folk, the Eifalians, were the first to agree to go. Then the Falcory, ancestors of the Umatilla. Next were dwarves, giants, and, yes, even the witches—all given a choice. Stay behind in your realm and lose their powers, or leave and be cut off from Midgard forever."

"What about the people who lived on those islands, the ones who didn't have magic?"

"Some left. The Orkadians who stayed were chosen to help oversee the new Orkney. That's how I got here. My great-great-great-grandfather served under Hermodan."

Sam let his history lesson sink in as the horses wended their way through the forest. After a while, he asked, "Do you know what happened to my dad?"

"The witches have never stopped trying to defeat us. Endera and her cronies are just the latest batch to attempt to bring us to our knees. Your father wanted to make peace, and he paid for it with his life. My own father served under yours, you know," he added. "He perished that day, fighting alongside Lord Barconian. I inherited my commission earlier than I would have liked."

"I'm sorry."

"That's all right. You're here now."

He said it like Sam mattered. Before Sam could ask why, one of the men rode up and called Captain Teren to the front of the caravan. Sam was left alone to ride in silence, wondering if his father had suffered before he died.

Chapter Ten

The trail left the river and began to wind through thick trees. Moss hung down and brushed his face. Thorny bushes caught at his clothes. Without the cooling effect of the river, Sam felt sweaty and irritable. A bee began to fly around his head. He swatted at it, but it persisted, buzzing in his ear.

"Go away," Sam said, as it tried to land on his nose. It flew off, and he relaxed. But then a buzzing sounded behind him. A flash of panic made him turn around in his saddle.

The bee had landed on his horse's rump. It stuck its tail up high, then sank down and stung the poor animal. The mare bucked once and then took off at a dead gallop, veering off the trail and bouncing Sam along with her.

Holding on to the saddle horn for dear life, Sam prayed to stay in one piece. He ducked to avoid getting blinded by slapping branches. The mare finally came to a stop in a wide clearing. She put her head down and began eating grass as if nothing had happened.

As he picked leaves out of his hair, Sam realized the clearing wasn't empty. A young woman dressed in a white gown sat on a rock in the center. Blond hair fell to her waist. She was beautiful, thin-limbed, and pale-skinned.

"Uh, excuse me," Sam said. "I think I'm lost."

The woman looked up at him, and he reeled. Her eyes were the color of milk.

"Yes, Son of Odin, I'm very much afraid you have lost your way."

"Do you know me?" Sam asked, wondering what had happened to make her eyes so blank. He eased himself off the horse, glad for an excuse to have his feet on the ground. He walked over and knelt down across from her. She looked at him as if she could see him, yet she had no pupils, nor irises.

"I know you, Samuel Barconian. I am Vor, the Goddess of Wisdom. There is a battle raging inside you. Which bloodline will win? That is the question on everyone's mind."

"What do you mean?"

She extended one arm and opened her hand. On her palm, a white butterfly fluttered. "The blood of your father leads you down one path."

Sam swallowed, dreading her next words. "And my mother's?"

"Her blood will take you down another path." Vor opened her other hand. A black wasp buzzed angrily. Its wings were laced with red-veined membranes. A large, pointed stinger protruded from its rear. It saw the butterfly and darted at it, giving chase as the butterfly took flight. Vor dropped her hands. "When the time comes, you must decide whom to save and whom to sacrifice. The fate of the world hangs on your decision."

Fate of the world? Sam looked back at Vor, feeling weak. "So, what am I supposed to do?"

Her hand waved gently in the air. "We cannot influence your decisions."

"We? Who's we?"

"The gods, Samuel."

Oh, just the gods. Great. He sat back heavily. "Then why are you here?"

"Because Odin has allowed you to ask one question of me."

Sam tried to think of something important, like how to rescue his friends or why the witches wanted him dead, but the words that tumbled out were filled with his shame.

"Sometimes, when I lose my temper, it's like I'm a different person. I can't control it. Why does that happen to me?"

She looked at Sam with those pearl-colored eyes and put her hand on his forehead, closing his eyelids. Her hand felt cool and soothing.

An image formed in his head of a baby lying in a crib. Sam was the baby, he realized, looking up at the small hands waving in front of his face. Over his crib, a woman appeared. He felt afraid.

No wonder. A younger Endera Tarkana smiled down at him and tickled him under his chin. He began to wail. As he did, she held a scorpion over the crib by its tail. He began to scream in earnest as the scorpion dropped onto his blanket and scuttled under the covers. A burning pain shot through his foot. Blue lights burst over his head, and then his mother appeared, looking scared. His father joined her, reaching down and grabbing the horrid thing, crushing it under his foot.

Vor took her hand away, and Sam gasped.

"I was stung by a scorpion?"

"Not just any scorpion. A Deathstalker," Vor explained. "The sting should have killed you. We cannot explain why you lived. Perhaps some venom remains inside you, circulating its poison."

"So it's not my fault," he said, feeling a rush of pure joy. There was a reason for his rage. He wasn't a monster.

But Vor dashed his sudden joy. "Yes and no," she answered. "A fire does not burn without fuel. You are easily brought to anger, Sam. The venom merely fans the flames. You must learn to control those feelings, or your path will be very dark, I'm afraid."

Voices rang out, calling Sam's name. He looked up to see Vor's reaction, but she was gone. In her place, a white dove sat cooing on the rock.

Captain Teren rode into the clearing. "Milord, there you are," he said, reining in his horse and looking relieved. "Is everything all right?"

"I don't know," Sam said with a puzzled sigh that reached into the soles of his boots. He had just met a blind woman who claimed to be a goddess, then turned into a dove. There were so many things that weren't "all right," he had lost track.

"Shall we proceed, then?" Teren asked. His horse pranced nervously as wind rattled the leaves in the clearing. The dove took flight through the trees.

Sam climbed back onto his horse and followed Teren to the trail. There was no more idle conversation between them. Sam hunkered down over the saddle. Not much about this place made sense. But one thought kept him going: rescuing Howie and Keely. His friends needed him to figure things out.

They made camp in a clump of trees as the sun set. Davis brought him a bowl of black cabbage stew, promising it was delicious. Sam managed a few bites before he grew too tired to chew. He stretched out on a rough blanket, his eyes closing before he could even take his boots off. It must have been some hours later when he awoke. Men slept in scattered lumps on the ground atop bedrolls, heads resting on folded saddle blankets. A few feet away, Sam could make out Rego's lumpy figure, snoring like a chain saw.

Sam stood, stretching the kinks out of his muscles. A large fire burned in the center of camp. A sentry warmed his hands over the flames. He gave Sam a nod. Tall trees pressed in close, surrounding the clearing. The moon was half full, spilling white light over the camp. The night was clear, the sky sprinkled with distant stars. A branch snapped in the woods behind Sam. He whipped around. An animal? He looked back at the sentry, but the man had wandered over to check on the horses.

A whispery voice drifted through the trees. "Saaaamm . . ."

His ears pricked up. Was that Keely? Uncertain, Sam looked at Rego's sleeping figure. It was probably nothing. The dwarf would be annoyed if Sam woke him. But if it was Keely, it was his chance, maybe his only chance, to rescue her. The sliver of moon was bright enough to see by. He would check it out and then go back to bed. He ducked into the stand of trees. Instantly, the thick canopy blotted out the moonlight. A cloak of dampness settled over him, making him shiver. He paused to listen.

There. Ahead. That sound was definitely Howie's laugh. No time to get Rego. Sam started to run. Branches whipped him across the face. He tripped over a root and hit the ground hard. He lay still, trying to catch his breath, listening for the voices. Pushing himself up, Sam grabbed a tree trunk, his fingers sinking into thick moss.

"Son of Odin," came a whisper through the trees.

"Who's there?" Sam called. His heart galloped in his chest. Fear made it hard to think. "Mavery? Is that you? Stop playing tricks. This isn't funny." Sam put his hands in front of him as he moved blindly toward the sound.

"Release us," the voice pleaded, a plaintive, restless sound that echoed inside his brain.

"Stop it," Sam said, straining to see in the near darkness. "Get out of my head."

"Release us, Son of Odin. It is time."

"I don't know what you're talking about," he yelled.

"Sam?" came a familiar voice, faint but real.

"Keely?" Sam instantly forgot his fear. "Keely, where are you?" he shouted.

"Sam, I thought you were my friend. Why won't you help me?" she called, her voice trailing through the wind and the branches.

"I'm coming!" Sam cried, and ran in the direction of her voice, crashing through the trees.

He broke into a small clearing. A figure stood alone in the center. Her head was bent and covered in a black, hooded cloak.

"Keely?"

"Sam, why don't you come?" It was Keely's voice, but as she raised her head, Sam stepped back in horror.

His substitute English teacher stood gloating, her eyes gleaming in the moonlight.

"I thought you were my friend," Endera mouthed, her face creasing into a smile as her voice lapsed back into her own. "Welcome home, Sam. We've been waiting for you."

Behind her, the clearing filled with a dozen figures in black cloaks. Sam took another step back.

"What do you want?"

"We want you to join us," she said, opening her arms wide. "You're one of us."

"One of us," the clan of witches murmured softly in agreement, while moving to encircle him.

For once, Sam wished Rego would show up unannounced. "Forget it! You're a bunch of evil, disgusting witches!"

"Ouch. I'm offended," Endera pouted, crossing her arms. "I thought we were getting so close."

"Where's Keely? What have you done with Howie?" Sam turned his head side to side to make sure they weren't sneaking up on him.

"Your friends are enjoying their time in our dungeons."

Sam lunged at her, wanting to wipe that smug look off her face, but Endera vanished, reappearing behind him to tap him on the shoulder. Sam spun around, prepared to swing at her, but her hand shot out and grabbed him by the throat. She lifted him off the ground easily, as if he weighed nothing, all the while keeping her eyes locked on his.

"What's. Your. Problem?" Sam choked out, pulling at the hands wrapped around his throat. "What did I ever do to you?"

She arched one thin eyebrow. "You don't know?"

"Know what?"

"Who you are." Endera pulled him closer, her eyes search-ing Sam's, as if seeking to know what thoughts were inside his head.

"I'm no one. I'm just a kid." That was what Sam wanted to believe.

Endera released him then, dropping him to the ground, and tilted her head back to laugh. The other witches remained silent, watching.

"Just a kid? No, Sam, that won't do. It's time you discov-ered who you really are."

The cloaked figures pressed forward, lifting him up by his arms and holding him tight. Their pale faces were shrouded in darkness, but Sam felt their wickedness.

Endera murmured some words. *"Fein kinter, respera, res-pera Barconian fils."* Her palm began to glow, and then a bolt of green light shot out and hit him in the chest. A sharp, lancing pain sent stars behind his eyes. Sam's body arched back as he let out a loud shriek, but a hand covered his mouth, muffling it so that he sounded like a mewling cat.

The witch drew nearer, keeping the sizzling bolt locked on Sam's heart. "All young witches undergo a ritual where they re-ceive their full measure of power. Haven't you ever wondered why strange words hover on the tip of your tongue?"

Sam shook his head, but it was a lie and she knew it. He heard them when he lost his temper, echoing like a muffled chant in his head.

"Why do you fight who you are?" She thrust her hands for-ward and increased the flow of energy.

It was agony, as if his soul were being ripped from his body, but Sam fought it. "I know who I am," he gasped. "I'm Sam Baron. And nothing you do is going to change that."

"Well, we'll see about that, won't we?" She stepped closer, until her scorching fingertips were only an inch from his body.

She murmured some final words and then touched one finger to his chest, just as she had done the first time he had met her back in Pilot Rock. Only this time, an explosion of dazzling green fire lit up Sam's brain. At the same moment, the witches let him go. He fell backward, boneless and faint. In slow motion, the sky came into view as he hit the ground with a thud. He couldn't move. His eyes were wide open, staring up at the sky. A jumble of words began filling his head in a language he understood hazily.

Endera leaned down next to him. "Welcome to the coven, Sam."

Chapter Eleven

Opening his eyes, Sam looked up into the bloodstained sun. The veins on its face throbbed in rhythm with his pulse, squeezing his heart with an angry fist. He turned away and saw Rego—except there were two of him. Sam had to blink several times before the vision merged into one annoyed dwarf. Next to him, Lagos let out an angry squawk as it fluttered its wings out, as if chastising Sam.

Rego squatted down next to him. "So, you want to tell me why you were knocked out cold in the woods?"

Sam sat up, groaning at the aches in his body.

"How did I get here?" He was back on his bedroll. Someone had taken his boots off.

"Lagos spotted you passed out in a clearing a click away. Teren and I had to drag your sorry hide through the woods. What on Odin's earth were you doing that far from camp?"

Sam tried to remember. "I thought I heard Keely's voice. I was trying to get to her. I must have run into a tree and blacked out." His fingers went to his chest, pulling his shirt open to look for any burn marks.

"Something wrong?"

Sam abruptly let go of his shirt. "No."

Rego glared at him suspiciously. "A tree, huh? Did you hear anything else?"

Sam hesitated. Telling Rego he had been zapped by Endera in some crazy ritual would just make the dwarf worry, or ask a lot of questions Sam couldn't answer. "Just my stomach growling," he lied. "I'm starving." That part was true. On cue, his stomach let out a loud grumble.

Rego abruptly shoved himself to his feet. "I don't believe a word you said, Sam Baron. Next time you wander off into the woods, I'll leave you to the wolves." He stomped off to join Amicus by the horses.

"What about breakfast?" Sam called after him.

Davis came up with a cheerful grin. "I've saved you some biscuits and sliced ham," he said, opening a checkered cloth. "Should tide you over till morning tea."

"Thanks." Sam bolted down two biscuits before asking, "Hey, Davis, can you tell me anything about magic?" If he was going to survive in this place, it was time he learned more about how things worked in the Ninth Realm.

Davis knelt down and helped put Sam's boots back on. "Not me, milord. But I know someone who can." He turned his head to search the camp. "There." He pointed. "That's who you're looking for."

Mavery. The little imp. She flitted across the clearing and darted into a tent. Sam thanked Davis, grabbed another biscuit off the plate, and then jogged after Mavery.

Edging around behind the tent, Sam snuck in through the back opening. Mavery was scarfing down a freshly baked pie, her face smeared with cherry-red filling.

Sam cleared his throat. "Gotcha."

She looked up guiltily, then smirked when she saw who it was.

"Get yer own pie," Mavery said, and went back to her snack, finishing the entire dish in a matter of seconds.

For a waif, the girl could eat. She scraped the tin until there was nothing left but crumbs. Then she let out a loud burp and a small bubble floated toward Sam. It was green and smelled faintly of apple. He snicked his fingers at it so it popped harmlessly in the air.

"Davis says you can tell me about magic."

She licked her lips greedily. "What's in it for me?"

"How about I don't tell Teren that you ate one of the cook's pies?"

The girl shrugged it off. "I'll just tell them you ate it."

"So don't help me," Sam said indifferently, giving a shrug. "You probably don't know anything, anyway."

Mavery stomped her foot. "I know all about magic. I was one of the Tarkana witches. I know why they're after you. I know why they'll make you pay for—" She stopped at his triumphant grin. "You tricked me." A smile crossed her face. "You're not as dumb as you look."

"And you're a little pig, so let's make a deal. You tell me what I want to know, and I'll make sure you get all the pies you want."

"I have been wanting to try a giblet pie," she said dreamily.

"Giblet pie, apple pie—whatever you say. I am a Lord of the Ninth Realm," Sam boasted, hoping she wouldn't ask him what that meant, since he didn't have a clue.

She fell for it. "That you are, milord." She gave a little curtsy. "Son of Odin, I am your humble servant." She stuck out her hand.

Sam stepped forward, reaching out with a smile, and failed to notice her little trap. Using her foot, she knocked over a lantern, spilling its oil on the ground. He promptly slipped in the puddle of slick tallow and landed hard on his sore bottom.

He wanted to curse her, but *oomph* was all that came out of his mouth. Sam reached for Mavery, but she danced away, laughing as if her gut would burst.

Suddenly, they heard voices outside the tent. The girl dove under a pile of blankets as Captain Teren walked in. He took one look at Sam sprawled on the floor and put his hand on his sword.

"Mavery!" he shouted. "I warned you, witchling!"

Sam picked himself up. He was fine, and since he needed the girl to trust him, he lied. "Teren, it's only me. I was just looking for something to eat."

Teren eyed the empty pie tin, then looked at Sam, one eyebrow raised.

Sam gave a shrug, lifting his hands. "Sorry. Ever since I got here, I've been starving." A muffled snort came from the blankets. Sam coughed to cover it up.

Fortunately, the captain let it pass. "We are a half day's ride from the capital, Skara Brae. The High Council is eager to meet with you. We will be leaving before the men break camp to expedite our journey."

"Then let's expedite," Sam said cheerily, waving at the door.

Teren looked at him like he was a bit loony, but the soldier exited the tent.

Sam swung around and pulled the blanket off Mavery.

"I saved your nasty little hide; now you owe me." His hand wrapped tightly around her thin wrist. Her pulse raced under his grip. The little witchling looked scared. Feeling bad, Sam relaxed his hold, and she immediately slipped away to the tent's opening.

Mavery stopped and flashed him a grin. "Bring a giblet pie to the stables later, and I'll tell you one secret." Then she disappeared.

One secret, my foot. She was going to spill a truckload if Sam had his way.

Davis helped him onto his mare. Sam's backside was raw from the previous day, but he just grimaced and kept quiet as he followed along behind Teren. Their party was small; only Rego and Amicus joined them. The rolling hills gave way to farmland and scattered villages where smoke rose from the chimneys atop small stone cottages. Teren pointed out the towns as they rode along. The names were simple. Potters Hill. High Town. Bright Hook. Sam felt like he had been dropped into a medieval time warp where electricity and flush toilets had not been invented—and apparently, here in Orkney, they hadn't. The fields were brown and filled with shriveled stalks of grain.

"Why is everything dead?" he asked Teren.

Teren jerked his head upward toward the smoldering red sun.

"The sun did this?" Sam found himself sneaking frequent glances at it. The glowing ball both attracted him and repelled him.

"Aye. It spreads a poison over the land, tainting everything it touches. The crops were the first to be affected."

"What happens next?"

Teren pulled up his horse and turned to face Sam. "From what is written in history, animals will start to perish. Livestock. Fish. Every living creature will become sickened."

"And the people?"

"They will go mad," Teren said quietly, then gave his horse a kick and moved on, as if he couldn't bear to think about it.

They drew near a farmhouse. A couple stood out front, watching them. There was a cheerlessness about them, as if they knew that ruin and destruction were coming. Sam stopped his horse, curious. The man gave him a long look, then ushered his wife inside their home, shutting the door and, with a loud clank, barring it.

Sam kicked his horse in the ribs to catch up to Teren and the two dwarves.

The horses seemed eager to reach Skara Brae, trotting so fast that every bone in Sam's body felt shaken out of place. As they crested a hill, the land fell away before them. He saw the stone walls of a fortress ahead, red flags flapping in the breeze. Beyond it, the ocean crashed against the stark cliffs guarding the seaward side.

Teren reined in his horse. "Welcome home, Sam. The people of Skara Brae await you. I sent ahead word of our arrival. Your father was much loved here. You will find it a warm welcome."

A curious mix of excitement and dread churned through Sam at the thought of returning home to a place he had no memory of.

Chapter Twelve

The riders entered the city through tall wooden gates and found themselves in a wide courtyard. The horses' shoes clattered on the paving stones, uprooting a flock of pigeons. A crowd of well-wishers jammed the square. They waved small flags and let out a cheer when they saw the group. The flags of red silk bore a white heron, wings outspread, clutching an olive branch in its beak.

The people were chanting something. It took Sam a moment to realize it was his name. Not Baron. The other one, the one he had apparently been born with.

Bar-con-ian! Bar-con-ian!

People reached out to touch him as he rode by. Women patted his legs, tears in their eyes. Brawny men shouted out that they had known his father. A silly grin was plastered on Sam's face. This was the coolest thing that had ever happened to him. They treated him like a hero.

The horses stopped in front of the wide stone steps of a palatial building where a group of official-looking people had gathered. A boy ran up and took his reins, helping Sam down before leading his horse away. Sam's legs were wobbly, but he was too awestruck by the sight in front of him to care.

"Wow."

The assembly of officials appeared in all sizes and colors, including some angry-looking warriors that reminded him of the Umatilla. They seemed to be waiting for Sam to do something. He felt tongue-tied and out of place, suddenly ashamed of how they had cheered for him. The truth was, he wasn't a hero. That had been his dad.

Then the crowd began to clap, and one by one, the groups waiting on the steps joined in, until the walls of the city echoed with their cheers. Sam couldn't help it. He smiled. They clapped harder, and Teren slapped him on the back, then grabbed his hand, thrusting it up in the air victoriously.

Captain Teren gave him a short bow. "Ready to face them?"

"Don't leave my side," Sam said in a panic.

"Never, milord. I am sworn to protect you." He winked, but there was an earnestness to his words that the soldier couldn't hide. Teren turned to face the assembly of officials and rubbed his hands together. "Right. Introductions are in order. First up are the Falcory."

Sam followed him, eyeing the pair of men standing motionless and silent at the end of the line. They looked like the Umatilla, with their long black hair and leather leggings embroidered with colorful beads. When they got closer, Sam gasped. Their noses were shaped like the curved beaks of falcons.

Teren stopped in front of them. "Samuel, this is Beo, the Falcory representative to the High Council."

Nervous, but eager to get it over with, Sam stuck out his hand with a smile. "Nice to meet you."

Beo ignored his hand, staring at Sam with flinty eyes that overflowed with suspicion, which was strange, since they had just met. Then, suddenly, Beo grasped Sam's hand, mashing Sam's fingers under his.

Up close, Sam could see Beo's hardened beak. It curved down slightly, ending in a sharp point. Small silver hooks dangled feathers from his earlobes. Sam's smile faded as the pressure on his hand increased until he nearly cried out in pain.

"Welcome home," Beo finally said, releasing Sam's hand. A muscle ticked in the warrior's cheek, as if the words were being dragged from him.

Sam let out a sigh of relief as blood flowed back into his fingers. Teren pushed Sam along and introduced him to Beo's brother, Geb. Geb looked scarier than Beo. His hair was cut close to his scalp, revealing a web of crisscrossing scars, as if he had tangled with a wildcat. Geb wasn't the friendly sort. He grunted once at Sam and folded his arms.

As they approached the next group, Teren whispered in Sam's ear, "These are the Balfins."

A cluster of somber-looking men in heavy black robes awaited them. All had shaved heads and the same round, scowling faces.

"Emenor is their representative to the council," Teren continued. "He's a nasty piece of work. I don't think the Balfins should be allowed a seat, what with their alliance with the witches, but your father wanted peace with them."

"They take the witches' side?" Sam's feet slowed.

"Aye, the Balfins shelter them on Balfour Island and marry them. In exchange, the Balfins receive trinkets of power."

Sam disliked them on sight, but Teren was already introducing him to the Balfin representative.

"You should not have brought him to Skara Brae," Emenor said in a low voice, his eyes shifting from Sam to Teren.

"Emenor, mind your manners," Teren said lightly, his hand casually moving to the hilt of his sword.

"It was a mistake, and you know it. He is not safe." Emenor's eyes slid over Sam like those of a snake sizing up its prey. "The witches will come for him. That blood will be on your hands."

Thankfully, Teren moved him along. "Beware of Emenor," he warned. "He's not happy unless he's plotting something."

"Does anyone in this place actually like me?" Sam grumbled.

Teren stopped, pitching his voice low. "They don't know what to think, Sam. Your mother is a witch, after all."

Teren had a point. Around here, witches were about as popular as the plague. "Okay, who's next?" Sam said.

"Next are the Eifalians. They're the elven folk to the north. They live on the island of Torf-Einnar. I'm pretty sure they don't hate you." Teren winked.

Sam stared at the tall, translucent-skinned men and women. Their oversize eyes were fixed on him as they whispered to one another. The Eifalians were reed-thin and wore long robes of shimmering greens and aquamarine that changed color in the light. Their pale skin glowed faintly as they eyed Sam up and down. But their hair was the most striking, an alabaster white, like the color of the moon on a clear night.

"Greetings, young master," the tallest one murmured in a low-pitched, singsong voice. "The Eifalian Kingdom welcomes you back to the Ninth Realm. I am Gael, son of King Einolach, who sends his greetings. This is my wife, Rayan." A beautiful woman with haunting eyes of luminescent blue smiled kindly at Sam.

"Welcome home, Samuel. Your father was a good friend to the Eifalians." She squeezed his hand gently, and Sam smiled, feeling marginally better from the warm greeting.

Gael closed his eyes and placed his hand on Sam's head. His scalp tingled under the Eifalian's touch.

Rayan elbowed her husband. "Stop reading the boy's aura, Gael. It isn't polite."

Gael lifted his hand. "You are right, as always, my wife." But his words were terse, and suddenly he didn't look happy at all.

At that moment, Sam's stomach rumbled loudly enough for Rayan to notice.

"Husband, the boy is famished. He needs refreshments."

Gael bowed. "A thousand pardons. Please, enter the Great

Hall. Someone will show you to your room." He swept his hand forward, his long fingers giving off a faint turquoise light.

Sam looked around for a friendly face, but Beo held Teren's arm, speaking urgently in his ear. Sam made his way slowly up the stairs, feeling alone and unprotected. At the top, a man stood off to the side, staring intently at Sam with narrowed eyes. He was dressed in long red robes. Anger radiated from him, as if from a furnace. Whoever he was, he was not one of Sam's fans.

In his mind, Sam heard the echo of Vor's prophetic voice: *There is a battle raging inside you. Which bloodline will win?*

Sam felt paralyzed with doubt, suddenly feeling the weight of this world upon him. But before he could turn around and head back to Teren, the man in the red robes reached out and grabbed his arm.

"We need to talk." He dragged Sam forward, away from the crowd. His hand gripped Sam's bicep like an iron manacle.

Thankfully, Rego came to his rescue, butting his head between them and pushing them apart.

"Apologies, Lord Orrin," the dwarf said loudly. "Didn't see you standing there. The boy needs some rest, so, if you'll pardon us, you can speak to him later."

Orrin gave the dwarf a blistering glare but said nothing, tilting his head slightly to signify his permission.

Rego pushed Sam along through the main doors into the entry of the Great Hall. Ceilings arched high overhead. Twin sets of stone staircases went up both sides, lit by candelabra set into the walls. The floor was a mosaic of black and white tiles. Freshly cut flowers stood on a table. A maid curtsied before hurrying past with platters of what looked like ham. Sam's stomach rumbled again as he looked longingly after her.

"Keep walking," Rego said, shoving him down a long corridor. It was dark; the ceilings were low, lit only by the widely spaced candles. They passed several open rooms, but Rego didn't stop until they came to a heavy wooden door that he pressed open with one hand, shoving Sam inside with the other.

"Seriously, you can lay off the pushing," Sam said, secretly relieved to be out of the spotlight. They were in a large chamber. An ornately carved canopy bed took up one corner. A large wardrobe stood open, a row of crisp white shirts hanging inside. A table had been set with a platter of fresh fruit.

Rego checked under the bed and behind the curtains, as if he suspected someone might be hiding there, before turning to warn Sam. "You stay away from Orrin. He's a serpent in disguise."

"You mean he's worse than that Falcory guy who looked like he wanted to punch me? Or that Balfin who said I shouldn't have come here?" Sam muttered, eyeing the fruit hungrily. There were clusters of plump grapes, and he grabbed a fistful, stuffing them in his mouth.

Rego grunted. "Your father loved jookberries, too. Seems you have something in common with him."

Sam looked at the purplish grapes and put them down, suddenly finding their sweet taste cloying. He settled on a plum and bit into it. It was sweet and juicy, like an Oregon plum from home. Sam sat down, feeling the wear and tear of the past couple days sink in. He propped his boots up on the table, trying to ease the ache in his bones.

"We're not in a barn, boy." Rego used the point of his sword to knock Sam's feet off the table. "So don't act uncivilized."

Sam couldn't do anything right for this dwarf. "What do you want from me?" he griped, wiping his mouth with his sleeve. "You brought me to this medieval place and have told me nothing about what I'm supposed to do. People treat me like I'm some kind of hero or hate me on sight, and all you do is yell at me!"

Rego waited till Sam was done, then sheathed his sword, letting out a sigh. "I suppose you've a right to be upset; it's your parents who created this mess. It's not fair you're in the middle of it, but there's nothing to be done about that now."

"When am I going home?" Sam asked, feeling a spell of homesickness.

"This is your home now, lad."

Sam shook his head, slamming his hand down on the table. "Orkney is not my home. I don't belong here. And my friends don't, either. We should be going after them. Those witches killed my father—doesn't that mean anything to you?"

Rego glared at him from across the table. "Your father cared more about the safety of this realm than about his own life. As for your friends, I told you, Endera took them for a reason. Try to rescue them, and you'll play right into her hands."

Sam stood up abruptly, knocking over his chair. He was done being bossed around by this dwarf. "Well, I'm going after them!" he shouted, feeling his temper soar. "And you can't stop me. I'll get Teren to help me."

Rego drew a dagger from his waist and slammed it into the wooden table, spearing Sam's half-eaten plum.

"You go right ahead." He leaned in, his whiskered face inches from Sam's. "Captain Teren will willingly follow you to his death, the same way his father and twenty other men followed your dad to their deaths. They think you're a hero come to save them. So you take Teren, and you lead him to his death, and see how it feels then."

Sam's anger deflated like a popped balloon.

"I can't just abandon them," he said, righting his chair and slumping down in it. "Howie's my best friend, and Keely . . ." The words dried up, but he pressed on. "They didn't ask for this."

Rego sighed sympathetically. "No, they didn't. But they're in it now. You have to make a choice, just like your father. What do you care about more—your friends or the safety of your realm?"

"It's not my realm," Sam protested.

A knock at the door interrupted whatever the dwarf was going to say next. A maid curtsied, apologizing for the intrusion. She carried a jug of hot water and a change of clothes.

Rego took the opportunity to hightail it for the door. "We'll talk more about this later," he said, pausing on the threshold. "I promised Captain Teren a word before supper." And then he ducked out, leaving Sam feeling more frustrated and confused than ever.

Chapter Thirteen

Keely pressed her face against the bars of her cell, trying to see into Howie's. He was imprisoned across the corridor, behind a wooden door, but she could just make out his body through the barred window. He was sprawled on a thin layer of hay. He hadn't spoken since a pair of brutes dressed in black armor had tossed them in here.

"Howie, answer me. Are you okay?" she repeated for the tenth time.

Howie didn't move. His eyes were open, looking at the ceiling. Every so often, he blinked, his only signal that he was still alive.

"Come on, Howie, snap out of it. We have to make a plan to escape. Sam's going to need our help."

He blinked once but didn't move.

"Or maybe you don't care about Sam. You know, your best friend? The one who always has your back? The one who protects you from bullies like Ronnie Polk?"

That got Howie moving. He sat up. Clumps of hay stuck to his stray curls. His glasses were tilted sideways on his nose. He pushed them into place, breathing in deeply before he spoke. "I can't protect Sam."

Keely breathed a sigh of relief. It was good to have company. "Sure you can. We both can. We can do it together."

He laughed. "In case you hadn't noticed, I'm a coward. That's why Ronnie picks on me. He knows I won't fight back."

"So prove him wrong. Prove them all wrong. Help get us out of here."

But Howie sat frozen, staring at the wall.

Keely gripped the bars on the door. "Howie, say something."

"Quiet," he said.

"I'm not going to stay quiet. Sam needs us."

"Rats," he said, scrabbling back on all fours. "Giant rats."

That's when Keely heard it: a scratching noise coming from the stone walls of her cell. She turned slowly. Howie was right. Giant rats had crawled out of some dark corner. They advanced on her, their small paws brushing their whiskers, as if they were assessing her. They weren't ordinary rats. Their teeth were long and sharp, their bodies the size of a small cat's.

"Howie, what are these things?" she shouted.

"Why're you asking me?" Howie shouted back.

Keely searched for a weapon. The only thing in her cell was a wooden bucket. She grabbed it by the handle and swung it at the closest rat as it tried to run at her. She sent it flying against the wall. It hit with a satisfying thump, but another rat moved in, scurrying across the stone floor to bite down on the soft flesh of her ankle.

She yelped in pain and heard Howie do the same.

More rats appeared, flowing across the floor. Keely crouched down, backing up against the wall. She kicked at one and threw the bucket at a bunch. She put her arms up, fearing they were about to run her over, when they stopped and sniffed the air, turning to fade away into their hidden nests.

Keely lowered her arms. Outside her door, Endera's eyes glittered at her.

"How do you like my *rathos*?" she asked.

Keely grabbed the bucket and threw it at the bars, enjoying the look of surprise on Endera's face. "Where's Sam?" Keely demanded.

"Sam is tied up at the moment, but he'll be here soon," Endera quipped.

"When he gets here, he's going to kick your butt." That came from Howie. Keely smiled at him over Endera's shoulder.

He winked at Keely. "My buddy Sam is the most righteous dude I know. He's not scared of you. Even if you are wicked-ugly."

Endera just laughed. "I shall count the minutes till he arrives to save you. Until then, enjoy my hospitality." With a swirl of her skirts, she stalked off.

Keely looked across the hall at Howie. His whole demeanor had changed. His face was still pale, but his jaw clenched as he spoke. "Don't you worry, Keely-pie. Sam's going to come for us, and when he does, you just watch. These witches are going to wish they'd never been born."

"You really think so?"

"I know Sam. And don't forget, that Leo dude was there with his Umatilla warriors. They aren't going to just leave us here."

For the first time since Endera had showed up on her porch, Keely felt a flicker of hope. In her pocket, she found the rune stone Sam had given her in the library. She pulled it out, rubbing the jagged $\lessgtr$. *Howie's right*, she thought. *Sam will come for us, and he'll find a way to fix everything.*

Chapter Fourteen

reshly dressed in a clean white shirt and breeches that tucked into soft leather boots, Sam opened the wooden shutters to his room, letting in the weak evening light. The sun hung low, clinging like a red blister to the horizon.

Questions swirled in his head. It was starting to sink in that nothing about him was normal. His parents had kept their incomprehensible, not-to-be-believed, straight-out-of-a-movie heritage such a big secret, Sam was completely in the dark about who he really was. One thing was certain: ever since Endera had shot that electrifying green fire at his chest, a strange language had been whispering constantly in the back of his head.

A young boy showed up at his door to take him to dinner. The boy held a candle to light the way down corridors lined with stone. The place was like a mausoleum. Sam stopped to look at a spear mounted on the wall. It was bronze, very old looking, sort of dull and dusty. A plaque underneath it read GUNGNIR.

Sam reached out and felt a rush of cold air as his fingers touched the shaft.

"You like it?" a voice said.

A man dressed in a black cowl, the hood loose around his neck, appeared next to Sam. His face was smooth under a sheaf of white hair, but his eyes were watery and yellowed with age.

"I'm sorry. I didn't mean to touch it." Sam snatched his hand back. He looked for the boy with the candle, but he had disappeared around the corner.

"It's okay. Take it. It's yours." The hooded man's voice was as dry as paper.

"Me? No, I've never even seen it before."

"Some things belong to us whether we like it or not," he wheezed with a deep sadness, as if his words weighed on him.

"Did Vor send you?" Sam asked, thinking that the old man reminded him of the pale Goddess of Wisdom, because of the stillness and the suddenness with which he had appeared.

"So, you have received Vor's counsel? You are most fortunate," the man answered. "I am Forset, the God of Justice. I provide fairness when none can be found." He coughed once, a deep, phlegmy sound, and wiped his mouth with a white handkerchief he pulled from his pocket. "It is rare for me to leave my home. But I have been sent to give you a gift." He lifted the spear down and handed it to Sam. "This belonged to Odin."

"Odin? Really? That's so cool." Sam eyed it with renewed respect. It felt heavy in his hands but really like nothing special. Still, a spear of the gods!

Forset nodded. "It is said to always find its target. When you most need it, raise your hand and call its name, Gungnir. It will appear." He stepped back, and a wave of panic washed over Sam. This stranger was leaving him holding a priceless artifact.

"No, they'll think I stole it." Sam tried to put it back, but the bracket was gone and so was the name plaque. When he turned around, Forset had disappeared. Sam looked down at the spear. It began to glow in his hand, turning red-hot, singeing his palm. He dropped it, and the spear vanished into thin air, leaving only a puff of smoke.

Shaking his head, Sam hurried to find his way to the banquet. After several wrong turns, he ended up in the kitchen. A blushing maid took pity on him and led him to the dining hall, curtsying quickly before fleeing.

He stood in the entrance, taking it all in. The crowded hall was blanketed by a haze of smoke emanating from a large stone fireplace where crackling flames leaped six feet into the air. Rough-hewn beams lined the ceiling. Hundreds of flickering candles dripped wax down from swaying chandeliers. Long tables lined both sides of a carpeted walkway leading to a head table at the other end of the room. The table was draped in Orkadian red, with the symbol of the white heron displayed prominently in the center.

Captain Teren hurried over to join Sam at the entrance and bowed. "I was beginning to think we'd scared you off. May I escort you to your seat?"

Relieved to see a friendly face, Sam nodded rapidly. "Who are all these people?"

Teren slapped him on the back and turned him around to face the crowds. "These are the people of Orkney. Don't worry, you'll get their names straight soon enough. But there're a few things you should know if you're going to live long enough to save us all."

Save them all? Sam wanted to ask what Teren meant by that, but the soldier was already moving him forward down the center aisle. Conversation died as they walked toward the head table.

Teren whispered in his ear as they slowly made their way. "The Chief High Council is that large man in the center, Lord Drabic—looking a bit into his cups, I might add. He took over after your father perished."

Drabic was fat and balding and had long jowls that wobbled as he drank from his goblet. This was his father's replacement?

"Drabic might seem a fool, but beware—he has strong al-liances," Teren added at Sam's skeptical look. "He should have been on the steps to greet you earlier. A calculated move on his part to put you in your place."

As Teren led Sam past a table of dwarves, Rego eyed Sam closely over a tankard of ale, then rose abruptly from his seat to move into the aisle, blocking their way. He bowed low. Teren elbowed Sam, and Sam bowed back awkwardly.

Rego took the moment to grab him by the arm. "Don't trust anyone, boy," he whispered in Sam's ear. "You hear me?"

His words were sharp and intense. Sam nodded, seeing fear in the dwarf's eyes. Rego resumed his seat as Teren pulled him along.

Sam focused on the head table. The man in the red robes who had accosted him earlier sat watching his approach with narrowed eyes. "Who's that to the left of Drabic?"

"That's Lord Orrin. He's High Regent. Advises the council on matters of importance, which is to say he spies on everyone. He has Drabic's ear. You should avoid him. He and Emenor are too close for my comfort."

Emenor's shoulders were hunched under a heavy black robe, but his beady eyes were pinned firmly on Sam.

"Why does Emenor hate me so much?" Sam whispered.

Teren gave a slight shrug. "It's not a question of hate; it's one of trust. The Balfins have the same concern we all do about you."

"Which is?"

They stopped a few feet from the head table. Teren looked at Sam. His eyes were kind but troubled as he leaned forward and whispered in Sam's ear, "Which path will you choose, Samuel? Which path will you lead us all down?"

A gong sounded, and the large hall grew quiet. Lord Drabic stood up, a little tottery, and raised his glass. Sam could feel Orrin's eyes impaling him. Gael looked worried, a small frown pinching the Eifalian's forehead. And Beo—well, the Falcory looked at Sam over his beak nose as if he would like to eat Sam's liver.

"We welcome the return of a Barconian to the Ninth Realm." Drabic waved his glass in Sam's direction. "May Odin smile upon you with his good fortune."

Glasses clanked together as applause broke out, and then conversation resumed. Teren bowed and left to join a table of Orkadian soldiers. Sam made his way up to the dais.

Drabic grabbed his arm, speaking so only Sam could hear. "Don't get any ideas about who's in charge. Your father is gone, and I run this city. Now take your seat and smile nicely, like a good boy." He pinched Sam's cheek roughly and gave him a little shove. Sam burned with anger and embarrassment, but he gritted his teeth and moved along toward the only empty seat. It was sandwiched between the scowling Emenor and the less-than-friendly High Regent, Lord Orrin.

Servers marched in with platters of steaming food, dropping them down in the center of each table, and the room was soon abuzz with the sounds of eating and drinking. Ravenous hunger had Sam reaching for a fat drumstick. It was good—much better than the black cabbage stew and hard biscuits he had been eating since he got to Orkney.

Lord Orrin waited until Sam was on his second drumstick before he spoke. His breath smelled like cloves. His face was smooth and oily and gave off a sheen in the candlelight. A thin scar ran along one cheek.

"I can help you rescue your friends," Orrin murmured in a low voice, keeping his eyes on the crowd, as if his attention were elsewhere, "but you have to do exactly as I say."

Sam choked on his food. An offer of help was the last thing Sam had expected from the High Regent. Across the room, Rego set down his mug, his eyes on the two of them.

"How do you know about my friends?"

"Word spreads fast in our world. The High Council is going to send you on a suicide mission," Orrin went on. "You must be gone before morning, or your friends will die at the hands of the witches."

The turkey turned to sawdust in Sam's throat. Here he was,

feasting, while Howie and Keely were being held hostage in some drafty dungeon.

"Why do you care?" Sam asked, pushing his plate away.

"Let's just say our interests are aligned." His next words surprised Sam even more. "The Balfins have agreed to assist."

Sam looked to his right at Emenor. So far, the Balfin had showed him only contempt. Why would a witch-loving Balfin lift a finger to help him?

Orrin rushed the words out. "Your friends are being held on Balfour Island. Emenor will provide a map to the Tarkana fortress. Without it, you will perish in the never-ending bogs and swamps that surround it."

Before Sam could ask how he was supposed to get to this Balfour Island, Lord Drabic pushed back his chair. The council members all rose and began filing out as the rest of the diners continued their meal.

"Be ready tonight," Orrin whispered to him, before hurrying to catch up with Drabic.

Rego and Captain Teren began heading intently toward Sam. No doubt Rego wanted to know every word the High Regent had been whispering, but before they could arrive, Gael took his elbow.

"Walk with me," the Eifalian said.

They left the dining hall and walked down a long hallway lit by softly glowing sconces. The walls were lined with portraits. The faces were a blur, old men with inscribed names whom Sam had never heard of—until he came to one he recognized. Sam stopped, his breath catching in his chest.

It was his father. LORD ROBERT BARCONIAN, the nameplate read. In the picture, he looked young, noble, alive.

"Your father was of the old bloodlines, a true Son of Odin," Gael said. His long robe shifted colors from emerald to shimmering aquamarine when he moved. "A direct descendent of Baldur, Odin's most favored son. He embodied many of Baldur's qualities: a brave warrior, strong and courageous."

So his father really had been a hero. If his father had had these traits, then maybe there was hope for Sam to follow in his footsteps. He looked at Gael, expecting warmth, but instead something flinty gleamed in the Eifalian's pale eyes.

"What's wrong?" Sam asked.

Gael shrugged. "I have read your aura. You are clouded. Too much of your mother's blood, I suppose." He moved away, gliding down the hall in his flowing robe.

Sam was speechless as he glared at Gael's back. If his aura was cloudy, maybe it was because he had been lied to his whole life. He looked back at the portrait of his father, and this time a wave of bitterness washed over him. They treated his dad like he was a full-on hero, but Robert Barconian had left Sam behind. Abandoned him. Lied to him. And never come back.

A real hero would have had the guts to say goodbye before he took off through a stonefire to another realm.

"Sam, the High Council is waiting for you." Captain Teren stood outside a set of double doors.

Sam gave his dad's portrait one last, bitter glance and then moved on.

Chapter Fifteen

Teren ushered Sam into a room with high ceilings and no windows. The room was stuffy and warm. Orrin's eyes burned into Sam from where he stood behind Lord Drabic. The Council members were seated around a long, oval table ringed with high-backed chairs. Teren motioned Sam into an empty seat and sat down beside him.

Drabic poured himself a generous portion of wine and then planted his hands on the table. "So, how soon can he leave for Asgard?"

Asgard? Wasn't that the land of the gods? Sam was about to remind them that he had just arrived in Orkney, when Rego jumped up. "You're not sending him off on a wild goose hunt after Odin. He's just a boy."

"Things have changed, dwarf," Drabic said. "Have you not seen how the red sun has spread its veins? Its poison destroys the crops. Soon there will be food shortages. The boy is a Son of Odin. Who will save us, if not him?"

The Council all began shouting at once. Everyone seemed to have a different opinion about what Sam was supposed to do now that he was here in Orkney.

Rego put his fingers in his mouth and let out a shrill whistle. The room quieted down, and all eyes turned to Sam. "Tell him," Rego urged from his seat. "He deserves to know what you're asking."

Gael waved his hand, and a cloud of fog rolled across the table. When it cleared, in the center Sam could see a hazy image of a circle of large stones. He sat forward, suddenly interested. "Is that the Ring of Brogar?" It fit Rego's description of the place where his father had been killed.

"You've heard the story of how Catriona and her sisters were entombed?" Gael asked.

Sam repeated what he remembered. "A long time ago, some guy named Hermodan defeated them with Odin's Stone and sent Orkney away from my world, into the Ninth Realm."

"Exactly." Gael waved his hand again, and the cloud shifted to show a young man standing in the middle of the Ring of Brogar, holding a large stone in the shape of a shield in front of him. "Hermodan used Odin's Stone to defend against the witches." A burst of green lightning flowed over Hermodan, but he was safe behind the stone. "Odin's Stone was powerful enough to trap Catriona and her cronies inside the stones of the Ring of Brogar."

Sam watched as the crackling energy bounced off the shield and returned to a group of women dressed in black gowns, their long, nasty fingers shooting green fire. Hermodan thrust the shield into the sky, his lips moving wordlessly. Blue fire exploded out of Odin's Stone, and the giant ring of stones began to glow.

Sam leaned in, watching breathlessly as the witches were pulled toward the rocks; their backs stuck against the sides like magnets. And then they vanished, sucked inside the stones.

"Cool," he whispered.

"The witches have waited a thousand years to take their revenge," Gael continued. "A few months ago, the sun began to shimmer, and then the first red vein appeared. It is spreading like a poison across the realm, killing the land and tainting the spirit of the people. Endera and her cronies wish to drive Orkney to its knees. They have sent a letter demanding our immediate surrender to their rule, or they will allow the curse of the red sun to spread until all of Orkney perishes."

He let his words hang in the air. The eyes of the Council continued to stare at Sam, as if they were waiting for him to come up with a plan.

Sam looked into the wisps of fog. "Rego said Odin cut off Rubicus's head and solved the problem. Can't you just do the same? Take an army and go after the witches?" Sam wouldn't mind seeing Endera's head on a stake.

Beo spoke then, spinning a knife in his hand as he vented his frustration. "Even if we killed every witch, we'd need Odin's magic to end the curse. Hermodan went to Asgard, to the island of the gods, to beseech Odin for his help, but one cannot find Asgard, let alone enter, unless one shares the blood of Odin."

There was silence after Beo spoke. It took a moment, and then the importance of his words hit Sam. "I'm a Son of Odin," he said, looking around the table.

"The last known offspring," Gael added softly.

Every adult stared at him expectantly, waiting for him to jump onboard with their plan.

Without thinking it all through, Sam blurted out, "Look, I'm happy to help, but first I have to pay a visit to Endera to get my friends back."

There were angry grumbles from the group. Beo slammed the tip of his blade into the table. "See how he runs to the witches' side," he said angrily. "His blood is tainted."

"Beo is correct," Gael added. "We don't know where the child's loyalty lies."

Rego jumped to his feet, his face red as a tomato. "His father was Robert Barconian. You know *spleeking* well where his loyalty lies: with the realm."

"He is also one of *theirs*." Beo practically spat out his words. "We can't be sure."

Confusion laced with a ripe dose of anger hummed through Sam. One of theirs? Tainted blood? His cheeks began to tingle with that familiar sense of rage at the injustice of how they were treating him. He rose out of his chair. "Hey, I said I would go on your stupid quest as soon as I get Howie and Keely back."

But the council kept speaking as if he weren't even there.

"The boy is the first he-witch in generations," Gael said. "There is no telling what powers he will achieve when he matures. Odin ended his kind for a reason."

Sam was about to tell them where they could stuff their quest, when an arm went around his neck and a sharp knife pressed against his throat. It was Geb, Beo's brother with the scarred scalp.

"I say we kill him now and be done with it," he muttered, his breath hot on Sam's neck. "Then we don't have to wonder what he'll turn out to be."

Rego jumped up, drawing his sword and placing its tip against Geb's ribs. "Do it, and the last thing you'll feel is my blade running through your heart."

"Now, now," Emenor said, his bald pate sweaty and shiny in the candlelight as he waved his pale hands. "We can't go around killing Robert Barconian's only son."

The room quieted, as if Emenor had dropped a bomb.

"Since when do Balfins support Barconians?" Gael said in the stillness, steepling his long fingers together.

"Emenor speaks the truth," Lord Orrin said, stepping forward and placing a hand on the dour-faced Balfin's shoulder. "The boy is too valuable to kill."

The room was eerily silent. The knife still pressed into Sam's skin. He didn't move, not even to breathe.

"Enough," Drabic said, waving Geb away irritably with his wine goblet.

The Falcory savage released him. Sam sank down in his chair, feeling his anger grow. He had tried to be nice, but they seemed to think he was on the wrong side. Sam hated those witches as much as these guys did for killing his father—more so if they laid even a finger on Keely or Howie.

Drabic continued, "I say he goes to Asgard. If we don't find a way to break the curse, it won't matter whose side he is on."

"Then the Falcory will escort him," Beo said, his black eyes fierce. "We will make sure he doesn't stray."

"And the Eifalians will come along as well," Gael stated.

What riled Sam was that he seemed to have no say in this. He felt like a lamb being led to slaughter. His eyes slid over to Orrin's and caught his satisfied sneer. The High Regent had been right. They didn't care one penny about his friends.

Rego picked up Sam by the collar and dragged him out of his seat. "Come on, lad. Let's leave it to them to fuss over who's going to ride with you."

"That was fun," Sam grumbled, as Rego pushed him along darkened hallways. "They act like I'm the bad guy here."

"Not out here, lad. The walls have ears." The dwarf seemed to have a sixth sense about which corridor to take. Finally, Rego placed his palm on a rough wooden door and pushed it open. Sam stumbled inside and turned on Rego as he shut the door.

"I thought you said I was safe here." His neck still stung from Geb's sharp blade.

The dwarf shrugged, levering himself up on the window ledge so he could look through the shutters out into the courtyard. "You're alive, aren't you?"

Sam's temperature spiked at the feeble apology. "That Falcory was about to skin me alive!"

"They need you more than they fear you." Rego kept his eyes on the courtyard. "You're safe enough."

Sam paced the room, unable to sit still. "What about Howie

and Keely? I can't just leave them with Endera and her pack of witches. Someone has to rescue them."

Rego sighed. "I'm sorry about your friends, Sam. Really, I am. But there's no time to go after them. The sun worsens every day. The High Council is right to send you to Asgard. You are our only hope of survival."

"I don't want the job!" Sam shouted. "Find someone else."

"There is no one else!" Rego shouted back. "If you don't find a way to end this, Orkney will perish."

"Well, that's not fair," Sam said, kicking a chair. "I just want to get my friends and go home."

There was silence. And then Rego dropped a bombshell. "There is no going home."

Sam's head snapped up. "What do you mean, no going home?"

Rego rubbed his whiskers before answering. "I ordered Chief Pate-wa to destroy the stonefire from the other side."

"You mean I'm never going home?"

Rego shook his head and resumed his study of the court-yard. "Once the witches discovered it, we couldn't risk their using it again and causing mischief and mayhem."

Never going home meant never playing video games again. Never eating at Chuggies. His friends would be stuck here. And what about his mom? A familiar flush of rage came over him, sending tingles through him as if his skin were on fire.

Sam flipped over the table, sending the bowl of fruit rolling across the room. "You had no right to ruin my life," he raged. "This is all your fault!"

"My fault?" Rego turned from the window and crossed his arms. "I'm not the one who got my friends involved. That was all you, lad. And I didn't put you in the middle of this; that was your parents' doing. A Son of Odin marrying a witch." He let out a snort of disgust. "Anyone with half a brain could have predicted that would turn out for the worst. But your parents didn't care;

they let their hearts rule their heads, when they should have been thinking about the consequences."

The dwarf was right. Sam unclenched his fists as the mist slowly receded. "I'm sorry." He took several deep breaths as he picked up the table. "It's just, my friends are counting on me to rescue them. Please help me, Rego, and then I'll go on your stupid quest."

The dwarf shook his head. "The red sun is spreading its poison. Soon, it won't be just the crops that die; it'll be the animals and the people."

"How long before that happens?"

"Don't know. But every day you delay, things get worse."

"So there could be time to rescue them. Come on, Rego."

"What's more important to you, Sam? Saving your friends or saving this realm?"

"What's the point in saving Orkney if I lose my best friends?" he shouted, glaring at Rego across the room.

The dwarf didn't flinch. "If you don't save Orkney, the red sun will kill us all, your friends included."

Chapter Sixteen

Leo lay on his back, staring up at the stars, waiting for his heart to slow down. His father had tried to stop him from coming through the stonefire, but in the end, Leo had convinced him that it was his duty. *And duty is everything to the Umatilla chief*, he thought with a trace of bitterness.

It wasn't easy being the son of the chief. Leo's life had been mapped out for him since the day he was born. Stay on the reservation. Become a great leader. Bear a son or daughter to carry on the tradition. Sacrifice any personal dreams for the good of his people. It had been drilled into Leo since he was old enough to walk.

Traveling to Orkney was Leo's one chance to escape, to do something more with his life and not let his father down. A smile crossed his face as the realization sunk in that he had done it. Crossed over to another realm. If Leo hadn't seen Endera turn that lizard into a monster, he would still be stuck back in Pilot Rock, training to take his father's place. Instead, he was here, in a realm of the gods, on a quest to save his friend.

He held his arm up, tracing the twisting scar that ran from his elbow to his wrist. Although he didn't know it yet, Sam had been there for Leo when he had needed it most. Now it was up to Leo to return the favor.

The stonefire lay in pieces. His father had destroyed the portal once Leo was safely through. As much as Leo wanted to escape the burdens of his heritage, the thought of never going home again gave him a sharp pang of regret. He would miss his mother's warm smile and his younger sister's annoying habit of braiding his hair.

A twig snapped at the edge of the clearing. Sitting up, Leo searched the shadows. The moon was only half full, but it was easy to make out shapes. Was that someone lurking behind a tree?

Leo got to his feet. He had brought along his prized bow and a quiver full of arrows, which he had wrapped in deerskin to protect them from the flames. Unwrapping the bow, he notched an arrow.

"Come out," he called. "I know you're there."

"Brave warrior, do not be afraid." A woman emerged from the shadows. Her hair was as pale as the white gown she wore.

Leo lowered his bow. "Who are you?"

"I am Vor, a friend to you and to the one you seek." She stepped into the clearing, and Leo bit back a gasp. Her eyes were white and sightless.

"You know where I can find Sam?"

She nodded. "But you must not stop him from undergoing his journey. There will be a time when he needs you. Then you must be ready."

Leo believed her. There was something about her that was otherworldly, but he felt no malice in her. "How will I know where to find him?"

"There is a road that runs along the coast. Follow it south three days, until you reach a large fishing village. Travel by night. The days are cursed by the rays of a powerful sun. Stay out of sight until you are called."

Leo hesitated. "I can't just stand by and do nothing. What if you're wrong? What if Sam needs my help sooner?" He itched to take action, to jump in with both feet to help defeat whatever demon Sam faced.

But Vor turned away from him toward the darkness of the woods. "Then all will be lost, brave one. Your help won't matter. Sam must learn to choose the right path on his own."

She began to shimmer, dissolving into pinpoints of light. Like fireflies, they floated away through the trees.

Leo waited to see if she would return; then he picked up his bow and the few things he had brought and began jogging along the trail. The moon would be his guide. He would take Vor's advice and wait for Sam's signal.

Chapter Seventeen

S am lay awake in his big four-poster bed, listening to Rego snoring a few feet away. The dwarf was curled up on a rug next to the bed. Sam's mind swirled, thinking about Howie and Keely. If something happened to them, he would spend the rest of his life feeling guilty. There was time, he told himself, time to make a side trip to rescue his friends and still get to Asgard to ask Odin for the cure for that cursed sun. Keely knew a lot about Odin. She would be a big help, and Howie, he could keep Sam from losing his cool. All Sam had to do was get out of Skara Brae and find them.

A hand covered his mouth. Sam opened his eyes to see the High Regent himself, Lord Orrin, standing over him, one bony finger to his lips.

Sam's first thought was that he should wake Rego. Sam would sooner trust a rattlesnake than this Orrin. But he was torn. His only shot at rescuing his friends was to go along with this slimy manipulator.

The bed creaked as he stood. They both froze. Rego snorted once, rolled over, and began to snore again.

Sam's boots and a cloak were next to the bed, as well as the knife he had brought with him. Sam picked up his things and, still barefoot, followed Orrin to a covering on the wall. Orrin pulled it aside to reveal a small door.

Beyond the door was a narrow corridor lit by a single candle on a shelf. Orrin picked it up, and they made their way silently to another door. He tapped once.

It opened. Sam wasn't surprised to see Emenor. The Balfin's round face was locked in its perpetual scowl.

"Quickly, boy, get dressed," he ordered.

Sam clumsily put on his boots and slipped the cloak over his shoulders.

Emenor's face glowed in the candlelight. He held out a folded piece of parchment. "This is a map of Balfour Island. It will guide you safely through the swamps and bogs that surround it to here"—he stabbed a gray *X*—"the Tarkana fortress. Don't lose it, boy. If you stray off course, you will surely die."

Sam studied the map, trying to make sense of the marks. "I'm not sure I understand . . . ," he began, but shouts sounded in the hallway.

Rego had awoken and alerted the guards.

Orrin gave Sam a shove. "Get him out of here, now," he said to Emenor. "I'll delay them as best I can."

The Balfin hauled Sam into the secret passage and pushed him farther along the corridor, until it ended in a solid stone wall. Sam groaned. They were trapped.

Emenor looked at Sam impatiently. "Open it," he demanded.

Sam put his hand on the cold stone. "How?" The wall was made of granite blocks. He didn't see a door or any secret opening.

The Balfin shook him roughly. "Use your magic, boy."

Confused, Sam stepped away. "I don't have any magic. You've got the wrong kid."

Emenor's face grew dark as he planted both hands on Sam's chest and shook him. "You are the son of a witch. You have all the magic you need inside—all you have to do is open the door in your mind."

The sound of voices in the corridor grew louder. They were

running out of time. Pretty soon the entire city would be awake and looking for Sam.

With a disgusted sigh, Emenor released him and hurriedly unbuttoned the top of his robe, revealing a heavy black medallion dangling on a silver chain. The medallion was made of polished black flint and carved with intricate symbols Sam didn't recognize.

"This is precious magic. Using it will drain its powers," he sniped. Then he passed the medallion in front of the stone and whispered, "*Fein kinter, terminus.*" At his words, the flint emitted a streak of light that bounced off the wall and bathed them in an emerald glow. The stone began to shimmer, changing substance until it simply faded away.

"How did you do that?" Sam asked in awe, waving his hand where the wall had been. The night sky glittered with stars. His breath fogged in the cold air.

Emenor slipped the medallion back inside his robe, buttoning up the collar. "Balfins receive trinkets from the witches. It's weak magic, but it comes in handy. Part of our arrangement for sheltering them."

He pushed Sam forward until the boy teetered on the corridor's edge. The ground was two stories below.

"Get to the stables across the courtyard. There's a horse waiting. Follow the back alley to the main road, and head for the gate." Then Emenor gave him a shove. Sam fell, arms flailing, expecting to splat on the paving stones. Instead, he landed in a cart filled with hay that had been parked below.

Spitting out bits of straw, he peered over the side of the cart. As Emenor had promised, the stables were just across the courtyard. The problem was, two guards stood at the bottom of the steps, watching the area. They were craning their heads at the cart, looking to see what had caused the noise.

He needed a distraction to reach the stables. Emenor had

promised Sam had all the magic necessary inside him, but if that was true, how did Sam turn it on?

The guards drew closer. Any second now, they would see him and he would be sent back to Rego.

The pouch holding his dad's stone hung heavily around his neck. He could throw it at them, Sam thought in desperation. He fingered it, feeling it warm at his touch. The guards were mere steps away.

The stone had belonged to Odin and had once possessed great power. Maybe it still did. What did he have to lose?

Standing up, Sam took the pouch from around his neck and started swinging it, figuring he looked crazy enough to startle them. But, strangely, as he swung it, a wind picked up and began to blow, scattering the hay. He swung it harder. On a whim, Sam tried out the words Emenor had just used, whispering, "*Fein kinter*."

Something kicked Sam in the chest, like he had just been hit with a fast pitch. Immediately, the wind blew harder. A tingling feeling came over him, and the meaning of the words clicked in his brain.

Fein kinter. I call on my magic.

Cool. Odin's potent stone was working, but it was unleashing something inside him, opening the door to something Sam had never known existed.

Closing his eyes, Sam let words flow through him from a base of knowledge he could access with ease. He imagined what he wanted, and then words spilled into his head. "*Fein kinter ventimus*," he whispered, and a sudden wind roared in his ears, picking up speed and spinning like a tornado, knocking the men off their feet and sending them tumbling head over heels across the courtyard.

He stopped, stunned by what had happened. The men lay in a heap on the ground, dazed and groaning. Lights began to blaze from the windows overhead. Sam needed to get moving. He tucked the stone back inside his shirt and ran across the court-yard to the stables.

Inside, a horse waited, saddled up and tied to the wall, just as Orrin had promised. He untied it and put his foot in the stir-rup, when a voice rang out.

"Where's my pie?"

Mavery stood blocking his horse, arms crossed. Sam could hear shouts from the entrance to the Great Hall.

"Not now, Mavery," he hissed.

"I could scream, you know. I want my pie."

Stepping back down from the horse, Sam was tempted to stuff her mouth with hay, but he tried reason instead. "I don't have your pie. Please get out of my way."

She opened her mouth to scream, and Sam had no choice. He grabbed her, muffling her with his hand. "Would you knock it off?" Their faces were an inch apart. He felt her eyes looking through him, their black depths staring into his own, and some-thing else—a recognition. In that moment, they both knew they were the same. Misfits. Outcasts. Magic-born.

Sam relaxed his grip. "I need to go. Give me a break. Please don't tell anyone."

"Take me with you."

His first instinct was to say no. She would just slow him down, but he humored her. "Give me one reason."

"I'll give you five." She held one grimy hand up, ticking off her answers. "I'm smarter than you. I know my way around. You don't know anything about this place. And I can get you out of the city."

"That's only four," he countered.

"I know about magic," she whispered.

Sam wavered. After that little scene in the secret passage, it was obvious that he was clueless about magic, in spite of what he had just done. And she was right: he had no idea where he was going. "Fine, you can come with me." He could always ditch her later, although secretly he was glad for the company.

Lifting Mavery up onto the back of the horse, Sam pulled himself onto the saddle and gave the horse a solid kick in the ribs. It lurched forward, and they slipped out through a back gate and trotted down a side street. The narrow cobblestone alley was deserted. Sinuous clouds crisscrossed the waning moon like snakes loose in the sky. It was well past midnight. They probably only had a few hours before the sun rose, and then they would be easily spotted.

"Turn here," Mavery said at the first intersection. Sam followed her directions through serpentine alleys until they had moved far from the center of the city. The path became narrower and filthier. It stank of sewage and rotting garbage.

They had entered the poorer part of the city. Even this late at night, taverns were still open and raucous shouts could be heard from drunks teetering down the alley. One of them tried to grab at Sam's boot, but he kicked the sot away and urged the horse on.

After another turn, the road came to an abrupt end. Rising above them was the block wall of the city's perimeter. At that moment, they heard excited yelping.

"They've sent the dogs after us," Mavery said.

"We're trapped." Sam sawed hard on the horse's reins. "We have to turn around."

"No, keep going. Head straight for the wall." She kicked her heels in the horse's ribs. The horse took off, rearing up its head as if to ask what they were thinking.

"Are you crazy?" Sam croaked.

The wall loomed ahead. He could hear the howling and yapping of dogs and the shouts of the men running behind them. He tried to pull in the reins, but Mavery just kept kicking her heels, urging the horse forward.

"Open the wall, Sam!" she shouted in his ear. "Use your magic."

"I don't have any magic!" he yelled.

Then he remembered the wall in the secret passage. Emenor had opened the stone with his medallion and made it disappear. Sam had done something magical back in the square, when he had swung Odin's Stone. But would the talisman be potent enough to open a stone wall?

Ripping his father's pouch from his neck, Sam spun it around his head, repeating Emenor's words.

"*Fein kinter, terminus!*" he shouted, then closed his eyes, expecting to smack headfirst into stone.

But there was no collision, just darkness and a cold breeze. Then they were galloping across a grassy field, holding on for dear life.

Mavery let out a whoop, and Sam did, too. It had worked. They weren't dead in a broken heap on the other side of the stone wall.

They raced across a field to the edge of the woods. To their right, steep cliffs led down to the ocean. The sun was rising over the blue sea, and Sam felt the beauty of Orkney in all its glory.

He had escaped one fate and now had to face a more perilous one: rescuing his friends.

Chapter Eighteen

They headed south. After a while, Sam heard soft snoring as Mavery slumped against him. The trail hugged the cliffs for a couple of hours and then turned inland and began to climb. A bank of fog rolled in, covering the sun, and the temperature began to drop. Mavery roused with a loud yawn.

"I'm cold," she mumbled to his back. "And I'm hungry."

Sam stopped the horse, needing a break himself. Tying it to a tree, he searched in the saddlebags for any provisions. Emenor had put in some rolls, a hunk of cheese, and a full leather waterskin. There was also a small bag of gold coins.

He took a seat on a rock across from Mavery, who had found a patch of grass to sit on. Using Leo's knife, Sam carved off some cheese and split a roll, giving half to Mavery. They ate in silence. The gray fog grew thicker, settling around them until it blocked out the trees and cocooned them in a ghostly whiteout.

"So, where are we going?" Mavery asked, gnawing on her hunk of bread.

Sam pulled out the map Emenor had provided and spread it out. "Balfour Island."

Mavery dropped her bread. "Are you crazy? I'm not going back to that nest of witches."

"I have to rescue my friends. I thought you wanted to help me, but if you're scared, you can walk back to Skara Brae."

"Scared? Do you know what Balfour Island is like? You'll die there. It's crawling with sneevils. Have you ever seen a sneevil? It has tusks as long as your arm and pointy teeth that will tear your guts out and eat you while you're still alive. Then there are the biters: giant insects that can drain all your blood in less than a minute."

Sam gulped, pointing stubbornly at the map. "But I have a safe route. The Balfin who gave it to me said if I followed this map, I'd survive."

Mavery snorted. "If a Balfin said it, it's a lie. Guaranteed. And if you do survive, how are you going to save your friends? You can't just walk up and knock on the door of the witches' fortress and say, 'Excuse me, Endera, can I have my friends back?' She must have taken them for a reason. Endera always has a plan."

He bristled at her lack of confidence. "I'll come up with something."

"Just because you're a witch doesn't mean they'll go easy on you."

"I'm not a witch," Sam snapped, irritated at her assumption. "I am a Son of Odin. My father descended from Baldur." Somehow, being related to the same guy who had fathered the mighty Thor was a lot more palatable than being part of a family of evil witches like Rubicus and the ever-horrible Endera.

But Mavery just laughed, almost splitting a gut. "Doesn't matter who your dad was. You're a witch, same as me."

Sam's anger rose, along with his blood pressure. "My mother's the witch, not me. I don't have magic."

"Then how'd you get us out of Skara Brae? By wishing upon a star?" She kept laughing, and Sam grabbed the pouch around his neck, whipping it off to shove it in her face.

"I used this. It's a piece of Odin's Stone," he yelled. "Emenor did the same thing with a trinket back in Skara Brae. I am not a witch, no matter who my mom is." But his words sounded hollow, even to him.

"Not all witches are bad, you know," she said indignantly. "It's not magic that makes you evil."

"What would you know about it?"

Her eyes grew shiny. She bent her head and mumbled, "My mother was evil, but I'm not."

"How do you know?"

Her head came up to glare at him. "I just do."

"But what if you turn out that way?"

"I won't," she said, jumping to her feet. "Because I'm nothing like her. I know who I am."

Sam tried to think of a comeback, but the truth was, he was having a harder and harder time figuring out who the heck he was. Son of Odin. Lord of the Ninth Realm. And maybe a witch. He let the thought sink in. "We should go," he sighed. "That is, if you're still coming."

They rode on, following the coastline. The fog had settled in like a thick blanket. It felt as if they were gliding through soup. The horse came to a stop and whinnied nervously, turning to look at them.

"I can't see anything." Sam waved his hand to clear the air. "Is it always like this?"

Mavery clutched his arm. "Shh," she whispered. "We're not alone."

Sam strained to hear. The mist blanked out all noise, leaving them blind and deaf. The horse startled, looking left, its eyes flaring.

"They're coming," Mavery said, her fingers digging into his skin.

"Who?"

"Wraiths. Whatever you do, don't look at them."

Sam kicked the horse and prayed it could see where it was going better than he could.

Mavery's arms locked around his waist. The horse jolted and pitched over the slippery, rocky trail. Branches whipped at his face.

He heard high-pitched screeching and the sound of rushing wind, as if the air was filled with flying creatures. Sam risked a glance to see if they were about to go off a cliff, and in front of him a ghostly woman flew by, her long hair trailing behind her like wisps of fog and her face as beautiful and perfect as a runway model's.

He was transfixed by her beauty until her eyes locked with his; then he reeled back in horror as her face hollowed into a ghostly skull.

"I said don't look at them!" Mavery shouted. "They can't hurt you if you don't see them."

Too late. The wraith's empty eye sockets sent out bolts of ice. Sam ducked, but a shard entered his shoulder, cutting it deeply. He shrieked in pain, then grabbed the shard and grimly pulled it out. It melted in his hands, leaving a burning pain behind.

A wraith appeared in front of them, and the horse reared up, terrified. Sam struggled to keep his grip on the saddle horn. Mavery screamed as she tried to hang onto him, but her arms slipped. He tried to grab her but missed, and she fell to the ground with a thump. Then the horse jolted forward, leaving Mavery behind.

"Mavery!" he shouted, sawing back on the reins awkwardly.

He had to open his eyes, even if it meant a hundred wraiths impaled him. Fighting to control the horse, he kept repeating, "Whoa, girl, whoa," until finally the animal halted.

Sam slid off and ran back, slipping over loose stones on the trail and scuffing his palms. When he found Mavery, the wraiths were swirling around her, creating a ghostly whirlwind. She sat in the middle of the maelstrom with her hands over her eyes. The creatures were singing to her, creating a shrill cacophony of sounds that was strangely captivating. He could see Mavery hesitate, fighting the urge to look; then her hands began to peel away from her eyes. They were enchanting her.

Sam grabbed the pouch hanging from his neck and swung Odin's Stone around.

"*Fein kinter, ventimus*!" he shouted, running forward, repeating the words he had used in the square. A sharp wind suddenly sprang up, blowing the wraiths back. The ghostly figures screeched angrily. Sam swung harder, sending a tornado toward them. But they hovered on the edge, trying to approach, as if they were drawn to the magic, not afraid of it. The pouch didn't seem to be enough.

Sam's own anger began to rise within him, and a cold chill filled his bones. Words sprang up in his head, lighting up like highway signs.

"*Spera nae mora*," he shouted, ordering the wraiths to leave this place. He could feel them calling, whispering to him to join them in a strange language they shared.

"*Spera nae mora*," he repeated, and they wavered, wanting to stay, until eventually they let out a mournful wail and trailed away, taking the entire fog bank with them.

"Mavery, are you okay?" He ran to her side, crouching down.

The little girl had her eyes covered, and she was crying. "They called to me. They told me to look at them, that I was one of them, but I'm not."

"It's okay. Don't cry."

She snuffled and wiped her nose with the back of her sleeve. "You were using your magic—your witch magic. I heard you. Now do you believe me?"

Sam touched the stone hanging around his neck. The stone had helped unlock something, but the power and the magical words had come from somewhere deep inside him. Like it or not, he was a witch. A sudden wave of dizziness came over him, and he sank back on the ground, dropping his head between his knees. Using magic was like burning a candle at both ends; he felt wiped out and weak.

"You're bleeding," she said, touching his shoulder gingerly. "Why did you come back for me?"

"We're a team, aren't we?" he said gruffly, lifting his head.

"We are?"

"Sure. You got me out of Skara Brae. You told me how to beat the wraiths. And I'm guessing you can get us to Balfour Island, because I don't have a clue."

She grinned through the tear-streaked dirt on her face. "I know where we can get a boat."

Chapter Nineteen

They found the horse grazing on clumps of grass just down the trail. Sam loaded Mavery and climbed wearily into the saddle. As the fog burned away, the sun returned, shining brightly down on them with its red-mottled face.

The trail wound its way out of the woods and away from the coast up a steep hill, switching back and forth. The horse began to tire, wheezing loudly, gray flecks of foam on its mouth. Sam got off and led it by the reins, feeling blisters rise up on the backs of his heels after he had taken a handful of steps.

To pass the time, he asked Mavery about the wraiths. "Have you ever seen any of those creepy skeleton ladies before?"

"No, just heard the other witchlings talking about them, back when I lived on Balfour Island. They used to tease me, say they were going to leave me in the swamps, tied to a tree, for the wraiths to take away."

"That's harsh." He looked up at her. "Did you get picked on a lot?"

She lifted her chin. "Didn't bother me. Witchlings are a bunch of stupid girls. Just meant I wasn't like them."

"So, what's a wraith, anyway?"

Mavery's eyes lit up as she chattered away. "They're soulless creatures who used to be a race of beautiful women. They bragged all about their good looks to Freya; she's the goddess of beauty. They said they were ten times more beautiful than she was. Freya got mad and stripped them of their souls and left them in limbo. I'm thirsty," she finished.

Sam stopped the horse. The air tasted like dust and the acrid smell of dead grass. There was nothing green covering the land. The shrubs had turned to brittle, dried-up shells. Sam passed Mavery a waterskin. She took a long sip and passed it back. He tilted his head to take a swig. As he did, he caught sight of the sun and the world came to a stop.

The red veins had spread in the few days he had been in Orkney. A new branch had sprouted up, forking off in a new direction, pulsating brightly.

As the red fingers of light licked at Sam's face, a sudden madness drew him in, as if the sun were a magnet and he its target. The water ran down his shirt as he forgot where he was. He stared at the throbbing face, feeling a surge of power in his veins. The first time he had seen those red veins, he had been scared. Now he hungered for the sun, wanting its power for himself.

"Stop it," Mavery said, throwing a hunk of bread at him.

It bounced off Sam's head, but he ignored her, continuing his worship. His eyes began to feel warm, as if two hot coals were burning a hole in his head.

"Sam!" Mavery slid down from the horse and kicked him hard in the shin.

He hardly felt her feeble kick. His brain swelled with power; his eyes felt molten, as if he could shoot out fire. His blood was pumping as fast as a steam engine. At that moment, Sam could have torn the sun from the sky and devoured it. Mavery didn't let up, pounding her fists on him, screaming at him to stop.

"What is wrong with you?" he shouted, finally tearing his eyes away. "They should have left you to the wraiths. You're just a whiny brat nobody wants around." Something was happening to him, a humming in his veins. The palms of his hands itched.

She opened her mouth to snap back at him, and without thinking, he raised his hand. A slim bolt of green lightning erupted from his palm, burning him and sending Mavery yelping backward. She hit the ground and let out a cry.

Sam's legs were shaky. He looked down at the tendril of smoke rising from his palm. What had he done?

"Mavery?"

He ran to her side, but she scooted away.

"You used magic against me," she said. Tears ran down her cheek. "Witchfire can kill. And your eyes were glowing a scary red color."

"I'm sorry. I didn't mean to. I don't know what happened." He felt sick and dizzy. He had only ever been able to do something with Odin's Stone in his hand. This was new. Thrillingly so.

"You can't look at the sun," she sniffled. "It will poison you, make you a bad person."

"I'm sorry," Sam repeated, reaching for her hand to help her up, but she jerked her arm back.

Guilt swamped him. A thin trail of blood ran down her knee where she had skinned it. Mavery limped over to the horse and waited, holding herself rigid as Sam lifted her up. He took the reins and resumed trudging uphill. He kept his eyes firmly downward, away from temptation. He suddenly longed for nighttime, when the sun would be tucked away, out of sight.

Sam's blisters grew blisters as they climbed steadily up the steep grade. After hiking for hours, they finally crested the hill. A sharp gust of salty wind blew in from the ocean. Below them was a small seaport, hemmed in by tall cliffs. Fishing boats bobbed off the coast. In the distance, a layer of clouds clung over an ominous dark mass. Jagged cliffs surrounded the island. In the center, the spires of a distant fortress rose into the sky, spearing the clouds.

"Is that Balfour Island?"

Mavery nodded mutely, keeping her eyes averted.

"Come on, then." He climbed back into the saddle in front of her. "Let's get on with it."

They rode into the town, which consisted of some ramshackle buildings lining a pocked dirt lane. Boats bobbed in the harbor. The smell of rotting fish permeated the air. No one paid much attention to a couple of kids on a broken-down horse. A fight broke out in front of the town store. A pair of men tussled over a bag of grain. It tore open and spilled on the ground. The crowd of onlookers rushed in and started scooping up handfuls of grain.

Rego had said food supplies were running low. Sam swallowed back his guilt. There was still time to rescue Howie and Keely, he convinced himself, and get on with his mission to stop this disaster from happening.

"Where to?" he asked, looking at Mavery over his shoulder.

She pointed toward the docks, her lips pressed tightly together.

"You have to talk to me eventually, you know," he said, trying to pick out a boat that looked inviting. "I said I was sorry. I don't know how to control magic."

"Don't care. I'm not going with you." And with that, she slipped off the back of the horse and sprinted away, disappearing into the crowds.

Sam let her go. She had every right to leave him. He had really messed up. But without the little witchling, he quickly felt lost. He rode along through the town, checking buildings on either side for a sign that would tell him where to hire a boat. Howie and Keely were getting closer. He just had to get across the ocean to Balfour Island, follow the map Emenor had given him, stay away from sneevils, whatever they were, and not get eaten by bloodsucking bugs.

Piece of cake.

Sam tied the horse to a post in front of a wooden building. The sign out front claimed it was Dorrian's Fine Tavern and Inn. Grabbing the small bag of gold Orrin had stashed in the saddlebags, he tucked it safely in his cloak. He had Leo's knife and the stone around his neck. He was as good as across the ocean already.

Pushing open a set of swinging doors, Sam stepped inside. It took a moment for his eyes to adjust to the dim lighting. A cloud of tobacco smoke hung over the room. A couple of dwarfs sat at the end of the bar. There were several round tables, each filled with coarse-looking men holding cards. Piles of coins were in the center of each table.

A long bar stretched across the back of the room, where a bartender was pulling a draft of beer. Silence rippled across the space, reaching a barrel-chested man at the bar. He turned and eyed Sam, lifting his mug of beer to his lips to blow off a layer of foam.

"Come on in, boy. Get out of that cursed sun," he called out.

Sam stepped inside, suddenly unsure this was a good idea. The men looked rough and unfriendly. He wanted to turn and run, but he had to find a boat. He slowly approached the stranger at the bar. The man wore a soiled blue coat. A three-cornered hat sat jauntily on his head.

"Name's Lionel Hawkins, but you can call me Hawk." He pulled out a barstool for Sam, and Sam sank down, licking his lips, hoping for a cold drink. The bartender slid a tankard of beer in front of him.

Hawk slapped him on the back. "That'll put hair on your chest." He laughed, and the men in the saloon laughed with him. "The way things are going, the red sun's going to kill us all. Might as well enjoy your last days."

Sam smiled weakly but pushed it away. "No, thanks. I'm looking for a boat to get to Balfour Island."

Hawk's eyes shifted away. He lifted his mug to his lips and

took a long drink. Wiping away the foam with the back of his hand, he let out a long, deep belch before answering. "There's nothing but witches and wild animals on that cursed island. Nothing for a boy like you."

Squaring his shoulders, Sam turned to face the rest of the room. He cleared his throat, hoping he didn't muff the little speech he had prepared. "I am a Son of Odin, Lord of the Ninth Realm. The witches took my friends, and I'm going to get them back. I can pay you. I have gold."

Conversation stopped, as if every ear was tuned in to the word *gold*.

"Show me your gold, boy. I'm sure we can make a deal." Hawk's eyes glinted with greed. A niggle of doubt ate at Sam. He stepped back.

"I left it with friends . . . ," he began, but Hawk leaned forward, roughly grabbed the leather pouch from inside Sam's cloak, and held it up, clinking the coins inside next to his ear.

"Yes, that will do nicely." He gave a nod, looking over Sam's shoulder as he did.

Sam glanced up in the mirror behind the bar and saw one of the seamen standing behind him. Before he could react, the sailor swung his tankard down on Sam's head.

Chapter Twenty

A cup of water thrown in his face made Sam sputter. He struggled to sit up, but his hands were tied behind his back. Worse, someone had tied a gag around his mouth that made it hard to breathe. The smell of horse manure and hay filled his nostrils.

He opened his eyes to see Mavery hovering over him.

"You're alive," she grunted, not sounding all that happy about it. She untied the gag, and Sam gulped in a lungful of air.

"What happened?" His head was pounding.

"You don't remember?"

It was fuzzy. "I remember talking to some guy, trying to hire a boat to Balfour Island."

"Yeah, I heard all about it. Here, roll over." She untied Sam's wrists and then worked on the rope on his feet. He sat up, rubbing his hands to get the blood back into them.

"Someone hit me from behind," he said, remembering the barroom he had entered. He searched his pockets. "The money's gone." He reached around his neck and was relieved to find the stone pouch there.

Her dark eyes searched Sam's. "Did you really brag you were a Son of Odin and pull out your gold in Dorrian's? Hawk's the biggest pirate in the seas of Orkney."

"I'm pretty stupid, huh?"

"Yup."

He looked at her crossly. "You don't have to agree."

"You're the talk of the town," she smirked.

"Glad I amused you." He rubbed the knot on his head. "So why'd you come back, anyway?"

"You said we're a team. Besides, you clearly can't get on without me." Mavery lifted her eyes to Sam's. She needed a friend as badly as he did.

"I'm sorry about before. It won't happen again."

"Better not, or I'll show you my magic. You'll be walking around with a pig's tail." She helped him to his feet.

"So now what?" he asked, feeling dizzy, but at least his legs still worked.

"We get a ride to Balfour Island. Come on."

Taking his hand, she led him through the stables. It was near dawn. The sun was just climbing over the horizon. Men slept, scattered around the barn. Sam recognized that pirate Hawk, the man in the soiled blue coat. Hawk lay on his back, arms flung wide, snoring like a logger. He had Leo's knife tucked in his waistband. Sam reached down and carefully stole it back, resisting the temptation to give old Hawk a kick in the nards, then followed Mavery outside.

She took his hand and pulled him toward the dock as the sun creased the horizon, casting red fingers of light. They ran past sturdy fishing vessels and tugboats until they came to the most rickety, run-down, ramshackle boat in the wharf.

"No," Sam said, shaking his head. "I am not crossing the ocean in that hunk o' junk." Its brown sails were full of holes. The small cabin had no windows, and it listed to one side.

Mavery ignored him. She slipped onboard, lifted the hatch on the deck, and disappeared below.

Angry voices rang out from the tavern up the hill. Sam

thought he heard his name bandied about. Maybe it wasn't such a bad idea to follow Mavery. He ducked under the rope and hopped on deck. It felt solid enough. He made his way along the railing toward the cabin.

"That's far enough," a voice said. The sharp edge of Sam's own knife pressed against his neck. The stranger had pulled it out of Sam's waistband so quickly, he hadn't even noticed.

"Hey, I don't want any trouble. My friend came onboard," he said.

"Jasper!" Mavery's head popped up through the hatch, and the knife returned to Sam's waistband like lightning.

Sam turned and saw an elderly man. Long gray hair spilled down his back in a wild mass. His wiry beard stretched to his belly. He had knobby hands, a hollow chest, and canvas shorts tied around his waist with a length of rope.

"Mavery? Is it really you?" he croaked, a smile creasing his face.

"This is Samuel," she piped back. "He's a witch."

Jasper looked at Sam with watery eyes that were full of fear—or maybe it was pity.

"Never thought I'd see the likes of you—a boy witchling. Show me your magic."

But a loud bird cry above interrupted them.

Lagos, Rego's sharp-eyed *iolar*, flew overhead. The shouting at the tavern got louder, and Sam could now make out a crowd of men gathered outside the building. Rego had found them.

"Uh, we should get moving," Sam said, trying not to sound desperate. Then it hit him—there was no wind. The boat was dead in the water. He groaned. They were as good as captured.

Mavery grabbed Jasper's hand. "Please, Jasper?"

The old sailor smiled down at her, giving her a wink. "Can't say no to you, Mavery." He cast off and quickly raised the sail. His stringy arms were roped with muscle. He pursed his lips together and blew toward the sail. At first nothing happened; then the sail flapped a bit.

Sam risked a glance up the hill and spotted Rego's sturdy figure running full speed toward them. Behind him, the Falcory representative, Beo, sprinted like a deer, passing Rego. Close behind Beo, another pair of Falcory men raced.

Sam was trying to decide whether he should jump overboard and try swimming or just turn himself in, when a strong breeze snapped out the sails and the boat jerked away from the dock. Sam stared in wonder as Jasper puffed out his cheeks and blew wind into the sails, creating a roaring gust that kicked across the sea.

They were a good fifty feet away by the time Rego skidded to a stop at the edge of the dock. He shouted at Sam, but his words were lost in Jasper's magic wind. Sam waved sheepishly back at the dwarf, hoping Rego didn't hate him. Beo notched an arrow to his bow, aiming at Sam, but Rego put his hand on the Falcory's arm and Beo slowly lowered the weapon.

Sam held on to the rigging as the boat cut through the water, sending up a white splash of spray. The boat looked rickety, but it sure was fast. He worked his way to the back, where Jasper held the wheel. Mavery had wriggled in between Jasper and the helm and was trying to steer.

Dropping down on a mat, Sam tried to catch his breath. "I'm Sam. Sam Baron," he started.

"I know who you are," the old seaman replied in his gravelly voice.

"I'm glad you do, 'cause I'm not so sure anymore," Sam said, half joking.

Jasper spun the wheel, turning them into the wind. "See that sun up there?" Jasper pointed a finger at the sky.

After his little incident with Mavery, Sam refused to look at it, but the power of the rays warmed his face.

"The fish are dying because of its poison," Jasper continued. "The boats come back empty every day. You're the one responsible—that's who you are."

Sam's jaw dropped open. *That is so unfair*, he thought. His mother might be a witch, and okay, so maybe he was one, too, but that didn't make him responsible for the red sun. Rego had said the sun had been that way for months. Sam had been in Orkney only a few days.

"You've got it backward. I'm going to save Orkney from the red sun. Some guy named Rubicus started it."

Mavery yawned, and Jasper patted her head fondly. "Run along to the cabin and get some rest."

She scampered down the stairs like she had been on the boat a thousand times.

"I found her adrift one day," Jasper commented, his eye on the distant horizon.

"At sea?"

"Holding on to a couple of sticks. They'd tossed her overboard."

"Who?"

"The witches."

"I thought she was a witch."

"There's witches and then there's witches."

Sam was more concerned with Jasper's crazy accusation. "You can't blame me for the curse on the sun. I was only a baby when I left Orkney," Sam challenged.

"Not just any baby—the first he-witch since Rubicus. Your parents thought they could protect Orkney by taking you to Midgard."

Sam felt a sudden chill. "You knew my parents?"

"Aye, I spirited them away the night they fled. You were sick from that Deathstalker venom, squalling your head off." Jasper squinted at the horizon. "You should have died from that scorpion bite. When you didn't, they knew. Your mother knew you were a threat."

"Me? How? I wasn't even here. And it's not my fault I got bit by a stupid scorpion." Sam really didn't want to lose his temper, but the old seaman was being unreasonable.

"It might not be your fault, but you're still responsible for it," Jasper replied. "And only you can stop it."

Sam climbed to his feet. "I am going to stop it; I just have to save my friends first."

"Then you've killed us all," Jasper said grimly.

"Why do you keep blaming me?" Sam shouted.

Jasper pointed a stern finger at Sam. "You are the red sun. The red sun is you. It will destroy everything and everyone here in Orkney if you don't stop it."

All Sam could do was shake his head in denial. *It's not my fault,* he told himself over and over. But no amount of rationalization could stem the tide of anger swelling inside him. Sam felt his fingers curl into tight fists at his side. A strong desire to smash something, anything, became all-consuming.

Jasper's watery blue eyes never left Sam's face. "You want to hit me, lad? Go ahead. But it won't change the truth."

Sam did want to hit the seaman. He wanted to plaster Jasper like he had done to Ronnie Polk. He wanted to make Jasper take back his harsh words. But Sam resisted the urge to lash out, and that caused his arms to shake uncontrollably.

"There's your evidence right there." Jasper pointed at the sky.

Sam looked up and watched as another thin vein appeared on the sun, spreading like the roots of a tree.

He was about to protest, but suddenly he wasn't sure. He did feel a connection—a boiling anger that flowed through him into that red, pulsing, poisonous vein on the sun. He had a sudden flash as he remembered the rune stone Rego had tossed at him in his garage. The one Keely had looked up in the library.

Sigel.

The holder of this rune stone is the source of energy for the sun.

A jolt of realization moved through Sam. Rego had known all along. Or suspected. As fast as it came on, the rage drained out of Sam, leaving him hollow inside.

"Get some rest, lad," Jasper said, with just a pinch of sympathy. "I'll need your help when we get close to Balfour. The *akkar* are not to be trifled with."

"What's an *akkar*?"

But Jasper didn't answer, keeping his eyes on the horizon, and Sam gave in to the bone-deep weariness. He went down into the cabin and found Mavery curled up on a narrow bunk. He took the one above it. Closing his eyes, Sam quickly and mercifully lost himself in the sanctuary of sleep—but not before a blazing image of the sun, encrusted with red, splotchy veins, had rooted firmly in his mind.

Chapter Twenty-One

The ship rolled steeply, knocking Sam out of the bunk. He blinked, clearing the dreamy image of the red sun from his eyes. They were in the middle of a storm; the seas tossed the boat about like a pinball. Mavery leaned over the top of the bunk and chucked up her breakfast all over the floor at Sam's feet.

"Stay here," Sam ordered, stepping carefully over the mess. Mavery flopped back on the bunk, pulling the blanket over her head. Struggling to steady himself, Sam grabbed a slicker off a hook on the wall and poked his head out of the deck hatch.

The wind aboveboard gusted hard enough to knock Sam backward. Thick black clouds dumped a torrent of rain. He made it up to the deck when a wave crashed over the side, washing him into the railing.

Sam grabbed at the rigging, but his feet went over and he dangled above the roiling sea, hanging desperately onto the badly weathered rope with two hands.

Just when Sam didn't think he could hold on another second, Jasper was there, leaning over and hauling him back onto the deck with a long grunt.

"What's happening?" Sam shouted over the storm.

"We're getting close to Balfour Island."

Jasper pointed ahead at a landmass rising from the ocean like an angry black slash. Up close, the jagged cliffs lining the shore made a safe landing seem impossible.

But that wasn't their biggest problem.

"What's that?" Sam asked, trying to shield his eyes from the blinding rain.

A swelling, murky blob rose from the frothy sea. Gray and bulbous, with long, trailing arms, it slashed at the ocean, spraying them with cold seawater. A single, swollen yellow eye blinked at them from its massive head.

"The *akkar*," Jasper warned with unmistakable dread. "They guard the island."

Jasper grabbed a long spear from a rack by the mast and thrust it into Sam's hand.

"Aim for its eye, boy. When I say the word, let it fly."

He's gotta be joking, Sam thought, looking down at the weapon in his hand. The spear was heavy and had a razor-sharp metal tip, but it felt feeble compared with the giant squid-thing that bobbed on the surface in front of their ship. How was Sam supposed to stop an enormous sea monster with a fishing spear?

The boat tilted sideways as the *akkar* rose up and thrust a slithering tentacle at them. Its hideous eye glared over a gaping mouth that belched out a noxious odor. Water frothed through long, spiny teeth. Ignoring the danger, Jasper navigated the boat directly toward the creature. Sam clutched the rigging with one hand and held the spear with the other.

The *akkar* gave a loud, resounding roar, blasting them with spray. A slimy tentacle skidded on deck, trying to sweep Sam off his feet. Gripping the spear, he stabbed at the groping limb but missed. The creature quickly coiled its tentacle around Sam's weapon, sending the spear flying into the ocean. Just then, a familiar squeal sent his heart into his shoes. Mavery had opened the hatch, and a tentacle scooped her up and locked a tight coil around her, holding her ten feet above the deck. She screamed, punching at the slimy limb.

Another tentacle crashed down on the deck. Sam ran forward, dodging it while he tried to get closer to Mavery. He skidded to a stop as the creature loomed two stories above him, rising out of the ocean in a gray, jellylike mass and letting out a timber-rattling shriek.

Long, spindly arms wrapped around the front of the boat, pulling them toward that awful, gaping maw crowded with hundreds of sharp, glistening teeth. Sam froze up, paralyzed with fear. This was the closest he had ever been to death.

"Do something!" Jasper shouted, whipping the wheel in his hands as he struggled to keep the boat from capsizing.

Rain lashed Sam's face, and his fingers were numb with cold. He heard Jasper yelling, but the words didn't move him. In fact, they actually amused him. *Does he think I can just pull another spear out of thin air?*

But then Sam straightened, remembering the words Forset, the God of Justice, had spoken back in Skara Brae. Forset had told him that spear in the hallway was a gift from Odin—that it would come if Sam called it.

Sam felt a little foolish, but as Mavery screamed again, he figured there was nothing to lose. So he held up his right hand and called out the name: "Gungnir." Nothing happened. The squid's teeth began gnashing on the long prow, tearing away the piece of wood like a toothpick and coming back for another bite. Desperate, Sam tried again, turning up the volume and thrusting his hand in the air. "Gungnir!" he shouted.

His palm tingled. There was a crackle of energy, and then— in a flash of light and heat—his fingers were wrapped around the solid shaft of Odin's spear.

"No way," Sam whispered, hardly believing his eyes.

"Don't just stand there!" Jasper barked at him. "Aim for the eye, boy! Aim for the eye!"

Sam nodded, then hefted the spear in his hand. After a deep breath, he took a run forward and launched it at the creature's rolling black eye. The spear wobbled off course; then, just as Forset had promised, the spear changed direction in the savage wind, and the sharp point hit dead center. The creature's eye burst open, spewing gray, gelatinous liquid.

Sam covered his ears as the *akkar*'s deafening wail shook the boat. The *akkar* dropped Mavery onto the deck as its tentacles withdrew in a frenzy, lashing the boat about as the creature retreated into the watery depths. As fast as the onslaught had come, it was over. Then they were free, bobbing in the water.

"We did it," Sam said, shocked that they were alive.

Mavery sat up woozily. "Is it gone?"

"It's gone," Jasper confirmed. "Your witch-boy came through."

Sam stepped forward to give Mavery a hug just as a stray tentacle broke the water's surface and swept the deck, knocking Sam into the sea. Thrashing around in the watery tumult, he tried to swim back to the boat. Mavery stretched through the railing and reached out her hand for him. He grabbed for her fingers, but a tentacle gripped one of his legs and dragged him under.

The cold seawater submerged him, leaving him gagging and choking for air. He tried to free himself, but the *akkar* wrapped another tentacle tight around his waist. Pink suction cups latched onto his hands as he pried futilely at them.

He needed air. Fast. Leo's knife was still in his belt. Fumbling, he managed to snag the blade, then stab at the throbbing tentacle. After the third jab, the monster released him just as black spots sprouted behind Sam's eyes. He couldn't tell which way was up. He swam a few strokes, then stopped, confused which way to go.

Then the water began to glow with a bright sheen, and Sam

had a flash of hope. But as the glow swirled and formed shapes, Sam realized who had joined him.

Wraiths swarmed around him, trailing their icy fingers along his face. Sam closed his eyes, not wanting a repeat of the ice bolt in his shoulder. This was all he needed: a bunch of soulless beauty queens showing up when he was on the brink of death. Then Sam's survival instincts kicked in. He pulled off their fingers, kicking hard to swim away, any direction, but he could hear their eerie call in his head, inviting him in.

"Join us," they whispered.

He stopped, letting himself float in the water. His lungs burned with the need to breathe. He was fading fast and had no hope of reaching the surface. Sam gave in and opened his eyes, turning to look into the skeletal face of the wraith closest to him.

"Help me," he whispered back, in the silent language they shared. He stared into her empty sockets, seeing the flesh ripple back to life as she looked at him with pity. Her long, grayish hair undulated in the water. She raised one bony hand to his cheek. Sam bit back the disgust as his lungs screamed for air.

"You are one of us," she whispered, taking his hand and tugging him downward. He had no strength to fight her off. A coldness settled over him as she dragged him down.

Then the water exploded into thousands of bubbles, and Sam's lungs gave out.

Chapter Twenty-Two

Something nibbled on Sam's toe, a sharp pinch. He lifted his head out of the sand. He was lying facedown on a beach, the surf rolling around his ankles. A large sand crab was investigating his toe. He had no idea why he was still alive. He remembered the wraiths twirling around him, pushing and prodding.

"That's twice I saved your life."

Turning his head, he saw Mavery. Wet hair clung to her head in clumps. Her arms were wrapped around her knees as she shook with cold.

Spitting out sand, he said, "That's why I keep you around. Where are we?"

Sam pushed himself up. They were on a narrow spit of beach boxed in by sheer cliffs. The tide was rolling in quickly. In a matter of hours, maybe less, they would be without dry land.

"Balfour Island, dummy. Where else? The wraiths were trying to take you with them. I stopped them."

He looked at her, seeing how pale she was.

"How?"

She shrugged. "I wouldn't let go of you. When the *akkar* knocked you over, I jumped in, too. Jasper tried to stop me, but I'm too quick for him," she said proudly.

"Thank you." The words were hardly adequate, but they made Mavery smile.

Sam reached for his pouch, reassured to feel it around his neck. One of his boots had come off and was half-buried in the sand. He dumped out the water and pulled it on, then stood on wobbly legs and helped Mavery up.

"So, how do we get off this beach?"

"We climb," she said, pointing at a low cleft in the face. "Race you to the top!" Mavery took off, her feet pounding in the sand.

"Hey, not fair!"

Sam gave chase, and they ran across the beach, laughing as Mavery got to the base of the cliff first and started scrambling up like a monkey. Sam felt strangely giddy. They were alive, and his friends were close. Once he rescued them, together they would find a way to stop this cursed sun from destroying Orkney.

But by the time they reached the top of the cliff, exhaustion had replaced Sam's excitement. His hands were raw, and his whole body ached. Behind them, the black clouds boxing in the shore had dissipated, leaving the day clear and cloudless. Before them, a flat valley spread out, covered in stumpy dead trees and boggy water.

Unfortunately, Emenor's map of Balfour was a sodden mess. Sam laid it out to dry, but the ink had run together, smudging the lines. He tried to recall where the big X had marked the Tarkana fortress. He traced the faint line Emenor had drawn through the bogs and the swamp.

"You don't need a stupid map to find the Tarkana fortress," Mavery said, scuffing the ground with her toe.

"Well, how are we going to get there?"

"I was born here, remember? I hid in these swamps when I wanted to escape," she mumbled.

"Did it work?" he asked.

"They couldn't tease me if they couldn't find me. This way, dunderhead." She struck off down the hill.

Sam caught up with her as they reached the edge of the swamp. A layer of mist clung to the ground. The mud let out loud pops as it released gas of some sort. Brown shriveled shrubs stuck out of the water.

"Is it always this . . . dead around here?"

Mavery held her skirts up as she waded. "It's usually thick with vines that snake across the ground and try to choke you, and trees that toss their thorns at you. Be grateful things are dead. The red sun's doing us a favor here."

Insects buzzed around Sam's head, and the shrieks of birds filled the air. They kept to higher ground when possible but had to wade through the murky swamp water between low-lying mounds of dry ground.

After only a few minutes of marshy trekking, Sam's boots were so full of water that he gave up and took them off, carrying them over his shoulder. Mavery hopped along like a toad, not seeming to mind that her toes squelched in the thick, slimy mud.

The first solid piece of ground they came to, Sam threw himself down in the shade of a scraggly tree. His stomach growled loudly. He thought of the last hamburger he had eaten, when he and Howie had gone to Chuggies. If he closed his eyes, Sam could almost smell the greasy fries and charbroiled meat patty. His mouth watered as he dreamed about a thick chocolate shake to wash down his meal.

"You don't have anything to eat, do you?" he asked.

Mavery reached into the pocket of her skirt, pulled out a small green apple, and waved it in front of his nose. "You mean like this?"

Sam snatched it from her, then hesitated. "No . . . it's yours."

She waved it away. "I ate two waiting for you to wake up."

Sam bit eagerly into the fruit. It was tangy and crisp. Similar to an Oregon apple, but even more flavorful and fresh. That was pretty much how Sam would describe most things in Orkney, compared with his home: similar but different.

"What's she like?" Mavery asked, taking a seat across from Sam.

"Who?"

"Your mother."

"She's great. A lousy cook—she usually burns dinner. And she can't do math for beans, but I guess growing up in Orkney, she didn't study geometry." At that moment, Abigail's complete lack of math skills finally made sense. Sam smiled at the memory of her struggling to help him. He tossed the core in the water and watched the ripples spread out in a circle. "You know what I don't get? How she left all this behind—her magic, her powers, this entire realm—and never said anything to me. It's like she erased everything she knew. Until some shreeks attacked us, I never saw her use her magic."

Mavery plucked a skinny white flower and twirled it in her fingers. "Watch," she said, cupping her hands and then blowing into them. She opened her palm to reveal a yellow frog in place of the flower.

"Is it a frog or a flower?" She looked at him with earnest eyes.

"I'm not sure."

The frog quivered in her hand, the size of a thumbnail.

"And neither was your mom." Mavery blew on the frog, and it hopped away into the water . . . where it turned back into the flower, now floating on the surface. "It's hard to remember what's real and what's not. Maybe she wanted your life there to be real."

"How'd you get so smart?"

"How'd you get so dumb?" she answered back, with that impish grin.

Sometimes Mavery was a real pain, but Sam couldn't imagine being here without her.

By late afternoon, they came to the edge of the bog and found themselves on solid, dry ground. A pair of crows flew in a lazy circle overhead. To the left were steep hills, and to the right, a thick tangle of bramble and thorny trees.

"Which way, Mavery?"

She pointed to the left. "On the other side of those hills is a road that winds around all this. It's longer but safer."

"What if we go that way?" He pointed at the bramble.

"That way will get you killed. Guaranteed. It's full of sneevils. A sneevil can use its tusk to tear your guts out and—"

"I know, I know, eat you while you're still alive. But look, if we go the safe way, how much longer will it take?"

"Another day."

"Another day? No. I can't wait another day."

"Better another day than dead."

"If we go fast, maybe we'll get lucky and not run into any sneevil things."

"That's wishful thinking," Mavery warned. "The kind of thinking that will get us both killed."

"My friends are waiting to be rescued. I can't make them wait another day because I'm afraid of something that might not even be there. Besides, another day, and who knows what the red sun will do? We don't have time to go around."

"I'm not going in there," she said, but Sam had already started walking into the bramble. He was pretty sure she would follow.

"Sam, you're being an idiot!"

"I know. You coming?"

Chapter Twenty-Three

ndera stared at the portrait of her ancestor that hung over the fireplace in her chambers. Catriona's piercing green eyes stared back at her under a mane of thick gray hair that flowed down her back. Catriona was the greatest witch ever to stalk the nine realms. Now she was trapped inside a rock, her powers shackled by Odin's magic. Endera reached a hand up to stroke the canvas, imagining what it would be like to possess Catriona's ancient magic, magic that had been lost to them in the centuries since she and her sisters had been entombed.

A light tap at the door sounded, and Lemeria appeared. The young witch was ditzy but useful. She had her spies, a network of ravens she used to keep an eye on things for Endera.

"What news, Lemeria?"

Lemeria skipped across the floor and took a seat on a spindly chair by the fireplace. "My pretty birds are full of tidings." She clapped her hands like an excited schoolgirl.

Endera bit back her impatience, seating herself across from Lemeria. "Do tell."

"The boy is here, just as you said he would be." Her eyes glowed. "He's got a child with him. I know her. She's that little orphan we got rid of."

Endera went to the window and breathed in the smell of the swamps. Yes, the boy was indeed out there. She could smell the faintest odor of his magic. "We must be sure to make them feel welcome."

She cast about for the pets she had in mind and sent a silent command. From across the murky depths of the bogs came a returning buzzing sound.

"Hestera is plotting against you," Lemeria said from behind her. "She doesn't believe you can do it."

"She is wrong." Endera turned to face her young protégé. "Everything is in motion. Even now the boy comes to us. He will deliver me what I seek. What do the others say?"

Lemeria shrugged, standing up, her hands twisting in her skirt. "They'll wait to see who's right. You know how witches are. You really think he can do it? My ravens tell me he is quite scrawny."

"Samuel Barconian has Odin's blood and that of Rubicus, the most powerful he-witch ever to live. You see how the sun glistens with his rage. How can you doubt he has the magic to break the ancient curse that keeps our ancestors prisoner?"

Lemeria shrugged, then giggled. "You're right, of course."

Endera waved her off. Soon enough, the boy and his little imp would be running for their lives and straight into her hands.

<hr>

It took only half an hour for Sam to cut every inch of his upper body on brambles with thorns the size of his thumb. Mavery walked mutinously behind him, avoiding the worst of it by staying close. He kept waiting for her to say, "I told you so," but she held her tongue. That didn't stop her from snorting with disdain every time Sam yelped in pain from a new cut.

He was about to proclaim the bog sneevil-free when they ran into a pack of them—six, to be precise, and each of them as ugly and vicious as Mavery had described. Their tusks were the length of his arm. Canine teeth jutted up from their lower lip. Only the filthiness of Sam's and Mavery's skin and clothes saved the children's lives. The sneevils were so busy sniffing the ground for roots, they didn't catch wind of the two mud-encrusted kids. Sam and Mavery slowly backed away into the brambles. Then, like an idiot, Sam stepped on a branch, snapping it in half, and the sneevils' heads jerked up with a chorus of snorts.

Mavery started to run, but Sam decided to test out his magic. The sneevils began to circle him. He raised his palm and cleared his throat, before shouting, *"Fein kinter!"* He thrust his hands forward as he shouted the words, but nothing happened. He tried again, feeling increasingly foolish, then gave up and grabbed his pouch as the sneevils drew closer, emboldened by his feeble efforts to stop them.

"Sam, run," Mavery shouted, but Sam held his ground stubbornly, determined to make this magic of his work.

"Fein kinter, ventimus," he said, swinging the pouch. A wind began to blow, stopping the surprised sneevils, but then one broke from the pack and charged him, intent on goring him.

Sam stumbled back and accidentally let go of the pouch. It sailed into a tree. He faced off against the sneevil while Mavery kept screaming at him to run.

The sneevil bared its snout at Sam, making a snuffling, growling sound. Sam dug his heels into the dirt, making himself tap into that other part of him. As the sneevil got within arm's reach, Sam raised his palm, this time feeling the connection to the pulsing of his blood.

"Fein kinter," he said again, and thrust his palm forward. This time, his whole hand tingled with energy, and, as the sneevil lowered its head to gore him, a bolt of witchfire shot out of Sam's palm, nearly knocking him backward, and seared the sneevil. The beast began to shake uncontrollably as smoke rose off it, and

then it incinerated in an odorous puff of black smoke. The other sneevils backed away and ran off through the trees.

Mavery didn't even thank Sam for saving her life. "Told you there were sneevils," she sniffed; then she stalked off through the brambles.

Sam's legs were shaky but held him up. He grinned lightly to himself. He was starting to get the hang of this magic stuff. Snatching his pouch from the low branch, he hurried after Mavery.

"Look!" he said excitedly, as the thorny bushes thinned out. In the distance, the tip of a dark tower thrust up from the swamps. "We made it."

Sam smiled smugly down at Mavery, but she was looking over her shoulder.

"Don't move," she whispered.

He froze. *Please don't tell me it's another sneevil*, he thought. Then he heard a buzz, like the humming of a generator. The sound grew louder.

Mavery grabbed his arm. "Run!"

She took off through the brambles, ignoring the thorns that caught at her dress. This time Sam didn't hesitate; he ran after her, but not before he turned around and saw a roiling black cloud snaking through the trees, arrowing after them with furious intent.

"What is that?" he asked, as he raced to catch up to her.

"Biters," she called back.

Up ahead, he could see a pile of rocks split by a black gap.

"There!" He pointed to the dark slice and veered toward it.

From behind, Sam could hear the buzzing grow louder. But he figured they might just reach the cave before the bloodsucking bugs overtook them. As the opening yawned in front of him, Sam heard Mavery scream.

Skidding to a stop, he turned and saw her sprawled facedown. She tried to get up, but her ankle was stuck in a hole. Mavery turned her head as the swarming cloud reached her, breaking apart into green bugs with wings the length of his finger and long, pointy beaks. Like mosquitoes on steroids. One of the biters landed on her arm, and she screamed as it drilled into her.

Giving up the refuge of the cave, Sam ran back to her side to pick her up, but the bugs were everywhere. They landed on his face and arms. He swatted at them, trying to fight them off long enough to get Mavery to safety, but there were too many.

All over his body he felt stinging sensations, followed soon after by light-headedness as dozens of malevolent vacuum cleaners sucked his blood out of him. He tried to help Mavery, who just kept screaming, a thick layer of bugs now covering her arms and face.

Weakness invaded Sam's legs. The biters were draining his life force, rapidly swelling in size as they engorged themselves. Sam swayed, his vision starting to blur. He knew that if the biters kept attacking, he would die. Mavery would die. And all of Orkney would be destroyed.

Sinking to his knees, he put his arms around Mavery, sheltering her. Deep inside, an anger began to build.

It's so unfair, Sam railed silently. *These stupid bugs are ruining everything!*

He turned his face to the sun, letting the rays soak into him, fueling him with the poisonous power the sun strangely provided him. As his eyes began to burn, anger coiled inside him, bubbling up, making his head rise as he gave voice to his molten rage.

"*Elie nistrasa liem golum!*" he ordered. *Harm her and I will destroy you.*

The voice was not his own, the words unrecognizable to him, but they came from somewhere deep inside him. From that dark source of his ancient bloodlines.

The clearing grew silent as the swarm paused, hovering, as if the bloodsuckers were waiting to see what he would do.

Sam climbed to his feet, staggering but feeling the strength gathering inside him. The boiling rage the red sun had ignited erupted into a fire that blazed from his eyes, sending a line across the clearing, toward the swarm of bugs.

"*Elie nistrasa liem golum*!" he roared. Raising his arm, Sam held his hand up and thrust his palm forward. A burst of witch-fire leaped from his palm and splintered the tree across the clearing. The swarm ascended, as if heeding his warning, then turned in unison and flew away.

Sam sagged, his energy spent. Mavery had lost consciousness. Her face red and swollen, she was bleeding from dozens of puncture marks on her arms and legs. He lifted the girl into his arms. She was dead weight, an enormous strain on his overtaxed muscles. He felt woozy, teetering on the verge of unconsciousness himself, but he was determined not to give up. It was his fault Mavery was out here. He made a vow to himself that she wouldn't die. He wouldn't let her.

He started walking—more like staggering—toward the distant castle. His arms burned with the strain of her weight, and his throat was parched, but he somehow kept putting one foot in front of the other.

Sam's own body had endured hundreds of bites that oozed blood and swelled up, making him look grotesque and leaving his skin tingling with numbness. Beneath his feet, the ground leveled out into a trail of hard-packed dirt. . . .

A road. He stepped onto it and kept moving. One foot in front of the other.

His arms were quivering now under Mavery's weight, threatening to give way any moment. The sun blazed down on his head. The insect bites had left him feverish. But he kept telling himself that he couldn't let Mavery down. He wouldn't. She had faced the wraiths for him, come back for him. So Sam pushed himself forward.

Until he stumbled over a loose stone and his arms finally

gave out. With a pitiful groan, he crumpled, dropping Mavery on the ground in front of him.

She lay there, still and pale. She hadn't moved since she had been attacked. Gripped with sadness, Sam just stared at her, not even sure she was still alive. He wanted to cry but didn't have the energy.

Feeling dizzy, he let his head drop to the hardened dirt next to Mavery. The Tarkana Fortress couldn't be far. They would help Mavery. She was one of them—a full-blooded witch. The poor girl didn't deserve to die, not like this.

Sam's eyes closed. Under his cheek, a deep vibration rumbled in the ground. His eyes fluttered open long enough to see a group of men on horseback, their bodies encased in dark armor, galloping toward him.

Rough hands lifted him from the ground. He struggled feebly, trying to tell the riders to take care of Mavery. Then something hit him over the head and everything went black.

Chapter Twenty-Four

As consciousness flickered inside him, Sam slowly became aware of his surroundings. The first thing he felt was cold stone biting into his hips; his back rested against a rough wall. Then he felt his head throbbing from the lump he had received. He could smell the pungent salve someone had slathered on his bites, but they still itched like crazy.

Cracking open his eyes, Sam saw a floor littered with rat droppings and filth. His wrists dangled painfully from chains clipped onto rusty wall rings. An old wooden bucket sat in the corner, with the smell of an outhouse wafting from it. Clearly, he was in some kind of dungeon.

"Samuel, how nice of you to come calling."

Sam raised his eyes and looked into the smirking face of Endera Tarkana. She sat on a chair in front of him, wearing a long, high-collared red dress and looking like a cat that had just slurped up a bowl of rich cream.

"I knew you would join us sooner or later," Endera gloated.

"Where's Mavery? What have you done with my friends?" He strained against his chains. "I swear if you've hurt them, I'll make you pay."

She lifted his chin, smiling. "Mmm, there's that temper I find so endearing."

He jerked away from her cold touch.

"What is your interest in that grubby imp?" she continued.

"Mavery's my friend. You better take care of her—not dump her in the ocean like garbage."

Endera smiled. "I saved her life, and that's the thanks I get? She's feasting on moldy bread as we speak. And your friends, they're having the time of their life. Just yesterday, your girlfriend was bitten by one of my *rathos*. What you call rats, but oh so much bigger and nastier, with teeth the size of . . . well, you get the picture." She waved her hand carelessly.

"Let them go. Take me instead."

"Dear boy, I have you already," she crowed. "And I've every intention of sending your friends back to their pathetic life of grammar lessons and homework . . . just as soon as you do me one little favor."

Sam knew there was nothing little about this favor. "Why would I help a witch like you?"

She pouted. "Is that any way to talk to your auntie? How is my sister Abigail, by the way? We used to be like two peas in a pod."

Sam lunged forward, rattling against his chains. "My mom is nothing like you. You're evil and cruel. You turned Mr. Platz into a lizard."

She gave a little shrug. "I turned that pudgy little teacher into a fearsome monster. He should be thanking me for giving him a taste of real power. As for your mother, she was supposed to deceive the Son of Odin, not marry him. Abigail and I might not be blood sisters, but in the coven we're all one big family."

"What did you do to me back in the woods?" Sam shuddered as he recalled her tearing into his soul with her powerful magic.

"I gave you a little push, is all. A crash course in magic. Your mother should have taught you how to use your powers, but she was scared to find out who you really are."

"I know who I am. Just because I have witch blood doesn't make me like you. Mavery and I, we're different. We can choose to do the right thing with our magic."

"The red sun says differently. Have you seen it lately? It's bursting with poison. I swear two new veins popped up when you took on those nasty biters. The High Council thinks we caused the red sun to return, but you and I both know"—she leaned her face in close—"it was all you, Samuel."

Sam didn't try to deny it, not after Jasper's words.

Endera leaned forward. "You should have died when I dropped that Deathstalker in your crib—I was so hoping you would. But you survived, and do you know why?"

His heart skipped a beat. He feared the answer.

"It's because you were meant to be one of us. The day you turned twelve, you didn't just gain your powers; you declared your true nature."

"What do you mean?"

"The first red vein appeared on your birthday. I remember the day vividly. Poor Ronnie Polk took the brunt of your anger, but here in Orkney, we felt it as well. And when I looked up into the sky and saw that first poisonous vein, I knew. I knew who was responsible and that it was my duty to bring you home to your family. Your *real* family."

"You're not my family."

"You belong here with us. Why do you fight your true nature?" Her voice was hypnotic, and he couldn't look away from the gleaming green of her eyes.

Sam's hands clenched at his side, his fingernails digging into his palms as he clung desperately to his truth about who he was. "Vor told me I get to choose which path I go down—"

Endera hissed at the mention of Vor's name. "I don't care what that pompous goddess says; she's a puppet of Odin. You are a Son of Rubicus; you share his temper and his flair for a big, splashy curse. You can't deny the connection when you look at the sun. That hunger you feel, the thirst for power."

Sam squirmed. Her words were like ants under his skin.

How did she know so much about him? How he felt, how he thought?

"Tell me, Sam, when you look into that throbbing red face, aren't you just dying to devour the whole world?"

There was silence. A drop of water fell from the damp ceiling.

Sam shook his head and looked away. He kept shaking it in denial, hoping Endera would end this torment.

"We should not be enemies, Samuel. We are more alike than you realize."

"I want to see my friends. And Mavery. You better not have hurt her."

"Or what?" Her voice was cold.

He answered, challenging her with his eyes, "If I am a Son of Odin and Rubicus, I . . . I probably have powers even greater than yours."

Endera's eyes sparked with fury, and Sam realized he should have kept his mouth shut. Color flashed in her cheeks, and her hand tightened into a trembling claw on her lap. The witch had the same hair-trigger temper as he did. She muttered something ominous under her breath, and Sam heard tiny feet skittering on the stone. Something knocked the wooden bucket over. And then he saw them. . . .

Rathos. Her army of giant rats. More than a dozen of them poured into the cell out of a hole in the wall and ran around Endera's chair. Their brown, hairy bodies brushed up against his feet and legs, their beady black eyes coveting his tender flesh. They were twice the size of normal rats, and their jagged teeth looked as sharp as a piranha's.

One of the *rathos* ran up Sam's leg inside his pants, its slimy feet skimming along his skin, tickling the hairs. He writhed, trying to stop it, but his hands were chained in place.

"Knock it off!"

"You have such power, boy—make them stop."

The vicious rat bit down on the soft part of his thigh, making Sam cry out in pain. Another ran across his chest and up to his neck, biting down hard on his ear. He could feel warm blood flowing down his neck.

Sam thrashed, trying to get away. "Stop it! Make them stop," he pleaded, as a swarm of *rathos* ran up his legs, toward his face.

Endera hissed at them, and the filthy rodents dispersed, disappearing back into the hole they had emerged from.

She leaned in, her finger jabbing into his chest, paralyzing him with that venomous magic of hers. "You will never have greater powers than I. You will serve me, and I will decide whether you live or die."

When she finally withdrew her finger, Sam gasped, drawing in precious air. "I'd rather eat worm guts than serve you."

The witch snapped her fingers. A guard appeared at the door.

"Kill the imp," she said.

"Wait, no!" Sam lunged forward, straining at his chains until the rusty metal cut into his wrists. "Don't hurt Mavery. I'm sorry. I didn't mean it. I'll do whatever you want."

The guard waited. After a long moment, Endera waved him away.

"When you're feeling better, we can discuss the price for your friends' lives." She left, sweeping her skirt in a garish swirl of red silk, and the door clanged shut behind her.

-------◁◎▷-------

Endera leaned against the cell door, dragging in a deep breath of satisfaction. It had taken longer than she had expected, but the boy had broken, precisely as she had hoped.

A rustle of skirts and the telltale tap of a cane alerted her she was not alone.

"Hestera, what brings you to the dungeons?" Endera asked, clenching her jaw to affect a normal tone at the unexpected sight of the old crone.

"I wanted to see the boy for myself, interrogate him." She made a move with her cane to brush past Endera, but Endera blocked her way.

The older witch bristled. "Step aside, Endera."

"You may enter, of course," Endera said, as lightly as she could. "It's simply, when the *rathos* attacked the boy, he grew queasy, and you know how children are. He made quite a mess in there. I thought to leave him to wallow in his own filth, to teach him a lesson. But please"—Endera stepped to the side—"perhaps you would enjoy the challenge?"

Hestera hesitated, her gnarled hands gripping the knobby, emerald-topped cane. "I'll wait until he's cleaned up. But I warn you, Endera, if he is not who you say he is, the coven will tear him to pieces."

Endera looped her arm in Hestera's and walked the old witch down the cobweb-laden hallway, out of earshot of the boy's cell.

"Hestera, I swear on my life, he brims with a power I have never felt before—I daresay power that will one day rival ours. And he is on the edge of joining us. I can feel it. He will go to Odin and receive the power needed to free our sisters."

"Why do you care so much about Catriona? She was a horrid creature. As cruel and merciless as her father, Rubicus."

Endera stopped to grip Hestera's shoulder. "Oh, I agree wholeheartedly. But Catriona holds what's left of our ancient magic. She can free us from being under the thumb of every living creature in Orkney. Or would you wait until they hunt us down and exterminate us like *rathos*?" Endera's voice rose to a high pitch.

Hestera tapped her cane vigorously. "We shall not go quietly, Endera. You are right to remind me of the threat. If the boy can deliver, then we will have the advantage."

Pleased, Endera patted her arm as they continued on. "I have a plan in mind to ensure he betrays Odin. When he does, he will have nowhere to turn but us."

Chapter Twenty-Five

Keely lifted her head from a fitful nap when her dungeon door opened. A swarthy guard dressed in black leather regalia dragged a young girl into the cell, tossed her on the thin pile of hay, and then left, slamming the heavy wooden door behind him and keying the lock with a dispiriting clank.

The girl smelled like eucalyptus. Insect bites spotted her face and arms. Her skin glistened with some kind of salve. She sat up, looking woozy and confused. One eye was nearly swollen shut. When she saw Keely, she scooted back.

"Who are you?" the girl asked suspiciously.

"I'm Keely."

Her face lit up. "You're Sam's friend. I'm Mavery."

Keely crawled across the stone floor as far as the chain around her ankle would let her and knelt in front of the girl. "You know Sam?"

"'Course," Mavery scoffed. "We're partners. I've been traveling with him for days. I brought him to Balfour Island." She scratched at the bites on her arms, leaving long red marks.

"He's here?" Hope flared in Keely. Sam was going to rescue them. "Howie," she shouted, "Sam's come for us!"

Howie let out a whoop from his cell. "I knew my man wouldn't let us down!"

"Where is he?" Keely asked.

Mavery shrugged. "Don't know. I kind of blacked out when the biters started draining me." She held her arms out, showing raised bumps from what must have been some nasty bloodsucking insects.

"So he's probably a prisoner, too," Keely said, her hope fizzling. "Those witches are horrible. I wish I could throw them all from the highest tower."

Mavery's eyes narrowed. "Yeah? That so? I'm a witch. You gonna toss me over?"

Keely moved back a safe distance. "You're one of them?"

"Yeah, I'm a horrible witch." She waved her hands in the air, mocking Keely. "Be careful, or I'll turn you into a pig."

It took a moment of terror before Keely realized the girl was kidding. "Very funny. If you're a witch, what are you doing locked up here?"

"Maybe I'm spying on you," she said, brushing her dirty dress down over her knees.

Keely doubted that. The girl was young and looked genuinely frightened by her circumstances. Not much of a threat. Keely began to regret her harsh words, but before she could apologize, Howie shouted from across the hall, "Does she know where Sam is?"

"No," Keely and Mavery answered at the same time.

Mavery glared at Keely. "I told Sam coming here was a mistake, but he wanted to save his friends. So whatever happens to him, it's your fault." Then Mavery turned on her side and curled up, folding her arms and closing her eyes.

Keely didn't know what to think. The girl said she was a witch, so she could be lying about Sam. But if she wasn't lying, then Sam was in trouble, and no help was coming for Keely and Howie. Sighing in despair, Keely rested her head back against the stone, fighting the tears. She would give anything to be home in her own bed, away from this nightmare.

It seemed as if Keely had barely closed her eyes when the clanking sound of keys awoke her again. Two guards rushed in, and one hauled her to her feet while unlocking her chains. Mavery yowled like a wet cat, kicking at the other guard as he dragged her away.

"Get your hands off me," Keely said, yanking her arm free. "You don't have to be so rough."

In the corridor, Howie was already unchained, looking skinny and pale.

"Don't worry, Keely-pie," he said, giving her a thumbs-up. "Sam's coming for us."

"Put me down!" Mavery screamed, pounding at the guard's armor with her fists. The guard had had enough and cuffed her upside the head. The girl went limp. Another guard threw a black hood over Keely's head and gave her a shove. It was hard to breathe, and disorienting, but Keely fought back panic with rapid rationalization. It didn't make sense that Endera would harm them. The witches obviously needed them for something, something to do with Sam. So Keely kept her head up, controlled her breathing, and followed where the guard led her.

The sound of a door clanging shut echoed like they were in an expansive room.

Someone clapped his or her hands. "My wonderful hostages."

Endera, thought Keely. That malevolent voice was unmistakable.

Keely's hood was ripped off, and she caught a first glimpse of her new surroundings. They were in a great hall, two stories at least. It was dim and musty, lit by flickering candles that seemed to animate the eerie carvings around the alabaster support columns. Not exactly welcoming, but a definite upgrade from the wretched dungeon.

Endera sat before her prisoners on a raised dais with a pair of other witches on each side of her. More witches filed in behind the children as the guards marched them forward into the center of the hall.

"I hope you have enjoyed your stay so far," Endera said with cruel glee.

"Where's Sam?" Keely asked.

"We know he came here to rescue us," Howie added.

"And look how that worked out," Endera mocked.

Mavery let out a low growl. "He's going to . . . to tear your head off when he gets here!"

Endera fanned herself. "Oh, dear sisters, we should all be trembling at the thought of a boy who doesn't yet know how to control his magic."

The other witches tittered with laughter.

"Now, if you're quite finished, let's play a little game. It's called Don't Get Eaten," Endera jeered.

Keely took a step back, instinctively putting one arm around Mavery's shoulder. Howie rested his hand on her back.

"We don't want to play any games," Keely said.

"Now, where's the fun in that? We're going to put on a show, and you are to be my stars."

Endera went to the back wall and dragged a long black curtain to the side. All Keely saw at first was a shimmery web. Mavery must have known what it meant, because the girl let out a keening sound of terror as a long set of jointed legs unfolded into the candlelight, carrying a car-size, brown torso covered in thick, oily hair. With deadly grace, the creature crawled from the dark corner, spreading more legs and clacking its ferocious mandible jaws at the presence of live prey. Before Keely could scream in horror, someone tied a gag around her mouth.

Chapter Twenty-Six

In the morning, a guard brought Sam a bowl of cold gruel and unchained his hands and feet. As soon as he was released, Sam reached for the familiar pouch, disappointed to find it gone. He felt naked without its power hanging from his neck. He forced himself to eat, even though the gruel tasted like swamp water.

There wasn't much to his dungeon: the smelly bucket, some bones from a small animal, and the chains he had been bound with. A single window covered with rusted bars perched high on the wall. He jumped up, grabbing hold of the iron rods, and pulled himself up so he could see out.

Sam was eye level with the ground. Across a courtyard, Endera stood talking to a man on a horse. He was bald and round, dressed in black robes. A Balfin, no doubt, judging by his clothes, but Sam couldn't see if it was Emenor, the High Council representative who had conspired with Lord Orrin back in Skara Brae to help him escape. Had this been their intention all along, to drive him into the witches' clutches?

Dropping back down, Sam paced his cell. He felt naked without his dad's pouch and the precious piece of Odin's stone, like he had been stripped of his powers. But then something occurred to him—something empowering. *Maybe I don't need it to do magic.* Maybe, thought Sam, that gift from his father was just like training wheels. A starter kit.

He was the son of a witch, after all.

"*Fein kinter*," he said, facing the door.

Nothing happened.

He tried again, shaking his hands out to get the energy flow-ing. "*Fein kinter* . . . something, something."

His mind was blank. The problem was, he couldn't con-jure up any spells. When he was in trouble or angry, the words flooded his brain, but now he couldn't even make the door rattle.

Guess I'm a pretty lousy witch, Sam realized, his spirits sink-ing again.

The sound of boots clomping down the hallway broke his gloom as the door to his dungeon opened. A guard dressed in a black leather breastplate, with a black cowl covering his face, grabbed Sam by his collar and shoved him into the hall, where three other guards waited.

"What's going on? Where are you taking me?"

Offering no answers, they pushed him along. Sam kept his head down, looking furtively side to side, hoping for a sign of his friends. But the cell doors were all firmly closed, and the narrow slit-windows were too high to give him a chance to see inside.

The guards trudged Sam up a set of spiral stairs lined with cobwebs. At the top, the first guard unlocked a heavy, reinforced door. Sunlight burst through the opening, and Sam threw his arm up, shading his eyes as they entered an enclosed courtyard. He in-stantly recognized this place as the one where he had seen Endera talking to the horseman earlier.

Stark gray walls rose up three stories around him, leaving a large, open space in the middle. It was planted with lush green grass and neat flower beds, with scattered benches set under wil-lowy trees. Not at all what Sam expected from a witches' fortress.

As they walked down the corridor, doors opened up, spilling out girls of all ages. They wore identical gray dresses, and each clutched an armload of books. Their long black hair was twisted into braids down their back, and they looked at him wide-eyed and slack-jawed, as if they had never seen a boy before. Strange as it seemed, it appeared to Sam to be some kind of school.

Reaching the far end of the courtyard, the guards ushered Sam into a quiet hall that led directly to a set of ornate metal doors. Two more guards stood in front, holding tall lances.

As Sam approached, the two guards pushed on the handles so the metal doors swung open. The other guards, his escorts, gave Sam a shove, sending him stumbling forward into the room as the metal doors swung closed behind him.

This place is humongous was Sam's first thought. The ceiling had to be two stories high, held up by carved alabaster columns. A narrow red carpet led to the opposite end of the room, where a raised dais stood in front of a large, black-curtained wall. He caught a faint whiff of something familiar—cherry, like the Chap-Stick Keely liked. His friends were close. Joy shot through him. He searched the room, scanning every inch for a sign of his friends.

Endera sat on a throne-like chair in the center of the room. Around her were five witches of varying ages, all seated in a semi-circle, their eyes fixed on him. Endera was speaking to a man in black robes—the same one from the courtyard. This time, Sam recognized Emenor's scowl as he drew nearer. He was right—the Balfin had betrayed him, just as Rego and Teren had warned.

Emenor turned as Sam approached. His fleshy lips twitched, and beads of sweat shone on his forehead. He smiled, seemingly pleased with his treachery.

"My dear nephew, how did you sleep?" Endera said cheerfully.

"I'm not your nephew," Sam said, adding, "How does it feel to be a traitor, Emenor?"

"That's rich calling me a traitor," Emenor said, not looking the slightest bit guilty. "You've come running after your friends and left all of Orkney to suffer. Who's the traitor, I wonder?"

Sam felt like he had been punched in the gut, but Endera cut in.

"You can go now, Emenor. You have done well," the hateful witch said.

Emenor nodded, avoiding eye contact with Sam, and said, "Yes, milady." He bowed and then seemed to hover, as if he were waiting for something.

Endera sighed and beckoned him forward. The Balfin eagerly stumbled to her chair and knelt down. She waved her hand over the medallion he pulled out from his cloak, the same one he had used to open the wall back in Skara Brae. A flash of green transferred from Endera's hand to the medallion. The Balfin was getting his little token recharged with magic.

Sam shook his head in disgust as the Balfin bowed reverently and backed away behind the black curtain.

"Where are my friends?" Sam demanded.

"Silence!"

The shrill voice came from one of the other witches, an older woman with gray streaks in her hair and the same piercing eyes as Endera. She clutched a cane with an emerald knob, which she rapped on the ground in sync with her voice. The sharp crack echoed in the room.

"Where are your manners, boy?" Endera murmured. "You haven't even been properly introduced. Hestera, meet Samuel Barconian, the brat with the bloodline of Odin and Rubicus."

Hestera spat at his feet. "He's an abomination. He should be put to death immediately."

The other witches nodded. Sam could see the bloodthirst in their eyes.

"And what of our quest?" Endera said. "Shall we give up on that?"

Another witch next to her, younger and pretty, with luminous eyes, sat forward, simpering, "How do we know this little child can do it?"

"Now, now, Lemeria, give the boy a chance," Endera chided.

"I'm almost thirteen." Sam stretched his age by a few months. "And who says I want to help you witches anyway?"

The witches cackled with laughter. But Sam wasn't trying to be funny.

The youngest witch, Lemeria, pointed her finger at him and said, "Dance."

Sam felt an electric current jolt through his body, which inexplicably began to shuffle side to side, as if someone were pulling strings, making him move in a crazy jig like a marionette.

"Knock it off." He tried to fight the magical forces moving his limbs but ended up tripping over his feet, landing hard on his backside. Now the witches' laughter became a stinging cacophony.

Endera raised her hand to quiet them. "Enough! Sam, we will make you a deal. We need something only you can obtain for us, and you want something that we possess."

"Forget it," he said, getting back on his feet. "I'm not making any deal with you."

"The boy is insolent, like his father," Hestera hissed. There were murmurs of agreement.

"And here I thought you would do anything to keep your friends alive. . . ." Endera clapped her hands. The black curtain that lined the wall behind them fell to the ground with a loud swoosh.

Sam gasped. Keely, Howie, and Mavery were suspended in a silvery spiderweb that stretched from the ceiling to the floor. They were gagged and wrapped so tightly in webbing that they couldn't move their hands or feet. They were alive—their imploring eyes wide with fear—but probably not for long.

In the upper corner of the web, a black spider the size of a Volkswagen Bug perched. Its long, nimble legs furiously spun more webbing. Red bands circled each leg. Giant mandibles on either side of its head looked as if they could devour all three kids in a single bite.

"Let them go!" Sam lunged forward to help his friends, but

Lemeria raised her finger, and his feet were instantly glued to the ground.

"Take another step, and one of them dies," Endera said. She made a kissing noise, and the spider skittered forward a few feet on the web, clacking its mandibles in anticipation of a meal. The creature stopped directly above Keely, who screamed through her gag.

"Did you know the Tarkana witches get their name from this beautiful specimen?"

Endera went on as if she were merely reciting an interesting bit of history while Sam's friends were about to be eaten alive.

"One bite paralyzes her victims so they can't move, but they can still feel everything. Then she slowly sucks their blood, savoring every drop. I'm sure the pain is unimaginable."

"Stop it. Don't hurt them," Sam pleaded. "Please, just tell me what you want."

Endera steepled her fingers under her chin and then smiled to her sisters. "The High Council wants this boy to seek out Odin and ask him for a cure for the red sun. It's ironic, isn't it? Those hapless Orkadians send the one who brought the curse to find the cure."

Another cackle of laughter broke out among the witches.

Endera continued speaking to Sam. "We seek the Horn of Gjall. It's buried somewhere near the root of Odin's sacred Yggdrasil tree. You will have to steal it. Odin will never give it to you."

"What do you want it for?"

"This brat asks too many questions," Hestera said, rapping her cane on the ground in a deliberate cadence. The spider veered left, toward Mavery. The little witch screamed, her eyes wide with terror as she thrashed in the webbing. The spider was right over her now, its powerful jaws poised to snap off her head.

"I'll do it!" Sam said frantically. "I'll do whatever you ask. Just don't hurt them."

Endera made her kissing noise again, sending the spider into retreat. "Wonderful. I knew we could work together. Bring us the

Horn before the moon wanes, and your friends will live to see another day. And, Samuel, if the High Council finds out about our deal, or if you fail, I promise each of them will die screaming your name."

Sam met Howie's eyes across the dais. Howie nodded at him, like he was trying to let Sam know it was okay, even though there was nothing remotely okay about any of this.

How was he supposed to find Asgard on his own? He flashed on the book in the library back home. The one Keely had shown him. It had mentioned the Yggdrasil tree. Keely might remember something that would help them.

Lemeria released the spell that bound his feet, and Sam took two steps closer to the dais. "I need my friends to come with me."

"Now, why would we ever permit that?" Endera said airily.

"What you want me to do, I can't do alone," Sam insisted. "I never would've made it here without Mavery. She knows this place much better than I do. And Keely's an expert on Odin and his tree."

Endera tapped her fingers on the armrest of her throne. "And your other little friend? Is he so worthless?"

"No, he's the best friend I'll ever have," Sam proclaimed. "I'd do anything for Howie."

The witches whispered among themselves, and Hestera finally nodded. Endera turned back to Sam.

"We agree. You may take the girls, we'll keep the boy, and everyone's happy."

Sam looked at Howie's face and saw his fear, but Howie managed to raise his thumb, signaling his agreement. "No, I didn't—"

"Or we could kill him now and keep the girls. Make up your mind. I'm getting bored."

The enormity of what he had just done sank in. Howie would be all alone in a dungeon for what could be days. "You have to swear to me you won't hurt him."

"Don't make me wait too long," Endera warned. "A boy could get eaten alive by the *rathos* in my dungeons."

She snapped her fingers, and the guards cut the three kids loose from the web.

Sam ran over to them. Keely grabbed him, nearly breaking one of his ribs.

"Sam, I've been so scared.." She seemed relieved and angry at the same time. She pushed him away to look at him. "We can't leave Howie here; you don't know how awful it is."

"I didn't have a choice." Sam turned to Howie. His friend's glasses were bent, but he managed a grin.

"Don't worry about me. I get to kick back and enjoy the fine cuisine in this place while you guys do all the work," Howie joked.

Sam hugged his friend. "I swear I'll come back for you soon as I can."

"I know you will, bro. I'm not worried. Just, you know, hurry. Like, get here yesterday, if you know what I mean."

Sam nodded and smiled—Howie could always make him smile, even now. Then Sam turned his eyes to Mavery, who looked mad and sad at the same time.

"I'll stay and your friend can go," she said, her lips quivering.

"I meant what I said," Sam told her. "I need you, Mavery."

She rushed forward and threw her arms around him, then stepped back self-consciously, swiping at her tears with the back of her hand. "We can't split up the team, right?"

"Right," Sam said.

Keely hugged Howie, and then guards pried Howie away. The last thing Sam saw was Howie's uncertain face as he clung to the door frame on his way back to the dungeon.

"See you when I see you," Howie said, pushing his glasses up on his nose.

"Not if I see you first," Sam answered.

"How touching," Endera said, standing as the other witches trailed out. She swept down the steps to where they stood. "I've arranged a Balfin ship to take you to Asgard—one of the fastest in the fleet."

"So, how do I find this place?" Sam asked.

"There are no maps. Odin's island appears and disappears according to his whims, but this will help you locate it." She handed him a leather satchel.

Opening it, Sam saw a heavy brass compass inside, dull and scratched with age.

"I need my pouch," Sam said, as Endera turned to go. She paused. "If you want me to find Odin, I need all the help I can get. That pouch might help me." When she still didn't respond, he added, "Please, Endera."

She gave a little shrug and turned back toward him, reaching into the pocket of her gown and pulling out the pouch, holding it up by the string as if she found it distasteful. "Why would a powerful witch like you rely on such a meaningless piece of stone?"

Sam didn't answer; he snatched it from her hand before she changed her mind. He took out the stone and smoothed its rough edges, before putting it back and looping it around his neck.

"You have one week to return with the Horn of Gjall before I feed your spineless friend to my pet." Endera turned and swept out of the room.

Mavery took his hand and squeezed it. "It's okay, Sam. We'll get your friend back."

Sam wished he shared her confidence. But they were heading out on a quest for Asgard, an island that had no map, to confront the most powerful god in Orkney. And if he somehow found Odin, he had to convince him to help Sam end the curse that was poisoning the land and then secretly steal one of Odin's prized objects, the Horn of Gjall.

Piece of cake, Sam lied to himself.

Chapter Twenty-Seven

Guards escorted Sam and the two girls along an arched corridor. No one spoke. Keely kept her head down, arms folded tightly across her chest. Mavery skipped along next to Sam. A set of iron gates appeared ahead. Rust-stained sunlight filtered through the bars, casting long, striped shadows. Keely picked up the pace, practically running toward the gates, no doubt eager to get away from the memories of that spider and all the other horrors she had faced here as a guest of the Tarkana witches. Mavery trailed close behind her.

But Sam's feet dragged. He kept looking over his shoulder, wishing guiltily for another glimpse of Howie. Had he made the right decision leaving his best friend behind? What if the witches broke their promise and fed Howie to the spider just for sport before Sam could return?

Busy imagining every possible painful end for Howie, Sam failed to see the shadowy figure lurking behind a pillar until a hand reached out and yanked him into a hidden recess.

It was Emenor. The black-robed Balfin looked anxiously over his shoulder down the corridor. The others kept on marching toward the gates.

"What do you want?" Sam asked angrily.

"You must not retrieve that horn," he hissed.

"Back off. You're nothing but a traitor. All you care about is your stupid trinkets."

"You need to focus on what's important, Barconian." Emenor's bloodshot eyes were intense as he gripped the front of Sam's shirt. "Do you even know what the Horn of Gjall can do?"

Sam shook his head slowly.

"Blasting the Horn summons an army of the dead. Hestera craves the power to rule over Orkney. With a legion of unstoppable corpses, she will have her way. Would you risk all of our lives to save one friend?"

Sam shrugged. "I don't know. I'll think of something."

He made to leave, but Emenor gripped his arm, stopping him. "Your father is alive."

Fresh grief rippled through Sam at the bold-faced lie. "No. Rego told me he's dead. He wouldn't lie. Not about that."

Emenor's grip tightened. "The dwarf wasn't there; I was. Lord Barconian was badly wounded. But Endera cast an enchantment and imprisoned him in a stone at the Ring of Brogar before he died. She wanted him to feel the same pain her ancestors do, trapped alive, with no hope of escape. Your father lives. I saw it with my own eyes."

Sam couldn't help but feel a flicker of hope. "How . . . how do I save him?"

"Odin's magic can break the spell that keeps your father trapped in that stone."

Sam nodded, still not sure he believed Emenor but confused about why the Balfin would lie about such a thing. "I have this. It contains Odin's magic." Sam pulled the pouch out, dumping the rock into his hand, but Emenor closed Sam's fingers over it, crushing his hand.

"That shard won't break a curse as powerful as that which holds your father in the stone. Go now," Emenor said. "Follow the road to the harbor. A ship has been arranged for you. You can trust my men. I swear it on my life."

He gave Sam a little shove back into the corridor and hurried away. Sam's mind was spinning with thoughts of his father. He stumbled through the gate outside, blinking at the sullen light of day. The sun's veins had blossomed, spreading across the face of the sun so much that the day had an eerie red cast to it. Endera had been right; the poison was spreading.

Keely and Mavery were already on horseback. Sam climbed onto a waiting horse.

"Let's go," Keely said impatiently, and turned her horse away. "I don't want to spend another minute in this place."

They trotted the horses down the road. Sam looked back once at the high stone wall encircling the fortress. A pair of crows flew overhead, letting out harsh caws. "I promise to come back for you, Howie," he whispered. He urged his horse forward and pulled up next to Keely. Her face was puckered into a frown. She didn't look happy to see him at all.

"I want to go home, Sam. I want to go home right now. I don't want to see any more witches or rats or giant spiders. I just want to go home."

The words spilled out of Sam. "Rego told me my father was dead, but Emenor says he's alive and there's a way to rescue him."

"Don't be stupid, Sam. They're just telling you that to get you to do what they want." Her eyes flashed with anger. "The witches are using you. You can't believe anything they tell you."

"But what if it's true?"

"It's not!" she shouted, pulling her horse up so hard, the animal tossed its head sharply. "God, Sam, do you realize you've just sentenced your best friend to death?"

Sam shook his head. "No, Endera promised—"

Keely cut him off. "Endera is a witch! She laughed when

those *rathos* attacked us. She has no heart. They're probably feeding Howie to their spider right now."

"Stop it!" Sam shouted back at her. "What did you want me to do?"

"You should've left her." She jerked her chin over her shoulder at Mavery. The little witch sat on her horse behind them, watching them with narrowed eyes.

Sam cast a quick glance at Mavery and then lowered his voice. "I didn't have a choice. I need her. She knows Orkney better than we do."

"She's a witch, too. She even told me she was spying for them." Keely looked at Mavery, as if challenging the girl to deny it. "And you chose her over Howie? He would never have left you there. Never." Keely kicked her horse in the ribs and rode ahead.

"When are you going to tell her you're a horrible witch, like me?" Mavery said saucily.

"Soon." Sam turned his horse to follow Keely.

"She's not gonna like it," Mavery called after him.

Sam rode on, gritting his teeth at the thought of confessing his secrets to Keely. After everything she had been through at the Tarkana fortress, he could imagine her horrified response when she found out not one but two witches were leading her across a hostile land. She would probably hate him on the spot, and he wouldn't blame her. After all, the only reason she was in this mess was that she had tried to help him.

─────◆─(◇◇◇◇)─◆─────

After an hour of riding, they crested a hill. A small harbor with several ships sat nestled between steep cliffs. Mavery turned her horse away and headed down a muddy trail, away from the Balfin ships.

"Where's she going?" Keely asked irritably.

"Mavery, we have to go this way," Sam called.

"Not going on a Balfin ship," she piped over her shoulder, without stopping.

Sam kicked his horse and rode over to her, grabbing her reins.

"Mavery, Emenor has a ship waiting for us. We don't have a lot of time."

"We can't use a Balfin ship." Her chin trembled like she was about to cry. "The Balfins hate the witches as much as they hate the Orkadians. We have to find Jasper. His boat can't be far. He would have waited for me."

"Sam, the ship is right there," Keely said. "Think about Howie. We don't have time to go running around just because this little witch says so."

A tingle of electricity passed over Sam's scalp. There was a crackle of energy in the air, and it hit him. That little witch was about to do something with her magic. Something bad.

"Mavery, stop!"

But he was too late. Mavery flung her hands out, muttering a spell. Keely squealed from atop her horse.

Sam turned around and groaned. Keely sported a face full of mud. Blobs of it clung to her hair and spattered her face. She wiped her eyes, looking at Sam in total disbelief, as if it was all his fault.

"I told you," Keely sputtered. "She's a horrid little witch."

Sam got down from his horse and walked over to her, tearing off the bottom of his shirt so she could clean her face.

"Try being nicer to her," Sam said. "It's not her fault she's a witch. She was born that way. Being a witch doesn't make her like Endera."

After Keely cleaned up, they followed Mavery, mainly because she wouldn't turn around, and also because, after giving it serious thought, Sam didn't like the idea of a Balfin ship, either. The trio snaked silently along the ridgeline bordering the coast. The day was hot, not a cloud in sight, leaving them exposed to the red rays of sun that seemed to sear a hole in Sam's brain as he clung to the saddle.

"Sam, what's wrong with the sun?" Keely asked quietly, shading her eyes to squint at it. "It looks . . . sick."

"Don't look at it," Sam said sharply. "It's been cursed. It's poisoning the land." He gathered his courage, searching for the right words to tell her the truth, but the sound of hooves pounding down the trail made him spin around in the saddle.

A regiment of Balfin soldiers was riding hard down the trail.

Chapter Twenty-Eight

"Move it, Mavery!" he shouted. They whipped the horses forward. They rounded a short bend, and Mavery let out a cry.

"There's the ship—see?"

Below them, Jasper's rickety ship, with its tattered brown sails, bobbed in the sea.

"That's our boat?" Keely's voice was loaded with doubt.

"No time to explain," Sam said, jumping down and helping her off her horse. Behind them, the Balfins were a hundred yards off and closing. "If you really want to go with the Balfins, we will," Sam said. "But I think this is a better way."

"Hurry up!" Mavery called, making her way down a narrow path.

"I swear, Sam Baron, you're going to be the death of me," Keely said, and then she ran after Mavery.

Sam grinned, scrambling after her down the path that led to the beach. He carried the leather satchel Endera had given him with the compass in it. They ran across the sand to where Jasper had a rowboat waiting. Shouts rang out from the clifftop as the Balfins appeared.

"Time to go, Jasper," Sam shouted, as the girls clambered onboard. He helped shove off the boat and jumped in.

Jasper rowed them out to his ship, his sinewy arms pushing

the oars easily through the surf. Sam waved at the helpless Balfin soldiers left standing on the beach.

The old seaman hauled up the anchor, and in moments they were under sail, helped along by Jasper's magical lungs.

"So where to, lad?" Jasper asked.

Sam pulled the compass from the satchel. "Asgard. This compass belonged to Odin. It should guide us there."

Jasper eyed the compass suspiciously. "Where did you get that?"

"The witches gave it to me. They need me to end this curse as badly as the rest of Orkney does."

Jasper grunted, taking the compass and turning it in his hands before handing it back. "Seems mighty hospitable of them. Where's the other one? The witches took two hostages."

Before Sam could think of a lie, Mavery piped up. "Jasper, you know Endera. She always has a plan. She wants to make sure Sam doesn't chicken out."

Jasper grunted again and returned to his helm, turning the ship into the wind.

Sam grinned at Keely. "Well, that was close."

Keely eyed the rickety boat. "Are you sure we shouldn't have gone on the Balfin ship? This boat looks like it's about to sink."

"Don't worry. Jasper knows what he's doing. You have to trust me."

Her eyes filled with tears. "I do, but . . . I just don't understand what's going on. A cursed sun? Witches? I feel like this is a bad dream and I can't wake up. Why does it seem like you're in the middle of it? Like this is all about you?"

Sam hesitated. Over Keely's shoulder, Mavery glared at Sam. "It's all about him because he's a witch, like me, so there." She headed below, slamming the hatch behind her.

"Keely, I can explain," he started.

She laughed. "Explain what? It's not true, right?"

Sam's throat constricted. He couldn't speak.

"Right?" she repeated, her voice growing tense. "Come on, Sam, tell me she's lying. I mean, you can't be a witch, right?"

Sam tripped over the words. "It's not . . . I mean, it is . . . I didn't know." He let out a groan of frustration.

"He's a witch, all right."

Jasper's gravelly voice cut in. The old seaman sat at the helm, his feet resting on the wheel as he steered. Sam closed his eyes, not wanting to see the look of disgust in Keely's eyes. He badly needed her support, needed her friendship.

"Explain," Keely said, her voice sharp.

Sam hesitated so long, Jasper added, "You gonna tell her, lad, or do you want me to?"

Sam cleared his throat before he started in. "Okay, so . . . you remember that book you showed me about Odin?"

She nodded. "Yeah, back in the library. What about it?"

"Well, Odin's sort of my great-great-grandfather."

She laughed. "You think you're related to Odin? Has the sun scrambled your brain?"

"I'm serious. My dad was born here. He's a direct descendent of Baldur, Odin's favorite son. People call him Lord Barconian. I was born here, too."

Keely looked at him as if he had grown two heads. "That's the stupidest thing I've ever heard."

"Oh, you haven't heard the half of it." Sam chose his words carefully. "My mom . . . she's from Orkney, too. She's apparently a witch. A good one," he added hastily, as Keely pulled away in horror. "I think. I mean . . . I don't know for sure." He ran a hand through his hair as confusion jumbled his thoughts.

"So you're really a witch?" Keely's voice was hoarse. She stared at him as if he had turned into a giant cockroach.

For a moment Sam couldn't answer, didn't want to answer, and then he nodded stiffly and admitted the truth. "Yeah, I am. I'm a witch."

It was the first time he had said it out loud. It was strange to say the words, but they fit. Like it or not.

Keely was silent, her brows pinched together as she processed his words. Sam waited for her words of disgust, of rejection, but all she said was, "I guess you can't pick your parents, can you? Just tell me you're a good witch, and not like those others."

Relief flooded Sam, and he chuckled, feeling his tension deflate. "It's funny, I thought my parents were the most boring people on Earth. I had no idea about any of this. They took me away when I was a baby and never told me I was from Orkney." He hesitated, then confessed, "But there's more. A long time ago, this he-witch, Rubicus, wanted to challenge Odin's power. He's the one who cursed the sun. Odin had to cut off Rubicus's head to end the curse. To stop it from happening again, Odin cursed the witches to never again have another son."

Keely was smart enough to see the problem right away. "So how can you be a witch?"

"You could say I'm special. I've got Odin's blood and Rubicus's blood. The combination somehow broke one curse and started another."

"What do you mean, 'started another'?"

This was the hard part. "When I was a baby, Endera dropped a scorpion in my crib to try to kill me."

Keely rolled her eyes. "Jeez, Sam, what is it with you?"

"She wanted to see if I would live or die. Obviously, I lived." He gave a short bow at that achievement.

She didn't smile at his antic. "So?"

"So it meant I had great power, magic, whatever you want to call it." He waggled his hands in the air. "Enough that on the day I turned twelve and pounded on Ronnie Polk, I caused that." He pointed up at the cursed sun.

She glanced quickly at the sun, then back at him. "No, I don't believe it." When he didn't retract the words, she grabbed his arm. "Look, I don't care what they say you did—there's no way you meant to do it. You're a good person, Sam. You protect Howie. You care about people. You might have caused this stupid curse, but it's not your fault."

Her support was a relief, but it didn't stop Sam from feeling the power, the connection to dark desires, that his magic offered. He wanted to control the sun. He wanted to do things that he couldn't put words to. But what he wanted now were more answers to questions haunting him.

Sam turned to face Jasper. "You said you knew my parents. What else can you tell me about them?"

Jasper spoke with a raspy voice while keeping both eyes on the water. "I knew your parents back when they lived here in Orkney. They were very different then."

The seaman tied a rope around the wheel to the rail, setting a course, and came to sit across from them. From inside his tattered shirt, he pulled a knobby piece of yellow fruit and peeled it with a knife, carving them each a slice.

"What is this?" Sam asked. The fruit tasted funny, a little bitter, like it wasn't quite ripe.

"Kava fruit. Keeps away the scurvy."

The wind blew Jasper's stringy hair off his forehead. The lines on his face were deep crevices.

"I remember the day your father went on a peacekeeping mission to meet with the coven on their home turf," Jasper began. "The witches were stirring up trouble, spreading discontent, damaging crops. Orkney was like dry kindling. Anything could upset the balance. Your father wanted to strike a truce, and that's when he met your mother. There were rumors it was a trap, some kind of powerful enchantment by Abigail. Your father was nearly thrown off the High Council when he announced he was marrying her."

"Do you think she tricked him?" Sam asked, chewing slowly.

Had his mother been living a lie all this time, pretending to be kind and loving while hiding her real witch self?

Jasper shrugged. "Who's to say? All I know is they married and your mother tried to make things work in Skara Brae."

Keely cut in quietly, "I've met your mom, Sam. She brought meals over when my own mom was sick. She's a good person."

Sam didn't know what to think anymore, and it was frustrating.

"How do you know so much, anyway?" he snapped, feeling out of sorts and irritable. How could an old sea captain know more about his life than he did?

"You're not the only one who's descended from the gods," Jasper replied.

"You're a Son of Odin?" Sam asked in disbelief.

"Not Odin. Aegir." Jasper said the name with pride.

Sam took another one of the slices of fruit Jasper proffered and broke off half for Keely. His tongue tingled, but the flavor was growing on him.

"Aegir was ruler of the ocean," Keely said with a touch of awe. "He lived in a beautiful coral palace under the water."

"Aye. And swam with ravishing mermaids all the day, taking his pleasure and making mead for the gods." Jasper sounded envious when speaking of his ancestor.

"So you have the sea in your blood," Keely remarked, nibbling on her fruit.

Jasper nodded. "Been on the water every day of my life. I was there the night Sam's parents needed help getting away from Balfour Island, when he was barely alive from that scorpion bite and squalling his head off."

"Do you think my mom knew what would happen if they had a kid?" Sam asked, looking at the sickly rays of the sun. Was he slurring his words? He seemed to be dizzy.

"No one predicted she would have a boy. They tried to keep

it secret, but word got out. Endera wanted to know if you had your mother's blood. I think that's the reason she dropped that Deathstalker in your crib. When you lived, she knew it was only a matter of time before the curse was reformed. I think your mother knew it, too. That's why she spirited you away from here."

Sam snorted. "Well, fat lot of good that did. It just keeps on getting worse."

"That's because you keep losing that temper of yours," Jasper said, handing him another slice of kava fruit.

Keely leaned forward, her words spaced apart. "You mean, hish temper . . ." She shook herself. "His temper's to blame? For that?" She pointed up at the sun.

Sam wanted to object, but, oddly, he couldn't get the words out. His jaw opened and closed as if he were a fish out of water, gasping for a little gulp of oxygen.

Jasper's voice sounded to him like it was coming down a long tunnel. The seaman leaned in, putting his face close to Sam's. "You lied to me, Sam. You made a deal with the witches. To save your friend, no doubt. They would never have given you the compass unless you're working for them."

The compass. The truth suddenly struck Sam: Jasper had barely looked at Odin's compass. Panic gripped him. He turned his head and looked out toward the horizon. Something wasn't right. It looked like they were getting closer to the main island, Garamond.

Jasper wasn't taking them to Asgard. He was taking them back to the High Council.

Sam's mouth felt completely numb, his lips useless as he tried to object.

"Sam, I don't feel good," Keely said, her head swaying side to side. A piece of kava fruit dropped from her hands.

What was that fruit? Sam thought, as he fell face forward onto the deck.

Chapter Twenty-Nine

Leo was restless.

His first few days in Orkney had passed quickly as he navigated his way to the small fishing village where Vor had sent him. He had taken her advice, sticking to the road that bordered the coastline. After a long night's walk, his feet grew sore and blistered. The second night, he stumbled on an encampment of Orkadian soldiers. There were eight of them, passing a bottle of ale around a fire and talking about how much they hated witches.

Leo remained hidden, peering out between trees as he studied their camp. Their horses were tethered in a makeshift paddock constructed from branches. Moving stealthily around the fire, he let out a soft clucking sound to reassure the horses. One of them moved closer to him, tossing its head in a greeting. Leo rubbed its nose, letting the horse get his scent. Quietly removing some of the paddock branches, he led the animal out.

A skilled rider from the age of five, Leo pulled himself up easily, urging the horse quietly away. His father would not like his stealing a horse, but it would do Sam no good if Leo arrived too late to help him, or worn to the bone by the walk.

Leo rode by night, taking cover from the cursed sun during the day. Game was scarce. He hunted as best he could, using his bow to take down a young pheasant early one morning. It took another two days before he arrived at the small fishing village Vor had described. He made camp in a cluster of trees in the hillside above the edge of the town and hunkered down to wait for the sign Vor had promised.

It came on the morning of the fourth day. Leo was dozing in the lower of branches of a tree, trying to ignore his hunger pangs, when he heard rocks tumbling. Someone was coming. Taking his bow, Leo notched an arrow, peering down from his vantage point.

Relief shot through him. It was only a girl. Ten or so. She had short, dark hair and wore a ragged-looking dress. She was eyeing his horse.

"Hey there," she said in a crooning voice to the mare. "Would you like to take me for a ride?" She rubbed her hands together and then blew on them. A bubble appeared and wafted through the air.

Leo leaned down, curious. He had never seen anything like it. The horse seemed entranced, sniffing at the bubble. Leo sniffed the air. It smelled of carrots.

She clucked softly, backing away, drawing the bubble and the horse along with her.

The pair had gotten a dozen feet away before Leo shook himself out of his fascinated trance. "Hey, that's my horse," he said, swinging his legs over the branch to drop down in the dirt next to her.

She jumped back, a guilty flush rising to her cheeks. "Says who?"

"Says me. I stole her first."

She looked at him, cocking her head to the side. "You look like a Falcory, but you're not. You're not from here, are you?" Her eyes lit up. "Are you a friend of Sam's?"

Excitement gripped Leo. This must be the sign Vor had promised. "Yes, I'm Leo. My father sent me to warn Sam. Vor said I would find him here."

"He's here, all right. Down there." She pointed at the small town. "But it's not going to be easy to rescue him. We'll need Keely."

"Keely's here, too? What about Howie?"

Mavery gave him the rundown on how Sam had left Howie behind with some witches and how an old sailor had double-crossed them and brought them back to this town. "I ran off before those rotten soldiers could capture me. They're gonna take Sam back to Skara Brae, but he needs to get to Asgard to see Odin so he can fix everything."

Leo's father had said as much to him, only the situation now seemed even more dire. "So, you got any good ideas?" he asked.

Mavery grinned. "I always have good ideas."

Chapter Thirty

For a moment, just before Sam regained consciousness, he dreamed he was back home in his own bed, the familiar smell of his mom cooking breakfast wafting through the air. He inhaled deeply, a smile on his lips, until the smell hit his brain and he groaned.

Horse manure.

Lifting his head, Sam forced his eyes open, taking in the dirt floor, rough wooden rails, and piles of hay. It looked an awful lot like the stable floor behind the inn where Mavery had found him tied up and robbed blind.

Rego sat on a stool, whittling.

"You had to run off and get yourself in trouble, didn't you? You just couldn't listen to me."

"Can you please spare me another lecture?" Sam's mouth felt like it was packed full of sour cotton. He pushed himself up and leaned back against the stall.

"Do you *spleeking* care you put people's lives in danger?" Rego replied furiously. "We've wasted precious time hunting you down." His stick snapped, and he tossed it aside.

"I'm sorry. But I couldn't turn my back on Howie and Keely. It's not who I am."

He pointed at Sam. "You don't know who you are, and that's the problem."

Anger stirred Sam's insides. "I know I'm not the kind of person who leaves his friends to die. I couldn't live with that."

"How about killing everyone in Orkney? Can you live with that?"

"I get it, okay?" Sam shouted, leaning forward. "I should never have been born, but here I am. What do you want me to do about it?"

Rego's face softened a bit. "Start listening to me, and stop running off and playing hero."

Tears stung Sam's eyes. He was trying to do the right thing, but no one seemed to care.

"Endera still has Howie," he said.

"Howie's not what's important."

Ice flushed through Sam's veins, but he held Rego's gaze. "He is to me, and I won't let him die."

"In case you haven't noticed, the red sun's getting worse by the day. Crops have turned to dust. Food lines in Skara Brae wrap around the town square."

"I'm sorry."

"You're sorry?" Rego bellowed. "Everyone's scratching their head, wondering how it is the witches got enough power to curse the sun, and it's only a matter of time before Gael and the rest of the High Council figure it out it was you. Then God help you, lad."

Sam slouched back against the stall. "How long have you known it was me?"

"When that first red vein appeared, the witches boasted it was them, but I had my doubts. So I looked up the records. The red sun returned on the twelfth anniversary of your birth."

"Does the High Council know?"

"You think you would be alive if they did?" he answered,

standing up. "And unless you want Beo to mount your head on a stake, I'd keep your piehole shut. They've ordered you back to Skara Brae. Gael and his Eifalian armada will try to find Asgard alone. Gael thinks he can beseech Odin for an audience."

"No, I have to get to Asgard," Sam pleaded. "Please, Rego, give me another chance."

"It's not up to me. How is it the witches let you leave with Keely? You want to explain that?"

Sam didn't. Not if he wanted Howie to live. The dwarf stared at him.

"Didn't think so," he said, reading the lie on Sam's face. "You're holding something back, and that's going to get us all killed."

"Emenor was there with the witches. He told me my father's still alive. Trapped in a stone at the Ring of Brogar."

Rego's eyes flared with shock; then a scowl came over his face. "I wouldn't believe a word that lying Balfin utters. Your father can't still be alive, Sam. I wouldn't lie to you."

The dwarf was probably right, but Sam held on grimly to his belief, needing to have a sliver of hope. "Where's Keely?"

"She's resting in the inn. I'm taking her north to Torf-Einnar. She'll be safer in the Eifalian kingdom until we can find a way to send her home."

"What about Mavery?"

"Ran off. Slippery as an eel, that one." Rego knelt down and grabbed Sam by the ear to make sure Sam received his message loud and clear. "Be warned: Beo has Falcory warriors stationed around the stable. They'll kill you if you try to escape, and I won't be able to stop them."

Sam glared at him but remained silent.

Rego stood. "Get some sleep. We leave first thing in the morning. There's food on the shelf for you."

Rego left him alone in the stall. Sam picked at the bowl of

cold stew. It was official. He hated black cabbage. He needed to be moving. Find Keely and catch up with Mavery.

Sam crept to the corner of the stall door and peered around it. He was alone, except for the horses. Sam patted their noses, feeling the velvety smoothness, as he slid past them.

At the edge of the barn, the double doors were slightly ajar. If he moved along the side, he could make it to some barrels stacked up by the wall of the inn. He took a step—and an arrow pierced the wood above his head.

Beo stood fifty feet away in the shadows of a tree, another arrow notched in his bow. Rego hadn't been kidding. The Falcory brave was waiting for him to escape so he could put an arrow through Sam's heart.

Sam put up his hands and stepped back inside the barn. He needed a better plan.

Back in his stall, he paced. A distraction would come in handy, something that would divert their attention long enough for him to find Keely, steal a horse, and get to wherever Mavery was hiding.

While he was still trying to come up with something brilliant, a loud *thunk* shook the rafters. The horses stomped their feet and whinnied nervously. Sam cocked his head to the side. Was that smoke he smelled?

A burning ember landed on the ground next to him, and he looked up to see that the hay in the loft was on fire. A flaming arrow had embedded in one of the bales.

Was Beo trying to get rid of him by burning down the barn around him? Sparks began to shoot over the edge, scaring the horses, making them stomp and kick the edges of their stalls.

Sam slid the bars on their doors. They stampeded through the double doors of the barn as the bales of hay exploded, sending flames shooting through the roof as the walls caught fire.

Shouts and screams came from the inn as it ignited, too. Sam ran with the horses, trying to blend in with them as people raced toward the barn. The inn was fully ablaze, sending waves of heat as Sam raced away from the ruckus. He skidded to a stop near some trees and turned back.

"Keely," he whispered. She could be trapped inside the inn.

"Hey, loser, looking for me?"

In the shelter of the small grove, Keely stood next to Mavery, both girls looking pleased with themselves. Behind them stood a Falcory with his back to them. His long black hair hung in a single braid, and he was wearing leather leggings and a leather vest. He held a bow with a flaming arrow in the notch. He drew back and let go. As he did, Sam saw the scar on his arm.

"Leo?"

The boy turned around to face him, and recognition made Sam want to leap for joy.

"Leo, what are you doing here?"

He shouldered his bow. "Not now, Sam. We need to get moving. I have horses waiting."

They ran through the trees to a spot where Leo had three horses tied to a tree. Two of them had saddles. They mounted up. Keely pulled Mavery up behind her. Leo rode bareback, gripping the mane. With a quick dig of their heels, they were on their way. It was dark; only a sliver of moonlight helped them see where they were going.

Leo led them up a trail that wound through the trees, quickly climbing in elevation. By the time they came to the top of a hill and stopped for a moment, the horses were panting. A red glow lit up the night below them as the inn burned to the ground.

"We can rest here a moment," Leo said, slipping off his horse.

Sam jumped down and gave Leo a hug, slapping him on the back.

"When did you get here? I can't believe you found me. And Keely and Mavery."

Leo had a silly grin on his face. "I met this goddess named Vor.

She told me to wait for you here. And Mavery found me when she tried to steal my horse. She helped get Keely out of the inn."

"But how did you get to Orkney?"

"My father sent me to help you. And pass on a message."

Excitement shot through Sam. "So the portal's not closed?"

"No, it is. After I went through, my father destroyed it like Rego ordered him to."

Keely jumped down and grabbed his arm. "Sam, you said we could go home when we got Howie back. My dad's probably worried sick about me."

"We'll figure out a way, Keely. If there's one portal, there have to be more, right, Leo?"

Leo just shrugged. "I don't know. But if we don't stop the red sun, it won't matter. My father said to tell you the curse must be broken or . . ." His words ran out when he saw the expression of dread on Sam's face.

Keely had no such qualms. "Or what?"

"Or . . . it will keep going. After it destroys Orkney, the red sun will begin to poison our world. My father says our worlds are connected. Through the roots of the great tree."

"The Yggdrasil tree," Keely whispered. "When Odin created the Nine Realms, the roots of the Yggdrasil connected them all."

"Does anyone care what I think?" Mavery sat sideways on Keely's horse, kicking her feet.

"You got us in enough trouble already," Sam said. "You made me lose the compass that would get us to Asgard, so you don't get a say this time."

"You mean this compass?" she said, pulling a heavy satchel from the saddle.

Sam's eyes bulged as she lifted the heavy compass out.

"How did you—"

"I stole it from Jasper. When I saw what a double-crosser he was. I know a way to get us to Asgard."

"We have a compass but no ship," Sam pointed out.

"I know a way," Mavery said.

She sucked in her lips and blew a bubble. It grew to the size of a grapefruit, and then she ran her hands around it, whispering a spell to herself. The bubble floated over to Sam and Keely, who saw dolphins splashing in tiny waves inside.

"Is that real?" Leo asked, his eyes big.

"How did you do that?" Keely added in awe, reaching out to touch it, but Sam flicked it impatiently so the bubble broke.

"Dolphins? How does that help us?"

"Simple. We build a raft, and the dolphins will take us where we want to go."

Keely snorted derisively. "Call dolphins? I get you guys are witches, but really, you can do that?"

"We just have to ask nicely," Mavery added.

Sam looked at Leo, and the boy nodded in agreement.

"We'll need logs to make the raft," Leo said. "And something to lash them together."

Mavery clapped her hands. "I know the perfect spot." She swung her leg over the horse and looked down at them. "Well, are you coming or not?"

"Bossy much?" Keely said as she passed by.

Leo elbowed Sam. "Girls," he said knowingly.

Chapter Thirty-One

The foursome rode through the night, fighting exhaustion but determined to put distance between them and the tavern Leo had burned down. In the early-morning light, they skirted a village, sticking to the trees that bordered it. The fields around the village were brown with dust. Even the trees were showing spots of disease, losing their leaves and becoming bare.

From the shelter of the woods, they could see men and women crowded around the town center, shouting at someone dressed in a red robe. An Orkadian official of some sort. The sound of children crying punctured the air.

"Please, everyone calm down!" the official shouted. "We are searching the land for crops that have not been destroyed."

"Our children starve!" a man shouted, holding up a small child for him to see. "What are you doing to end this cursed sun?"

"The High Council is even now sending an emissary to Odin," he replied. Immediately the crowd quieted.

"A Son of Odin has returned to us. We must all place in him our hope that he will be victorious and return with a cure for the curse."

"The witches are a plague on the land!" another man shouted. "We should kill them all." There were loud shouts of approval at that.

Sam looked over at Mavery. She looked pale.

"Don't listen to them," Keely said. "It's going to be okay. You'll find a way to fix this."

Sam stared at the sunken faces of the children, swamped with guilt. "I should have listened to Rego and gone directly to Asgard."

"Then you wouldn't have the compass," Keely pointed out. "And you wouldn't have all of us to help you. Together we can figure this out, Sam. I know we can."

Leo added, "She's right, Sam. We are stronger together. We need to keep moving. The faster we get to Asgard, the faster you can stop this." He pointed at a distant set of hills. "We should head to high ground so we can see which direction to go. We'll be able to find cover in those trees."

They pushed on somberly, staying out of sight, with Leo in the lead. No one spoke. As they wound through the woods, a terrible odor reached them, carried by the afternoon breeze.

"What's that smell?" Mavery groaned, wrinkling her nose.

Leo stopped the group and sniffed the air. "It smells of death."

Sam dreaded what they would see when they crested the hill. They pushed on till they reached the top. He drew up his horse at the horrible sight before them. Black shapes littered the hillside below: cattle that had fallen over dead where they grazed. The earth was barren of life. Sam didn't need to look up at the grotesque face of the sun to know what had caused the herd to die. The poisonous effects of the solar curse were spreading.

He swallowed back fear, feeling his heart jerk erratically in his chest.

"Are we too late?" he choked out. "Are we next?"

"No. It's not going to come to that," Keely said firmly.

Behind her, Mavery wrapped her arms around Keely's waist. The little witch looked scared but didn't say anything.

Leo stared at Sam from atop his horse, his dark eyes showing nothing.

"Stop staring at me," Sam said gruffly. "I'm fine."

"You can't blame yourself," Leo said. "It's just who you are. I blamed my father for making me the son of a chief, but that's just the way it is. Your mother is a witch. You can't change that, only accept it and figure out what it means for you."

Leo was probably right, if your life was as simple as being the son of an Umatilla chief. Kicking his horse hard in the ribs, Sam rode ahead, feeling like he had been lashed with a whip.

Howie made a game out of keeping the *rathos* from biting him. He stocked up on his meager food supplies; moldy bread crusts were easy to pass up, and after having older brothers steal his food on a daily basis, Howie was used to skipping meals. One of the rats was larger than the others. It led the charge when the *rathos* swarmed. Its left ear was torn off, probably lost in a fight.

"Hey there. I'm calling you Bert," Howie said, tossing it a large piece of crust. The *rathos* looked surprised, sniffing it suspiciously, before picking it up and gnawing on it. Howie threw more bread crumbs until Bert was sated and scampered back out of the dungeon, taking the other *rathos* with him.

The next time one of the monster rats bit him, Howie gave the cold shoulder to the boss rat when he came sniffing around for food. "Suck it, Bert. Your boys bite me, you get nothing."

It took only a day before the big rat figured it out. After that, it attacked any of the vermin that wanted to gnaw on Howie.

"You're learning, Bert. Brains are better than brawn," Howie said, breaking off a large piece of crust from his meager dinner tray and feeding it to the salivating creature. "Find me a key out of here, and I'll personally deliver a pizza for you and your buddies. Stuffed crust, extra cheese, whatever you want."

The sound of clapping echoed in the hall outside his cell. "Well done," a girl said. She was slender and tall, her face pressed against the bars. "But what are you going to do when you run out of bread?"

Howie sat up, pushing his glasses in place to see better. A visitor was exciting. Especially one who didn't seem prepared to torture him. The *rathos* greedily pawed the air for another piece of bread.

"What do you care?" Howie said, playing it cool. He tossed the boss rat his last piece of bread.

"My mother's *rathos* are ravenous. One day you won't have enough and they'll eat you alive," she announced. "Unless you starve first."

Howie gestured to Bert that mealtime was over, and the big rat squeaked loudly, then led his army back to the hole from which they had come.

"Not much of me left to eat," Howie joked. "Who's your mother, anyway?"

"Endera Tarkana."

Howie couldn't help it—he snorted with laughter. But the young witch wasn't amused.

"Why is that funny?" she asked coldly.

Howie pushed up his glasses, remembering every evil thing Endera had done. "Because Endera's not just a witch; she's like the Godzilla of witches. Not only did she try to feed me to her pet spider, she turned my English teacher into a lizard and . . ." But before he could get the next sentence out, Howie realized he was alone. The girl, whoever she was, had left.

That night, Howie fell asleep with the image of Endera as a mother floating in his mind. He had a nightmare he was being chased by her children: a pack of *rathos* as large as buses. Howie ran for his life down the street as they chased him, their spiny whiskers bristling over bared teeth.

He awoke with a shout as his breakfast was noisily shoved through the slot in his dungeon door. At the end of his dream, one of Endera's children had finally caught him, dangling him in the air with one paw, about to drop him in its gaping mouth. He shook off the cobwebs, shuddering at the images that peppered his brain. He pulled the tray toward him, expecting the same thin gruel and moldy bread, but this time there was a hot scone and an extra-large serving of moldy bread. He bit into the scone, savoring its buttery sweetness, and found he was chewing on something that tasted like paper. He spit it out and looked at the scone. There was a note tucked inside. The corner was chewed, but the words were intact.

My mother is not a monster.

Howie smiled and shoved the entire scone into his mouth.

Chapter Thirty-Two

S am awoke in the morning to the sun rising over the horizon. The foursome had made camp the night before near a stream, in a small clearing away from any nearby farms. The sun sat low in the sky, like a bloodshot eye, mocking him with its red cast. More veins had sprouted, branching and twisting across its face. Sam turned away, running his hand through his hair. He felt gritty and dirty all over. He hadn't bathed in days.

The sound of rushing water reached his ears. Sam had a sudden desire to get clean, to wash away all the filth and grime. Leaving the others to sleep, he made his way down to the water. A bend in the stream had formed a swimming hole. It looked cool and inviting.

Sam slipped his shirt over his head, undid his pants, and set them on a rock, along with his boots and his father's pouch. Goose bumps rose up on his skin as he stepped to the edge, and, with a whoop, he ran and dove under.

The water did more than cleanse his body—the bracing cold cleared all the restless thoughts from his mind. He surfaced, swam out a few strokes, and floated on his back. For the first time since he had been blasted through a rock into Orkney, Sam enjoyed a moment of peace. The dawn sky looked purplish, the red and blue mixing to make streaks of lavender. The day was ahead of him. Anything seemed possible. He ran his hands back and forth across the surface, floating idly.

Something brushed against his leg, but he paid it no mind. *Probably just a fish*, he thought. If it was anything like the perch in Indian Lake back home, it would be nibbling at his toes next.

Suddenly, bony fingers grabbed Sam's ankle and jerked him down. He flailed, trying to stay afloat, but whatever it was had a firm grip and dragged him below the surface. Sam thrashed and kicked, precious air bubbling from his mouth and nose as he fought to get free.

Opening his eyes under the water, Sam saw several shadowy figures twining themselves around him.

Wraiths.

They trailed their skeletal fingers around his torso and leaned in to kiss him on the cheek with their ghastly lips.

He tried to swat them away, but they kept coming. And then a face emerged from the ghostly mob. His father, swimming straight at Sam. He looked pained, confused. His lips were moving. Sam strained to hear what he was saying.

"Why don't you come, Sam?" he said, looking anguished as he moved toward Sam. "Why? I've been waiting for you. Son, please. I need you."

Sam tried to reach him, kicking furiously at the bony hand holding his ankle. Here was proof at last: his father was really alive. He had to get to him. He kicked harder, reaching down to pry the fingers off. He freed his ankle and began to swim forward as fast as he could. He stretched his fingers out to his father's, but before he could touch him, his father's image dissipated in a cascade of ripples as someone dove in and disrupted the water.

Leo's arms wrapped around Sam's midsection, dragging him upward. Sam wanted to hear what his father was saying. He fought and twisted against Leo, but Leo was stronger and Sam was nearly out of breath.

As they broke the surface, Sam turned and swung his fist at Leo, landing a blow on his cheek. "Why did you do that?" Sam shouted.

"You were drowning!" Leo said, treading water and looking at him like Sam had lost his mind.

"My dad was there. He was talking to me."

Leo shook his head. "I didn't see anyone. You were alone."

Sam dove defiantly back down and searched. The pond was murky, but visibility was good. The wraiths were gone, along with his father. Sam floated a moment, feeling bereft. Then he surfaced and swam for shore, not waiting for Leo to follow.

Throwing on his clothes, Sam ran through the brush back to camp before Leo could catch up. *I saw my father*, he told himself. He was alive, as Emenor had said, and waiting for Sam to help him.

Back at the camp, Mavery and Keely were making breakfast: a roasted squirrel Leo had trapped the night before. Ignoring the girls, Sam threw his saddle on his horse. Leo came back, dripping wet, and spoke quietly to Keely. She nodded and then came over to where Sam stood.

"Leave me alone," he said, before she could speak.

"What's going on, Sam?"

"Nothing."

He focused on tightening the saddle cinch.

She put a hand on the saddle, staying him. "Leo says you took a swing at him?"

Sam stared straight ahead. "He surprised me, that's all."

"He was just trying to help you."

"Help me?" He turned to glare at her. "The wraiths showed me my father. He was speaking to me."

She looked at him with pity. "You don't know it was him. It could've been a trick."

"You weren't there. You don't know anything."

He tried to muscle past her onto the horse, but Keely held her ground. "Talk to me, Sam. You've been acting weird, even for you. You hardly talk to anyone or smile."

"Have you seen how people are starving because the sun is poisoning them? Not a good reason to smile, Keely. Have you forgotten I created that sun?"

His anger swelled, making him breathe heavily.

She paled but remained steady. "No, but Sam, you need to calm down. Please."

He looked over at Mavery and Leo. They stood by the fire, staring at him warily.

"Calm down? Did I mention my father is trapped in a stone and wants me to come help him but I don't know how?" He stepped closer to her. "Do you know how that feels?"

She stared back into his eyes, not flinching. "No one's blaming you."

He let out another bark of laughter. "Well, I do! My best friend is going to be eaten by a giant spider if I don't steal some horn from Odin. And even if I do, I could make things worse than the red sun already has. So maybe you're right—I should just lighten up."

Keely gripped his arm tightly. "I'm not the enemy, Sam. I'm here to help you."

"You wanna help me? Then leave me alone!" Ripping his arm loose, he put his foot in the stirrup, leaped on the back of his horse, and gave it a swift kick.

Sam had come a long way in his equestrian skills since that first day in Orkney. His rear was no longer sore from bouncing around all day. But not long after he rode out of sight, guilt began to prick at his conscience.

If he was honest with himself, Leo and Keely were just being good friends. And he had overreacted, as usual, to their efforts to help. He knew he should go back and apologize, but Sam was reluctant to face them, scared of what they must think. He pulled up his horse, wrestling with what to do.

"Hello, Samuel."

Vor's soft voice took him by surprise.

The Goddess of Wisdom stood next to his horse, her hand on its bridle, rubbing its nose. Her long blond hair fell over her shoulder. She wore the same gauzy gown of snowy material that flowed to her feet.

"Vor, I saw my father," he blurted out.

She turned her pale eyes toward him. "You saw what the wraiths wanted you to see. Be mindful of the path you are on, Son of Odin. I see great darkness before you."

"I'm trying. But I have to help my friend if I'm going to get this right. And my father. I can't just leave him in that stone."

"I cannot influence your decisions, Samuel, but think before you act. The darkness grows inside you. If you give in to it, there will be no deliverance."

Her image shimmered and then dissolved into a thousand white butterflies that fluttered away through the barren branches of the trees.

A girl's scream made Sam's horse rear up, nearly unseating him.

Keely, Sam realized.

The scream was followed by a snarling screech that echoed through the woods. He pulled hard on the reins and kicked the horse, forcing its head around and digging in with his heels.

Charging back down the trail toward camp, he ran head-on into a creature unlike anything he had ever seen.

Black as night, with wings that spanned the length of its body, it towered over Keely, stalking her on two legs. Its beak was lined with razor-sharp teeth that glistened with blood. It had a long, thin tail with a spike on the end that looked like it could impale him with one jab. It looked to Sam like a cross between a winged dragon and a giant raptor.

Leo shielded Keely and Mavery, an arrow notched in his bow. On the ground before them, a horse lay dead, its stomach ripped open.

Sam tore the pouch holding Odin's rock from around his neck and swung it around his head, driving his horse in front of the beast, cutting it off from his friends.

"*Demos mora dinfera*!" he shouted, feeling the ancient words come to him as his rage rose up. A few feet from the creature, he slid off the horse, which bolted away.

The beast slithered a forked tongue at him.

"*Demos mora gestera*," Sam said, calling it to stand down. He swung the rock harder above his head, trying to drive back the beast. The wind began to rise as Sam's pouch gained unnatural velocity and became a blur of motion like the eye of a tornado.

The beast tossed its head, unleashing another angry screech.

"Sam, watch out!" Mavery shouted, pointing upward.

Another winged creature dropped from the sky with a thud, landing next to its mate. They stalked the kids from both sides, their tails swishing and jabbing. Sam stood in front of his friends, still swinging the rock and relishing the tide of darkness rising up inside him.

A strange heartbeat echoed in his head, slightly out of sync with his own. Hungry thoughts of destruction flashed behind Sam's eyes.

Somehow these creatures were connected to him. He could feel their rage, their hunger, their call to join them. It was sickening and exhilarating all at once.

Blocking out the darkness, Sam closed his eyes and swung the pouch holding Odin's rock and then threw it down on the ground with all his might, shouting, "*Fein Kinter tentera demos morte!*"

As the rock hit the ground, the earth shook and split open, forming a wide crack that ran from his feet, across the clearing, to the beasts.

In tandem, they launched themselves at Sam. He swung his hands over his head, gathering the energy around him, and threw his palms forward at the beasts as he repeated, "*Tentera demos morte.*"

A bolt of green energy shot across the clearing singeing them in their chests. The creatures shrieked and pulled off, veering into the sky in tandem, before turning to dive-bomb again.

The other kids stood transfixed, staring helplessly as the battle unfolded.

Grimly, Sam stood his ground, swirling his hands around, using his powers to draw on the energy in the air. Like a living thing, it shimmered around him. For the first time, he felt in control of the magic tingling under his fingertips, waiting to be unleashed. Someone came to stand next to him.

Mavery.

He nodded at her as she started to follow his moves, saying the words with him. "Together, on my count!" he shouted.

The beasts descended, leading with their fierce talons. As they closed in, Sam began to count.

"Ready, set, go!"

Mavery and Sam stomped the ground and threw their hands forward at the same moment, their magic in sync. A ball of witch-fire exploded from their palms, a burst of light that incinerated the beasts this time, destroying them in an emerald blaze of crisping flesh.

There was a stillness in the clearing when it was over, and then Sam could swear Endera's laughter cackled at them through the leaves. He looked up at the sun. The throbbing veins had grown thicker, sprouting in new directions and clogging the light, leaving less than one-fourth of the sun's face clear.

His shoulders sagged. This should be a victory. But no matter what he did, Sam seemed to make things worse.

"That was amazing," Mavery said, looking at her palms in awe. "I've never used magic that powerful before."

Sam's legs had turned to jelly. He gave her a half smile and then sank down to the ground. Leo brought him his leather pouch and slipped it back over his head.

"Be careful, Sam," he said softly, his dark eyes concerned. "My father says magic will change you in ways you can't understand."

Sam knew he was right, but before he could answer, Keely rushed over.

"Nice work, hotshot." She knelt down next to him with a grin. "I kind of like having a powerful witch on our side."

Sam attempted a smile. That was the strongest magic he had used by far. He felt spent and exhausted. Within seconds, he fell into a deep sleep filled with dreams in which he was chased by a giant beast with gnashing teeth, trying to devour the world.

———◦(〇XXX〇)◦———

Endera sat in the nook of a tree, looking down at the unsuspecting children. "Why don't you come, Sam?" she repeated in a mocking voice to herself, laughing out loud as she recalled Sam's frantic fight to get to his father. The arrival of the Omera had been unexpected, but she had enjoyed seeing the boy use his magic in such a powerful way. He was teetering on a very dark edge. Soon, very soon, everything she had planned for would be delivered into her hands.

She wished she could follow the boy and his little band of rebels farther, but she had pressing business to attend to back at the Tarkana Fortress. The war between the hapless Orkadians and the army of witches she had assembled was about to begin.

Chapter Thirty-Three

By midafternoon, Sam awoke refreshed for the first time in days. Leo managed to get one of their horses back. Keely and Mavery climbed up onto the saddle, and Leo led the horse as they continued on their journey.

"Sorry about this morning," Sam said gruffly as he walked alongside. "I didn't mean to hit you; I just . . . something came over me. I can't explain it."

Leo kept his eyes on the trail. "You weren't yourself. It was the wraiths. Mavery told me about them." They walked on farther, before Leo added, "But these powers you have—the way you destroyed those creatures. You could easily kill me, or any of us, if you lost control."

Sam bristled at Leo's comments. He looked up at Keely. She didn't say anything, but he knew she had heard Leo. "What was I supposed to do? Let those things eat you guys?"

Leo slid him a glance and then went back to watching the trail. "I'm not saying you did the wrong thing, Sam. But I felt a difference in you when you were using your magic. Like you were someone else. Someone to be feared."

Sam wanted to argue, but the words didn't come, because Leo was right. Sam *was* changing. He craved magic like an itch that needed scratching, and the more he tried to ignore it, the stronger the urge to use it grew.

Fear gnawed at his guts. What if Leo was right and he lost control? He snuck a peek at the sun, shuddering at the strength it gave him. Leo didn't understand the burden Sam carried. They lapsed into silence as they wended their way along the trail. The trees began to thin out, and they emerged from the woods onto a bluff.

"There!" Mavery shouted, pointing. Below them, a blue inlet lay sheltered from the sea by a crescent-shaped bay.

The foursome made their way down the bluff. Hard ground gave way to white sand. The beach was littered with branches and logs that had washed up from storms. Keely and Mavery ran into the surf, getting wet up to their knees.

"Come on, Sam," Keely called. "It feels great."

Sam smiled but shook his head. After his run-in with the wraiths, the thought of going back into the water was unappealing, to say the least. Then, from behind, Leo tackled him and threw him over his shoulder, running into the ocean and dropping Sam into the water.

He came up sputtering and fuming. But seeing his friends splash around, chasing each other and playing in the surf, made Sam feel like a kid again. He surrendered and joined in, forgetting his cares for a few precious minutes.

Afterward, they built a fire from driftwood and dried their clothes. Leo was able to catch two small fish with a spear he fashioned out of a stick. Mavery gathered fresh greens while Keely wrapped the fish in some leaves and cooked them over the fire. Sam studied the compass, turning it in his hands, trying to get the needle to move. He polished it with his sleeve until the brass shone and the runic symbols were clearly visible under the glass. The symbols were as familiar as the words he spoke when he used magic. He recited them aloud, wondering at the knowledge he'd never known he had but no less able to make the compass turn on.

As the sun set, Sam leaned back on one elbow and watched Mavery do a little dance in the light of the fire. She stomped her feet and waved her hands, imitating their fight against the winged creatures.

"Those black-hearted beasts are known as the Omera," she said, pretending to fly like one. "They share a dark magic with the ancient witches. 'Course, only two powerful witches like me and Sam could defeat them." She blew a bubble of blue energy that floated over Keely's head. Inside the bubble, the battle replayed, showing the beasts exploding into black confetti. Even Leo laughed at Mavery's antics.

"So, what's the plan?" Keely asked, as the embers of their fire burned down. "How do we build a raft?"

"We can cut vines from the trees and use them to lash those together," Leo answered, pointing to the pile of logs that had washed up. "It won't hold up in a storm, but it should last a couple of days."

"How far is it?" Keely asked, turning to Sam.

He shook the compass lightly. The needle floated around, moving aimlessly in whatever direction he tilted it. He sighed in frustration. "I've tried everything. I don't know how it works."

"Give it to me," Mavery said, snatching it out of his hands. "Oh, mighty compass of Odin," she chanted, holding the compass in front of her, her eyes squinched shut, "take me across the seas to the island of the gods."

The compass needle fluttered. Sam sat forward, excited. The needle began to spin around and around, whirling one direction, then stopping to spin in the other, never settling in one spot.

"Great job, kid—you broke it," Sam said, snatching it back from her. The needle slowed and hung limply. Disgusted, Sam shoved it into his saddlebag.

Keely cleared her throat. "Look, Endera wants you to find Odin and bring back the Horn of Gjall, right?" Sam nodded, and so did Mavery and Leo. "So, the way I figure it, the compass will work when we need it to."

It wasn't much to stake on a perilous journey on.

"In the morning, we start the raft," Sam said firmly. "We should be finished by sunset, and we can sail at night, safe from the sun's rays."

———— (◦◦◦◦◦) ————

At the first sliver of light, they began work in earnest. By midday, they had a sizable raft assembled. To Sam's eye it appeared flimsy, but Leo seemed proud of it. It took another hour to knot enough vines to make the net Mavery had in mind.

While Keely and Leo filled up the waterskins, Sam lashed their meager supplies to the raft. They set the horse free and slapped its rear to send it home. The late-afternoon tide was going out when they pushed the raft into the water. Leo jumped on behind Keely.

Sam helped Mavery onboard, then hesitated. This was the point of no turning back. He looked back at the safety of the shore. If the compass didn't work, or if their raft collapsed in the waves, they would be done for, along with all of Orkney and maybe the rest of Planet Earth. Sam swallowed his fear, gave a hard push to launch the raft through the small waves, and climbed on. Leo had a long pole he used to navigate them through the surf. They broke over a wave and then dipped the paddles they had fashioned out of wide strips of bark.

Another wave crashed, nearly capsizing them.

"Maybe we should go back," Keely said anxiously.

"No, we keep going," Sam said grimly, digging in with his paddle. "Just hang on."

He and Leo battled through the waves, nearly getting washed off as the next set came down over them. There was a splitting sound, but the raft held together. After another few minutes of tense paddling, they were away from the current that pulled them back to shore.

Mavery stood up, put her fingers to her lips, and whistled. It was a lilting sound, trilling across the water. They waited. Nothing happened. She whistled again, and a tiny splash sounded behind them. Sam whirled around to see a shiny gray bottlenose break the surface, followed by the curve of a fin, then another.

A bolt of euphoria shot through him. It was working. The dolphins were heeding Mavery's call.

The witchling leaned over the edge and patted the dolphin on the head. It skittered back to her in its language and splashed the water. She laughed.

"Get ready," she said to Sam.

Leo and Sam lifted the net of vines they had knotted together. One end was tied to the front of the raft.

The sea churned as three, then four, then a large pod of dolphins broke the surface and backpedaled. They threw the net, and the dolphins grabbed it with their noses and dropped back and began to swim. The raft jerked forward, and they sat down in a state of awe to watch the dolphins.

Sam grinned and gave Leo a high five.

"Nice job," Keely said, ruffling Mavery's hair.

After a few minutes, Leo elbowed Sam. "See if the compass works now."

Sam pulled the brass object out of his bag. The needle spun crazily. Sam grasped it tightly, wishing with all his might that the compass would actually work. It stopped abruptly in one place, on a runic symbol shaped like an upside-down pitchfork.

"Hey, I think it's working! It looks like Asgard is that way." He held it out in front of him, pointing it at the red sun as it sank low on the horizon. Leo steered the raft with the rudder. As night set in, the large island of Garamond drifted from sight.

Keely lay back, resting her head on her hands to stare up at the stars. "I think it's cool you guys can do magic stuff. I mean, I wish I could talk to dolphins like that."

Mavery settled down next to her. "I might be able to teach you a coupla things, like how to whistle and make the dolphins come to you."

Keely looked at her with a smile, then went back to staring at the stars. "Cool."

Leo and Sam exchanged wry glances. Finally, the girls were getting along. It didn't take long for the pair to drift off to sleep.

Sam took the rudder from Leo. "Get some rest. We don't know how long it's going to take to find this place."

"No. I'll stay up and keep you company. I don't mind."

Sam put his hand on Leo's shoulder. "Look, you've been going at it for three days straight now. You rescued us from the inn, stopped me from drowning myself, and built this raft. I got this. That's an order," he added, as Leo hesitated.

A wide yawn creased Leo's face. "Okay, but only for an hour or so. Then you can rest."

Leo stretched out next to Keely, and in less than a minute, his breathing was evenly spaced as he slept. Sam took the moment to revel in a little excitement. The stars glittered brightly overhead, keeping him company. For once, the sun was out of sight, safely tucked away for the night. He checked the compass in the light of the moon, following the course the needle pointed to. They had to get to Odin to stop the sun, but the thought of saving his dad never left his mind.

He imagined the look on his dad's face when he caught sight of Sam, two years older and about four inches taller. Yet as he imagined their reunion, anger blossomed in Sam's heart. His resentment at having been left behind, having been lied to, lingered. Maybe he wasn't ready to just forget it and forgive his father. Sam shook his head, wishing away the bad thoughts.

As the night wore on, the stars faded and a cold fog settled over them. Sam's eyes grew so heavy, he couldn't focus. The rhythmic movement of the dolphins splashing through the waves lulled him into a deep sleep. He slept, one hand on the rudder, clutching the compass in the other.

Chapter Thirty-Four

S am had a dream so vivid he was sure it was real. He could see his father. Robert Barconian was smiling, his arm around Sam's mother. He looked dashing, dressed in the red, royal Orkadian uniform, while Abigail wore a long, white silk gown woven with lilies.

It was their wedding day. They were outside in a garden filled with people in their finest clothes. Sam heard a hissing sound and turned his head, expecting to see a snake. A black raven sat in the tree next to him, watching him with shiny green eyes.

His parents turned to each other and kissed; then his mother raised her bouquet and tossed it into the air. The raven launched from the tree and caught it in its beak, carrying it away from the outstretched hands of the ladies-in-waiting.

The raven morphed into Endera, dressed in a black dress of feathers, looking beautiful as she landed beside the newlyweds. Endera took Robert's chin in her hand, turned him away from Abigail, and kissed him. As she did, the bouquet dropped in slow motion and bounced on the ground.

Sam watched the flowers turn into rats that ran toward his mother, spreading like a black stain over her white gown and smothering her in darkness.

He awoke, biting back the scream on his lips as the raft

bumped up against a rock. They had reached land. The dolphins were gone; they had left the net behind. Fog shrouded the island, penetrated in a few spots by weak morning light. Sam sat up and scanned his surroundings, unable to make out more than the boulder in front of them.

Leo and the girls were sound asleep. Mavery was curled up in the crook of Keely's arm. Sam tried to shake Leo, but his friend didn't wake. Grabbing the pole to push them around the boulder, Sam let the tide carry them onto the beach, then dragged the raft as far up as he could. He jumped back on and shook Mavery. For once, the little witch was silent.

He turned to Keely, grabbing her shoulders.

"Hey, wake up, come on."

Her face was pale, her body limp. For a terrible moment, Sam thought she was dead. He pressed his head to her chest and felt for a heartbeat, sighing with relief when he heard it. He tried splashing water on her face, but even that didn't rouse her. He grabbed Leo, shaking him roughly.

"Come on, man, let's go exploring. I need someone to go with me."

Sam's heart pounded as he sat back on his knees. They were all in a deep sleep—bespelled by something.

He was on his own.

Looking around, Sam wrinkled his nose, taking in the smells. The fog covering the thick jungle that bordered the strip of sand made it impossible to see anything of the interior of the island. He stood up, flexing his fingers, trying to decide what to do. What if an Omera came by and attacked his friends while he was off searching for Odin? Or *rathos* swarmed out of the jungle and bit their sleeping bodies?

He wavered, wanting to stay, wanting desperately some company on his journey, then resigned himself to the fact that he would have to go it alone. He dragged downed palm fronds from the beach and covered up his friends, shielding them from the sun and any predators. It was the best he could do. Sam crossed to the edge of the dense tangle of trees. As he pushed aside the foliage and stepped forward, everything changed.

The fog wiped away, leaving the day bright and sunny. Turning back, he could see the gray screen of fog behind him. He put his hand through it, feeling the dampness. He turned again and faced the interior. The air was hot and humid and made his brow sweat. Insects buzzed in his ear, animals yipped, and strange birds darted through the foliage.

Dreading the red streaks, he looked up, but the sun was like a golden sunflower, bright and pristine, free of the red stain smothering Orkney. He stared at it until his eyes burned, drinking it in. He felt a crazy kind of hope. This must be Asgard. Home of Odin. Trees towered overhead like skyscrapers. Oversize plants with purple and orange flowers littered the floor.

Sam started walking, trusting his instincts to guide him. Streams of water ran through the jungle. He knelt beside one and scooped up a handful of water, then another, reveling in the fresh, cold drink. Pink fish swam in the shallows. The fish looked up at him curiously, hovering in a cluster to watch him seemingly without fear. He reached a hand in to touch one, and it swam into his palm, nestling there. Curious, Sam lifted it up out of the water. As he did, it changed into a frog and leaped out of his hand, disappearing into the bushes. He laughed. Life here was abundant, untouched by the poison killing everything in Orkney.

Walking on, Sam plucked what looked like juicy blackberries but tasted like nothing he had ever eaten before. They had a tangy sweetness that defied explanation and left him hungrier for more. The birds sang in the trees, and he began whistling with them. He faintly recognized the tune, some kind of melody that played in his head. Sam felt free of burdens, free of the load he had been carrying since he had traveled through that stonefire. He was happy.

A bird flew down to a low branch and chirped. Its chest was bright yellow, and its back was blue and orange. It shook out its feathers, preening in the sunlight. Its eyes met Sam's.

Touch me, it cheeped, or at least Sam thought he heard the words in his head.

He reached out a hand, and then he hesitated. Was the island really safe? Every place he had been to in Orkney had dangers. Sneevils. Biters. Why would Asgard be any different? Warning bells went off in his head. He looked around, seeing things differently. The bird let out another encouraging chirp, but underneath it, Sam heard malice. Tucking his hand into his shirtsleeve, he touched the bird through the fabric and felt a prick and a shooting pain in his hand.

The feathers were barbed. One had pierced his sleeve and hooked in his skin. The bird chirped again. This time it bared a row of spiny teeth and let out a vicious shriek before launching itself up into the sky.

Sam looked around, his fears realized. The beauty of the day seemed false, as easily ripped away as a paper covering.

A hissing sound revealed a poisonous snake coiled around that same branch where the bird had been. The harmless insects hovering over his head were now large biters, thirsting for his blood, waiting for the right moment to strike.

Sam looked down at the berries in his hand and saw they were rotting. He let them drop to the ground and sank to his knees.

Nothing was what it seemed in this place. He had let his senses get bewitched. Sam knew he had to stop thinking that what he was seeing was real. He touched the pouch that held his one connection to Odin.

"Odin," he said out loud, "It's me. Sam Baron. I need your help. Orkney needs your help. They sent me to ask you for a token, like this one." He opened the pouch and shook the stone out, holding it up. "Remember Hermodan? He got a stone like this from you. If you have another like that, I could sure use it."

The jungle grew quiet. The animals stopped calling to each other, as they also seemed to be waiting for an answer to the boy's request.

Sam sat back, closing his eyes and letting the pure, warm sunlight bathe his face. He clenched the shard of rock tightly in his fist, squeezing it with all his strength as he made his plea.

"Odin, please help me," he whispered.

When he opened his eyes, Sam was on a rocky plain. The jungle had vanished, as if it had been nothing more than a figment of his imagination.

He stood up slowly. Surrounding him now were jagged mountains. No trees, no sign of any living thing. A harsh wind began to blow, kicking coarse sand into his eyes. Carefully tucking the rock back in his pouch, he pulled up his shirt to cover his face from the blowing grit. *What now?* he wondered.

Shelter, his brain supplied, as grit began to dig into his skin. He started walking, blindly searching for an escape from the wind.

What felt like hours passed, and the terrain didn't change. After a while, the sandstorm mercifully died down. Visibility restored, Sam followed a narrow, rocky trail he found that led higher up the mountain to a low saddle between two peaks. He staggered the last few steps to the crest.

The mountains stretched as far as he could see. He spun around, searching for a destination, something to aim for, but every mountain appeared the same from his vantage point. The narrow trail he was following split into two, heading to the left peak or the right. *Eeny meeny*, Sam whispered to himself, then chose the trail on the right and soldiered on. He continued uphill for an eternity; then the trail ended abruptly at a blunt rock wall.

Sam checked for handholds or false doors, but it was a dead end. The wall was solid.

Ignoring the aches and pains in his feet, Sam retraced his steps to the saddle. This time, he headed up the other trail toward the other peak, moving as quickly as he could.

And found himself back at the same wall of rock.

Turning in a circle, he told himself he had to be mistaken. He had taken a different trail but ended up in the same place.

Tearing off a scrap of fabric from his shirt, he tied it to a fist-size stone and retraced his steps back to the fork and tried the other route. As he suspected, it led back to the same place. Sam picked up the rock with the fabric tied to it and weighed it in his hand.

"Somebody's got a warped sense of humor," Sam grumbled aloud, searching for any clues. He looked up at the rock face. It rose above him, impenetrable and foreboding. The thought that he was supposed to ignore the obvious crossed Sam's mind.

He stepped back several paces from the wall, shaking his hands out, and then ran at it full speed. His shoulder crashed into solid rock, and he landed on his backside, winded and bruised.

"This is getting really old," he snarled out loud.

Behind him, tittering, childish laughter rang out. Turning, Sam saw a small creature seated on a rock. Pale green fur covered its body. Its drooping ears were long, like a donkey's, and its large, almond-shaped eyes glittered with mirth. It sat double-jointed on its haunches, its knees reaching its ears, chewing on its own toenail.

"Where did you come from?" Sam asked. He had seen nothing else alive in this barren place on any of his trips down this trail.

"Where did you come from?" it responded cockily.

"I asked you first," Sam said, stepping closer.

"I asked you second," the creature retorted, "and two is greater than one."

Annoyed, Sam tried a stronger approach. "I am a Son of Odin. I command you to answer me."

The creature laughed so hard it fell off the rock. Tears streamed down its face, and it began to turn purple.

Sam grabbed the creature. "Answer my question," he demanded.

Still laughing, it fended off Sam with its arms, remaining just out of reach.

"Answer my question," it parroted, escaping to jump nimbly up onto the rock.

Sam dove at the creature. "Stop copying me!" he shouted, but he came up with only handfuls of air.

Sam whirled around. The creature had jumped to a rock behind him. *Through him.*

"How did you do that?" Sam asked.

Its lips pulled up into a wide grin, and it shrugged its crooked shoulders.

Sam was trying hard to control his anger, but it wasn't working. He had walked for hours without getting anywhere, and he was sure this little avocado-colored pest knew where he needed to go.

"Tell me what to do," Sam said, his voice rising.

The creature's face turned red, mimicking Sam's expression, and its eyebrows drew together. "Tell me what to dooo," it mocked.

"Stop it!" Sam shouted, blood pounding in his ears. "Tell me how to find Odin, or I'll shut you up for good."

At his words, the creature's face drooped and its purplish lips trembled. Tears began to roll down its cheeks, and its whole body shook.

Sam was taken aback. This was not the reaction he had been expecting.

The sad beast hopped down from the rock, scooted past Sam, and walked away down the trail, its hands dragging, shoulders slumped.

Sam felt like the worst sort of bully. "I'm sorry," he said, feeling the anger drain from him.

The creature kept dragging its pitiful self away.

"I said I'm sorry!" Sam shouted, desperate to be forgiven and not left alone in this desolate place.

The creature slowed, glancing back. "You are right, sir, to be angry," it said softly, sounding much more intelligent and mature than Sam had given it credit for. "I deserve no form of kindness."

Then it continued dragging itself down the trail.

Sam rolled his eyes and threw his hands up in the air. "Come on, just give me a second chance."

The creature stopped, squaring its shoulders back a little. "Second chance?" it said hesitantly. "I've never had a second chance. Banished I was, the first time I made a mistake."

"Banished? By who?"

They were communicating. *Okay. This is progress*, Sam thought.

The creature climbed onto a rock and sat back on its haunches. It lifted one foot and nibbled delicately on its toe. "You know who. The one you seek."

"Odin?"

Sam sat down on the ground before the creature, ignoring its disgusting habit of chewing on his toenails, eager to hear what other information it had. "You know where he is?"

The little fella's ears twitched, and it seemed to shrink down a size before answering. "Know, yes. Regrettably, I cannot take you there." Its words were bitter; then it went back to toe nibbling.

"My name is Sam. What's yours?"

"I am called Fetch. Pleased to meet you, Sam."

"Fetch? That's not a name."

"It is indeed, sir. His Superior High Being calls me by my name whenever he sees me. Fetch me my pipe. Fetch me a glass of mead. Fetch me my eyeglass."

"So you're Odin's servant?"

The creature bristled, its fur standing on end. It dropped its toe to glare at Sam. "I am much more than a lowly servant. The same way you are much more than a lost boy."

Sam leaned forward. "So help me find Odin. I must speak to him."

"Yes, you must. But you must find him on your own."

"How? I'm stuck on this mountain, and it's a dead end. Where do I go? Come on, Fetch, there has to be a reason you're here."

The creature snapped its fingers, as if it had just remembered something. "Yes. A reason. A message I was sent to deliver to you. That's why I'm here."

"Okay, so deliver it," Sam insisted, annoyed that Fetch had kept him waiting so long.

Fetch stood up straight, cleared his throat, and then repeated the words it had clearly memorized with great care. "Be warned, Samuel Barconian. The journey ahead is dangerous. You will be tested."

Sam waited, hoping for more words of wisdom from the great Odin. But when nothing else came out of Fetch, he got annoyed.

"Is that it?"

"There is more, but I must have your word you will not be angry with me again."

"Yes—I mean, no. I won't be mad, I promise," Sam sputtered, impatient to get the rest of Odin's message. "Just tell me everything."

"First, we must agree to part as friends," Fetch said, extending a spindly hand.

Sam didn't want to touch him. Something about the creature's furry flesh—that unnatural green color—reminded him of that barbed bird in the jungle. On the other hand, he figured Fetch would find his refusal rude, and he was the key to finding Odin. So, pushing past his unease, Sam slowly reached out and gripped the little paw.

An icy chill that reached to his bones ran through him.

"Remember, you promised . . . ," Fetch worriedly reminded him.

Those were the last words Sam heard.

The world began to spin dizzily as Fetch gripped his hand tightly now with two paws, its soulful eyes burning into the boy's. Sam tried to pull free, lifting the creature off the ground, but Fetch held firm, dangling in the air.

For Sam, the world spun faster, until everything around him blurred. All light and color receded into pinpricks as a black curtain completely engulfed him. Sam felt Fetch finally release his hand, and the boy fell backward, down into absolute darkness.

In free fall, Sam tried to grab at something, anything. But there was nothing solid, just the rushing of air as he dropped into a bottomless abyss.

Chapter Thirty-Five

S am lost track of time and direction as he tumbled head over heels in the dark void, picturing a landing that was bound to be fatal—or, worse, incredibly painful and crippling. He frantically reached out to stop his fall, but there was nothing, just infinite blackness and an icy current of air rushing past that chilled him to the bone.

"Hello?" he shouted. "Can anyone hear me?"

Hear you, hear you, hear you, came an echo that sounded like his own voice.

"Help me!" he yelled, flailing his arms as if they were wings that would slow his descent. If this was Odin's idea of testing him, it seemed the god wanted to see if he could fly.

Help you, help you, returned the echo. *Help you help me.*

"What do you want?" Sam shouted, feeling nauseated and dizzy from the interminable plunge. "Who are you?"

Who are you? Who are you?

Fingers of freezing air swirled around Sam, probing at him, feeling the lines of his face, as if the darkness were trying to familiarize itself with him.

"I'm Sam. Sam Baron."

The wind whipped harder, spinning him like a propeller, making each word he spoke a considerable effort to enunciate.

Who are you?

The echo was demanding an answer. Sam tried again.

"I am Sam Barconian, son of Robert Barconian . . . and Odin!" He had to shout to be heard above the roaring wind. "Also son of Abigail Tarkana . . . and Rubicus. I've got a witch's and a god's blood in me. Is that what you want to know?"

Sam wasn't sure if he was imagining, but the current of air felt warmer, and softer, as if it was slowing down.

"I need to find Odin so I can save Orkney. Please, help me!"

The rushing wind rapidly slowed, and then it was as if there were no air at all, and Sam was just floating, suspended in darkness.

His feet settled on something solid, and light began to fill the chamber from an unseen source. He was in a room with a desk and a single chair. Sam walked over to the desk and sat down. The walls were covered in stained, yellowed wallpaper. The desk was bare, except for a layer of dust and a single lamp. He pulled on the string and was surprised when the lamp turned on, even though there was no cord or electrical outlet.

Sam drummed his fingers impatiently on the desk.

"Okay, I'm here," he called out. "What now?"

No response. He rolled back the chair and saw a desk drawer he hadn't noticed at first. Sliding it open, he found a single sheet of paper and a fountain pen. Sam laid the paper on the desk and picked up the pen, searching for inspiration.

Was he supposed to write something?

"Dear Odin," he wrote, figuring it couldn't hurt. "Please help me end the cursed red sun."

That was stupid. Odin wasn't Santa Claus.

He crumpled up the paper and tossed it over his shoulder. He opened the drawer and magically found a new sheet of paper waiting.

Sam started again. "Dear Odin, please show me the way so I can help my friends and find my father."

Twice as stupid, Sam lamented.

He tore it in half and let it flutter to the ground. He got up and paced the room, checking to make sure there were no hidden exits. Sure enough, there was nothing more than what he saw: four walls, a desk, a chair, and a lamp with no cord. Not even a door.

"Great," Sam muttered.

Finding another fresh sheet in the drawer, Sam tapped the pen on the desk. This was worse than a pop quiz in English, when his mind usually went blank.

It occurred to him that maybe he wasn't looking for words. Maybe it was something else, something he could only visualize. Closing his eyes, Sam tried to clear his thoughts. It took a few moments, but an image of Leo floated up and hung there.

Sam saw himself punching Leo at the lake because his friend had stopped him from going with the wraiths. He remembered the rage he had felt, and he began to sketch, feeling a trancelike quality take over his hand, as if he were recalling a memory.

The picture that formed was of a young boy, a boy like Leo, around ten years old, with long black hair, walking down a trail. Sam made a crude drawing of a moon and stars, so it must have been dark. The boy Leo was smiling as he walked, happy and safe. Sam hesitated and the pen wavered, and then it flowed, and he drew a creature, a black, shaggy wolf, lurking in the bushes.

A Shun Kara.

And Leo was walking right toward it.

Suddenly scared, Sam took the pen and threw it against the wall, but as it hit, it exploded in black ink. Then the room tilted sideways, awash in blackness, and he found himself on earthen ground, rocks pressing into his back as he stared up into the cold night sky of Pilot Rock. Familiar stars winked down at Sam, and he could see the outline of the red rock against the sky.

A low growl snapped Sam to attention. Rolling over, he looked through the bushes. A flashlight bounced along the trail.

He could make out the faint image of a boy holding it. It looked just like the young Leo in his drawing.

Is this a dream? Sam wondered. *Or some kind of memory?*

Across the trail, Sam could smell the scent of the Shun Kara as it lay in wait for an unsuspecting Leo. Sam's heart raced. Whatever this was, the moment felt real, and in his heart he knew if he didn't do something, young Leo was going to die.

Leo's steps drew inexorably closer. The Shun Kara let out another growl, louder this time, and Leo heard it. He stopped in the center of the trail, waving his flashlight at the bushes.

"Is somebody there?" he said.

The wolf growled again and stepped out onto the path in front of Leo, a foot taller and a hundred pounds heavier than its young prey.

Leo should have screamed and run, but he faced the wolf, holding the light in front of him, and dropped into a fighting stance.

"I am not afraid, Shun Kara. I am a warrior of the Umatilla," he said bravely.

The wolf howled once and drew back on its haunches. Sam knew it was about to pounce on his friend. He had to do something. He had no weapons, nothing to help him at all, so he sprang from the bushes into the path in front of the Shun Kara as it leaped, tumbling with the creature into the cactus.

The Shun Kara snarled in rage. The beast's feral scent overwhelmed Sam's senses; its rotten breath made him gag. He held on to it tightly, wrapping his arms around the predator and tried to get hold of its neck. Its fur was so thick, it was hard to find a choke point, but Sam's thumbs dug in as its teeth sank into his shoulder, sending blinding pain through him.

Leo stared at the boy and the wolf in shock.

"Run!" Sam shouted at him. "Get away from here!"

Typical Leo—he didn't listen. Instead, he ran straight at them, trying to kick the Shun Kara off Sam. The wolf released

Sam and bit down on Leo's arm, twisting it as it tried to drag him away into the bushes.

Leo let out a scream of pain, and rage boiled up inside Sam. His friend was not going to die because Sam was weak.

Fighting past the pain from the deep wound in his shoulder, Sam staggered to his feet. Holding one hand in front of him, he shouted, "*Fein kinter deomora, Shun Kara spera, spera nae mora.*"

The wolf dropped the boy, glaring at Sam with its emerald-green eyes. It took two wary steps toward Sam, its sinewy shoulders bunched to leap again.

Sam held his ground and drew his hands together, trying to summon whatever magic he could, though the pain in his shoulder left him light-headed and weak.

"*Deomora, Shun Kara!*" he shouted. "Come get me, you ugly mutt. I'm right here."

The wolf leaped at him as Sam shot his hand out and released the sphere of energy he had gathered in his palm. The Shun Kara yelped in pain as the witchfire burned its chest, but it landed on Sam, knocking them both backward onto the ground. Razor-sharp teeth descended onto Sam's neck.

Sam hadn't stopped the attack at all, and now he was the prey.

Bobbing lights rushed into the dark clearing. Voices called out for Leo.

A floating numbness cushioned Sam as the night sky faded to black.

Chapter Thirty-Six

The sun beat down on Keely's face, waking her from a fitful slumber. She opened her eyes, grimacing from the brightness. She was on a beach, lying in the sand, inexplicably covered with palm fronds. She brushed them off and sat up. Next to her, Mavery snored loudly. There was no sign of Leo or Sam. How long had she been asleep? It could have been days, for all she knew. Keely brushed off the sand and stood stretching her arms.

"Mavery, wake up," she said, shaking the girl.

"Leave me alone," she grumbled, rolling over on her side.

Keely shook her again. "Get up. We're here."

Mavery sat up, her hair standing on end, and looked around in awe. "We're here? On Asgard? Why didn't you say so?" She jumped up with instant excitement. "Let's go exploring. Where's Sam? Where's Leo? Come on." She grabbed Keely's hand and dragged her forward. "What are you waiting for?"

Keely laughed, holding her back. "Stop. I don't know where they are. We should be careful. Who knows what's out there?"

Mavery pulled harder. "Nah, there's nothing dangerous on Asgard."

As if on cue, a screeching roar creased the air like fingernails on a chalkboard. The girls saw a black arrow streak across the distant sky.

"Nothing dangerous, huh?" Keely remarked pointedly.

"It's a long way away," Mavery said, unconcerned. "I want to see Odin. You coming or not?" She stood at the edge of the tree-lined border. A rim of fog clung to the interior, blocking the view of what lay beyond. Mavery held back a big branch that offered a glimpse of the island's enchanting interior.

"Don't be so bossy," Keely snapped. "I'm the oldest right now, so I'm in charge. We need to find the boys first and make a plan."

"What we really need to find is food. I'm starving. And I'll bet there's some in here. . . ."

Mavery disappeared into the gap in the branches. Keely let out an exasperated groan, certain this was a bad idea, then followed.

Pushing through the leafy border, Keely walked into a different world. The ocean sounds faded away, and they were in a humid jungle. Birds squawked, and strange animals let out howling calls. Mavery was just ahead.

"Maybe we should go back and wait on the beach," Keely said.

"Are you crazy? We may never get a chance to come back here. I'm exploring," Mavery said, marching off through the jungle.

Keely followed reluctantly. Bright flowers sprouted from the lush plants that choked the forest floor. Tall trees blocked out the light, their branches strung with moss. Then she looked up and gasped in shock. The sun that shone through the leaves was a bright yellow, free from the stain.

"Mavery, do you see that? I think Sam broke the curse," she said, hurrying to keep up with Mavery.

"I don't know. Maybe. I hope so," Mavery answered distractedly, hopping over a stream. She stopped in front of a tree with thorny branches bare of leaves. The limbs were yellowish green, and the thorns looked sharp enough to poke through steel.

A songbird landed on the lower branch and let out a sweet trill, bringing Mavery to a halt.

"Pretty bird," she cooed, lifting her hand to pet the bird's chest. Upon touching it, she let out a squeal of pain, yanking her hand back, howling. "Ow, ow, ow!"

Keely lifted the girl's hand and saw a large welt. "What the—"

The songbird growled, revealing tiny, sharp teeth in its beak.

"Get away," Keely shouted, waving her hands to shoo it off.

"*Brunin*," the bird hissed.

After everything that had transpired since she had passed through the stonefire, Keely shouldn't have been surprised by talking birds, but this one rendered her speechless.

Mavery was not intimidated. "Listen, you, we don't mean any harm, so just get out of our way."

The bird flapped its wings, baring its fangs again. "*Brunin*," it repeated.

"Brunin? Why do you keep saying that?" Keely asked.

In the distance behind Keely, a tree crashed to the ground, shaking the earth.

Keely jumped. "What was that?"

"It was just a tree falling," Mavery informed her, still glaring at the bird.

"Why does that not feel like a coincidence to me?"

The bird flew angrily into Keely's face, crying, "*Brunin*!" before it took flight, zigzagging between the tree branches.

Another tree fell down, this one much closer to the girls. Then another, as if something approaching was mowing them down.

Keely and Mavery instinctively moved closer together, holding hands. Even the little witch was scared now.

"Shouldn't we run?" Mavery asked.

"Run where?" Keely said, scanning the area. Suddenly, nothing looked familiar.

The next falling tree was so close, the girls felt the rush of wind as it toppled to the ground. Keely made a decision. "You're right. We're running." Hand in hand, the girls started to sprint, ducking into the brush away from the falling trees.

After a few moments, Keely slowed, listening. The falling trees had stopped. For a moment, she thought they were safe. But then a hulking shadow loomed over them.

Both girls turned slowly to confront their pursuer.

Brunin was a bear. Not an ordinary bear, but a giant one, at least two stories tall. Standing upright on its hind legs and dressed in leather armor, the beast let out a terrifying roar. It clutched a round wooden shield in one paw and a broadsword in the other. Its stout head was encased in a helmet of metal and leather. One eye was adorned with a black silken patch.

"Who dares enter my forest?" Brunin bellowed.

"I-I am Keely; this is Mavery. We're looking for our friends," Keely said, her voice quivering.

The bear plunged his enormous sword into the ground, spraying the girls with dirt. "There are more trespassers? I will skin you all alive!"

Behind the bear, a pair of ravens circled the sky, cawing what sounded like a warning.

"We didn't mean to trespass, I swear," Keely said, but the words had hardly left her mouth when Brunin howled in pain. An arrow pierced its cheek, sending the beast into a frenzy as it pawed at the shaft.

Leo stepped from the bushes, notching another arrow in his bow. "Stay back, Keely."

"Leo, don't," Keely warned, but Leo unleashed the arrow. The bear moved fast; in a blur of motion, it spun and held the shield in front of it so the second arrow landed squarely in the center of the wood. Then it raised its paw and threw the sword it held, sending it spinning across the clearing at Leo. The boy dropped adroitly to the ground, and the blade embedded in the tree behind him, wobbling back and forth.

The enraged bear swiped its mighty paw at Keely and scooped her up, dangling her between two claws.

"Put her down!" Mavery shouted. She quickly rubbed her palms together and sent out a weak blast of green fire. The sizzling bolt hit Brunin in the knee, but the beast didn't flinch. Instead, it swiped its other paw across the clearing and scooped up Mavery.

Keely tried to pry apart the bear's claws, but its grip was unyielding. She desperately searched the area for Leo but saw no sign of the boy.

"Leo, help!" she shouted.

The bear grunted as it turned around in search of its attacker. But the beast was focused on the ground, so it didn't see that Leo had climbed a tree and was now eye level with his target. Leo waited for the perfect moment, balanced upon a branch, and then jumped out, grabbing hold of the bear's armor and pulling himself up to its shoulder.

The bear stumbled back, startled by the boy's bold assault. One of the crows dive-bombed Leo, trying to knock the boy off. But Leo batted the crow away and jumped onto the bear's cheek, gripping its fur with his hand and drawing a knife with the other.

"Put them down, or lose the other eye," Leo said.

The bear held the two girls as the pair of crows circled and cawed angrily. After a tense moment, the beast let out a chuffing noise of humor, as if it found them entertaining, then released Keely. She dropped to the thick grass with a thump, followed by Mavery.

Leo jumped down and helped Keely up. "Are you all right?" he asked, eying her for any sign of injury.

"I'm fine," Keely said, her fear wiped away by Leo's dashing bravery.

Mavery didn't wait for a hand up. She walked over and kicked the bear in the shins. "I wanna see Odin. Take me to him, or I'm gonna tell him you were a meanie."

The giant bear sat down, laughing harder. It scooped up Mavery again in its paw, holding her up to its nose. It bared a row of fangs at her, but the little girl was not intimidated. She leaned forward, putting her hands on his black nose, ignoring the sharp teeth.

"I know who you are," Mavery said. "You're—"

"Shh, child." Brunin held one claw up to his mouth, silencing her. "What is it you wish from Odin?" the bear asked Keely, setting Mavery down gently.

"We're looking for our other friend," Keely said.

"His name's Sam," Leo added. "He needs our help."

"Your Sam is perfectly safe," Brunin said. "For today. But the day will come when he will need strong allies."

Keely looked at Leo, then back at the bear. "I'm strong," she said confidently. "I won't turn my back on him."

"You must learn more about this world before you are ready," the bear chided gently. "And you, young warrior. Will you fight for your friend?"

Leo held up his bow. "I am a warrior of the Umatilla. I am not afraid."

"Both so brave," Brunin said, scratching his chest with a thick row of claws. "But the day will come when he is not himself. Will you stand beside him then, when he needs you most?" The bear seemed lost in thought. The two crows landed on his shoulders. One whispered in his ear.

"Quite right, Hunin," the bear murmured. The crow let out a loud caw, and Keely felt a sudden grief as she glimpsed a future so bleak it sent a chill through her.

Sam in pain, Sam torn in two. Taken from them. The images were like camera flashes, bright pops that briefly illuminated the darkness that awaited.

She stepped closer to the bear. "I get it, it's going to be hard, but Sam is our friend, and we'll do whatever it takes to help him." Mavery nodded emphatically at her side.

Brunin seemed pleased. He levered himself to his feet, stretching his arms wide and letting out a loud growl. "Then it shall be as it shall be. Return to the beach before you lose your way. This island can be treacherous for the uninvited."

The three kids watched the bear turn away and begin to walk on two legs, then lope on all four, crashing through the trees and disappearing from sight.

Mavery was already heading back to the beach.

"I thought you wanted to explore," Keely said. "Meet Odin and all that?"

Mavery kept walking. "We just did," she called out.

Chapter Thirty-Seven

When Sam opened his eyes, it was daylight. He was no longer in the wasteland around Pilot Rock. He was now reclining on a bed of moss next to a babbling brook.

Sam touched his neck, expecting to find a gaping wound where the Shun Kara had bitten him. Instead, the skin was tender but otherwise fine. But Sam knew it had been real, that the twisted scar on Leo's arm had been a result of that night. It didn't make sense—there was no way Sam could have been there two years ago—but nonetheless, he believed it had happened. And Leo must have known and kept it to himself. His friend had some explaining to do.

Feeling parched and sapped of energy, Sam drank heartily from the stream and washed his face. He wanted to rest, but he knew that sitting here wasn't getting him any closer to his goal of finding Odin. Maybe the Yggdrasil tree was in this ancient forest.

A woman's scream came from Sam's left. His heart lurched. The voice was familiar—it sounded like his mother's. Was this another of Odin's tests?

At the mere thought of Abigail, a wave of longing washed

over Sam. He missed her so much. He began running toward the sound, alarmed that she might be in danger. He jumped over a log, slid down a mossy bank, and tumbled into a wide clearing. He stood up and tried to see her.

A wave of waist-high grass undulated like a bright curtain as far as he could see, shifting in the gentle breeze.

"Samuel, come here." Her voice floated across the grass, carried by the wind.

Definitely his mother. And she sounded excited.

"I'm coming!" he shouted, wading forward through the grass.

"Samuel, I'm over here. Come on, you have to see this."

"Mom, wait for me!"

The sharp blades of grass nicked his skin as he hurried forward, making him wince.

Where was she? Why couldn't he see her?

Sam made it to the middle of the wide field. There was no sign of anything but rippling green waves. No trees, no rocks, nothing.

"Mom!" he called. "Where are you?"

"Over here," came the reply.

He headed in the direction of her voice, running as fast as he could.

"Where?" He was sweating and agitated. "I can't find you!"

"Can't you see me, Samuel?"

Sam wasn't getting anywhere. *This can't be real*, he reasoned. Putting his hands over his ears, he tried to block her out, but he kept hearing her calling to him, and he couldn't help himself from continuing his search.

"Please! I can't take this anymore!"

Pushing forward, fighting back tears, Sam searched frantically for her. His shins were raw from slapping at the thick blades of grass. He ran and ran, chasing the voice that was just out of reach, until he could run no more. He came to a stop, breathless and spent.

Sam looked around and once again couldn't see anything but

waves of grass spreading in every direction. He had to face the facts—this was just another of Odin's magical manipulations. His mother wasn't here in Asgard.

"I'm right here."

And just when Sam had nearly given up all hope of finding his mother, he looked up and saw Abigail standing in front of him in a yellow dress, her dark hair falling around her shoulders. White flowers were woven into a crown around her temple, and the sun cast a golden halo around her.

"Mom?" Sam stepped forward incredulously, reaching a hand out to touch her. She felt warm—she felt whole and real. Still, he hesitated. "Is it really you?"

"Of course it's me, silly. Who else would it be?"

It seemed too good to be true, but at the moment, Sam was so overjoyed, he refused to believe it was another one of the island's traps.

Taking her son's hand, Abigail drew Sam forward. "Come with me. I have so much to show you."

He followed her through the grass until they came to a clearing with drooping willow trees and floating insects that danced around her head. She laughed and held out her finger. A fat purple insect landed softly.

"How did you get here?"

His mother just looked down and smiled at him. She looked beautiful, radiant, and happy—as if this was where she belonged, and he belonged here with her. But something wasn't right. A feeling of unease tickled the back of Sam's neck.

"What's wrong?" she asked, setting the insect free to flutter around her head.

"It doesn't make any sense. You shouldn't be here."

"Of course I should," she replied. "I belong with my son. That's how it should be."

Sam stared at her, hoping and wishing with all his being that this was real. He was about to tell her the incredible news that Robert was still alive, when a terrible screech interrupted their reunion. The heavy sound of flapping wings rustled the leaves in the trees. Sam turned to scan the area, sensing danger.

"Mom, you need to leave right now."

Sam pushed her away from him, but it was too late. A black, winged beast—an Omera, Mavery had called it—dropped out of the sky. It dug its claws into his mother, picking her up and launching itself away.

"Mom!" he cried, running after them, reaching futilely for her dangling feet.

The beast flapped its wings and dragged her higher into the sky.

Sam's heart felt like it had been ripped out of his chest. He couldn't bear losing her—he couldn't. Not now.

Anything but this.

"No!" he shouted at the sky. "Take me instead!" But he was pleading with an empty field.

Then, behind him, a second beast landed with an earthshaking thud. Sam turned as it arched its wings high, hissing as it prepared to charge. Sam didn't hesitate as it launched itself at him, claws extended—he ducked and rolled under the creature and grabbed its tail as it passed over, twisting it to the ground.

It sprang back up, pulling free of his grip, and paced around in a circle, its spiked tail arching high in the air as it hissed at Sam. He dodged a jab from its tail and rolled back on his feet. He was desperate to retrieve his mother, but he had no weapons, only his instincts and reflexes.

That's when Sam remembered he had magic. He was not just a Son of Odin; he was also a Son of Rubicus. In that moment, Sam knew exactly how to get his mom back: he must fly like that black demon that had snatched her.

Sam positioned himself in front of the hissing creature and

shook out his hands, preparing to cast what would be his greatest spell.

"*Fein kinter*," he whispered, searching deep inside him for the ancient words he needed. He had to let himself go completely to tap into this kind of black magic.

"*Fein kinter, tempera similus, tempera morpheus, tempera transfera*," Sam called out as words flooded his brain, and a tingle raced to his fingertips as he called on ancient Tarkana magic.

The creature before him reared back with a hiss, as if it recognized the threat in his words, then launched at him.

At that very same moment, a powerful force compelled Sam to dive headlong at the winged demon. The boy and the beast met in a thunderous midair collision. Sam's hands hit its scaly skin and passed right through as the black-magic spell took hold and made it possible for him to meld with the creature.

Sam felt a burning sensation as his own body dissolved into the Omera's, mixing his essence with the liquid evil, the primal blackness, of the creature. It fought him for control, but Sam kept the upper hand with a higher awareness and greater power, refusing to let the Omera be in the driver's seat. He felt the presence of arms and stretched out his new wings. Where he had once had feet, there were now talons.

Taking in a deep breath, Sam let out a mighty roar, arching his wings at the sun.

He was demon. He was winged. And he was going to kill anything that stopped him from saving his mother.

Chapter Thirty-Eight

S am felt invincible. Power coursed through his veins as he launched the hijacked demon into the sky. He felt the creature's feelings and sensations: its hunger, its desires, its malevolent heart. Furiously beating his wings, Sam flew faster and faster. He was determined to find his mother at any cost. Movement below on the ground caught his sharp vision. Was that she?

He flew lower and spied a small animal, a meek rabbit, nibbling on the grass. He hesitated, gripped by a primal need to feed. He flew on, clinging desperately to his mission, and then the need overtook him. In an instant he changed course and dove straight down, the wind rushing past his beak as he extended his claws.

The rabbit had no idea of the danger it was in. Sam tucked in his new wings and let his body fall like a rocket. At the last second, he unfurled his wings, pulling up and stretching his claws out. Remorse hit him as his talons wrapped around the warm body of the rabbit. What was he doing? He was supposed to be looking for his mother, not hunting rabbits, but the smell of fresh blood made his nostrils flare with hunger. Before he could stop himself, he tossed the rabbit in the air and swallowed it down his gullet.

A thrill of pleasure ran through him. A few rabbits wouldn't hurt. He needed to stay strong. Sam took to the air, scouring the land from the skies, searching for more prey. He spied a herd of deer moving through the trees. A thrill of excitement raced through him as he hunted a buck. It ran swiftly, dodging side to side. Sam flew after it, flying hard to stay on its tail, tilting left and right to avoid branches. Tiring, the buck pulled up and tried to gore him with its pointed antlers, but Sam swung his spiked tail around and knocked the buck to the ground. With a triumphant dive, Sam pounced on his prey.

After he had fed, he made a lazy circle in the sky, sated and full. With the sun on his back, the power coursing through his veins, he felt cunning and capable, as if he had landed in his own skin and this was who he was meant to be—this black-skinned demon with teeth that could rip flesh from bone.

The sun rose and set. He hunted again, gaining skills and cunning. Somewhere along the way, in the midst of hunting and feeding, Sam forgot what he was looking for, who he had been before. He forgot his own name.

He had a new name.

Omera.

Top of the food chain. Nothing in Orkney dared challenge the fearsome power of his bone-crushing jaws and deadly talons.

The creature flew a lazy spiral in the sky, feeling the rays of the sun warm his wings. As Omera, he was king of the sky and all he surveyed. Yet an unquenchable desire gnawed at him, something bigger than his hunger.

Someone, he realized. Someone who mattered to Omera.

He couldn't recall the name, but he saw a face, pale and insignificant but persistent, pricking at him so much that he grew irritated and restless. He tried to hunt a rabbit, but it evaded him, and that made Omera even more annoyed. Ravenous and in a rage, he raced through the forest, intent on satisfying his desire.

The air carried a faint scent, a scent he recognized somewhere in the recesses of his brain. He turned and flew silently through the trees and landed in front of a wretched green crea-ture. It had big, terrified eyes and long, drooping ears.

Pathetic, thought Omera.

One snap of his jaws, and this thing would be breakfast.

The little creature clasped its hands in front of itself, plead-ing, "Please, great Omera, do not eat me. My pitiful bones will surely stick in your throat and cause you distress."

Omera growled at his prey, circling it, enjoying the way it trembled when he roared.

"I am on my way to His Supreme Being," it continued, turn-ing to keep its eyes fixed on the winged demon that stalked him, "to ask my master if Fetch can have a second chance. Have you, sir, ever needed a second chance?"

Wanting to pounce, to taste his furry green flesh, Omera found the words made him curiously hesitant. They sounded vaguely familiar.

Fetch took a cautious half step forward, reaching one small hand toward the winged beast. "You, sir, seem to have lost your way. Fetch can help you. Just, please, don't eat me." It took another step, hand trembling now, as it tentatively stroked the rough, pebbled skin of Omera's cold nose. "You have friends, sir. Remember?"

As Fetch's hand touched the creature's skin, a wave of long-ing washed over Omera. Friends? Omera had no friends. But Sam did.

Sam, the creature remembered.

The name coursed through him with a longing and a sadness so strong, he shrieked with a sudden rage that made the leaves on the trees overhead shudder on their stems. Fetch shrank back.

"Please, sir—Fetch can help you find what you're looking for."

Blind with rage and pain, Sam pounced on the little pest, determined to swallow it in one bite and end its wretched chat-tering. With one taloned claw on Fetch's chest, Omera opened his jaws to devour his prey, when their eyes met, and for a brief moment, Omera saw something powerful in this pitiful creature, something hidden from sight. A fire within, as if it were testing him, waiting to see what he would do. This made Omera pause, and in that pause, a calmness settled over him.

This Fetch is right, the creature realized.

Omera needed help finding what he was looking for. He controlled his rage, holding back a snarl as the little green creature hopped onto his back, grabbing hold of the spikes behind his ears.

Fetch guided him with his knees, sending Omera toward the distant mountain range that bordered the forest. Omera flew higher and higher, suppressing his hunger, letting a higher purpose drive him forward.

As they approached a jagged peak topped by a thin rim of snow, an aerie came into view. Omera landed on the ledge, seeing an unattended nest and eggs at the same time as he saw a human female.

Her arms were pinned in place against the rocky wall with some kind of mud paste that held her captive. Three eggs the size of ottomans were in the throes of hatching. The woman was to be dinner—a ready-to-eat meal so the new hatchlings could feed.

Omera's ravenous appetite surged inside him. He could get to the human first and feast. The woman looked weak, desperate, and filthy. Blood streaked her face; her yellow dress was torn and dirty.

This is wrong, Omera felt.

But the hunger pangs overrode that thought. The woman was a meal. Nothing more.

Omera launched himself forward. One of the three hatchlings was already poking its small black head out, desperately snapping at the air, seeking food. As Omera closed in on its human meal, the hatchlings' mother, a female Omera, zoomed out of nowhere, nearly causing an aerial collision of winged creatures. Fetch shrieked in surprise, nearly falling off.

The female Omera had shorter, sleeker wings, but she quickly proved herself more agile than the male invader.

Omera ducked and jabbed at the female with his tail spike, landing a satisfying blow to her chest.

"*Traitor!*" she screeched in their shared language, then spun adroitly and whipped her tail around, ripping a tear in Omera's left wing and sending him off course, toward the nest.

The three hatchlings were nearly out of their eggs now, and they were ravenous, nipping with sharp teeth at the invader's legs and wings.

Omera reversed course to avoid the hatchlings, sending Fetch sliding off his back and into the snapping mouth of one of the chicks.

Fetch's pitiful cry tugged at Omera as the chicks' vigilant mother swooped in again. With another swing of his formidable tail spike, Omera sent the winged female spinning away.

But now, the human woman screamed as another hatchling broke from its egg and lurched toward her on wobbly legs, beak outstretched.

Confusion careened through Omera.

Too many conflicting desires. Eat. Save. Destroy.

Eat, he resolved.

He roared deep from his chest and trampled over the hatchlings to reach the woman first, using his talon to tear her from the mud encasement.

Omera drew his prey nearer, preparing to rend her human flesh with his razor-edged beak, as he had done so many times. But when he looked down into her face, his beak an inch from her, she whispered a name.

"Sam."

Omera stopped.

Sam.

Why did that name matter?

Shaking himself, Sam felt his grip over Omera breaking apart. He had to choose—human or demon—but he was torn. Indecision pulled him in every direction. His wings shuddered as his hold over the creature splintered, and he faltered, feeling it slip away. And then Sam was expelled from the winged demon.

The boy lay on the ground, coughing and gagging, as the feeling of being inside the Omera faded, and he came back to the present, to the aerie. There were two black-winged creatures—male and female—stalking around the nest, their wings flared for combat and beaks bared, exposing rows of sharp teeth.

All three hatchlings were now out of their shells, crying hungrily. One of them had Fetch in its toothless maw, trying to swallow him as Fetch tried vigorously to squirm away.

Sam's mother knelt by her son's side, running a soft hand over his forehead.

"What happened?" Sam asked groggily. "Is this real?"

"Get up, Sam. We need to fight."

The two adult Omeras had stopped fighting each other and now circled the humans, ready to pounce. Abigail lifted Sam, and they stood back to back. Inspired by the warmth of her body, Sam regained his focus.

"*Sepera tantriona,*" she said. As she spoke the words, Sam felt the force of her magic. A powerful tingling swept over him as she unleashed her spell, energizing him and making his blood surge. He repeated her words, copying her magic as best he could but feeling like a novice.

The pair of Omeras leaped at mother and son as they chanted in unison and drew their hands over their heads, pulling the energy from around them and then thrusting their glowing hands forward to unleash the coiled magic.

Blasts of blue-and-green light erupted from their palms, singeing the wings of the Omeras and causing them to scream in pain as they were pushed backward and cast over the edge of the cliff, spinning into space.

Abigail turned to the hatchlings and, with a thrust of her palms, swept two of the chicks after the adults, their useless wings flapping helplessly.

Fetch and the last demon hatchling were still battling. One of Fetch's legs was already down its gullet, and Fetch was keeping its jaws pried open with his spindly fingers. Sam gave the chick a kick in the belly. It choked and spat out Fetch; then Sam used his mother's spell to thrust it over the edge.

Fetch sat dazed, covered in spit but alive.

They were safe for the moment, but they all knew the Omeras would be back when they recovered from the attack. Sam ran to his mom and hugged her. It was like the best kind of homecoming when she wrapped her arms around him, squeezing him tight.

"I was one of those things. I was inside it—I almost killed you," he confessed.

"But you didn't."

"I wanted to. I didn't even recognize you. What kind of person does that?"

She put her hand on his cheek. "You are my son. And I love you very much."

Sam closed his eyes. "I can't believe you're here," he said, shedding tears of relief.

"I'm not," she whispered.

"What do you mean?"

She ran a hand over his hair. "You've only conjured up my spirit. You need to let me go."

"Let you go?"

"Send me back. I can't leave unless you let me."

"No. I won't." Anger washed over him. How easily she abandoned him. "You have to stay. I need you. I don't understand what's happening to me."

They stared at each other. Her eyes looked bruised with guilt. "I should have prepared you better," she said, "Your father and I, we didn't think it through." She gripped his shoulders. "I don't regret a thing, Sam. You are the best thing in my life. But if I'd known, if I'd felt the kind of power you have, I would've prepared you. I swear it, Sam."

Sam couldn't stay angry at her. "I believe you."

She pulled him close. "I will find a way back to Orkney. I won't leave you here alone." Then she held him away from her, her eyes boring into his. "Swear that you believe me."

"I swear," he said. "I know you'll come back."

"Then let me go."

Sam nodded. And in that moment, as he was about to say goodbye, she shimmered in his arms and then disappeared.

Keep moving, Sam. He heard his mother's voice in his head. *You are not safe here.*

A heavy sadness sapped the energy from Sam. But he knew he must get away from this nest before the Omeras returned to feed on him. Without his mother's magic, he was sure he could not hold the demons at bay again.

"See any way down?" Sam asked, joining Fetch at the ledge. The cliff face dropped over a thousand feet into a steep ravine. No chance of climbing down.

Fetch slipped his undersize hand into Sam's.

"The way down is easy, sir." Fetch tugged with a strength Sam didn't expect, and they fell over the ledge, tumbling together straight down into the rocky ravine.

Chapter Thirty-Nine

He should have expected it. The last time Fetch had taken his hand, Sam had spent hours falling through a black void. This time, it took only a few seconds before he slammed into water and went under, swallowing a gallon before he gathered his senses and kicked his way to the surface.

Cold water carried him past rocks and logs. He was in a river, and that devious Fetch was nowhere to be seen. Sam kicked and flailed through rapids, avoiding the boulders as he bounced downstream.

Several minutes later, the rapids ended, and the water settled down enough for Sam to swim to the shore and climb out. The forest was calm here, tranquil. He found himself in a familiar clearing.

There was the tree with the snake in the crook, and the rock where he had knelt and pleaded with Odin to help him. After an exhausting wild goose chase, Sam was right back where he had started. Soaking wet and despondent, he dropped to his knees in the same spot as before.

"Please, Odin," he said wearily. "If you won't help me, just tell me to go. I can't take any more of your tests."

For a moment, all sounds in the forest ceased. Even the rushing noise of the river quieted. Then the earth shook and tree limbs crackled as a powerful uprising moved rocks aside. The young sapling before him began to grow, stretching its branches, turning into a mature tree, sprouting broad leaves to create a vast canopy overhead. By the time the tree stopped growing, it towered several stories above Sam.

A loud hiss got him on his feet. The snake had increased in size as well, growing from the width of his arm to the girth of a sewer pipe. Its sinuous body wrapped around the redwood-size tree trunk. The snake's yellow eyes fixed on Sam while its forked tongue probed the air around him, measuring the boy's fear.

"State your bussssssinesss," the snake hissed.

"My business? I'll tell you my business," Sam said, feeling cranky after having been jerked around for what felt like days. "I want to see Odin. Have you seen him?"

"Sssssilence!" the snake spat, whipping its tail out to coil around Sam's neck, choking off his air. "Ssspeak with resssssspect or ssssuffer."

Sam tried to peel the snake's tail off his neck, but it was useless. The blood vessels in his head felt ready to pop, and he nodded helplessly at the creature.

The snake loosened its hold and settled itself into a shimmering, red-and-gold coiled pyramid that was still twice as tall as Sam. The reptile raised its shovel-shaped head on a slender neck and stared into Sam's eyes, waiting for him to speak.

"I am Sam Barconian, Lord of the Ninth Realm and Son of Odin," he stated loudly. "I need to see Odin."

"What for, Sssson of Odin?"

"I have to stop the red sun. You may not see it here, but it's messing up the rest of Orkney pretty bad."

The black ovals in the snake's yellow eyes narrowed to menacing slivers. "Odin has no patience for a fool'sss errand."

"You're not the boss. The boss is the boss. The boy should see the boss."

This new, manic voice came from over Sam's head. In the branches of the tree, a bushy-tailed squirrel with fat cheeks sat nibbling a walnut at high speed, turning it over and over in its hands before tossing the bare shell to the side.

"Sssilence, Ratatosk!" snapped the snake.

But the squirrel had run around the trunk in a brown flash and disappeared from sight. Leaves rustled as it climbed higher.

"Who was that?" Sam asked.

"Sssssomeone with delusssions of grandeur," the snake replied.

The branches rattled overhead, and a streak of brown raced down the tree trunk.

"Boss says he should come up, so he should come up." Ratatosk zipped around the trunk, gesturing at Sam with his tail to come forward, then waited for Sam to follow.

"Guess I've been invited," Sam boasted, and stepped past the snake.

Reaching up into the branches, he found a knot and pulled himself up, stepping from limb to branch to knotty hole, following Ratatosk.

"Hurry, hurry," the squirrel said, stopping to peer around the trunk. "Don't delay. Mustn't keep His Lordship waiting."

Sam tried to keep up, but it was hard going, and as he got higher, he made the mistake of looking down. The ground seemed an alarming distance away. He felt clammy, paralyzed with dread. This was a bad time to develop a fear of heights.

The squirrel raced back, urging him on. "Come on, come on, it's quite safe. He's waiting; you don't want him to leave."

Sam pushed himself on until the branches began to thin out and bend under his weight. He was near the top. He balanced, with one arm wrapped around the trunk, and looked up.

At first he didn't see it. Perched on the highest knob sat a noble-looking bird. Brown feathers with white tips covered its solid body, which stood about three feet tall.

Is this the boss? Sam wondered.

Somehow it didn't surprise Sam that the person in charge was a bald eagle. When the bird turned its head, Sam was taken aback by the fierceness in its gaze.

"Uh . . . hello. I'm Sam. Sam Baron—Barconian, I mean. I need your help."

The bird listened to him, or at least Sam thought it did, and then it turned away to stare off into the distance.

"Hey!" Sam shouted after a few moments. "I'm talking to you. Just please don't give me any more tests. I failed every one of them."

The eagle turned its head back toward Sam.

"Tell him," Ratatosk urged Sam. "Tell the boss what happened."

"Okay. The first one, I got frustrated, and I took it out on Fetch. The next one, I couldn't protect Leo from the Shun Kara. And the last one—well, I almost ate my own mother. So if that's why you won't talk to me, I get it. But just so you know, all of Orkney is counting on me to end this red-sun curse, so . . . ."

Sam let the last and most important point hang in the air, hoping it would generate some sympathy. Instead, the eagle flapped its expansive wings, fanning so much air at Sam that the boy lost his balance and nearly fell from the branch on which he stood.

"Oh no, oh no, the boss is mad, he's mad, you should go." Ratatosk scurried down the tree trunk a safe distance, but Sam wasn't going anywhere. He clung to the trunk until the wind from the wings subsided. He had nowhere else to go.

But when he looked back at the bird, the eagle was gone. In its place sat an old man with thick gray hair and the eagle's same blazing, blue topaz eyes. The man was barefoot and draped in a simple cloth sheath knotted at the waist like a toga. A crown of leaves wrapped around his forehead. It was evident that he had been strong and handsome in his youth.

"Are you Odin?" Sam asked.

"Who else would you expect to find?"

"I don't know. I thought you had only one eye."

Odin rubbed his face thoughtfully. "A vanity on my part. When I am here in this place, I appear as I choose. So you think you failed my tests," the god challenged.

Sam's heart raced. "Didn't I?"

Odin smiled, then threw his head back and laughed. "You are still alive, are you not?" He jumped down to a lower branch with a thud so they were now eye to eye. "Just like your father," he mused. His eyes were as dazzling as the ocean, shifting and changing from sea foam green to bright blue.

"You knew my father?"

"Aye, I keep track of all my offspring. Bloody hard at times, but I liked Robert. He reminded me of my son Baldur, a great warrior. They both understood you must fight for what you want in this life."

"Emenor told me the witches put my dad into a stone."

Odin nodded wryly. "Your father had a blind eye for the witches. Came from loving one, I suppose."

"So it's true . . ." Crazy hope sprang up in Sam. "Please. Help me save him," he pleaded.

"Your father cannot be saved, Samuel. He clings to life in that stone, but no power in this realm can restore him. He was mortally wounded in battle."

Sam's hope fizzled, but he remained firm. "I can't just leave him like that. I didn't even get to say goodbye. Please. Give me something to set him free."

"Do you realize how much trouble you have caused me, breaking my curse against the witches after all these years?" Odin chuckled. "If that old goat Rubicus had not wanted to destroy this world, we would have been friends."

"He can still destroy the world." Sam insisted. "Maybe you

can't see it here on Asgard, but the red sun is killing everything: animals, crops, and pretty soon people. Then everything on Earth. And it's all my fault."

"That's a lot for one small boy. I suppose I could cut off your head," Odin said thoughtfully, rubbing his bearded chin. "It worked with Rubicus."

"What if another boy like me is born?" Sam argued desperately. "I say let's end it now, while we can."

"And you think you are the one to do it?"

Sam could hear Odin's skepticism. Drawing himself up as tall as he could, he tried to project confidence. "Everyone keeps telling me I am a Son of Odin. With your help, I can break the curse."

"Perhaps you are right." Odin sighed. "You are blood of my blood. But I warn you, it won't be easy to end this pox on the sun once and for all."

"Then help me. Tell me what to do," Sam pleaded.

"You must find the source of the dark magic. The curse was born in the Fourth Realm of Nifelheim, the underworld of lost souls. I always suspected its mistress, Sinmara, was behind the red sun, but cutting Rubicus's head off was less trouble. To steal her secret, you will have to get inside Sinmara, like you did with the Omera—only this time, do not linger. Being inside Sinmara too long could consume you."

The god's gentle chiding bemused Sam. Like he ever wanted to feel that oily darkness again.

Odin continued, "You will need powerful magic to withstand her darkness. Let me think . . ." After a moment, the god snapped his sturdy fingers. "My Fury. Where did I put it? Fetch!" he bellowed.

Ratatosk poked his head out of the leaves. "Fetch is not here, boss. You banished him."

"Oh, bother. Go on, then—get me my Fury."

The squirrel streaked off and rustled through the leaves.

There was a rattling and clanking sound down below in the canopy. Then the brown streak ran up Odin's leg to his shoulder, where it stopped. Odin held out his palm, and Ratatosk dropped a battered tin cup in his hand.

That's Odin's Fury? Sam wondered, unimpressed.

Odin stared down into the cup and murmured some incomprehensible words. After clearing his throat, he spat into the cup, raised it to the sun, and then offered it to Sam.

"Drink."

Sam took the cup, thoroughly grossed out by the idea of drinking Odin's spit.

"All of it," Odin ordered.

Sam stared into the cup. It was half-filled with an amber liquid. Steeling himself for a nasty taste, Sam took a small sip. There was no taste at all, but he felt a burning in his belly. The feeling was not painful; rather, it was empowering. So he tilted the cup back and swallowed all of the god's nectar. He instantly flushed as fire seemed to race through his veins, filling him with a searing energy and a strange desire to grab a sword and fight someone, anyone. Sam tapped the tin cup to get the last few drops of this precious and powerful fluid.

He felt invincible.

He felt like a god.

"Now what?" Sam asked.

"Now you must follow your heart. You did not fail my tests, Samuel. You passed them. Each and every one. You showed me that you have the power of mercy. The courage to sacrifice yourself for a friend. And, most important, the strength of self-control."

Sam smiled sheepishly. If only the tests in junior high were this easy to pass.

"But you must be careful, my boy."

"Why? What do you mean?"

Odin put one thick finger to Sam's chest. "You saw with the

Omera how easy it is to surrender yourself to darkness. Yes, you fought back. But never underestimate its power, or it will consume you." Odin smiled then, his eyes twinkling proudly. "I trust you to do the right thing, Sam. Stay the true course, and things will turn out."

As Sam tried to process all that wisdom, Odin began to change and shift again, his body shimmering, and then, in a blur of golden light, he transformed back into the eagle. The majestic bird flew up to his perch atop the Yggdrasil tree and stared at the pure sun.

Ratatosk scampered up next to Sam, then twirled a walnut in his little paws. "The boss likes you. You like the boss. Everything's going to change now." He split the walnut in half and held it out to Sam.

Inside the shell nestled a glowing emerald. It was a deep jade color, shaped like a perfect teardrop. Sam reached slowly for the jewel but pulled back when he saw, in the facets, Endera's glittering eyes. A chill stopped his heart for a beat.

Sam could hear her laughing at him somewhere inside his mind. She was mocking him, waiting for him to return so she could manipulate him. Sam seized the emerald and squeezed it tightly, feeling the jewel heat up from his touch. He tightened his grip, his arm trembling from exertion, until the emerald was reduced to dust. He let the glimmering remains sift through his fingers and drift down like sparking rain through the tree branches.

The squirrel was right. Everything was going to change now.

Chapter Forty

Sam shimmied down Odin's Yggdrasil tree and jumped from the last branch, hitting the ground with a satisfying thump. Everything felt different, starting with him. There was hope in the air, confidence in his veins. Twenty feet above the ground, he paused. The snake waited at the bottom. That wouldn't do. Sam picked a handful of brown nuts off the tree and threw them across the clearing so they landed in a scatter of clunks.

The nosy snake whipped its head around, then slithered off in a hurry toward the noise. Sam was alone. Now was the time to steal the Horn of Gjall. He hesitated, not wanting to betray Odin. *I trust you to do the right thing*, Odin had said. The god had trusted him with great power. Abusing it felt wrong. Then Sam remembered Howie's scared look as his friend had been taken away. He couldn't live with himself if he didn't at least try. He probably wouldn't find it, and that would be that.

Dropping to the ground, he felt around the base of the tree, searching for where Odin might have buried the Horn. He dug through the shrubs, pushing aside tall grass, and came up empty-handed. A familiar hiss echoed across the meadow. The snake was coming back.

Hurriedly turning over rocks, Sam desperately wished it to magically appear, but still nothing. Then he spied a yellow flower at the base of the trunk. It stood alone, with a thick stalk and the most perfect yellow petals. It reminded him of a sunflower. Its face was turned toward the sun, and it waved in the breeze, beckoning him.

Wrapping two hands around the stalk, Sam gave it a tug, straining to uproot it. The stalk was rubbery and tough. A large clod of dirt came up as the roots began to unearth and Sam fell backward as the plant finally came free.

He was shocked to see a mud-encrusted horn dangling from the roots. The instrument was made of brass, dulled with age, and elegantly curved like a ram's horn. Sam didn't have time to brush off the grime. Breaking it free from the root tangle, he shoved the Horn into his waistband, pulling his shirt over it to hide it, then hurriedly replanted the flower. Even after he had packed dirt around the roots, the stalk drooped. The bright yellow petals fluttered one by one to the ground, as if the loss of the Horn had sapped its life.

"Where are you, Sssson of Odin?" the snake called from nearby. "I can ssssmell you."

Leaving the wilted flower, Sam darted into the woods and ran as fast as his legs would carry him back to the beach where he had left his friends. He felt as if he had been gone for days. They would be sick with worry. The Horn bit into his waist where it was lodged under his belt.

Sam used the sound of crashing waves to guide him to the beach. He ran through the fog that separated the interior of the island from the rest of Orkney. A breeze began blowing, and he broke through the mist onto the narrow sand spit.

He expected to find Mavery, Keely, and Leo jumping for joy at his return, but instead he found them bound, captive, and huddled under a tree. An Orkadian warship was anchored in the harbor, its red-and-white flags flapping in the breeze.

The Falcory, Beo, looking fierce as ever, stood guard over

Leo and Keely. Another Falcory held Mavery by her nape while she kicked and screamed to be released. Rego stood near the captives, next to Gael, the tall Eifalian Sam had met in Skara Brae who had disliked his aura. Gael wore the same flowing aqua blue robe and had that disapproving look in his eyes.

Sam took in the situation, contemplating his next move. He was about to duck back into the bushes, when Rego's trusty bird, Lagos, squawked at Sam reprovingly as she flew over his head.

Rego and the rest of the Orkadians were alerted. Sam gave in and walked down the beach toward Rego and Gael. A group of Orkadian soldiers dressed in battle regalia trotted over and surrounded him. The blond-headed Captain of the Guard, Teren, was with them, looking pained as he clamped his hand on Sam's shoulder.

"Sam, I'm glad you are well," Teren said, though his left hand was at the hilt of his sword.

"Thanks for the welcoming party," Sam said jovially to Rego and the other adults. He couldn't help the enthusiasm, Odin's magic bubbled in his veins, creating a veritable fountain of confidence.

But Gael lunged forward. "You are responsible for this," he said, shooting an accusatory finger up at the clotted sun. "You did this to us."

Sam stepped back, overcome with guilt. The Orkadians had found out the boy from Pilot Rock, not the witches, had caused the red sun. Not even Odin's Fury could save him from that.

Did Rego betray me? Sam wondered, glaring at the dwarf.

Rego put a firm hand on the Eifalian's arm. "Now, Gael, calm yourself. The boy didn't plan this."

"He's no boy. He's a witch," Gael accused, jerking free of Rego's grasp. His eyes flashed with anger and something else. Grief. His voice was choked with it. "I should have seen it before. When I read his aura, I saw the darkness in him."

Sam backed away. "Hey, I didn't ask for any of this," he said, raising his hands.

"You are killing my people," Gael said, advancing on Sam. He drew a long sword from his robes and held the blade in front of him, pointed directly at Sam. "My own sister," he sobbed, the grief spilling over. "Dead because of you. She was weakened by illness, and your red sun finished her."

"I'm sorry. I really am." Sam took another step back as Gael advanced with his sword. "I didn't know who I was."

Captain Teren stepped protectively to Sam's side. "Let's not act hasty, Gael," Teren said calmly. "Witch or not, he's just a boy."

But Gael kept coming, murder in his eyes. "You must be stopped before it kills everyone!"

Before Teren could draw his own sword, Gael sprang forward and shouted, "This is for Orkney!" and drove his blade straight at Sam's heart.

There was no time for Sam to react, to feel horror or shock. The event seemed to happen in slow motion. Sam saw the grief and anger ripple over Gael's face as the man rushed forward. He watched the sun flash off the edge of Gael's blade, saw the tip heading straight for him. He heard Keely scream and Rego yell, "Nooooo!"

Through it all, Sam had one regret—that he would never see his father again, never get to ask him why he had abandoned his wife and son. His eyes fluttered closed, waiting for death. But the sword didn't penetrate Sam's chest. Instead, the hardened steel melted like butter and ran down the front of his shirt in a stream of liquid silver.

There was shocked silence. Stunned, Sam opened his eyes and touched the place where Gael had tried to skewer him. His finger poked through a hole in his shirt, but his skin was intact.

"What magic is this?" Gael gasped, dropping his broken sword hilt in the sand.

"Odin's Fury," Rego said in awe. "The boy must've drunk the nectar of the gods. He cannot be killed while it's in him."

The Orkadian soldiers traded looks of surprise.

"The boy did it!" Rego exclaimed. "We have our chance to end the curse. He found Odin."

Teren clapped Sam hard on the back, followed by hearty congratulations from Rego. But Sam couldn't take his eyes off Gael. The Eifalian looked stricken. Without another word, the elven leader turned, walked back to a waiting rowboat, and returned to the ship.

Rego turned to Beo. "Untie his friends. Sam is coming back with us to explain to the High Council how we're going to end this curse. Isn't that right, Sam?"

Sam knew it wasn't the right time to tell Rego he needed to go to someplace called Nifelheim to face a mistress of the underworld named Sinmara, so he nodded and said, "Sure thing. High Council. Can't wait." Anything to free his friends.

The Falcory didn't look happy, but he cut Keely and Leo loose. Mavery seized the moment to break away from the relaxed hold of her guard.

Keely raced to Sam and hugged him so hard, she nearly bowled him over. "I thought you were never coming back," she said. "We searched the island, but this giant bear tried to eat us, then he decided to help us, and . . . I know it sounds crazy, but Mavery thinks it was Odin."

Mavery cut in, squeezing Sam's leg tightly. "I can't believe you climbed the Yggdrasil tree without me."

Sam ruffled her hair. "Sorry, imp. Maybe next time."

"What was it like?" she said in awe.

"I met Odin's pet snake and a funny squirrel named Ratatosk."

"It's good to see you, Sam." Leo put his arm on Sam's shoulder, and Sam grabbed him back. Leo had a lot of explaining to do—like the fact that they had met before, when Leo was ten and attacked by a Shun Kara. But Sam knew that now was not the time.

"We need to make a plan," Sam said quietly to his friends, so Beo and the others couldn't hear. "We're not going back to Skara Brae."

"Did you steal that horn?" Keely asked.

"Shh," Sam said curtly, as Rego passed by. "We'll talk later."

In no time, the group boarded the ship and set sail for Garamond. Sam gave the island of Asgard one last look. It shimmered in the sunlight before vanishing from sight. He stared at the empty space where Asgard had been, remembering his mother and what it had felt like to be with her again.

The deck of the ship was smooth and clean, in far better shape than Jasper's rickety boat. The crew hoisted the sails, and in a snap, they were moving quickly across the windy seas. His friends were all feasting in the galley below, but Sam had no appetite and instead made his way to the prow of the ship, where he could be alone and watch the waves. Lagos perched on the rail next to him, cleaning her feathers with her beak. Sam ran his hand over her back.

A pod of dolphins breached the water alongside the ship, their silvery-gray bodies giving off an eerie red glow, reflecting the poison of the sun.

Time's running out, thought Sam.

He didn't know how much time they had until more people started dying. But he figured it was only a matter of days.

A shadow fell over Sam as Gael joined him at the prow.

"I apologize for my behavior on the beach," he said stiffly. "It is not the Eifalian way to use violence."

Sam gripped the rail. "Why do you hate me so much, anyway?"

Gael took a long breath. "My sister, Therese, died from the effects of the sun. Her son, Theo, is now an orphan. Your parents swore to me on the day you were born that you didn't inherit magic. It seems they lied. If they had told us, we could have taken actions to protect Orkney."

"You mean, get rid of me when I was a baby," Sam choked out.

Gael shrugged but didn't correct him.

Before Sam could tell Gael what he thought, Keely came up. Gael nodded politely and drifted away.

She slipped her arm through his. "You okay?"

He didn't answer, not trusting himself to speak. Gael had as much as admitted Orkney would have been better off if Sam had ceased to exist. How did he go on from that?

"So what's the plan? Where's that horn to save Howie?"

Sam shook himself and focused on what he could do, pulling his shirt up to show her the artifact. "It's safe for now, but I still have to deal with the red-sun curse," he said with a heavy heart. "And Odin said my dad is really in that stone, but he won't survive if I free him. I can't just leave him there, but I can't let him die, either. Argh!" He slammed his hand on the rail. "It's so frustrating."

"What about Howie?" she asked.

Sam shook his head, feeling overwhelmed. "I don't know."

She grabbed his arm, turning Sam to face her. "Hey, you promised me we were going to rescue Howie."

Sam shook himself free of Keely's grasp. "You heard Leo back at the inn. If I don't stop this curse, our home, Pilot Rock, Planet Earth, is going to be hit next by the red sun. That's bigger than Howie. You want your dad and everyone you know back in Pilot Rock to die? I'm not giving up on Howie; it's just . . . somehow I have to make it all work."

Keely studied his face a long moment and then softened. "If anyone can do it, Sam, you're the one."

Sam sighed, unconvinced.

"Let's look at the facts," Keely challenged. "I watched you incinerate a couple of Omeras. Mavery says you survived a giant-squid attack. Not to mention you met a god named Odin, and he gave you his Fury, whatever that is." She said the last part with understandable awe. "You'll figure out a way. I know it."

Sam appreciated her faith in him, but he didn't share it. At this point, a happy ending seemed impossible. Sam had seen first-hand that the dark side of his blood was strong. Even with Odin's Fury, he still felt enticed by the poisonous red sun, wanting to turn his face to it and draw its power into his veins.

But he couldn't tell Keely that. He couldn't risk letting her see who he really was, or, at the very least, who he was capable of becoming.

Chapter Forty-One

S am and his entourage arrived at the shores of Garamond the next morning. By Sam's estimation, he had been in Orkney for almost two weeks, but it felt more like two lifetimes. The capital city, Skara Brae, was still two days' ride away, according to Captain Teren.

Mounting the assembled horses, the group passed through villages that had burned to the ground and empty, barren fields. In the days since they had been gone, society seemed to have crumbled. What had once been picturesque countryside now seemed apocalyptic. People were nowhere to be seen, the life had been sucked out of the landscape, and the smell of rotting animal carcasses filled the air. The Eifalians rode silently while the Falcory dispersed through the forests like shadows.

Teren rode alongside Sam.

"This village was called Barlow's Hill," he said, his eyes grimly scanning the devastation. "I was here just last month. The vicar served me a glass of honey mead from his private stock. All gone now," Teren lamented.

"What happened here?" Sam asked. "Did the witches do this?"

Teren drew in a shuddering breath. "No. It was the madness set in."

"Madness?"

"It's what happens when you get too much exposure to the poisonous rays of the sun. It started with a fight over food supplies, then escalated to full-scale warfare between neighbors. I came with a regiment of men to help, but we arrived too late. They burned their own homes." Teren choked over the last words. "Sam, you have to stop this, whatever it takes. We don't want to become Barlow's Hill." Teren gave his horse a kick and moved on to ride with his men.

Sam sank in his saddle. Someone rode up next to him. He glanced over. It was Rego.

"Don't let it get to you, lad. You couldn't have known any of this would happen."

"You were wrong, you know, about my dad. He's still alive. Odin said he can't survive, he's pretty badly wounded, but he's in some stone with those witches."

Rego looked pained, muttering a curse under his breath. "I'm sorry, lad. I didn't know. But you can't go around messing with powerful magic like that. There's no telling what the consequences would be. You need to focus on whom you can save today. Your friends and all of Orkney."

"Yeah, that's why I'm not going back to Skara Brae. Odin told me what to do." He hesitated, then added, "I could use your help, Rego."

The dwarf's eyes glowed with excitement. He kept his voice low so the other Orkadians wouldn't hear. "What exactly did Odin say?"

"He told me to go to the Fourth Realm of Nifelheim. Have you heard of it?"

The dwarf snorted in disbelief. "The Fourth Realm? That's where souls who've been damned to eternal suffering go. That place is not for the likes of you."

"Well, that's what he told me to do. Find somebody named

Sinmara. Ask her for her help. He says she'll know how to break the curse."

Rego ran a hand over his whiskers. "And that's your plan?" he said. "Run off to the underworld, face the demons of hell, and hope for the best?"

"You got a better one?"

Rego shook his head. "There's something about you, Samuel, that makes us all nervous. You lack discipline and respect. And you have no idea of the kind of power you wield. But maybe, just maybe, you have something the rest of us don't."

"And what's that?" Sam asked.

"Blind faith."

"So you'll help me?"

Rego drew in a deep breath, as if weighing his odds of survival. "It's been a while since I visited the Fourth Realm. It won't be easy to get away from Teren and Gael. We'll need some kind of diversion. Let me think on it." He clicked his heels against his horse's flank and rode off.

Keely, who had been eavesdropping on the conversation, rode up with Mavery in tow. "Sam Baron, you're not going anywhere without us."

Sam took one look at the girls—they had *stubborn* written all over their faces—and he knew there was no point in arguing with them. "Fine. But don't say I didn't warn you." The truth was, he wanted them along, even if it was selfish.

The red sun beat down, burning the travelers' backs as they continued on through the desolate landscape. Sam could feel tempers rising around them as the Falcory and the Eifalians looked at him with mistrust. He had suggested to Gael and Teren that the group travel at night, safe from the sun's poison, but the Orkadians had insisted time was of the essence.

They rode until the sun sank low on the horizon; then they broke for rest. The horses were left to roam on a grassy patch protected by the shade of trees. Three horses collapsed that day. Gael and other Eifalians tended to the rest, reciting enchantments to keep them going, but the animals were glassy-eyed and wobbling.

Even Rego's mighty pet *iolar*, Lagos, looked weak, tottering on the roof of the supply wagon instead of soaring overhead.

Sam lay back on the shaded grass and stared up at the darkening sky. The moon was a quarter its full size. Soon Howie would be out of time. A few stars came out as the light faded. The familiar constellations were reassuring—they hadn't changed universes, even if they were in a different realm. Leo took a seat next to him.

"There's Venus," Leo said, pointing at one especially bright star.

"How do you know?" Sam asked, grateful for the distraction.

"The Umatilla often pray to Venus. She represents fertility and prosperity, a shining light for our people."

"Think she can stop the red sun?" Sam joked.

Leo, ever serious, just shook his head. "Only you can do that, Sam."

Sam sat up, clearing his throat. He wanted to talk to Leo about that whole Shun Kara attack, but he didn't want to sound like a loon. "So, a funny thing happened when I was on Asgard. Odin gave me all these tests, and in one of them he sent me back in time to Pilot Rock, to the day you were attacked by a Shun Kara. Sounds pretty crazy, huh?"

But Leo didn't laugh. He sat up slowly. "I wanted to tell you, but I didn't think you'd believe me," he said with relief.

Sam's eyes bulged. "So it really happened? I was there?"

Leo nodded, absently rubbing the scar on his arm. "If not for you, the Shun Kara would have killed me. You saved my life."

"Well, I did a pretty lousy job. It almost took your arm off. What was a Shun Kara doing in Pilot Rock?"

"My dad says it snuck through the stonefire when your father returned to Orkney. If you hadn't taken it back to the Ninth Realm with you, I'd be dead. When Rego showed up and warned us the witches were hunting you, my father sent me to the school to keep an eye on you. The moment I saw you, I knew it was you who had saved me, but you didn't look a day older. Not even my father could explain it." He shook his head, "Odin's magic. I can't believe the god sent you to save me," he said, a bit awed.

"Yeah, go figure." Odin had given Sam more than his Fury; he had given him a friend. "Looks like we're stuck with each other."

They went back to stargazing. Sam must have closed his eyes and dozed, because he woke to see Rego's whiskered face hovering above him.

"Let's go, lad," he whispered.

Sam sat up. Leo was already standing with Keely and Mavery.

They followed Rego, all of them hunched close to the ground as they crept into the woods. Rego had arranged for the guards to be busy tending to the ailing horses while they sneaked away. It meant they were stuck on foot, but the horses were too weak to be of much use anyway.

They jogged through the woods until Sam's lungs burned. He could hear Keely gasping next to him, while Leo ran, silent as a wraith, and Mavery skipped along as effortlessly as a jackrabbit.

"How far is it?" Sam asked, stopping to catch his breath.

Keely collapsed on the ground.

Rego's face was flushed red from exertion. "Nifelheim can be entered only through volcanic tunnels on the island of Pantros," he said, panting. Behind them, a loud fluttering in the trees made them all jump, but it was only Lagos. The bird looked winded and out of breath as it landed on a branch and let out a croaking squawk.

"No, Lagos, you have to stay behind," Rego said, taking the

bird on his arm and stroking her. "You can't come with us. Not this time. You're too weak."

The bird squawked again in complaint, but Rego threw her up into the air. "Go back now," he said, whistling sharply. The bird protested but winged off crookedly through the trees.

Keely stared at Rego. "Did you say we have to go to another island?"

Sam was concerned, too. "How are we supposed to get there?"

Rego shrugged. "If we keep a steady pace to the coast, we can find a ship—or steal one if we must—and sail across the firth to it. Two days, maybe three."

Sam shook his head. "We'll never make it in time. We need a ride."

"Well, I don't have any flying machines, do you?"

Sam thought about it a moment. "Maybe I do," he mused aloud.

Walking to a spot where he had a clear view of the sky, Sam raised his hands over his head and swung them around, drawing on the energy around him.

"*Fein kinter, Omera. Omera venus acai, acai.*"

Come here, my brothers, he called in his ancient language. Calling on his brethren, the Omera, reaching out to their dark spirit. His skin tingled as their primal response echoed across the clearing, heard only by Sam.

They were coming. They might eat them when they arrived, but they were definitely coming.

Chapter Forty-Two

"What did you do, lad?" Rego asked warily.

Above them, two shadows passed in front of the moon.

"I got us a ride," Sam said smugly. But he was hoping he hadn't been a complete fool for inviting them here.

"A ride from what?" Keely wondered aloud.

Leo stepped next to him, eyes searching the sky. "You called the dark ones."

Sam nodded.

"What?" Keely squealed in outrage. "Are you crazy? They'll kill us all."

But it was too late to take it back. A shrill cry cut through the night, and then there were two thumping sounds as the Omera landed on either side of the group. The beasts stalked around, their tail spikes curved over their backs. As the two beasts tightened their circle around the group, Sam reached out with his mind.

We need safe passage to Pantros, he called.

The female Omera let out a screech, but Sam understood her. *Traitor.*

The male one hissed at him, *Our children died because of you.*

Worse will happen if we don't get to Pantros, he answered. *If the red sun continues, first your food supply will die, then you and everything else.*

The male Omera stabbed its tail toward Sam's chest. Sam jumped back and tried a different sales tactic. *If you give us safe passage, I can stop the red sun.*

The beasts circled closer, hissing and stabbing with their tails. Their eyes glowed with menace and the same bloodlust Sam had succumbed to.

Rego drew his sword and Leo his bow, but the two winged demons were clearly more powerful than Sam's group.

"How's it going, lad?" Rego asked.

"Not good," Sam said, wishing he could take it back.

You shall die, the male Omera snarled, leaping at Sam.

Sam shouted, "Run!" as he stepped in front of his friends, shielding them from the Omera's imminent attack.

Its claws were outstretched, spiked tail aiming for Sam's head. Sam stood his ground, knowing if he ran, the Omera would just go after Keely or Mavery. Sam didn't want to destroy the beast, but he didn't have a choice. He had to fight back. But as he summoned his witchfire for an attack, the Omera's mate knocked it away from Sam.

No, the female said. *The boy is right.*

The two beasts wrestled each other violently. The male roared in protest, baring his fangs and biting into her neck so that she bled. But she was strong and cunning enough to wrestle herself on top until she pinned him, with her claws to his throat. Heaving in anger, the male Omera bit back once more, but his mate held him down until he surrendered.

The female turned to Sam and tucked in her sleek black wing, lowering herself so that the boy could climb aboard. After a moment, the male joined her in offering the other humans a ride.

The clearing was silent. Nobody but Sam was sure exactly what had happened.

Sam clapped his hands together, rubbing them to get the blood flowing. "Okay, the Omeras have agreed to take us to Pantros."

He stepped forward, grabbing the female's neck and hoisting himself onto her back.

"I can't guarantee anybody's safety. We have to meet some underworld hag named Sinmara, and Odin said she won't want to help me, so . . ." He made eye contact with each of his friends as he spoke. "I can't ask you to come with me, but I could sure use your help." He held his breath, holding back his fear that they wouldn't join him on this quest.

At first Keely looked at him like he was out of his mind, but then she cautiously took his hand and slid behind him on the female Omera. Mavery followed her, and they all waited while Rego approached the male Omera. The beast let out a low rumble as the dwarf stepped on its back, but it allowed him to take hold of its horned neck. Leo jumped up behind Rego.

They were ready to take the ride of their lives.

Sam dug his heels gently into the side of the Omera, and they flew off into the night sky.

The Omeras soared over the moonlit landscape of the island of Garamond, heading steadily toward the coast. The air temperature dropped noticeably as they glided over the water.

At one point, Sam looked over at Rego, who winked back as he leaned over the neck of his Omera. The dwarf was clearly enjoying himself. And he wasn't the only one—Sam kicked the sides of his beast and let out a whoop. He relished the feeling of freedom riding high above the troubled world below, and, for the moment, he ignored the dark connection he shared with the winged demon.

———◆———(◯✕✕◯)———◆———

Harsh morning light seared the edges of the horizon by the time the five riders saw the outline of a gloomy, foreboding island in the distance.

Pantros.

A jagged peak rose from the center of the island. Tendrils of smoke rose from the top. Sam figured it to be the volcano where Rego had said they would find the tunnels leading to the underworld. A shudder ran through him as he imagined the venomous spiders and hairy bats they would find down there. What if there were worse things than his imagination could conjure up? That was the thought that scared him the most.

They landed the Omeras on a field of black rock, dismounting the beasts with noticeable relief. The male took flight, bounding off with hardly a pause. The female lingered a moment, allowing Sam to silently thank her, before she launched herself into the air to follow her mate.

"Where to?" Sam asked, stretching out the kinks.

Rego pointed out a faint trail that led to the top of the volcano. "Up yonder. We had best start moving. The sooner we face Sinmara, the sooner we end this curse."

"But I'm so hungry," the little witch proclaimed, rubbing her grubby face with one hand. "I could eat a bowl of worms."

"Ditto that. Minus the worms," Keely said. "I would give my soul for a Chuggies burger right now."

Keely would have to be starving before she would lower herself to eat at Chuggies, so Sam knew she was desperate. "I've got some jerky," he said, reaching into his pouch.

Hungry hands grabbed for the dried meat.

"Here." Leo pulled out a plastic-wrapped granola bar and held it out for the girls. "I've been saving it."

Keely looked in awe at the remnant from their world. The bright blue package seemed out of place here in Orkney. "Where did you get that?" she whispered.

"I brought a bunch with me when I passed through the stonefire," Leo said. "My father taught me to be prepared."

"Where are the rest?" Sam asked, as Leo tore off the wrapper and they divided it up five ways.

"I ate them," he said between chews.

Leo had the grace to look embarrassed, but at the moment, none of them could complain. The melty chocolate granola was the best thing Sam had ever eaten. Mavery moaned in delight. Even Rego was taken by the tasty treat.

"Who's ready to raid the underworld?" Sam said, brushing his hands on his shirt.

The dwarf took the lead, setting a course across the black rock toward the base of the volcano. Ancient lava flows covered most of the ground, eliminating any vegetation save for a few stubby palms that poked through the cracks. The lava field was porous and sharp, like coral. Within the first few minutes, Mavery stumbled and scraped her knee, leaving a trail of blood flowing down her leg. But she didn't complain, just pinched her mouth shut and kept walking.

After an hour's walk, the terrain got smoother and steeper as they reached the base of the volcano. Serpentine tendrils of steam rose from the top.

"This isn't an active volcano, is it?" Sam asked, as they paused for a short rest.

"You mean will it erupt today? Probably not," Rego surmised, eyeing the smoking peak.

"*Probably* not?" Keely repeated.

"Hey, probably not is better than probably, right?" Sam said, trying to make her smile. But Keely's glare was as fierce as the red sun.

"Just so you know, Sam, if you get us killed, I will never speak to you again," she replied.

Chapter Forty-Three

After several hours of hiking, during which Sam had time to count all the reasons this was a bad idea, they came around a bend and stumbled on a large, oval breach in the side of the volcano. Hot air blasted out from inside the shaft. The ocean seemed an impossible distance below them. Waves crashed against the volcanic rock sending up a spray, but no cooling breeze reached them.

Sam fought a sudden urge to turn away from the dark, sulfuric-smelling cave and run down the trail, back to safety. Rego took a dead torch stuck in the side of the cave wall, lit it with a spark from a flint, and stepped into the long, downward-sloping tunnel. Leo shot Sam a look of bravado and hoisted Mavery onto his shoulders. Keely slipped her hand into Sam's and squeezed it once.

"You're sure about this?" she asked, searching his eyes with hers.

"Sure as you can be about going to an underworld full of demons," Sam said dryly.

"Hurry up," Rego called out, nearly out of sight as he descended rapidly into the volcano's depths. The kids hurried to catch up.

"I thought you said no one comes here." Sam eyed the torch.

Rego snorted. "I said 'no one in their right mind comes here.' Sinmara's the foulest creature in this realm, worse than ten Tarkana witches. But if you can pay her price, there is hope."

"So what made you come before?" Keely asked.

The light flickered off the walls, revealing a flash of anguish across Rego's face. "A lady friend in trouble. Bargained away her soul. Sinmara and I came to an agreement. But it cost me a pretty penny."

Sam knew what it felt like to bargain away his soul. The Horn of Gjall bit into his waist as he stumbled over a rock.

The air grew hotter as they descended. Sam heard a rustle overhead.

"Did you hear that?" he whispered.

"It sounds like bats," Keely answered, her voice shaky.

They looked up at the same time. In the flickering light of Rego's torch, Sam saw the shreeks.

Hundreds of them. Maybe thousands.

They hung upside down from the ceiling like bats roosting. These shreeks were larger than the ones he had encountered back in Pilot Rock, but they had the same vicious claws, glowing red eyes, and leathery wings tucked behind them.

Keely would have screamed, but Sam clamped his hand over her mouth. "Don't make any loud noises."

She nodded, and he removed his hand. "What are those things?" she whispered.

"Shreeks," answered Mavery. "They used to be people, but their souls belong to Sinmara now. They can't leave this place."

"Keep moving," Rego said. "Don't pay them any attention, and they won't bother you."

Keely shuddered, averting her eyes.

But Sam made eye contact with one the shreeks. As they locked eyes, there was an instant connection, an awareness that zinged between them. In that moment, Sam could feel its terror, its desperation, its rage at being trapped here. He forced himself to look away, but not before he heard its plea.

Release us.

Sam looked around, but no one else appeared to notice. He had heard it in his head, in the silent language through which magical things in Orkney had a way of reaching him.

Sam's thoughts drifted to the Omera. What if he had stayed trapped in the black-hearted beast?

What would I have become? Sam wondered.

"Sinmara's up ahead," Rego said, shaking Sam's thoughts loose. The dwarf stopped, twitching his whiskers as he scented the air. "She's alone for now. Her brothers must be off making mischief. This is our chance."

"Brothers? What brothers?" Sam said, concerned by the thought of multiple underworld enemies to overcome.

"A pair of giants with the smarts of a slug. But what they lack in brains, they make up for in brawn. They protect Sinmara by keeping her chained up. So there's no shortage of hatred in that family." Rego moved on.

"That might have been nice to know up front," Sam griped. He glanced at Leo. He had a bad feeling about this, but Leo merely shrugged in return and stepped forward.

No turning back now, Sam realized.

They followed Rego into a large, open chamber hewn from walls of black onyx. Heat emanated off the sides, back to the center of the room, where a pool of molten lava bubbled and popped noxious gas in the air. On a throne carved from the same onyx sat a woman.

Sinmara. Rego wasn't exaggerating. The underworld mad-am was enormous, with gray, flabby skin and a wart the size of a tomato on her nose. In her arms, she held a creature that looked like a large black puma. It snarled at the invaders, but she ran a fleshy hand over it, rubbing it into submission. On Sinmara's thick fingers, she wore rings of different colors: ruby red, emerald green, and a blue sapphire the size of a goose egg. At the sight of their little group, Sinmara's lips creased into a smile.

"Rego, you obnoxious dwarf, what brings you back to my slice of paradise?" she said casually. The wart on her nose wiggled as if it were alive.

"Mistress Sinmara." Rego laid the torch on the ground and gave an exaggerated bow to her. "I realize it's a merely trifling annoyance for someone as great as you, but the red sun has returned."

Sinmara's eyes widened for a moment, and then she waved one sparkling hand in the air. "I cannot abide the sun, whatever color. It damages my lovely skin. So why should I care?" Next to her sat a basket of large snails. She reached in, pulled one out, and popped it into her mouth, crunching down satisfyingly on its shell.

"You should care, you fat hog!" Mavery shouted, stamping her foot. "It's your fault the sun's killing everything."

Crimson lava flowed up around their ankles. Mavery squealed and leaped into Leo's arms. Sam jumped to the side, dragging Keely with him, but smoke sizzled off his boots.

"Silence, little brat!" Sinmara barked. The lava died down, and she stroked the head of the puma in her lap, her rings twinkling in the light of the glowing lava. "What makes you think I know anything about this curse? That old he-witch Rubicus concocted it."

"You're lying," Sam said, wishing he could shake the truth out of the old hag. "Odin told me Rubicus came to you, that you were the source."

"You spoke to that insufferable god?" Sinmara's thick brows drew together in a frown. "Then you must be a Son of Odin." She leaned forward, sniffing at the air. "But you've got magic." She sniffed again, and then a delighted look crossed her face as she crowed, "You're a witch. You broke Odin's curse."

She tilted her head back and cackled, her cheeks jiggling with fiendish glee. "Rubicus swore the curse would be broken and he would have the last laugh. Poor Odin must have been furious." She leaned forward again, her eyes bright with delight. "Tell me, did he threaten to chop off your head, like he did to Rubicus?" She roared with laughter at the look of confirmation on Sam's face.

Rego stepped forward. "Now, now, Sinmara, you've had your fun. The red sun is bad for business. If this world ends, you'll have no souls to lord over."

"It's a thankless job," she sniffed, popping another snail into her mouth and rolling it around in her cheek. "I'll need a better reason to get involved."

"Last time I visited, you were keen on being released," Rego said, looking pointedly at her feet. Her ankles were bound by a thick chain bolted into the ground. "It must get tiresome being locked up down here."

Suddenly self-conscious, she tucked her hideous feet under her gown.

"No mortal has the power to break these chains," she said, petting the puma so hard it complained loudly. "The black dwarves fastened these from iron ore dug from Gomara. No human weapon can break the steel."

"I have the strength of ten men," Sam proclaimed. With Odin's Fury running through his veins, Sam felt strong enough to tear the chain apart with his bare hands.

"Sam, we have a problem," Leo whispered at his side.

Sam ignored Leo, stepping closer to the underworld madam. "If I set you free, will you show me how to end the red-sun curse?"

"Sam," Leo tugged emphatically on his arm, but Sam shrugged loose, keeping his eye on the gray giantess.

Sinmara's eyes lit up at the idea of freedom. She opened her mouth to speak, when a noise echoed from the tunnel behind her.

Sam heard loud banging and snorting, then grunting. Sinmara leaned forward eagerly, almost desperate. "Now, boy; release me now," she said, sweeping the cat off her lap and knocking over the bowl of snails.

But it was too late. Two giants with bulbous noses rumbled into the throne chamber. One giant was bald as an egg; the other had a thick pelt of brown hair like a Mohawk running down its pate.

Sinmara's brothers. Baldy and Mohawk, Sam named them.

They stooped to avoid hitting the carved ceiling, looking as surprised to see the four visitors as the visitors were to see them. Baldy carried the carcass of a large deer, which he dropped with a thud. Mohawk held a giant club in his hand.

Sinmara moved fast for such an oversize sloth. She grabbed Keely and wrapped her thick arm around the helpless girl's throat.

"Release me, or she dies," she bellowed.

Chapter Forty-Four

$e$ven though he stood only as high as Sinmara's thighs, Rego unsheathed his sword. Leo drew his bow and notched an arrow. Sam held his ground between, wondering where Mavery had disappeared to.

"Sam!" Keely screamed, kicking her feet at the giantess.

The two giant brothers lurched into action, raising their clubs over their heads and yowling unintelligibly.

Baldy leaped and swung his club Sam's way. The boy alertly ducked and rolled while Leo launched an arrow, piercing the giant's throat. The giant wailed like a baby, pawing at the arrow lodged in his flesh.

Mohawk roared and raised his leg high, then brought it crashing down, aiming to stomp Rego to a pulp. The dwarf leaped nimbly to the side, then drew his sword and stabbed it into the giant's gnarly foot.

That's when Sam spied Mavery. She was clambering up the side of Sinmara's throne like a monkey. Once she reached the top, she took two steps along the narrow back and, without hesitation, leaped down on Sinmara's head.

"Let her go!" Mavery shouted, pulling at Sinmara's tangled hair and pinching her wart.

Sinmara shrieked and dropped to her knees.

"Not my beauty mark," she cried, holding her nose. Mavery had knocked the thing loose so it hung grotesquely from Sinmara's face by a thin strip of flesh. Sam could see something alive inside it, a parasite of some kind. She tried to smush the wart back onto her nose, but it wouldn't stay attached.

But Sam saw there were bigger problems at hand.

With Sinmara and her brothers all caterwauling, the army of shreeks had awoken and were now flying into the large chamber. Three of them swooped down on Mavery and Keely. The girls screamed, trying to bat them away.

Sam moved to help, but then he saw that Baldy had picked up a large boulder and was about to drop it on Leo's head. Sam dove at Leo, shoving him aside, and threw up his hands. "*Fein kinter movius,*" he shouted. The trajectory of the falling boulder shifted just enough to avoid crushing him, crashing to the ground one foot away.

Rego furiously battled the Mohawk giant with his sword, but it kept trying to bash him into the ground with his club. The agile dwarf leaped from side to side, but he was clearly running out of energy.

Sensing he needed to turn the tide, Sam grabbed the pouch from around his neck and swung it with furious intent. "*Fein kinter, ventimus enormous, ventimus destera nova!*" A wind rose up and began to blow the giants back while the shreeks spun and tossed in the air.

Sinmara remained chained to her throne. She looked pitiful with her hair blown back and her mole hanging limply on her face.

"Son of Odin, you will die for this!" she screamed, spittle spraying from her lips as she drew up her hands and sent a wave of lava at him.

"*Fein kinter, fereza, fereza nae movio.*" Sam swung Odin's rock so hard it was only a blur of motion. Odin's Fury was temporarily increasing the potency of what he could do. Everything in the chamber began to slow down. The droplets of lava heading toward him hung in the air. Keely and Leo both froze. The shrieks halted midflight, and Rego and the two giants remained locked in a frozen contest. Rego looked like he was about to be smashed by the rock the Baldy had dropped on him.

Sam blinked. He had stopped time. There wasn't a sound in the chamber—just the echo of his heartbeat in his ears. He shook himself, realizing he had no idea how long the spell would last.

First, he dragged Rego out of the way of the rock; then he lifted Mavery out of the open jaws of Sinmara's black puma.

Sinmara still had the solution to ending the red-sun curse. All he had to do was follow Odin's instructions. He closed his eyes, tapping into Odin's Fury, letting his senses become empowered. He envisioned the giantess and the mountain of gray flesh. He shuddered, then hardened his resolve. He would run at her, leap inside, as he had done with the Omera, and then exit as soon as he had her secret.

Before he could talk himself out of it, Sam ran, diving headfirst. He shut his eyes as he hit her rubbery blubber. The transition was easier this time. With a gasp, he melded with her behemoth of a body. He reeled at the ugliness of her mind, then steeled himself to look, delving into her horrid center, feeling the evil that held on to the souls of the underworld, the pain, the agony.

What did she prize? Where was her source of power? Sam searched her thoughts, her memories, but her evilness was like a black stain, spreading over him as he lingered. She was stronger than the Omera. She was fighting back, trying to consume his magic. Frantically, Sam attempted to force her to remember, pressuring her with his mind to tell him.

Then he saw a spark of memory, a handful of gems passed to her. He looked down at the fleshy gray fingers. The stones on her rings glittered back. She was screaming loudly now, pushing him out, but he had what he wanted.

Sam tore himself lose, landing facedown on the ground. He couldn't stop himself from retching. Wiping his mouth, he turned his head to look at her rings—one ring in particular, the red one on her middle finger. He could feel its power as he stared at it.

The ruby in her ring controlled the sun. He had to get it off her hand.

The ground began to tremble. His spell was fading. Lava rained down, and the rock that had dangled over Rego's head landed harmlessly beside the dwarf. The giant blinked at the spot where Rego had been.

Keely and Mavery scrambled to their feet.

Rego shook his head. "That was a mite strange. I think I owe you my life, but I'm not sure."

"You can thank me later," Sam said. "We need the ring off her hand—the ruby one."

"Distract her."

Sam drew on his powers, running his hands in a circle over his head as he concentrated, then pushed forward with his palms and tossed the rocks at Sinmara. She dodged them easily. Leo launched a volley of arrows at the pair of giants, who swatted them away but stayed a safe distance back.

"Hey, Sinmara, check this out," Sam said. He pointed at the pool of lava and drew it up into a thick stream in the air, letting it rain down on her head.

Wailing, the flabby priestess wiped the burning liquid from her eyes.

"You will spend eternity in this hole!" she screamed, then flung her arm out, trying to grab Sam by his shirt.

But Rego had snuck around behind her and climbed up on her throne. He raised his sword over his head and brought it down, grunting with effort as he lopped off her right hand clean at the wrist.

Sinmara let out a deafening screech that echoed off the onyx walls. Writhing in agony, she clutched at her butchered arm. Leo slid in and scooped up the hand, its fingers twitching, and tossed it at Sam. Sam grabbed the limb and stuffed it into the leather satchel that Rego threw at his feet. Keely and Leo were already running for the cave entrance, dragging Mavery along.

With the satchel flung over his shoulder, Sam was right behind his friends, only to be blocked by a swarm of shreeks that poured into the chamber through the tunnel. He knocked a few away and swung Odin's rock over his head, desperately searching for words to stave off this latest attack. He was tired, and his brain felt fuzzy.

Before he could mutter a spell, a large shreek flew straight into his face. Sam was frozen in place. His last thought was that it was going to scratch his eyes out, but it veered off and, as one, the swarm of shreeks parted in front of them, clearing a pathway to escape through.

Surprised and more than a little relieved, Sam stopped inside the tunnel and turned to see the shreeks descending on the giants and attacking them with all their fury. It was as if they were helping Sam and his friends escape, or maybe they just hated their keepers. He ran up the steep path with Sinmara's screams ringing in his ears.

Back outside, Sam sucked in all the fresh air his lungs could hold. Freedom had never tasted sweeter. He didn't even mind the sickly rays of the sun bearing down on him. Anything was better than the subterranean nightmare of Sinmara's cavern.

"What do I do with this?" Sam said to Rego, holding out the heavy satchel.

He wanted to get rid of the foul thing, but Rego said, "Only Sinmara can wield the rings. Leave them as they are."

The sun was setting, spreading scarlet trails of light across the horizon. Sam whistled into the twilight and heard the beating of wings. Within minutes, the two Omeras landed with a thump next to them, and the gang climbed onto their backs. The female Omera communicated to Sam silently, as she had done before.

Is it done?

Now it can be, Sam assured the beast.

A thin sliver of moon appeared through the clouds as they flew across the ocean. The seasons were changing. A chill hung in the air. Sam had an urge to pull Sinmara's hand out of his bag and admire the rings, but instead he focused on the warmth of Keely's arms around his waist.

"You were amazing back there, Sam," she said.

"You weren't so bad yourself," he replied.

He was getting stronger, more confident of his magic. He could feel the rock of Odin lying against his chest, but a deeper power hummed inside him. Odin's Fury.

I can finish this, Sam thought. *And I will.*

They would break the red-sun curse and destroy the witches. Sam grinned as the wind whipped at his face. He urged the Omera on toward Garamond. The end was in sight.

Chapter Forty-Five

The Omeras landed as the sun's sickly rays speared above the horizon. The four riders had fallen asleep on the backs of the beasts, trusting them to carry the group safely across the water. The exhilaration of the ride faded fast as they stood on the shore of Garamond. The rising sun cast a deathly glow on the day, washing them in its bloody stain and illuminating the current state of devastation. The once-pristine sand was littered with rotting fish. Birds lay dead on the ground in black, lifeless clumps. There wasn't a living creature in sight, not even a scavenger.

"I don't feel so good," Mavery said, swaying on her feet. Leo caught her before she fell over. He laid her gently on the sand.

"The sun's starting to make us sick," Leo said, looking up at Sam. "I feel it, too."

Then a faint squawk made them all turn. There in the low branches of a scraggly tree was the hunched figure of a bird.

"Is that Lagos?" Sam asked, recognizing the cinnamon-orange-tipped feathers. Rego had ordered the bird to stay back with Gael and the others.

The dwarf began to run, his short legs pounding the sand as he made for his pet. Sam and the others gathered around as Rego lifted her out of the tree and cradled the bird in his arms.

"There, now, Lagos. It's going to be okay," Rego crooned,

swaddling the bird close. "You just got too much of that cursed sun on you." He tried to feed the bird a sip from his waterskin, but the bird turned its beak away.

"What's that on her leg?" Sam asked, spying a small tube tied to her.

Rego tugged it loose and unscrolled a small piece of parchment. "It's a message from Gael. He's going to surrender to the witches. They've promised to end the red-sun curse if he does."

"You have to stop him," Sam said. "Endera's lying. She knows I'm the only one who can stop the red sun."

Lagos let out a weak call. Her eyes were glassy and unfocused.

"Lagos?" Rego asked, his voice breaking. "Hang on, girl."

The bird opened her beak one more time, as if there was something she wanted to say, and then she went limp in Rego's arms. The dwarf shuddered, gripping the bird tightly, then laid her gently back in the sand.

"Is she dead?" Keely asked, her voice wavering.

Leo dropped down and put his head to its chest, then sat back, shaking his head. "I'm sorry, Rego," he said.

"She held on until the end, waiting to deliver that message," Rego said, wiping a tear away. "Give me a moment to say a proper goodbye."

Leo herded them a short distance away.

"Look at Mavery. What if we're next?" Keely asked, her voice bordering on hysteria. "What if we all die before you break the curse?"

Sam looked at Leo, and his friend nodded reluctantly, reading Sam's intention. Sam had to do something. Now. Before things got worse.

Stalking back to the spot where they landed, Sam dropped to his knees and drew Sinmara's hand out of the satchel. It had grown cold, stiff, and rubbery to the touch, but Sam bit back his revulsion.

Leo and Keely sat down beside Sam. Mavery lay on the sand, eyes open, watching them, but the girl seemed too weak to move.

"Sam, are you sure about this?" Leo asked. "Rego said not to use the ring."

"Keely's right. We're all going to be like Lagos unless I do something."

Keely hugged her knees, eyeing the severed hand with disgust. "What exactly are you going to do?"

"I don't know. But the ruby and the sun are connected. I just have to figure out how to break the connection."

Sam pried the ruby ring off Sinmara's stiff, cold finger. He held it in the palm of his hand, looking at his friends' expectant faces. They were counting on him to save them. Swallowing back his fear, Sam slid the ring on his finger. It was three sizes too big, but as the metal touched his skin, the gold turned warm and shrank until it fit snugly on his hand. Then the ruby began to glow, lighting up with an internal fire. Sam felt a jolt of power as the ring and the sun made a connection.

His scared friends took several steps back, unsure what to expect.

Sam's hand rose over his head of its own volition as the power of the curse drew the ruby to the sun. In an instant, Sam realized he had made a mistake. The sun's poison flooded his veins with a seething electricity that spread through him, then returned to the ring and back to the sun in mere seconds. His connection to the curse was now complete. It felt exhilarating and terrifying at the same time.

Too late, Sam realized the sun was molting into a brighter shade of red, glowing the fiercest hue he had seen since he had arrived in Orkney. There was no trace of yellow left. His efforts to stop the curse had backfired, as if his blood were gasoline added to the cursed fire already burning in the sky above them. The sun had become a blazing ball of fury, shooting out rays more intense than anything they had seen so far.

Sam's eyes began to burn like hot coals, emitting piercing red light.

Keely ran at Sam, jumping up to grab at his arm. "Put it away, Sam! It's too powerful." She grabbed at the ring, but when her fingers touched the stone, a burst of crimson light flung the girl backward, planting her face down in the sand.

A part of Sam knew he should stop, but even if he wanted to, the power of the sun had taken hold of the ruby, as if it had been reunited with an old friend. He held the ring over his head. As the blazing connection intensified, wind began to whip around him, blowing sand into his friends' faces. He was like a living torch, sending out scalding rays of heat. Rego came charging across the sand, but the dwarf was too late.

Sam surrendered to the power that coursed through him. He flung his arms out, absorbing all the energy he could.

He was the red sun. The red sun was him.

Rego finally reached Sam, tackling him with his burly body and knocking him to the ground.

"Get the ring off him!" Rego shouted as Sam wrestled to get free.

Leo sat on his arm and pried the ring off his finger, then buried it under the sand, ending the connection.

"Why did you do that?" Sam screamed, trying to dive for the ring.

Rego kept him pinned him down and put his elbow across Sam's throat. "It was killing you. We had to stop it."

He shoved Rego off and sat up. "It was working! You ruined it."

"No, Sam, you were making it worse," Leo said. "Any longer and we would have all been dead." He held his arm out and Sam gasped at the blisters that pebbled his skin.

The dwarf was kneeling over a still figure. Sam's anger collapsed. "Keely?"

He scrabbled on all fours across the sand to her side.

"Keely, wake up." He shook her gently, but her face was as pale as the inside of a shell. Only the slow rising of her chest gave him hope. "I almost killed her," he whispered.

Rego looked Sam square in the eye. "Sam, if you put that ring on again, you will die. Mark my words."

"No. The ring is the key. Odin sent me to get the ring, so it has to work." Sam was so frustrated he wanted to punch a hole in the sky. "If Odin wanted me dead, he would have just killed me. I just don't know how to use it." He settled for pounding his fist into the sand.

Mavery's voice was a croak. "Sam?"

Sam moved to lean over her. "What is it, imp?"

"Endera always has a plan," she whispered.

Sam's heart thrummed. Mavery had said that before. "You think Endera has the key?"

"That's why she kept Howie," Mavery whispered, her eyes large in her pale face as she looked up at him. "So you would go find them. They'll know how to end the curse."

She was right, Sam realized. Endera had known he would need her help; the evil witch had figured he could be her errand boy and bring her the Horn of Gjall at the same time.

"Thanks, imp." He ruffled her hair. "Don't die on me." He stood up on legs that felt too wobbly for what he had to do.

"Let me come with you, Sam," Leo said, rising.

"No, I need you here, Leo. Get Keely and Mavery to Gael. Maybe he can help them. And whatever happens, don't let him surrender to the witches."

"We'll find Gael," Rego said.

Taking the pouch that held Odin's Stone, Sam carefully dug Sinmara's ring out of the sand and tucked it inside, putting the pouch safely inside his shirt. He still had the Horn of Gjall at his waist. He might turn to dust before this was over, but he was going to do his best to make sure Howie was safe and Endera suffered maximum pain.

Leo hugged Sam tightly, slapping him hard on the back.

Sam let Leo's strength fill him for a long moment; then he turned and started running up the trail that led to the top of the bluff. Pursing his lips, Sam whistled loudly and began running through the woods as the toxic sun rose higher in the sky.

The female Omera flew overhead as he raced through the forest. He barely broke stride as she flew low enough for him to leap onto her back. They flew over the tops of the trees as he whispered in her ear where he wanted to go.

Chapter Forty-Six

Howie and his new friend, Bert the rat, snoozed in the corner of his cell. The two of them had developed a strong bond based on mutual dependency. Howie served up his leftovers, and Bert alerted him if any of the other *rathos* came near. Lately, the other vermin had steered clear once Bert had grown fat and strong. Howie didn't see Endera's daughter again, but every so often a note appeared in his food.

Rat boy, said one.

Snore much? said another, as if she knew what went on in his cell.

For Howie, the torture was not the lack of TV or flush toilets, but the boredom. There were only so many games he could play with a rat. He paced his cell, hopping on one foot, balancing a rock on his head, and sang every verse to every song he knew. He craved daylight, but when he looked out the skinny bars of his cell, all he saw was the strangely toxic sun. Today it blazed with a brighter intensity than ever before.

"Your friend did that," a familiar voice said.

Howie turned, jumping down from the window. "Liar."

"I never lie."

Howie moved closer to his visitor at the door, pressing his face up to the bars. She was pretty, for a witch, with her red lips and large green eyes. A fringe of dark bangs crossed her forehead. Howie could see the resemblance to Endera in her high cheekbones and pointed chin.

"I'm Howie."

"Perrin."

"So, Endera's really your mom?"

Perrin gave a slight shrug. "Witches don't exactly have close families. We're raised by the coven."

"That's crazy. I can't imagine not having my brothers and sisters around."

"So, you're close to them?"

No one in Howie's family thought twice about him, but that didn't stop him from claiming them. "They're not perfect. But I bet they're worried about me." Or at least he liked to think they would be. "What do you know about Sam? Is he okay?"

She lowered her eyes. "My witch brother has put us all in danger. His anger is boiling the sun. But my mother will fix it. You'll see. Everything will be better when the stone witches are—"

Perrin stopped herself.

Howie gripped the bars. "Stone witches? What's Endera up to now?"

The girl backed away. "Never mind, rat boy. I shouldn't have come here." She turned and hurried away.

"What did you mean? Perrin!" Howie shouted, but she was gone.

A guard appeared at the door. "Time to go," he said.

Howie felt a flicker of unease. This couldn't be good. He hadn't left his cell since Sam had embarked on his journey. Bert let out a sad-sounding squeak as Howie was led away.

⚬⚬⚬ (✕✕✕) ⚬⚬⚬

Endera stood in front of the gathering. Every witch old enough to cast a spell was assembled on the grand plaza in front of the

301　ALANE ADAMS

Tarkana Fortress. Hestera stood at her side, leaning on her emerald-topped cane, allowing Endera to have this moment of glory.

"Sisters!" Endera called for silence. The gathering quieted down. "We are setting out on a journey that will restore us to our former glory. I promise you, we will return victorious. We will not leave our ancestors trapped in stone."

Shouts rang out in support.

"We have not forgotten the sacrifice they made for us. Catriona. Bronte. Ariane. Leatrice. Paulina. Nestra. Vena. Agathea. These eight sisters have endured eons of suffering, waiting for us to gain the strength to free them. Today is that day. The Son of Rubicus rises even now. See how the sun seethes with his magic."

The witches craned their necks toward the boiling face of the sun.

"Samuel Barconian will free Catriona and the others from those stones. It is his destiny. We will destroy our enemies, the Orkney guardians Odin put in charge. The ones who have opposed us all these centuries. We will sweep them aside like the rubbish they are. No one shall be left standing when we are through."

Endera waved her hand at a guard dragging the pitiful friend of the Barconian spawn. "Bring him with us. This little brat has a very important role to play today."

"What's going on?" Howie challenged, searching the group of witches. "Where's Sam?"

Ignoring his questions, Endera turned to Hestera. "It is time we brought this to an end. If Sam succeeded in his cause, he will need our help to end the curse." She folded her hand over the emerald atop Hestera's cane. "When I give the word, act."

Hestera nodded, her face mirroring the bloodthirst in every witch's eye.

"And what of the Horn?"

"Not until the red-sun curse is lifted. He mustn't be distracted, or we will all perish. After he succeeds, then we can force him to deliver it, and then we will know which side he has chosen."

Hestera's eyes glittered with excitement. "Then let us be gone!"

"*Tempus ferro*!" Endera shouted, then thrust her fist into the sky as every witch did the same. In a green flash, they vanished, dragging Howie with them.

———— (◆◆◆) ————

The Omera flew doggedly across the barren land. Sam urged her on, racing to reach the Tarkana Fortress before another person succumbed to the poison of the red sun. All he saw in his mind was Mavery's pale face and Keely lying motionless. After hours in flight, the Omera finally tired; Sam could hear the female's breath rattle in her chest, but she flew on valiantly. They passed over barren hills and deep valleys filled with deadened trees, and then they were over the sea and the island of Balfour rose into view.

They flew over the lower tiers of the ancient castle as Sam guided his winged beast down to a corner rampart. The female Omera was panting, her mouth covered in foam, as Sam slid off her back. He ran his hand over her neck and put his forehead against hers.

Thank you for your service.

They shared a moment where he asked more of her. Then she butted his head with hers and took off, circling overhead once before heading north.

Sam jogged across the rampart toward a wooden door that he hoped would lead him down to the dungeons. He needed to know that Howie was all right before he took on a coven of witches. He didn't have a lot to negotiate with, but he wasn't the same clueless kid who had been here before.

The door creaked on its hinges and opened onto an unused storage room, dusty with cobwebs. Another door led to a narrow spiral staircase that was dark and smelled like rat droppings.

The door at the bottom of the spiral staircase was bolted shut. Sam ran his hands over the hinges and pressed down on the metal, saying a few magic words. The hinge pins began to shimmy and vibrate and then popped from the hardware.

Quietly prying open the door, Sam poked out his head and peered into an empty corridor. A familiar row of cells lined the hall. This was where he had been imprisoned. At the end, he saw a flickering light and heard some loud discussions. It sounded as if the guards were having a card game.

Sam moved quickly down the hall, peering into the barred window of each cell door. The first cell was empty, as was the second. In the third, a figure dressed in dirty rags lay on the ground. He squinted, trying to make out the shape.

"Howie?" he whispered. "Is that you?"

The scrawny figure sat up, straw clinging to his long gray hair.

"Jasper." Disappointment flooded through Sam.

"You shouldn't be here," the old man rasped. "Your friend is gone."

"Why should I listen to you? You sold us out to the witches."

"That was a mistake," he said heavily. "I should have had more faith in you, lad. I came back here to help, but they'd already left with your friend. From what I overheard, they took him to the Ring of Brogar."

"Ring of Brogar?" Sam's father was there in his stone tomb, along with the old witch Catriona and her cronies. "I don't get it. Why take Howie there?"

"Setting a trap, no doubt. You'd be a fool to go."

"I have no choice. I need their help. I can't end the red-sun curse on my own."

"And once you end the curse, what then?" Jasper pressed his wrinkled face to the bars. "They know you'll do anything to save your friend, even if it means the end of Orkney."

Sam stared at him, meeting his gaze. His mouth opened and

closed. He wanted to deny the truth, wanted to forget that he had betrayed Odin by stealing his horn.

"The witches want you on their side," Jasper added. "They're going to lead you down a path that there's no coming back from."

Sam slowly reached for the Horn tucked inside his shirt. His hands were shaking as he drew it out, lashed by his guilt, dreading the outcome that would face Howie if he surrendered it. "The witches asked me to steal this," he said, turning the ancient artifact over in his hands.

Jasper's eyes widened. "You know what that Horn can do?"

"Yes."

Sam was shaking. He stared at the Horn, seeing Odin's blue eyes twinkling at him as he placed his trust in him. "If I don't give it to them, Howie is going to die."

Jasper didn't speak. After a moment, he grunted. "I'da probably stole the Horn myself if I was you. Can't tell you what to do, lad. Just tell me how I can help."

Sam rubbed the Horn, seeing Howie's face, and, coming to a decision, tucked it away. "I say we go to the Ring of Brogar and end those witches."

Jasper squinted at the boy with those sea-blue eyes. "That's the first intelligent thing you've said. Now, why don't you break me out of here?"

Sam grinned.

Magic flowed from his fingertips as he summoned the energy needed to push aside the bolts holding Jasper's door closed. Once Jasper was free, they moved down the hallway toward the guards.

There were three of them clustered around a small table, playing a card game with rune stones. Sam cleared his throat, and the guards looked up, surprised, then jumped to their feet, drawing their swords. Jasper dropped a wooden jug on the head of one of them, and Sam grabbed a chair and smashed it over the head of another. The last one stood his ground until Jasper picked up another guard's fallen sword.

"Remember what I said I'd do to you if I ever got out," Jasper growled.

The last guard turned and ran, drawing an amused snort from Jasper.

They made it to the top of the stairs, expecting to find resistance, but the hallway outside the dungeon was silent and deserted. There wasn't a Balfin or a witch to be found, aside from the three guards they had found in the dungeons.

"They've all left, then," Jasper said. "Every last one of them filthy witches. This can mean only one thing."

"What's that?"

"They're going to war with Orkney."

They walked openly through the compound and found a pair of old nags in the stables.

"My boat is nearby," Jasper grunted as he hoisted himself up. "And the Ring is only a short sail around the east cape of Garamond."

"Then what are we waiting for?" Sam said as he mounted his nag. He kicked the horse's bony ribs to get it moving.

Chapter Forty-Seven

A rocky cliff pushed up from the sea as Jasper's ship pulled into a recessed bay. There were more than a dozen Balfin ships anchored, crowded with soldiers. They stared at Jasper's ship as it passed by but made no move to stop it. At the top of the bluff, the outline of tall, standing stones set in a broad circle came into view.

And a whole lot of witches.

Sam could make out their dark figures crowding the hilltop. The place was thick with them. They were waiting for Sam to bring them their Horn so they could call up some army of the dead and take over Orkney. Well, Sam wasn't about to let that happen.

"Why are the Balfins on their ships?" Sam asked, as Jasper rowed them to shore in his dinghy.

"They won't take sides until they know who's going to win."

They made their way silently up a narrow trail. Near the top, the seaman stopped and wiped his brow.

"You sure about this, lad?"

"It's okay, Jasper." Sam managed a weak grin. "I got this."

The old sailor nodded with admiration. "All right, then. Go send them witches to the Fourth Realm, where they belong."

Sam turned to him, handing him the Horn of Gjall.

"I want you to take this."

Jasper's eyes flared in surprise. "Are you sure, lad?" The sea-man held it up, admiring the carved whorls on the Horn. "What about your friend?"

"I'll figure something out. I can't make things worse. Just get it back to Odin for me. But watch out for his snake; he's as likely to swallow you whole before he asks why you're there."

"I can do that. I'm a Son of Aegir. Odin was fond of the sea god."

"Goodbye, Jasper." Sam stuck out his hand.

Jasper clutched him firmly, his hand warm and reassuring. "I believe in you, lad. You're doing a good thing."

Sam climbed the rest of the way to the top alone and looked down on the wide, grassy clearing below. A ring of ancient, flat-sided, rectangular stones stood in a wide loop, like surfboards stuck in the sand. He counted nine in all. In the center, an enormous, solitary stone loomed above the others.

Sam knew his dad was down there, trapped in one of those stones. He ached to find him, to save him, even though Odin said he couldn't be saved.

Which one are you in, Dad? Sam wondered.

But first, Sam had to deal with the throng of witches wait-ing inside the ring of stones. They stood arm in arm, dozens of them, maybe a hundred, in all shapes and sizes, old and young, dressed in black gowns, waiting silently, their faces turned to the red sun.

In the very center, near the large, solitary stone, Endera waited next to her elder, Hestera, and the young Lemeria, who had made Sam's feet dance not so long ago. A Shun Kara wolf stood menacingly over a small figure slumped on the ground.

Howie, Sam realized.

His friend didn't move. Sam hurried down the hill and ap-proached the gathering. The witches parted, creating an opening. He looked into their faces, seeing curiosity, excitement, and maybe a little fear. They had never met anyone like him, he realized, and they were curious. A sliver of longing ran through him as he marched past their silent faces. A desire to know them, to be connected to them. But he pushed that thought aside and continued into the center of the circle of stones. The witches filled in behind him, closing off his exit.

Sam stopped ten feet away from Endera.

He began the speech he had prepared. "The red sun is killing everything," Sam called. "Not even your precious Balfour Island is safe. The poison will soon destroy everyone but those few with powerful magic. What will you do then? Who will you enslave if everyone is gone?"

"We have no intention of letting it come to that," the old one, Hestera, said.

"Then help me end the curse," he said. "Before it's too late."

Endera shrugged. "We did not cause this curse; you did, so only you can end it. Did you not see Sinmara?"

"Yes. The dark magic was in a ruby ring she wore." His fingers curled around the ring in his pocket for security.

"Then use it, boy. What are you waiting for?"

"I tried. It's not enough."

"I see," Endera said, folding her arms. "So you need our help. If only the High Council were here now to hear your plea, they might see us as something more than savages. But, alas, we are alone. Ask nicely, and we might agree."

Sam gritted his teeth. "Please, Endera, help me end this curse. People are dying. My friends are sick."

Endera turned to Hestera, who nodded her agreement.

"Very well," Endera agreed. "But it must begin with you."

Sam took a deep breath. Part of him feared that seething electricity flowing through him again. But part of him, though, the dark part deep inside, thrilled at the chance to wield such power. With all the witches' eyes upon him, Sam slipped Sinmara's ring onto his finger. Before he could change his mind, he thrust his fist into the sky. The ruby glittered brightly, connecting him with the red sun. A jolt of the poisonous current hit him. It raced through his body, down to the soles of his feet, making every blood vessel rage.

He kept the ruby up high. Closing his eyes, he let the magic that bubbled through his veins reach his lips as he spoke the ancient words. *"Fein kinter, soleila, soleila diminus, mera diminus, mera nein kinter."* The other witches joined him in his chant, their voices rising together to fill the air.

The ruby absorbed the sun's blazing intensity. Fire flooded his veins until his temperature rose to a boiling point. Only the power of Odin's Fury kept Sam from bursting into flame. His eyes burned as red flames shot from them, searing the ground at his feet. His lips swelled and split. His skin felt like it was peeling off. His arms trembled uncontrollably, but still he held the ring high and repeated the spell.

Every beat of his heart sent fire through Sam's veins, burning so intensely that he could not remain standing. He dropped to one knee, teetering, desperately maintaining the connection with the sun.

⸺⬦⬦⬦⬦⬦⸺

Endera enjoyed watching the boy suffer. She wanted him to break, to beg for help. The sight of Sam's young body twisting and writhing in agony as the full force of the curse was released brought a cruel smile to the witch's face.

"Enough," Hestera said, raising her hand to drive the staff into the ground. But Endera stayed her hand.

"Just another moment," she said, her eyes dancing in the light of the sun's ferocious display.

"If he dies, your plan fails," Hestera reminded her.

Endera watched the boy immolate for another moment and

then nodded. "Very well," she said with a flick of her hand. "End this."

Hestera drove her staff into the ground and shouted, "*Test-era Tarkana, diminus solera, diminus solera, finis, finis, finis.*"

She repeated the words over and over, and on her third chant, the emerald atop her cane sent out a blaze of light that shot across the circle toward the ruby and destroyed it in a shower of light. Sam collapsed on the ground, his clothes smoldering, his skin blistered and raw.

A sudden chill filled the air.

Sam craned his head feebly toward the sun, staring in awe as it changed from red to a dark orange and then to a faint yellow.

Chapter Forty-Eight

Sam lay sprawled facedown outside the Ring of Brogar as the last remnant of the curse faded away. He wanted to soak up its unblemished warmth, but the witches weren't finished with him yet.

"Save your friend, and give us the Horn of Gjall." The voice was Endera's. Hestera grasped Howie by the neck, holding him up like a sack of potatoes. "We did our part to help end the red-sun curse."

Sam lifted his head and tried to focus in on Howie. Sam's eyes were swollen, and the heat had blistered his hands, but he was relieved to see Howie was alive, kicking and twisting in Hestera's grasp. For now. But what would happen when the witches found out he didn't have the Horn they so desperately wanted?

Endera held one hand out. "Give me what I ask, or your friend will pay for your insolence."

Sam pushed himself to his feet. Blistering pain made his eyes water. He swayed slightly but managed to stay upright. "I don't have the Horn," he declared.

The entire coven of witches hissed collectively, but Endera raised her hand for silence. "You're lying, child. You said you would do anything to save your friend. Give it to us now."

"Search me." He raised his hands. Endera snapped her fingers, and a pair of witches came over and patted him down roughly. They turned and shook their heads at Endera.

Murmurs of confusion spread across the assembly, but Endera had a cold smile pinned to her face.

"What. A. Pity." Endera spoke with contempt. "And here I thought you were one of the good guys." She snapped her fingers, and Hestera flung Howie onto the ground. They raised their hands, zapping Howie with green fire, making him writhe and scream in pain. Hestera did the same, followed by Lemeria. They were killing Howie. Sam threw his hand forward, sending a blast of witchfire at Endera to get her attention.

"Stop it!" Sam commanded.

Endera raised a hand, signaling the other witches to pause.

"Why should I?"

"I stole the Horn, like you asked. But Odin put his trust in me, and I can't break that."

Endera shook her head, making *tsking* noises at him. "You sentenced your friend to die, your very *best* friend, because of some stupid loyalty to a worthless god?"

Sam knelt by Howie, rolling his friend over. Burn marks streaked his arms, and one went across his face. Howie moaned a bit but didn't open his eyes. Endera was right—Sam's loyalty probably was stupid—but it was too late to change his mind. Jasper was likely halfway out to sea by now.

Endera continued taunting him. "You have the makings of a real witch, Sam. You might even be more heartless than I am." She laughed, and the rest of the witches laughed with her. "But now I am going to kill you *and* your friend."

Sam considered his options. He was down to his last few cards. It was time to play his last hand and see if he could save Howie once and for all. "You can't kill me, not with Odin's Fury in me. So I'm going to take Howie and leave." He reached down and grabbed Howie by the collar, but Endera's next words stopped him.

"So that's it? You're leaving without even trying to save your father?"

Sam's head came up. *Dad.* He looked around, remembering where he was. The Ring of Brogar. His dad was trapped inside one of those stones. He dropped Howie.

Endera sauntered over to run her hand over the closest stone. "Eventually Odin's Fury is going to run out; it doesn't last forever, you know. My guess is you have just enough left to free your father. Or you could escape now with your life. What do you care about a man who abandoned you, left you behind without so much as a goodbye?"

Guilt punched Sam in the solar plexus, making it hard to breathe. The years of anger and resentment washed over him like a bucket of acid.

She stared at him like she could see right through him. "You think I don't know the rage you feel? I watched you back in Pilot Rock; you seethed with it. You beat that poor Ronnie Polk into the ground, and you call *me* a monster?"

Sam flinched, but his feet carried him forward. He counted the stones. There were nine in total. He could do it. Somehow he would find the one that imprisoned his dad.

Sam ran his hands over the first stone. He felt nothing but cold granite.

"How will you know which one he's in?" Endera asked. "You might discover there's a witch waiting instead."

"I'll know," Sam said, trying desperately to believe that. He moved on to the next one as Endera kept pace inside the circle. The rest of the witches waited, motionless.

"You never got to say goodbye to him, did you?" Endera said. "Never got to tell him how it felt to be abandoned."

Sam tried to block out her words. He was so desperate to see his dad, he didn't want to think about the other feelings he had. The negative feelings. He ran his hands over the second stone. Cold again. If his dad was inside, shouldn't he feel something?

"I would be furious if my father left me and made my mother lie about it. How terribly unfair." Endera's words were like needles in Sam's skin.

"Just shut up!" Sam shouted, trying to stay focused as he arrived at the third stone. "You don't know anything about me."

"I know everything about you. You hate him, don't you?" Endera asserted. "You certainly have every right to."

Her words brought Sam to a halt. He stood at the fourth rock. It was awful and true. Some part of Sam did hate his father, for all the reasons Endera had mentioned. But he still wanted to see him one last time. He put his hand on the tall stone and felt a thrum, a warmth, an electric current.

"I hope you can, Sam. Free him, that is. It will be a pleasure to kill Robert Barconian twice."

Sam ran his hand over the fourth stone again, thrilling at the electric sensation. His dad was in there. He had found him.

He looked over at Endera. "When I release my father, we're going to destroy you." He closed his eyes and walked away, drawing in a deep breath and channeling his energy.

Sam focused on the Fury that Odin had infused his body with. He could feel it pumping through his veins. Could he do it? Could Odin's magic really undo the spell that held his father in that stone? There was only one way to find out. Sam planted his feet and then ran forward at full speed . . .

"*Fein kinter separas*," he shouted, and hit the rock.

Sam didn't bounce back on his rear, like he had half expected to. Instead, the rock absorbed the impact.

Silence hung in the air. Every witch in the coven watched breathlessly.

For a moment, Sam thought he had failed. He took a step

back, bracing for despair. Then the rock began to splinter. Cracks spread like black veins across the surface, slowly at first, then faster and faster, until, with a loud pop, the stone shattered into thousands of pieces, disintegrating into a squall of gray dust. As the air cleared, Sam saw a man curled up in a ball on the ground, wearing a tattered Orkadian uniform.

"Dad!" Flooded with joy, Sam dropped to his knees.

His father didn't move at first, then lifted a hand groggily.

"Sam?" he whispered though dry lips. "Is it really you?" His blue eyes burned with intensity as they searched his son's face. He hadn't seen Sam since the boy was ten years old.

"Yeah, it's me," Sam said, brushing tears away.

Robert Barconian's eyes clouded as he looked around and saw Endera with the rest of the witches. "Sam, what have you done?"

"I saved you," he said, confused by his father's tone.

"Yes, Sam. But . . . freeing me may have doomed us all," his father lamented. His face was gray with pain. Blood seeped through his clothing from a puncture wound in his side.

Before Sam could speak, a loud crack rang out, splintering the air as the tall stone next to them split down the center.

"It's happening," Robert murmured helplessly.

Sam looked up at Endera and was surprised to see her smiling. Then she tilted her head back, laughing triumphantly.

The stone finally shattered, and an old woman stepped out from the rubble.

The coven gasped at the sight, and a wave of witches began to kneel in reverence.

Then, in a chain reaction, each stone in the ring began to crack and shatter in succession. From the dust and debris, more female figures emerged.

Witches.

The last stone exploded with a boom that hurt Sam's ears and sent rocky shrapnel flying through the air. An older witch, with a shock of gray hair, took a deep, fortifying breath and then let out a high-pitched shriek, which the assembled mass of witches echoed.

"What's going on?" Sam asked his father.

"The Ring of Brogar was bound together by Odin's magic. Breaking one stone broke them all."

Sam looked around at the splintering rocks, and the truth hit him like a punch to the gut: Endera had planned this all along.

She hadn't wanted the Horn of Gjall at all. The Horn had just been a distraction, a way to appease Hestera and lead Sam here, to this place. She had banked on the fact that he would find Odin and be armed with the power to break the red-sun curse. And after he did, Endera knew, he wouldn't be able to resist rescuing his father.

Sam glared at Endera and the coven of witches, cackling and exhorting in raucous celebration as they welcomed back their malignant elders. She had played him. But the game wasn't over.

Robert coughed, drawing Sam's attention. "I'm sorry I left, Sam," he whispered. "Please forgive me."

Sam hesitated. He was full of so many conflicting emotions—anger, compassion, despair, and hope—that he couldn't find words to respond. All that sputtered from his mouth was, "It's okay." And suddenly, despite his more than two years harboring hate, it *was* okay. "But why didn't you say goodbye?"

Robert grabbed Sam's head, bringing him down close to whisper in his ear. "Because I never could have left." He released Sam and studied him closely. "Look at you, all grown up. . . . How old are you now?"

"Twelve. I'm taller, too."

His father smiled, and his eyes shimmered with pride, even as the life was fading fast from him. "You are the best of Abigail and me." A grimace of pain crossed his face. "You have a hard road ahead, son. I wish . . ." He grimaced in pain, then continued, "I wish it were not so, but you must accept your path. Tell your mother . . . I love her."

Sam felt his father's fingers lose their strength and slip away. Then he slumped back to the dirt with a soft, mournful groan.

Sam waited for his father's eyes to open again, but this time he was really gone.

Chapter Forty-Nine

Sam rocked back on his ankles, awash in grief. He had wasted so much time being angry. All the while, his dad had been trapped in a stone, trying to save his world. At that moment, Sam would have given anything to spend five more minutes with his father, just to tell him everything he had done in the years since he had been gone.

"Sam, buddy, time to move." It was Howie. Burn marks crisscrossed his arms and face, but he helped Sam to his feet. "They're busy having a reunion." Howie gestured at the witches, still in the midst of their repellent homecoming. "Let's go."

Swiping his tears away with the back of his hand, Sam put his arm around Howie to help his friend, and they began to run. But a blast of witchfire at their feet knocked them both to the ground.

"Leaving so soon?" Endera challenged.

Sam spat out a mouthful of dirt and pushed himself back to his feet. "Get out of here, Howie. This isn't your fight."

But Howie hauled himself up and stood next to him. "The heck it's not. I've been their prisoner for weeks now." Howie squeezed his hands into scrawny fists at his side.

"So it's you and me against an army of witches. I'm liking the odds; how about you?"

"Just like when Ronnie Polk and his thugs tried to smash a

grape jelly sandwich in my face. All I needed was my buddy at my side."

Sam nodded. The sides were set. He faced Endera and her horde of witches. "Go back to Balfour Island, where you belong!" he shouted.

"Or what?" Endera sauntered forward. "I have eight of the most powerful witches in history on my side. Who's going to stop us from taking over Orkney?"

Sam looked at Howie, and his friend gave him a thumbs-up. He turned back to Endera. "Looks like we are."

Endera began to back away, looking suddenly wary.

It was working. The other witches began to draw in closer, forming a tighter circle, giving Sam the crazy idea that they really did fear him. Then he heard a shout, and the onrushing rumble of stamping feet.

"The Ninth Realm will never fall into your wicked hands!"

The voice was Rego's.

I must be dreaming, Sam thought. Rego was supposed to be on the other side of Garamond.

"The Eifalians will not allow the Ninth Realm to fall," Gael echoed.

"The Falcory will not allow the Ninth Realm to fall," Beo grunted.

Sam and Howie watched in shocked relief as Captain Teren stepped up, sword drawn. "The Orkadian army stands ready to defend the Ninth Realm." He looked sideways at Sam, and Sam could swear Teren winked at him.

Behind Sam now stood an army. A legion of Ninth Realmers on horses, on foot: Falcory, Eifalian, Orkadian, as far as he could see. Men and women stood ready to do battle.

And there, pushing to the front of the horde, were Keely, looking pale but alive, next to Leo, and Mavery, standing with Rego, looking fired up enough to tear the witches apart.

Keely looked smug. "You're not the only one who can ride an Omera," she told Sam.

A bolt of green lightning split the sky, and Sam's gaze snapped back toward the witches.

"Let the fate of the Ninth Realm be decided!" Endera decreed.

Proud and defiant roars rose up from each side.

I've started a war, Sam thought.

Rego led the charge with a cry, followed by his one-armed brother, Amicus, brandishing his sword, leading a battalion of Orkadian soldiers.

"Let me at them," Mavery growled, marching forward, but Sam scooped her up over his shoulder and dumped her wriggling body behind a tree.

"Stay here," he warned the little witch.

"But I wanna fight," she said, her eyes determined.

Sam knelt down and took her by the shoulders. "I can't help win this if I'm worried about you, understand?"

She nodded reluctantly, leaning back against the trunk, arms folded in protest.

Sam left her and ran back to the fighting line, where he took a stand next to Leo. Leo held his bow and calmly launched arrows at the witches. Keely stood next to him, a bow in hand as well. She wasn't as smooth as Leo, and her arrows wobbled when they flew.

"Keely?"

"Leo's been teaching me," she said proudly.

"Where's Howie?"

She jerked her head to the right.

Sam searched and found him. Howie was in the thick of things, trying awkwardly to swing a sword. Sam moved toward him when he spied Endera making her way across the battlefield, blazing fire at soldiers that stood in her way. At her side, a Shun Kara loped.

She's going after Howie, Sam realized.

Sam raced toward his friend, but he was still fifteen feet away when Endera gave the signal, and the Shun Kara leaped straight at Howie, taking him down in a tumble of claws and fur. Howie made feeble attempts to defend himself, but the fight would be over in seconds. *Not now*, Sam thought. *Howie doesn't get to die while I stand by.*

In that moment, Sam knew what he had to do. The word flew to his lips. "Gungnir!" he shouted. Instantly, he felt a burning sensation in his hand, and then he was holding the mighty spear. He cocked his arm back and threw it with all his might straight at the Shun Kara. The spear flew through the air, steady and straight, hitting the wolf in the shoulder. The animal yelped as the impact carried it ten feet away and then impaled it in the ground. The mighty spear shimmered in the light and then disappeared.

Sam turned to check on Howie, but a sharp pain in his side knocked him back.

Endera stood gloating, ready to send another blast of witchfire Sam's way. And that's when it happened. When the last semblance of denial about who Sam really was snapped. A curtain of rage came down over his eyes, blocking out all thought and reason. A frenzy of hate and a towering need to destroy her filled every cell in his body. She had done this. Hurt Howie. Tried to destroy Orkney. Killed his father.

Sam slowly stood and turned to face her. He felt flushed with cold and heat at the same time, like he had ice running through his veins to keep him from exploding. As Endera sent another blast his way, he stopped it and then let out a scream of rage, the cords in his throat bulging as he vented his fury. He raised his hands. Witchfire burst from his palms. He thrust them at her, sending twin bolts of searing energy at her.

"You lured me here, just like my father!" Sam screamed. "But now you're going to feel what pain is."

Sam blasted her over and over again, putting everything he

had into destroying the witch who had made his existence a living hell. Endera screamed, her body contorting in pain, smoke rising off her. She fell back, twisting and tumbling to the ground, but he kept on, advancing on her and showing her no mercy as he recalled every evil deed she had done. He kept firing at Endera's writhing body until he felt a firm hand on his shoulder. It was Gael. The Eifalian looked at him with empathy.

"Don't be like her, Sam."

But in that moment, Sam wanted to be like her, wanted to be the one who had the power to inflict pain on others. He shrugged Gael off, but the curtain had lifted. After another few seconds of watching Endera writhe, he dropped his arm, feeling the rage drain out of him.

On the battlefield, Sam watched three men go down in a blaze of green fire as the witches lashed out at the Orkadian forces. Gael's band of Eifalians used their magic to defend the soldiers, steadily deflecting the deadly bolts and sending them back at the witches, but men were falling into smoldering heaps. Beo's Falcory had deadly aim with their bows; helped along by Keely and Leo, they dropped witches as fast as they could notch an arrow, but it was a neck-and-neck battle, with the fate of Orkney hanging in the balance.

Sam's eyes were drawn into the center of the ring, where one witch stood apart from the rest. She had waist-long gray hair and sharp, penetrating eyes that shot blazes of emerald fire.

Catriona.

The mother of all witches.

Daughter of Rubicus.

His great-great-grandmother.

For Sam, it was hate at first sight.

The matriarchal witch was muttering words and running her hands through the air. Sam could feel the pulsing current from where he stood. She had enormous power. Power she was drawing on to launch an unholy attack. As energy coalesced around Catriona like an electric tornado, the hair all over Sam's body stood on end. Endera and her cronies didn't come close to this kind of potency.

The Orkadians don't stand a chance, Sam realized.

Sam began to run, knocking witches to the side as if they were bowling pins. A Shun Kara jumped at him, and he punched it in the jaw, sending the creature flying. He still had the Fury of Odin, and, combined with his own witch magic, it made him feel invincible. He made it twenty feet away from Catriona before she sensed him and turned.

The ancient witch blazed a trail of fire in the dust, right up to his feet, where it stopped as he raised his hand and held her at bay.

"Stop!" he shouted. "Stop the fighting!"

The battle slowed to a halt as Catriona eyed him up and down. "Who are you?"

"Samuel Barconian, Son of Odin, Son of Rubicus."

Her eyes filled with fury and disgust. "There has never been a Son of Rubicus." She looked around at the other witches and shot her hand into the sky, letting loose a deafening clap of thunder. It was so loud the hundreds of shields on the battlefield rattled.

Sam's eardrums rang so strongly he thought he would faint.

Sam regrouped and unleashed a ball of witchfire, directing it at the old witch's head.

Catriona easily batted it away and spun back at him. "You have dark magic. How is that so?"

"There's a lot you don't know about me."

She tilted her head back and laughed. "I know you are puny and weak." She sent a blazing blast of witchfire at Sam, but he held his hand up, absorbing it in his palm, and then thrust it back at her. It singed the bottom of her skirt, making her yelp.

"I'm stronger than you think," he boasted. It was time to

put his plan into action. He put his fingers to his lips and let out a shrill whistle. He did it again, more loudly. Then again.

From the hillsides, Sam heard the beat of wings as the sky filled with black shapes. Omeras swooped down, more than fifty of them, and took up a stand around the circle of pulverized stones.

"You think these creatures will protect you? I created them." Catriona stalked forward triumphantly, shouting at the closest Omera, "*Catriona temerus, morbidio, morbidio Barconian.*" The Omera didn't move, didn't flinch—just continued to stand, poised, with its tail raised.

Catriona spun back to Sam, launching a wave of fire in his direction. "What have you done to my beautiful pets?"

Sam raised his hand and pushed back the fire with an invisible wall of magic. "I've made them my own."

Fury turned her face a putrid shade of purple. "Destroy them!" Catriona commanded. "Destroy them all. Leave nothing alive."

Every witch on the battlefield turned her magic toward Sam. But the Omeras launched themselves at the witches, diving with spiked tails and slashing claws. Sam grabbed the pouch from his neck, swinging it over his head, creating a wave of energy that blew back the witchfire and shielded his friends.

Catriona started singing in a soprano voice, joined by her recently released sisters. They sang in an ancient language Sam faintly recognized, drawing their combined strength together into a crackling ball of energy that floated over their heads, growing in size until it was as large as a hot-air balloon.

Gael stood next to Sam, chanting, trying to augment Sam's magic. Sam felt the other Eifalians do the same. Leo came to his side, joined by Keely.

"Take her out!" Leo shouted.

Catriona and her sisters released the lethal sphere of witchfire onto the Orkadian forces. Sam stepped forward in front of his friends and flung his arms wide, letting the blast penetrate his chest. It knocked him back a step, taking his breath away and sending jolts of electricity through his bones. He almost fell, but a stubborn need to prove himself to Catriona made him dig his heels in. Odin's Fury was in his blood, he reminded himself. He could beat her.

Sam pushed back against the enormous blast, and, slowly, he began to drive the blaze of energy away from him and back at the witches. He took a step forward, pushing with both arms, sending all of his magic into his hands, and finally, with a cathartic cry, he shoved his palms forward and said, "*Fein kinter dispera!*"

A great crash of light erupted over the battlefield. The witches' mass of energy shot up into the sky in an emerald blaze and then collapsed on itself like a black hole. When it did, the battle was over.

The witches had all disappeared.

Chapter Fifty

Sam ran straight to Howie. The boy lay like a limp dishrag on the field where the Shun Kara had attacked him. He turned Howie over, hardly expecting his friend to be alive. Howie's eyes were closed, and Sam couldn't tell whether he was still breathing.

"Howie, say something," he said.

His glasses lay next to him, and Sam slipped them back onto Howie's face. They were cracked and dirty, but he at least looked like himself when he had them on.

"Howie, come on, man. Don't leave me here alone."

Howie stayed limp, unconscious. Keely and Leo knelt down next to him. Leo had blood from a deep scratch on his cheek, but otherwise he looked okay.

"Sam, I think he's gone," Keely said softly, her voice trembling.

No. No. No, Sam told himself. *Not now.*

Sam shook him hard. "Come on, Howie—snap out of it. Or I'll feed you to the Shun Kara."

No response. Then, to everyone's surprise, Howie coughed once, his eyes still closed, as he mumbled, "Can't a guy take a nap around here?"

"Howie! You're okay!"

He opened his eyes blearily and let out a sigh. "The Howmaster lives."

"I am so sorry for dragging you into this," Sam started, but Howie cut him off.

"Dude, chillax. We're good. Besides, the witches weren't all bad. There was this cute one who visited my cell. I think she liked me."

Sam chuckled. "You fell for a witch?"

"Did I mention she brought me hot scones?"

Around them, soldiers were being helped to their feet. The bodies of the sacrificed Orkadians marred the grassy hillside. Too many were left dead on the battlefield. As for the witches, Sam saw no trace of them. Those who had perished had vanished, along with the surviving witches, probably back to their fortress on Balfour Island. The Balfin ships had already lifted anchor and set sail.

Rego strode over to Sam, limping a bit but in one piece.

"So you had to free the stone witches, didn't you, lad?" he started in. But he was interrupted by a whirlwind that tackled Sam.

"You're alive! You did it! I knew you could. I wish you would've let me help," Mavery babbled on, grinning up at him with a tear-streaked face.

Sam looped his arm around her shoulder and faced Rego, waiting for the lecture. The condemnation. The blame. He had really screwed up.

"Let me guess. Gael and Beo want me dead again?"

But Rego just snorted. "Dead? No. They're not happy those witches are loose, not by a long shot. But no one's blaming you this time."

"Really? They're not?"

Rego's whiskers twitched. "That's only because I convinced them you could help us defeat the stone witches. So they're willing to keep you alive. For now." He winked at them and walked away.

"Sam, I really need to go home," Keely said.

"I wouldn't mind seeing my parents again," Howie said, sitting up.

"I know how you guys feel," Sam said. "I want to go home, too. See my mom, take a hot shower, sleep in my own bed. But the portal that brought us here . . . we can't go back that way. The stonefire's been destroyed."

"Sam, you still have some of Odin's Fury in you," Leo said. "Maybe you can open another portal?"

Sam's eyes went to the center of the Ring of Brogar, where the last remaining stone stood. He walked toward the towering stone and ran his hand over it. He felt a shimmer. Could he do it? It shimmered again, and his hope soared.

He turned and looked at his friends. "Leo's right. I think I may have just enough left. Are you ready?"

Keely nodded rapidly. "I'm so ready for a bubble bath. Send me home, please!"

Leo stepped forward with an uncharacteristic grin. "I'm ready to see my dad and the rest of my family."

Howie slapped Sam on the back. "Dude, enough of these medieval times. Let's go play some Zombie Wars and eat Chuggies until we puke."

Sam grinned at the thought of the good times ahead in Pilot Rock. For extra measure, he pressed the pouch that held Odin's stone to the standing rock and murmured another spell.

"*Fein kinter, portola, portola envera amica*," he said, and placed both hands on the large chunk of granite.

The rock began to vibrate, growing warmer beneath Sam's hands. The hard surface began to soften, wiggling like Jell-O. Then, at his feet, a ring of fire burst into life, circling the stone and sending flames licking up the surface. Sam stepped back with the others as the flames burned more brightly.

"It's working," said an excited Keely.

The solid gray stone shifted into a transparent veil, and Sam could make out another field—it looked like the football field at Pilot Rock Junior High—just on the other side of this new stonefire.

"Go," he said, looking at his friends.

Keely stepped up, and Leo helped push her into the stone. She disappeared from sight, and then Sam saw her tumble onto the field of grass. Howie rubbed his hands together and then took a running dive, joining Keely in a heap on the sports field.

Leo nodded at Sam, then followed. "See you on the other side," he said, before disappearing.

Sam readied himself to follow, when a voice stopped him.

"You're not leaving us, are you?" Mavery asked.

He wavered. On the other side of the stonefire, he could see his friends waiting for him.

"Please, Sam. The witches will ruin everything if you leave."

Sam clenched his teeth. He was torn.

"Come on, Sam," Keely called from the other side, holding one hand out. "Come home with us."

But in that moment, Sam made a decision. With a resigned sigh, he pulled his hands off the stone. As the surface shimmer started to fade and the veil lost its transparency, Sam could see the confused looks on his friends' faces.

"I'm sorry, guys. They need me here. Tell my mom I love her."

"Sam, wait—don't do this," Keely pleaded, her voice muted and slightly distorted by the closing stonefire. "We need you, too."

But the rock sealed up, and the tantalizing view of Pilot Rock was gone.

Rego's voice came from behind Sam. "You did the right thing, lad. You're home now."

Sam surveyed the battlefield—the rolling green hills, the blazing yellow sun—and wondered if he could really call this place home.

There was no time to worry about that now. He had to bury his father and figure out how they were going to defeat the stone witches, because one thing was certain.

The battle for Orkney wasn't over.

The End

From the Author

Dear Reader:

I hope you enjoyed *The Red Sun*! It has been an incredible journey creating the *Legends of Orkney* series and catapulting my characters into action. Sam has learned so much about his past and how to overcome his anger. Will he continue to use his powers for good, or will darkness overcome him?

As an author, I love to get feedback from my fans letting me know what you liked about the book, what you loved about the book, and even what you didn't like. You can write me at PO Box 1475, Orange, CA 92856, or e-mail me at author@alaneadams.com. Visit me on the web at www.alaneadams.com and learn about the interactive digital game app you can download on your smartphone.

The adventures of Sam and his friends are not over. As a thank-you for being a loyal reader, I have included a preview of the next book in the series, *The Moon Pearl*, to be available soon.

Keep reading!

—*Alane Adams*

The Moon Pearl

North Shores of Garamond

Orkney

Chapter One

A burst of green fire exploded the tree next to Sam's head. He flinched, brushing splinters out of his hair. He had to move or end up incinerated into a pile of smoldering ash. Counting silently to three, he broke from his hiding place and sprinted across the clearing, weaving side to side to avoid the blasts.

War had come to Orkney.

Already Dunham Brook, High Town, and Potters Hill had been burned to the ground. The witches were terrorizing the countryside, which was still recovering from the deadly effects of the red sun. Striking at random. Driving the helpless Orkadians from their homes.

Sam dropped behind a fallen log and tried to catch his breath. His heart raced like a steam piston.

Catriona was extracting her revenge. The queen of evil. A witch so nasty, Odin had made sure she was permanently trapped inside a stone. Until Sam messed that up by releasing her trying to save his father. As if that Tarkana witch Endera hadn't been enough trouble, now there were eight more of them. Eight stone witches who possessed a powerful, ancient magic that threatened to destroy all of Orkney.

There was smelly old Bronte, a wizened hag, stooped with age, able to conjure up deadly potions that turned men to stone; crafty Agathea, with her wide stripe of white hair, who controlled the beasts they used in their attacks; and ghastly Leatrice, whose tongue had been removed in ancient days. Now, she poured out her silent rage in the acid rain that spewed from her fingertips, melting whatever she touched.

The rest—Paulina, Vena, Ariane, and Nestra—were like deadly tentacles, extending the reach of Catriona through all of Orkney.

The witches were holed up at the Tarkana Fortress on Balfour Island, training Endera's younger acolytes to be a lethal force, teaching them the old ways, and restoring the magic Odin had stripped away spell by spell. Then they sent them out to wage war, along with a legion of vicious creatures worse than any sneevil.

Oh, and plenty of sneevils. Those beasts could rip a person apart with one hook of their curved tusks.

Sam had come face-to-face with a sneevil just last week in a field on the eastern shores of Garamond. Out patrolling with a young recruit not much older than he, the boy had been in the middle of a colorful joke about a barmaid and a parrot. And then he was gone. The sneevil had sprung out from behind an elderthorn bush, charging at Sam. But his brave friend had thrown himself in the way and given his life in exchange for Sam's.

The last Son of Odin was to be protected at all costs.

Even now, it made Sam want to pound the ground in frustration. He was no hero. Not worthy of any sacrifice. He had as much hope of setting things right as getting an A on an algebra test.

The facts were the facts. This war was his fault.

He was the one who had released the stone witches.

Another stump exploded next to him. Sam rubbed the leather pouch around his neck. It held a shard of Odin's Stone. A gift from his father. Robert Barconian had been a good man. A man worth dying for.

Sam missed him every day.

Now he kept the stone as a reminder of who he was. One of the good guys. He fought for the Orkadian army. Just because witch magic flowed through his veins, it didn't make him one of *them*.

The battle lines had been drawn. Sides chosen.

Witches were vermin.

Endera Tarkana had said the Orkadians wanted to exterminate all witches, and now Sam understood why. All of Orkney would fall if Catriona had her way. The world could end, and she would laugh into the black void.

Sam gripped the pouch around his neck. Today, when they captured Agathea, they would strike a blow into the heart of Catriona's vengeance plan. Then the witches would know that Samuel Elias Barconian, Lord of the Ninth Realm, Son of Odin, son of Robert Barconian, was a force to be reckoned with. He would avenge his father and send Catriona and her ancient cronies back into the dark hole they had emerged from.

Sam peered around the corner of the log.

Agathea had been leading her acolytes on a series of raids along the northern shores of Garamond, Orkney's largest island and home to its capital city of Skara Brae. The witches acted with impunity, as if they feared nothing. Burning crops in broad daylight. Unleashing their wild beasts to terrorize. Casting a pox on the farm animals. Then retreating to some hole where they waited to launch their next strike.

But not this time. This time, Sam and company had tracked them back to their nest at the top of this hill in this drafty corner of Orkney where the stones fell into the ocean.

Captain Teren, the stalwart commander of the Orkadian Guard and Sam's friend and mentor these past few months, had a dozen of his best men creeping up the slope. If all went right, their ally, Gael of the Eifalians, would arrive along the flank side with his band of skilled archers.

The tables were about to be turned.

Sam might not like his witch blood, but he couldn't very well shut it out. The words of spells were written in the dust motes. They lit up like fireflies in his brain. The magic blew in the winds and was absorbed into his skin. As the witches grew in power, so did he.

Captain Teren signaled to Sam across the clearing, pointing up at the tree.

There.

A nasty little witch hid in the branches. She was preparing to launch another blast of witchfire.

Sam closed his eyes, centered himself, and then stepped out. He threw his hands forward, shouting, "*Mea ustrina.*"

A burst of virescent fire exploded from his palms, blasting the branch to pieces and cindering the witch dead.

They moved forward up the hill toward Agathea's roost. Two of Teren's men let out cries as the witches sent a wall of earth down the mountain, tumbling boulders and pinning the men underneath. Teren rallied his remaining men forward.

Sam raced up the far side, darting through trees. He had one thought on his mind: get to Agathea before she fled. He heard the whisper of the wings before he saw them. Black rain poured out of the sky, armed with fangs and claws.

Shreeks. *Witches' spawn.*

The men cried out as the vermin latched on and bit. Sam cut back toward Teren and his men.

Swinging Odin's rock over his head, he created a powerful windstorm. "*Fein kinter,*" he cried. *I call on my magic.* "*Fein kinter, ventimus, ventimus.*"

The wind blew off the flying black rats, giving the men a fighting chance to slash at them with their swords.

Too late, Sam realized his mistake. *Dumbhead*. He had run out into the open. A rain of fiery arrows arced up over the trees and came down, aimed directly at him. Two of the men closest to him fell to the ground. He threw up his hands, instinctively shouting, "*Concustodio*."

A bubble of blue energy formed, deflecting the deadly rain. He murmured to himself, focusing his strength on keeping the shield up over the men around him. The rain of flaming arrows slowed, then stopped.

Sam's shoulders drooped. Magic took a heavy toll. He was spent, but the witches weren't finished with his band of friends. While they were huddled under the shield, a pack of sneevils had surrounded them.

Sam drew his sword, followed by Teren and the handful of men left: the redhead, Heppner; brawny Tiber; dark and wiry Speria; and the steadfast Galatin. They huddled back to back in the center of the clearing, while eight, then ten, then a dozen sneevils crawled into the clearing, their lips drawn into a snarl. White tusks curved wickedly at the ends, tipped with sharp points ready to eviscerate them.

"Steady," Teren said. "Wait until they draw close. Aim for the heart."

In a puff of black smoke, Agathea appeared behind the creatures. A thick white streak marked her swath of black hair. Her little band of acolytes crouched behind her, ready to do battle. She tilted her head back, laughing at the sight of their little group.

"Come, my pretties; feast on some fresh blood," she cooed to the sneevils, urging them forward.

The beasts circled closer, heeding her call.

Her flinty green eyes met Sam's, hardening as she recognized him. "The witch-boy will make a delicious meal."

"Not this time, Agathea," Sam said, lurching forward with his sword. The sneevil closest to him bared its teeth and charged. Without thinking, Sam drew his sword up between two hands and plunged straight down, pinning the sneevil to the ground.

"Kill them," Agathea ordered. The sneevils charged. The young witches began blasting the small band of fighters with green fire. Sam tried to deflect it, but he was fatigued. His arms shook with the effort. Then a volley of arrows appeared high in the sky, aiming directly down at the witches.

Their Eifalian ally, Gael, had arrived with his archers.

The young witches shrieked as the arrows found their marks. Agathea took her eyes off Sam's group to deal with the Eifalians. Their pale figures moved stealthily through the trees, keeping up a stream of deadly arrows. Agathea cast a spell, puffing out her cheeks and blowing hard. The Eifalians tumbled backward, their arrows careening away. Teren and his men fought the sneevils, but they were in danger of being overrun. One of the sneevils broke through and scored Tiber's thigh with a deep gash before Teren put it down.

Sam tried to think. Agathea was winning. He had to stop her.

Think, Baron. Don't die now.

Then he had it.

"Gungnir," he shouted, and held his hand up.

Teren and the redhead, Heppner, looked at Sam as if he had lost his mind. Then their eyes widened as an old bronze spear appeared in his hand.

"Agathea!" Sam shouted, and threw the spear with all his might. It whizzed through the air and across the clearing, heading straight for Agathea's heart.

Acknowledgments

I created the magical realm of Orkney out of an abundance of love for my son, Alex, and to satisfy his challenge to write a book he would enjoy reading. Without his faith in me, I would never have had the courage to begin the journey of creating this fantastical realm and developing the characters whom I have grown to love so much.

A big thanks to my family for being my biggest fans and pushing me to publish these books so others can share in the legendary tales. A very special thanks to the editors who inspired me to get better at the craft of writing, especially Brent Friedman for his insight into story and world building and his invention of the word *jookberries*. Final thanks to the wonderful cover artist Jonathan Stroh, who brought *The Red Sun* to life in vivid color.

To Orkney! Long may her legends grow!

—*Alane Adams*

About the Author

Alane Adams is a social entrepreneur, philanthropist, professor and award-winning author. After retiring from a successful business career, Adams founded the Rise Up Foundation, which focuses on creating collaborations to empower people to make lasting changes in their lives with a special emphasis on improving literacy in children. A believer in the power of transmedia storytelling, Adams founded Alane Adams Studios to create more interactive, immersive experiences for readers of her books.

Photo credit © Melissa Coulier / Bring Media

About SparkPress

SparkPress is an independent boutique publisher delivering high-quality, entertaining, and engaging content that enhances readers' lives, with a special focus on female-driven work. We take pride in our catalog of fiction and non-fiction titles, representing a wide array of genres, as well as our established, industry-wide reputation for innovative, creative, results-driven success in working with authors. SparkPress, a BookSparks imprint, is a division of SparkPoint Studio, LLC.

CPSIA information can be obtained at www.ICGtesting.com
Printed in the USA
BVOW02*1924040116

431530BV00002B/2/P